QUEEN OF THE HILLBILLIES

Chronicles
OF THE *Ozarks*

Brooks Blevins, General Editor

Queen OF THE HILLBILLIES

Writings of
May Kennedy McCord

Edited by
Patti McCord and Kristene Sutliff

The University of Arkansas Press
Fayetteville
2022

ISBN: 978-1-68226-199-6
eISBN: 978-1-61075-766-9

26 25 24 23 22   5 4 3 2 1

Manufactured in the United States of America

Designed by Liz Lester

∞ The paper used in this publication meets the minimum requirements of the American National Standard for Permanence of Paper for Printed Library Materials Z39.48-1984.

Library of Congress Cataloging-in-Publication Data

Names: McCord, May K., author. | McCord, Patti, editor. | Sutliff, Kristene, editor.
Title: Queen of the hillbillies: writings of May Kennedy McCord / edited by Patti McCord and Kristene Sutliff.
Description: Fayetteville: The University of Arkansas Press, 2022. | Series: Chronicles of the Ozarks | Includes index. | Summary: "Queen of the Hillbillies is a vibrant, long-overdue collection of the writings of May Kennedy McCord, who documented the traditions and history of her native Ozarks as one of the twentieth century's preeminent folklorists. This capacious volume features McCord's own multifaceted writing alongside correspondence, recollections, and poems from her readers and fellow writers"—Provided by publisher.
Identifiers: LCCN 2021039342 (print) | LCCN 2021039343 (ebook) | ISBN 9781682261996 (paperback) | ISBN 9781610757669 (ebook)
Subjects: LCSH: Ozark Mountains Region—Social life and customs. | Folklore—Ozark Mountains Region.
Classification: LCC F417.O9 M33 2022 (print) | LCC F417.O9 (ebook) | DDC 976.7/1—dc23
LC record available at https://lccn.loc.gov/2021039342
LC ebook record available at https://lccn.loc.gov/2021039343

CONTENTS

ILLUSTRATIONS

SERIES EDITOR'S PREFACE

When the University of Arkansas Press launched this series with the publication of Wayman Hogue's *Back Yonder: An Ozark Chronicle* in 2016, it was a rare opportunity for twenty-first-century readers to revisit the genesis of a regional image. We could not only bring back crucial books that defined—and frequently mythologized—the Ozarks for a national audience, but also reacquaint modern Ozarkers with the writers and observers who crafted an enduring regional image. For the most part it was a good strategy. Legendary chroniclers like Vance Randolph and Otto Ernest Rayburn produced signature books that were long out of print, and more obscure writers like Hogue and Catherine Barker broadened the region's portrait with their own takes on life in the Ozarks.

But from the beginning I was disappointed that it seemed one giant of Ozarks chronicling would be left out. From the Depression days through the Eisenhower era, no Ozarks observer reached a larger audience or boasted a more loyal fan base than did May Kennedy McCord, the southwestern-Missouri native known as the "Queen of the Hillbillies." Through long-running newspaper columns and popular radio shows, her musings on the folk culture, history, and characters of the Ozarks reached tens of thousands of people across the region each week. Yet, despite cajoling from confidantes and fans, McCord never published a book, and time has obscured her legacy. More than four decades after her death and well over half a century after the end of her morning radio show, comparatively few people in McCord's beloved Ozarks even recognize her name.

Thus, it was exciting news when Kris Sutliff, my former colleague in Ozarks Studies at Missouri State University, told me that she and a partner were compiling a collection of McCord's writings. That partner turned out to be McCord's granddaughter, Patti McCord, who assures us that the Queen of the Hillbillies was no ordinary grandma. Singer, musician, storyteller, hostess, entertainer—McCord's light burned bright, and it shone on all who came near. Those outside the Ozarks might have been more familiar with Randolph and Rayburn, but back in the hills and hollers in the middle of the twentieth century no one rivaled her celebrity. McCord was regional royalty, and we are glad to welcome the Queen back to the realm.

Brooks Blevins

VOLUME EDITORS' PREFACE

An Ozarks Treasure

May Kennedy McCord is an Ozarks treasure, and we are indebted to her for preserving so much of our history and culture. It's unfortunate that she never wrote a book, but she never felt the need, though others (such as Vance Randolph) encouraged her to do so. She was an entertainer who preferred to publicize the works of others than to publish her own. Her husband was a successful salesman who supported her financially, so she didn't need to write for money. Nor did she need to publish a book to stoke her own ego; in fact, she was so unpretentious that when the editor of the *Saturday Evening Post* wrote to encourage her to let him see any future article she might write, she turned the letter over and wrote her grocery list on the back: "buttermilk, spinach, strawberries, butter, cream, lard"!

May was a trailblazer who kept her maiden name as her middle name; traveled across the Ozarks, state, and nation, often by train or Greyhound bus, on her own; and built a substantial career for herself after her children were grown. She was the unofficial PR manager for the Ozarks and spent her time promoting the land and the people she loved. "You can't go wrong in the Ozarks—you just can't," she wrote. There's "so much to do—there are rabbits to track and nuts to crack."

She believed that no one could own folklore, that it should be shared—so that's how she spent her time. She said some accused her of living in the past, but she made no apologies for that: "Believe me, it was some past to live in!"

I remember my family listening to May on the radio when I was growing up in Cabool, Missouri, and I regret that my move to Springfield came in 1979, six months after her death and too late for me to meet her. How I would have loved to sit in on some of those music parties at 817 North Jefferson! I don't doubt the writer for the *St. Louis Globe-Democrat* who advised that anyone interviewing May "bring along an overnight bag and stay a while, for May can keep anybody entertained—not just for hours, but for days." As Otto Ernest Rayburn once said, "May could find fun in swallowing a fish bone."

"Bless your hearts, here I am again! Bad pennies will bob up, you know," May declared. And it's a delight when this bad penny shows up again. Reading her columns makes me want to follow May's advice on any number of things: to prune my fruit trees in the light of the moon, to try witching for water (I have seen my father do this successfully and so believe I might be successful, too), to make dye from poke or sumac berries. By all means, I will now plant my lettuce on Valentine's Day and potatoes on St. Patrick's Day—though I will confess my disappointment that cutting sprouts on my property on May 9 and 10 seems not to keep them from growing back. I'm a fan, and I've enjoyed getting to know May through her granddaughter's eyes (and I've told Patti more than once that I'm jealous she got to have May for her Moomaw). This book has truly been a labor of love, and I appreciate Patti's sharing May with me—and now, with you.

May spoke the truth when she told a journalist, "They love me in the hill country, and I love them." I hope this long-overdue collection of the best of May's writings—heretofore scattered hither and yon, a bit like May—will help a new generation grow to love her as her contemporaries did. All royalties from the sale of this book will be donated to a scholarship in May's name at Missouri State University. To be eligible, applicants must be undergraduates minoring in Ozarks Studies or graduate students committed to working in Ozarks Studies, for we wish to encourage future generations to carry on May's love for Ozarks culture—past, present, and future.

Kristene Sutliff

My Grandmother

May Kennedy McCord loved life! She loved songs, and poetry, and dancing, and laughing and storytelling—especially hearing and repeating tales of "her people," the Ozarks hill people. She had no patience for conventions that got in the way of such things. At family dinners when I was a child, our mothers would start to stir to help with clean up as the meal was ending. But Moomaw (our name for May) always said, "Now girls, I don't get to see you often enough, and the hired girl will be here from Galena on Wednesday. So, fetch me my guitar, let Junior play the piano, and let's have fun the rest of this night." Then, if we visited on Tuesday, those dirty dishes that so threatened time that could be better used to enjoy life would still be on the table, waiting for the hired girl to come and remove them.

Her home was constantly full of visitors. I recall more than once when friends arrived unexpectedly, and she was always thrilled to see them. She would pull down her guitar, and they would laugh and sing old ballads and swap stories until late into the night. Such gatherings in her home were common, often with characters who were enchanting to me as a child. There was the old Polish sea captain, the man with the funny beard that got caught in his fiddle, the old lady without teeth who made such mournful sounds, and the undertaker who smoked a stubby cigar and cussed in every sentence. I would fall asleep in the middle of it all, and when my mother came for me the next morning, she would find that some kind soul had moved me to a bed, still dressed from the night before. And Moomaw would tell my mother about her friends, "We had a feast of a visit last night."

I remember several times when Jimmie and Cleda Morris (later Driftwood), their boys, Moomaw, and a few other friends came to my childhood home. My dad played the fiddle and piano, Jimmie played his mouth bow, and his son Bo (James)—on whom I had a huge crush at that age—played the guitar along with his dad. Of course, Moomaw and Jimmie sang, too. What memories!

Moomaw could "stir up a dinner" as quick as anyone, and after everyone was stuffed, she would inquire, "Do you want me to fry you an egg?" She had many sets of dishes, and after dinners, she often just moved them to the back porch where they would sit until the hired girl came to clean them. Not that she was raised in a family with servants—far from it. Today we would consider her early circumstances in the hill country of the Ozarks extreme poverty, especially after her father became too ill to work. He died when May was only twelve years old. A brother died as a toddler, and her younger sister was murdered by a jealous lover. Despite tragedies, she reached out and found joy no matter what life brought her. Perhaps it was Moomaw's positive attitude that caused her to end many of her columns and radio programs with the faith that she would be back next time, "The Lord willin' and the creek don't rise!"

The old ballads were as much a part of Moomaw as life itself. She collected the old songs from folks in the deep hills, and she shared them with anyone who was interested. I remember once when I was a child of about ten, we drove for miles over country roads to an old cabin where "the blind man" lived. He and Moomaw sang and laughed together for hours, and he shared with her the words to an old song he had heard as a child.

She titled her writings Hillbilly Heartbeats. It was not just a title. After rereading all of her writings that I could find, I understand that her own heart throbbed with love for everything and everyone she wrote about. She loved to be with people and loved and respected everyone without regard to their station in life. Once she wrote of Ozarkians, "I'm for them—every one of them. I love the whole clan. I love the hills. The call of nativity is the strongest thing in my body. I hunger to see the cows coming home at eve, and the lazy goats munching the sprouts at noonday on the rocky slopes. It's the 'call of the wool' I guess, for I long to climb the steeps with them. I love the people and their lore and language. My heart cries out for the misty hills and the overhanging cliffs, shadowed in colors far out upon the water."

Often late on a Sunday afternoon, my brother and I would be sitting on our porch swing when a taxi would pull up and Moomaw would emerge. It was then party time for us! Sometimes she brought her guitar, but often she just sang with us and played our piano. On summer evenings outside, she might just roll up a hickory leaf and whistle an old tune. Even though we were only children, we somehow knew that she brought the wisdom of our elders. It was a treasured life that few have been lucky enough to have lived.

Moomaw once wrote, "When I walked, last week, along the great cliffs of the virgin bluffs on White River, towering four hundred feet above the green waters, and looked breathlessly below at the staggering beauty of it all, it seemed almost that I might find a lost star in my hair— that I was dizzily near the infinite!"

Many of those streams are now long gone—buried deep under water created by a great dam, where speedboats and jet skis race to and fro. Of course, the folks of the deep hills have also passed, along with their log cabins, trails marked only by wood chips, and the fiddlers and ballad singers who played or sang with unaccompanied simplicity. Also gone are the peace and simple life of the hills, often retold in ballads and stories that had room to grow. The mountain life of the Ozarks could not endure forever, but our hearts can find joy in remembering those people and times.

Patti McCord

ACKNOWLEDGMENTS

We are indebted to many people who have assisted and encouraged us to bring this book to fruition.

This project would not have been possible without the resources available through the Local History and Genealogy Department at the Library Center of the Springfield-Greene County Library District. The librarians we worked with were incredible guides in accessing old newspapers on microfilm; we are grateful for your never-ending patience. We thank Gwen Simmons at the Lyons Memorial Library at the College of the Ozarks for your assistance in accessing and copying materials in your collection. Thank you, Gordon McCann, for sharing your extensive library of Ozarks material with us and for locating relevant articles in your collection.

For permission to use copyrighted material, we acknowledge and thank Ken Meyer, owner of Meyer Communications, for the use of articles from KWTO's *Dial* magazine; and Cheryl Whitsitt, news director of the *Springfield News-Leader* for the use of columns, articles, and photographs.

Many others lent their support in various ways: Wayne Glenn, Thomas Peters, Curtis Copeland, Laura Jolley, and Kim Lansford. We deeply appreciate your help. Brooks Blevins, thank you for encouraging us and for painstakingly reading our manuscript; your suggestions made this a stronger book, as did those of Jenny Vos and others of the editorial staff at the University of Arkansas Press. Thank you all!

Finally, we want to express our heartfelt thanks to Barbara Morelock for your hospitality while we researched and organized this material. Thank you for being a friend.

EDITORS' NOTE

May Kennedy McCord wrote hundreds of columns and articles over a period of thirty-five years. For May, writing was a group effort. Always crediting her contributors by their name and town of residence, she often quoted from letters her devoted readers wrote her about their lives in the Ozarks. What follows is but a small selection of May's work, published and occasionally unpublished, organized by topic.

Since May's writing appeared across many publications over many years, we have provided the date and source of each entry in parentheses immediately after May's text. The greatest number appeared in her columns in newspapers in Springfield. She wrote a weekly column in the *Springfield News and Leader* (*SNL*) from October 23, 1932, to April 1, 1938, when she began writing three times weekly for the *Springfield Daily News* (*SDN*).[1] She also wrote frequently for *Dial*, a magazine published by the radio station KWTO in Springfield.

While we have tidied up a few typographical errors and made light edits for clarity, we have preserved May's folksy style, including the dialect she often used. We introduce each chapter with contextual information and have organized the entries under our own headings. Otherwise, the book's contents are the words of May and her contributors.

QUEEN OF THE HILLBILLIES

Remembering
May Kennedy McCord

First Lady of the Ozarks...
Queen of the Hillbillies

Deep in the Ozark Mountains of the 1880s and '90s the only roads were Indian trails and the Old Wire Road, which was built to follow the telegraph lines during the Civil War. No hospitals, most medical care provided by country doctors, or by old grannies with local folk treatments. No electricity. Fresh water came from springs and wells. For sustenance, the clear streams and rivers were full of bass and jack salmon, and the woods were full of squirrels, possums, beavers, and wild turkeys. The people themselves were always full of music and stories. Families gathered to play fiddle tunes, sing the old ballads, and tell and retell the old, old stories in the colorful language of people who did not always understand words on paper. Town parties were held in schoolhouses that were then used for church on Sunday, for shoutin' the old-time Glory Hallelujahs.[1] Square dancin's and apple peelin's and spelling bees and horse swappin's and even revivals were times of entertainment, as was just plain visiting around. Everybody was as good as everybody else, and nobody was looked down on unless they were caught looking down on somebody else—being "uppity" they called it, and they didn't tolerate it.

This is the world May Anderson Kennedy McCord grew up in. More accurately, it is the ideal world she remembered and passionately shared with her readers and listeners for decades. The simple life of an Ozarker in the days of her childhood, May once told a reporter, required nothing more than "a little cot, a wife and kids, a houn' dog, a little patch of corn, a pipe to smoke, bread, fat-back and molasses, a little store sweetenin' now and then, a fiddle, a coon-skin hung over the door—and bliss complete."[2]

May was born on December 1, 1880, in Carthage, Missouri, and moved with her family to Galena, Missouri, when she was six. Although May proudly recognized Galena as her hometown, making her a daughter of the hills, her family background was not that of the poor, hardscrabble farmers and other humble people whose lives she would later chronicle. Her educated parents were not originally from the Ozarks and passed on to her somewhat of an outsider's perspective. Her own education and travel widened her reference for understanding her environment. May was intelligent and attractive, with a sense of humor that endeared her to people, and she had the rare ability to relate to people from all stations in life. She was outgoing and comfortable in the limelight. As her career later developed, these experiences and personal qualities put her in an unusual position as a mediator between the rural Ozarkers she loved, and who loved her, and the academic and professional outsiders who were interested in the culture of the Ozarks.

May had "a nation-wide reputation as an authority on American folklore."[3] Many worked in this field with differing agendas. May simply told it as she saw it. Her writings and lectures show that she, like many reformers in her time, shared a belief about the basic goodness of ordinary folk, but she showed no interest in changing the lives of common Ozarkers, nor do her writings suggest any effort to steer others toward more rustic Ozarkian values. May was friends with academics and often participated in their seminars, but her writings show her lack of interest in scholarly analysis or interpretation. Her straightforward reporting made her writings and lectures valuable to others who needed an unfiltered source for their work.

May Kennedy McCord. *Courtesy of the* Springfield News-Leader.

May's father, Jesse Thomas "Tom" Kennedy, was born in Palestine, Illinois, in 1843, and her mother, Delia Melissa Fike, was born in St. Clair County, Illinois, in 1845. Education was important to both, and they encouraged May's love of great literature and poetry and helped her develop the language to retell it all. Delia had graduated from the Greenville Female Seminary (now closed) and attended McKendree College, both in St. Clair County. Tom's educational background is unknown, but May wrote that both of her parents had been teachers. Music was also important in May's family; according to May, her mother had a lovely singing voice, played a small organ they had at home, and sang many of the old ballads that May would later perform.[4]

May wrote that her parents first moved to Carthage when her father was hired to teach in a local grade school, and he was later an auditor for the Robert Moore Lumber Company. When he developed tuberculosis, Tom was advised to move deeper into the Ozarks, and in 1886 the family settled in Galena, where Tom was a partner with Thomas J. Porter in a general merchandise business. When May was nine, her parents traveled west for a drier climate, for a time leaving May with their friend Aunt Polly Crouch in Dry Creek, a more remote area west of Galena. This was an important time for May's education about Ozarks heritage; she learned many old ballads and shared the daily life of rural hill people, learning their dialect and absorbing their philosophy and love of the hills.

Later, May went with her mother and two siblings to be with her father in Arizona, where they lived in the Salt River Valley near Phoenix for two years until her father's death in 1892. After Tom's death, Delia brought the family back to Galena and soon married Benjamin Yocum, a judge, attorney, and Civil War pensioner. May always spoke warmly about her stepfather.

May went to the little school in Galena and later graduated from Sheldon's Private College in Aurora, Missouri (now closed). In later years she often said her real education came from people such as Aunt Polly, who knew all the moon signs and how to cure ailments and sang the ballads that told the stories of old times. She embodied the wisdom of the ages that May absorbed as a child—including Aunt Polly's belief that "a lot of people knew things but a heap of what they knew hain't so."

May loved to participate in the theatrical events held frequently in her small town. She first sang in a public event when she was only six—an old temperance tearjerker, "Father, Dear Father, Come Home with Me Now." As told by scholar Robert K. Gilmore, "When she was a girl of sixteen in Galena, the family minister was upset with her title role in *The Gypsy's Daughter*. He called at her home after opening night and prayed over her, telling her parents that such a role would cause her to become 'worldly—may even lead her to be an actress!' A direr fate would have been hard for the Ozarker to imagine."[5]

May was well known in Galena for swimming her horse across the James River, chestnut hair streaming behind her; rowing a boat like a sailor; shooting the river's ripples fearlessly in the unsteady birch-bark canoe her stepfather gave her; sitting at the piano, her exceptional memory and singing spirit recreating every ballad she had ever heard. But she also had a philosophical side that sought the solitude of the hills and streams and found joy in the simple pleasures of working in her garden and in her Methodist Church, down on her "prayer bones."[6]

May had a brother, Leslie; a sister, Maudeva, who was murdered by a jealous lover at age eighteen; a younger brother who died as a toddler; and a half-sister, Vera Courtney Thomas, her mother's child from a previous marriage. Vera had a magnificent voice. In 1890, at age twenty-two, she ventured to Paris for voice training and later gained success singing leading roles with the Opéra Comique in Paris, had an opera written for her by Massenet,[7] and toured with the Metropolitan Opera Company, singing leading roles with Caruso. May and her half-sister did not grow up together—Vera was twelve years older than May and lived with her father in Clinton, Missouri, during her later childhood. Nevertheless, May often spoke of her half-sister's talent and her adventurous spirit that enabled her to travel abroad and pursue an ambitious career.

The 1900 census found nineteen-year-old May still living at home in Galena and teaching music part time.[8] The following year she decided it was time to do something with her future and set out for St. Louis, where she landed an office job as a stenographer that paid ten dollars per week. Her main weekly expense was four dollars for room, board, and a practice piano.[9] Her brother, Leslie, also struck out on his own at about this same time and went to California, where he found employment with the Los Angeles Bureau of Power and Light.

May returned to Galena for a Christmas visit in 1902, and on January 3, 1903, married her childhood sweetheart Charles C. McCord, son of the town doctor. In about 1908 they moved to St. Louis but returned to Galena by 1914 when the Shapleigh Hardware Company of

St. Louis hired Charles as their salesman for the Ozarks area. Back in Galena, Charles would pick up a horse and wagon on Monday mornings and travel through southern Missouri and northern Arkansas to sell his wares, leaving May alone in Galena. They lived only a couple blocks from the town square, and May loved being in the center of the community. While Charles was away, May spent her time with their three children: Charles Jr., born in 1903; Maudeva, born in 1905; and Leslie, born in 1913. May was active organizing social activities, plays, Women's Christian Temperance Union events, singing contests, and the like. She often traveled with Dr. McCord in his horse and buggy to help with a birth or see an ill backcountry patient. The country people generally trusted "old grannies" more than they did doctors, and it was during these trips that May learned many old remedies.

In 1918 the Shapleigh Hardware Company named Charles director of sales for the Springfield area, and the family moved from Galena to Springfield. May later wrote, "When we were forced to move almost with a club, because it is my better half's trade territory (he's one of those 'drummers,' you know) I thought my heart would die within me. Almost would I rather have been taken out on the hill of my little hometown and planted beside my beloved ones. No one knows what I experienced. But here I have made my friends and pitched my tent and loosed my shoes and found my sky. I love it."[10]

Charles's new position continued to require frequent travel. With extra time now available, May joined the Springfield Music Club, the local Women's Christian Temperance Union chapter, the Grace Methodist Church, and several local writers' groups. Soon she began playing piano accompaniment for other musicians, speaking about the hill country, and singing ballads at various meetings, such as ladies' social clubs, missionary societies, and veterans' and church groups. She even played a role in a musical comedy put on by the Shrine Patrol Association in the auditorium of Springfield's Abou Ben Adhem Shrine Mosque.

May had developed an interest in writing early in her life. As a child she wrote poetry but hid it because she thought her schoolmates would make fun of it as proof of her feeble mind. By the early 1920s, May's participation in local activities was making her known in the community. Thomas Nickel, a writer for a Springfield newspaper, "sought May out from her literary seclusion" and asked her to write a silly poem for his *Midget Magazine*. He printed her poem "Alarming" in July 1924.[11] This small success spurred May's interest in writing, and when she saw a notice in the *Sample Case,* her husband's trade magazine, soliciting submissions, she sent in a story. In December 1925, they printed her first story, "The Buryin'."[12] Although this story was fictional, her later writings were mostly nonfiction or at least based on actual events. She wrote using the dialect of the deep hills of the Ozarks.

By the 1930s May's writing career was well underway. In addition to her regular contributions to friend Otto Ernest Rayburn's *Ozark Life* and *Arcadian Magazine,* she was recruited by the *Springfield News and Leader* to write her weekly column, Hillbilly Heartbeats, beginning October 23, 1932. She moved to the *Springfield Daily News* on April 1, 1938, and wrote three columns each week through July 25, 1942.

A colorful array of characters and fascinating lore had evolved in the Ozarks, but May said "you must get it in the raw," and she believed that such stories would be ruined by any attempt at sophistication or academics. May believed that people in the hills and small towns of the Ozarks had stories worth sharing and recording. She invited her readers to send her their stories, and she devoted a large part of her columns to their contributions. Hillbilly Heartbeats became a forum for her people to reminisce about their past, and because May did not edit or embellish her readers' stories, they became an archive of authentic tales that could later be studied by academic folklorists. In her first Hillbilly Heartbeats column in the *Springfield News and Leader*, May wrote,

> This is a new column, and it is going to be yours as well as mine. Tell me what you know about this Hillbilly. We never tire of learning about him. . . . Come on, Hillbillies, let's get together. Let's rave about it all. Write some poetry and some essays and some love letters to the hills! Let's don't talk about our hotels and garages and banks and politics and the cosmic situation— let's go out into the flaming autumn and run the whole gamut

of human emotions. Let's hear from the idealists and the boosters and the poets and the dreamers—yes, don't forget the dreamers—and the religionists and the farmers and the pied pipers and spinners in the sun and the sorghum makers. Let's forget all else. This old world is progressing fast enough scientifically; it doesn't need us hillbillies to help along that line. It is simply amazing the geniuses that spring up out of these rocks when you go to stirring them about. You can roll a pumpkin under the bed down here in the Ozark hills and scare out more poets and fiddlers and dreamers and singers of songs than they have within the walls of Gotham itself![13]

May had a desk with pigeonholes where she stuck the mountains of correspondence she received. Many envelopes were simply addressed to "May, Springfield, Mo.," or "Hillbilly, Springfield, Mo." There were poems and prose, family stories, ghost stories, requests for old-time remedies and methods or the proper mix of greens for a poke sallet, questions about the best phase of the moon for plantings, words and music of ballads, and praise for her column.

The secretary of the Missouri Historical Society, Floyd Shoemaker, wrote a personal letter to May saying that he never ceased to be amazed at the wealth of material she crowded into her column. "Few persons," he wrote, "realize the extent of the contribution you are making to the folklore of the state and to America as well."[14] The *Missouri Historical Review* had this to say about May: "Hillbilly Heartbeats is a reservoir for Ozark folklore. Mrs. McCord, by recording notes about the superstitions, ballads, and history of the region, is doing much to preserve a rich heritage of the State that might otherwise be lost."[15]

Even while devoting most of her efforts to her weekly columns and speaking engagements, May continued to write for other publications and broader audiences. In June of 1936, her article about being the wife of a fisherman was published by *Field and Stream*,[16] and in April 1942 her short story "A Partin' in Smoky Holler" was printed by the *American Mercury*. In 1935 she received the following note from the editor of the *Saturday Evening Post*: "Someday when you get around to writing an article be sure to let us see it."[17] The ever-unpretentious May wrote her grocery list on the back of the note, which was found in her personal files.

Music was an essential part of life in the hills, where the old ballads were still sung and passed down from one generation to the next. As a result, the study of traditional ballads was an important element of folklore studies. In the 1930s and '40s ballad collecting had become popular among academics and laypersons, including Henry Marvin Belden at the University of Missouri, John A. Lomax and his cowboy songs, Olive Dame Campbell and Cecil Sharp in Southern Appalachia, and Robert W. Gordon for the Library of Congress. Carl Sandburg published *The American Songbag* in 1927, and Vance Randolph published in four volumes the old songs he collected during his forays into the Ozarks hill country.[18]

Calling May "an authoritative source for much Ozark Music," an article in the *Missouri Folklore Society Journal* noted that "when she performed what she had collected, she made a point not to change the songs."[19] Some academic collectors, such as Cecil Sharp, focused only on the old ballads of English origin. May honored those, but she believed that folklore "never stops flowing from the springs of the people's fancy." She was interested in folklore that covered a wide range of experiences— as she put it, "folklore of the cotton pickers, of the lumberjacks, of the western cowboy, the sailors and their chanteys, songs of the Nebraska pioneers, tales of the early Indians, the California gold rush . . . songs and lore of bandits and gamblers and outlaws, frontier characters and the little old log cabin on the claim."[20]

Considerably rarer than ballad collectors, wrote Marguerite Lyon in a column for the *Chicago Tribune*, is a "dyed-in-the-wool ballad singer, one who can sing these old songs with the fire and spirit with which they were meant to be sung. Fortunately, we have May Kennedy McCord who knows scores of old ballads and no one could sing them more effectively."[21] In the 1930s, the Resettlement Administration, part of Roosevelt's New Deal, sent field agents into rural areas to record the nation's musical heritage in authentic voices. Before coming to the Ozarks in December 1936, field agent Sidney Robertson was told that

May Kennedy McCord was the local authority on folklore in the Ozarks and that she was friends with families who knew the old songs of the Ozark hills. Robertson set up her equipment in May's home and used May's help to persuade those who were reluctant to deal with strangers, especially "government folk," to participate. Many of Robertson's ninety-six recordings were of May talking or singing,[22] and May also contributed ballads for the recording projects of Vance Randolph in 1941 and George Armstrong in 1963. These works are available through the American Folklife Center of the Library of Congress.[23]

By the mid 1930s May was speaking and singing her ballads across the country, from the Los Angeles Breakfast Club on Warner Brothers' radio to the English-Speaking Union in New York City. She was invited to speak at many universities, historical societies, festivals, and local gatherings in between—but not neglecting fish fries, town picnics, and basket dinners with her people in the Ozarks.

May's activity was often covered by the press. While she was visiting her brother in 1935, the *Los Angeles Times* wrote an article about her that included a photo with the caption "Humorist." The article referenced her authority of Elizabethan ballads, pride of Ozarks dialect, and Hillbilly Heartbeats columns, and referred to her as the "Will Rogers of the Ozarks."[24] During her visit in 1941 the *Los Angeles Times* ran a picture of May and an article, "Hillbilly Queen of Ozarks Recalls Customs of Hills."[25] Other newspapers printed biographical articles about May and reviewed her lectures. Many can be accessed through https://www.newspapers.com.

May's career continued to expand when, during the Golden Age of Radio, she was recruited by KWK in St. Louis for a weekday-morning broadcast. Springfield continued to be her home. On Sunday nights she took the Frisco Railroad from Springfield to St. Louis, returning the following Friday night. Her first program aired August 3, 1942, and the station's owners supported her through extensive streetcar and newspaper ads. The warmth of her personality caught on immediately, and in 1943 she was rated first among the best-known radio personalities in St. Louis. (Noted baseball announcer Dizzy Dean came in third.)[26] May was even a featured speaker on pregame baseball broadcasts on KWK.[27]

In September of 1943, May was devastated by the sudden death of her husband and, a year later, by the death of her beloved older brother. May's notes on her radio script say she had gone to California when notified of her brother's serious condition and, after his death, returned to St. Louis by train, arriving at 8:00 on the morning of November 27, 1944, in time for her 9:15 broadcast. She wrote "I was very ill, but I got through. I went into the station director's office and collapsed."[28] May's daughter, Maudeva Janss, took her home to Springfield, where she spent three months in recovery and decided not to return to her program at KWK. She gradually returned to her work and from December 1945 through July 1963 had a radio program on KWTO in Springfield, reprising the name Hillbilly Heartbeats from her newspaper columns. Fittingly, the call letters for the radio station stood for "Keep Watching the Ozarks." She was introduced by her theme song, "Hillbilly Heartbeats, tender and warm, down in the Ozarks, back on the farm . . ." followed by "Here is May Kennedy McCord, the Queen of the Ozarks."

May's youth and especially her developing career coincided with upheavals in the United States and in the world: wars, large-scale immigration, economic depression, and rapid urbanization. In response to immigration from Southern and Eastern Europe came a xenophobic belief that "Anglo-Saxon" communities and traditions were superior to those of newer arrivals.[29] During this time well-meaning reformers went into Appalachia, and later into the Ozarks, where they saw extreme poverty but also what they viewed as a strong culture of traditional Anglo-Saxon values. Such reformers wanted to improve, according to their own value systems, the lives of the people they met.[30] They thought the activities and values they found could be built on as a tool for social reform in other depressed population groups. According to one analysis, "The folk and their traditions seemed to offer Americans the foundation for a way of life that did not rely on material wealth. Traditional practices, many believed, might be restorative, uniting body and spirit, nourishing the soul, encouraging self-reliance, and upholding the family."[31] Though the Anglo-Saxon thesis emanated from the xenophobia of the early twentieth century and May repeated the thesis's phraseology, her writings are devoid of disparaging remarks about non-whites and foreigners.

She seems to have embraced this laudatory description of her fellow Ozarkers as a tool of regional defense and pride.

Social worker Catherine Barker spent time in the deep hills of the Ozarks during the Depression. She later wrote about the deplorable poverty she found, but she also described the people as proud, independent, and opposed to anything new. An educated newcomer to the region, Barker believed that intervention was necessary to give these people a better life.[32] Unsurprisingly, many of the proud people in the Ozarks were not in favor of such changes. Although May recognized the existence of poverty in the Ozarks and collected food, clothing, and toys from her readers to send to the hills, she never joined those who wanted to reform the lives of the people there.[33] This statement—perhaps an admonishment to reformers—sums up her position on this issue: "You can never quite modernize or absorb or transform the rock-ribbed Hillbilly, and there's no use trying; and thank heaven for it."[34] Another "hillbilly" who rejected the notion of reform was May's friend Dewey Short, whom a large section of the Missouri Ozarks sent to Congress for twenty-four years. He fought against the deep changes imbedded in Roosevelt's New Deal programs, even though some, such as the Rural Electrification Act of 1936, would bring what most would consider progress to his constituents. He said in Congress,

> I fully realize, as do you, that the world is now going through one of its periodic transitions. It is only natural, logical, and inevitable that following a catastrophe of such gigantic magnitude as the World War we should be compelled, as every other participant in the savage struggle that exacted such a toll in life and property, to make certain social and economic readjustments. . . . I also know we can never go back to the old order just as it was. New ideas cramp some peoples' minds just as new shoes hurt their feet but not so with me. I know that without change there would be no progress, but I am not going to mistake mere change for progress. . . .
>
>   . . . One does not have to kill his dog in order to get rid of

its fleas. In fact, a few fleas are good for any dog—they keep his mind off being a dog all the time.[35]

These troubling times set the stage for renewed interest in the folklore of the nation's past: stories of hardships and hard-working people, their old-time Protestant religious practices, folk tales, superstitions, dialect, crafts, and traditional music—especially ballads. Major universities began to recognize folklore as a legitimate academic discipline.[36] Folklore societies were blossoming all over, including the Missouri Folklore Society that H. M. Belden of the University of Missouri had first struggled to establish in 1908.[37] The Texas Folklore Society had been established by John Lomax and L. W. Payne in 1909, largely initiated by Lomax to formalize work on his collection of cowboy songs.[38]

May did not have academic credentials; however, she was included in meetings and seminars with those who did. She was a panelist in the academic workshops that were part of the National Folk Festivals, and she spoke at universities, such as Washington University in St. Louis. She was included in conferences such as the National Conference on American Folklore for Children held by Ball State Teachers College (now University), where she was a featured speaker along with noted folklore scholars Richard Dorson of Michigan State College and Alfred Shoemaker of Franklin & Marshall College in Lancaster, Pennsylvania. Since May was in touch with older Ozarkers, she used her columns to find stories that others wanted for their work. For example, in 1938, after May wrote about a sociology professor's lecture discussing the role of mail-order catalogues in rural life, May's readers sent her many examples, which she forwarded to the professor.[39] May wrote about sharing ballads with H. M. Belden at the University of Missouri and exchanging letters with Frederick Middlebush, President of the University of Missouri, about water witching.[40] The *Missouri Folklore Society Journal* dedicated its issue on ballad collecting to several academics and others, including May.[41]

In addition to the scholars and reformers, from the soil emerged a group of kindred spirits and friends who wanted to document the oral traditions of their past and trumpet the values of the common hill folks of the Ozarks. These groups were labeled "romantics" because their writings glorified the hillbilly and described their Ozarks country and vanishing culture in a sentimental and nostalgic manner.

May was very much at the center of a large circle of friends who shared her passion for folklore and the Ozarks. They got together through writers' groups, festivals, and organizations such as the Ozarkians and the Hillcrofters. They wrote for rural newspapers and published essays and poetry in local magazines and journals; several first gained wider recognition when May included their work in her columns. Described in the *St. Louis Post-Dispatch* as "reigning over all the hillbilly poets," she touched one local poet, Herb Duncan, "with her wand and gave him prominence."[42] Many of these friends are no longer widely remembered, but for some whose contributions are included in this book, short biographical sketches are provided in the endnotes.

Probably the best remembered of these romantics are two Kansans who adopted the Ozarks as their home after World War I: folklorist Vance Randolph and teacher-publisher Otto Ernest Rayburn. While Randolph became a valued friend, it was Rayburn who was important in launching May's career. Rayburn was a keen observer of his neighbors and how they lived in the hills, which provided material and understanding for his own writings; however, he needed other writers to provide material for his magazine. Early in his publishing career he met May, who shared his affection for the people of the Ozarks. In 1929 he recruited her to conduct a column for *Ozark Life,* his first publication. Rayburn once wrote, "History is only a rattle of dry bones in the secret closet of the past for a great number of people. . . . But there is poetry in history. . . . The over-all picture of a people in any age is best determined by the story of the human heart."[43] This romantic approach to history was capsuled by the title Hillbilly Heartbeats, which they selected for May's new column. For the rest of her career, May used this title for her newspaper columns and radio programs.

May, Otto Rayburn, Vance Randolph, and Mary Elizabeth Mahnkey (a published poet and writer) often got together and shared their stories for one another's books and articles. In 1932, May described the first meeting of these four:

> We made a pilgrimage one Sunday, a few of us, to the little crossroads of Oasis to see that wonderful hillbilly woman, Mary Elizabeth Mahnkey. You have read so much of her beautiful verse in this paper and other publications. There she was, a strangely quiet, sensitive gray-haired woman with a young face: a woman who was, plainly, all soul. At first she had that sort of unapproachableness of the true old Ozarker of pioneer lineage. Not an unfriendly sort, but just something you can't describe unless you go down into the hills and meet her. She lived above her little store. She received us with dignity and seemed a bit overcome that we should make a pilgrimage to her shrine, and her strange gray eyes struggled to hold back amazed tears. But she knew we were kindred spirits and friends though she had never met us. Vance Randolph and Otto Rayburn, both of whose writings she admired, were in the party. She invited us upstairs after a while, to the humble little roof-tree where on a small table sat the typewriter which clicked out the words of that great woman's heart in the far away, lonely little country store at the bend of the road. She longs for the beautiful things of the world and for the companionship and sweet understanding of those who speak her language.
>
> We came away silent, admiring, with no words to describe the woman with the light in her face from the candle within her soul. Mary Elizabeth Mahnkey, an Ozarkian, a Hillbilly whose poetry, to my mind, ranks with the very great.[44]

These friends contributed to one another's writings. Over several years Rayburn printed articles by and about May in his publications. May's files include very personal correspondence with both Rayburn and Randolph, some written in their aging years. When May was seventy-seven years old, Rayburn wrote to her, "How are you feeling, what are you thinking about, does life still flame for you as it has done through the years? I wonder if you know how much I treasure and adore you. Your soul has touched mine and that is a rare thing in this life. May, we are on the Twilight Trail. . . . Will you take time to write me a few lines? A letter from you is like a gift from the gods."[45]

In a personal letter to May, Randolph asked for "any old-time jokes. . . . It would be bad luck to publish a book about the Ozarks without your name in it somewhere." Randolph gave May a copy of his book *We Always Lie to Strangers*, which he signed with the message "To my good friend May McCord, to whom I am indebted for a lot of good stories."[46]

May corresponded with poet Carl Sandburg over several decades and shared the words of old ballads with him. In a personal letter to May, Sandburg wrote, "Time rolls on. You are right. We belong to some kind of a vanguard, you and I."[47]

The artist, writer, and creator of the Kewpie Doll, Rose O'Neill, was a friend and frequent guest in May's home. Jimmie (or Jimmy) Driftwood often visited May, and in a letter to her in 1959, asked her to write Alan Lomax about an upcoming folk festival concert in Carnegie Hall, noting, "You can tell him more about me than anyone could."[48] Congressman Dewey Short and May both grew up in Galena, Missouri; they remained friends as adults, wrote personal letters to each other over the years, and visited when their busy careers allowed.

May, like many Ozarkers, had a deep love and appreciation of folk music, both for its own sake and for the treasured traditions it recorded. Some social reformers of the time thought music could be used to improve impoverished lives.[49] Others, like May, simply wanted to preserve this music as folklore. In the 1920s several folk-music festivals emerged in Appalachia; the most enduring, the Mountain Dance and Folk Festival, was organized by Bascom Lamar Lunsford in Asheville, North Carolina, in 1928. Later, Sarah Gertrude Knott, then director of the St. Louis Dramatic League, founded the National Folk Festival, which was first held in May 1934 as part of the formal dedication of the St. Louis Municipal Auditorium. This festival was different from earlier ones because performers were presented from across cultural, religious, and racial groups.[50] Knott sought the prestige of an advisory group from the academic folklore community. When it came time to find participants for her show, however, she did not look to the academics in her committee but found individuals such as May, who were in touch with local talent and knew where the authentic musicians could be found in the Ozarks. Knott's organizational plan was to create minifestivals in communities across the country, with contests to select the best representatives to appear at the National Folk Festival. May was named Ozarks chair and helped organize festivals in Eureka Springs, Arkansas, and in the Missouri towns of Cape Girardeau, Rolla, Aurora, and West Plains. Winners from each local festival were invited to the regional festival in Springfield, Missouri, and the winners from there went to the national festival in St. Louis.[51]

How often we are not appreciated in our own land! May asked the Springfield Chamber of Commerce to help support the festival. Chamber president John T. Woodruff protested, saying "the Chamber would not be a party to putting on a 'freak show.'" This response caused quite a stir. The dispute was picked up by the Associated Press and covered in newspapers across the country, quoting May, a "folklore authority," as saying that Woodruff's statement caused her to "boil over."[52] May explained, "We are NOT staging a 'Hillbilly Show'; we are staging an Ozark Festival. We are not caricaturing the Ozarks or the Hillman. . . . Springfield is the HOST to its surrounding rural people, the best ever lived, in a festival of the old things: songs, dances, customs, arts and crafts, religions and lore that went into the making of this great Ozark Empire. And what is more, people are not coming here to this great playground to see our Empire Buildings and symphony concerts. People out in the world have plenty of these. They are coming here to see our hills and see the things which they have not."[53]

The festival was held in Springfield despite the lack of support from the Chamber, and as planned, the winning performers were selected for Ozark Day at the National Folk Festival in St. Louis. The following newspaper account describes May at work, directing performers on stage.

Yesterday was Ozark Day. It was more than that. It marked the inception of a true festival spirit. Informality and spontaneity were there in rare degree, making it difficult to answer the question as to whether the audience or the actors enjoyed the programs most. Homespun jubilation reigned supreme. With Mrs. May Kennedy McCord of Springfield, Mo., as the effervescent mistress of ceremonies, the hill folks of Missouri and Arkansas sat on the stage while groups of them performed, almost oblivious to the audience, as though the occasion were a real, old-time "play party" held in the Ozarks.

"We're plain and simple," declared Mrs. McCord. "We'd have to be, for half our blood is sorghum and the other half's turnip juice."[54]

Springfield's mayor praised the festival after it was over,[55] and in later years, the National Folk Festival was favorably recognized. Vance Randolph reminded May in a personal letter of their struggles to create the festival. "It's funny how public sentiment changes. Remember the hassle we had with the Chamber of Commerce back in 1934? They wanted to run me out of town for the way I had 'advertised' Missouri."[56]

May continued her support of the festival as a committee member and featured performer. Pete Seeger, a founding member of the New York City folk group The Weavers and a regular festival performer, became a good friend. In later years in a Christmas greeting to her, Seeger wrote, "I will never forget you nor the ageless songs you taught me."[57]

May's dispute with the Springfield Chamber of Commerce illustrates the tension that existed between those who respected the rural people in the hills and those who did not want to be associated with common "hillbillies." May had been selected "Queen of the Hillbillies" in 1931 at a meeting of the Ozarkians, and she forever kept this title, calling it the best anyone could have. But tension developed around the term *hillbilly* when it was commandeered for commercial exploitation in the late 1930s and '40s. May was indignant that the rural people of her country were being stereotyped as lazy, ignorant, whiskered moonshiners of low character.

Still, the same widespread fame and Ozarks expertise that often landed May in unexpected settings could on occasion unintentionally contribute to the stereotyping of her beloved hill people. An example was the 1951 court case of Rev. Guy Howard of Branson, Missouri, who sued the Capitol Records Distributing Company on the grounds that its record, "The Missouri Walkin' Preacher (With a Little Book in His Hand)," referred to him, since he was known as "the Walking Preacher of the Ozarks." After Howard's attorneys called May to the stand to confirm that the preacher's reputation had been damaged by the record, the cross-examining defense attorney proceeded to divert her "expert" testimony into a treatise on Ozarks superstitions. She told the court, "Some believe the cure for malaria is a jigger of whiskey to which three drops of cat's blood have been added. To stop a tornado, Ozarks farmers sometimes stick a knife in the ground with the blade facing the cloud on the theory it will cut the storm in two. You can keep the hoot of an owl from meaning that a sick person will die if you quickly throw salt on a fire. Hill folks have about seventy-five cures for warts, the most common of which is to rub them with a piece of potato." The bemused federal judge quizzed her about some of the remedies, but finally wondered aloud what her testimony had to do with the trial. The attorney explained that he "just thought it would break the monotony of the case." May's colorful testimony not only made the trial less monotonous but also gained the case national media coverage and at least a few headlines, such as the *Chicago Tribune*'s "Court Learns of 75 Ways to Cure a Wart."[58]

May's anguish over hillbilly stereotyping and commercialization in music predated her role in Howard's trial. She was concerned that radio was promoting loud "honky-tonk" songs as the music of rural people. In 1946 she wrote, "You know folk songs and hillbilly songs are not the same at all."[59] She was not alone in this view. Early organizers of the National Folk Festival, including May, hoped to show the dignity of traditional folk music, help preserve its tradition, and gain public appreciation of folk music over the "vulgar commercial imitations" represented by early radio barn dances and the recording companies' production of hillbilly records.

The organizers of the first National Folk Festival in 1934 limited performers to those who were rooted in the traditions they inherited or that had developed on the North American continent—common people whose songs, stories, or dances had passed down from parent to child or within a community. They included "folk expressions of Indians, British, Spanish-American, French, German, and Negroes, along with newer indigenous creations of the cowboy, lumberjack, sailor, and other such typical groups." [60] The festival performance standard was to stage folk expressions that had developed through oral traditions. Dr. George Pullen Jackson of Vanderbilt University was head of music for the festival and had the last word on all music that was presented. [61]

To meet these standards, performers in the Ozarks who came prepared with an act patterned after music they had heard on the radio were coached to revert to traditional sounds. May described working with a family that came to the regional festival in Eureka Springs in 1934. Dissatisfied with the family's modern sound, May, Knott, and Randolph coached them until, as May wrote, "a light broke in upon them and they began to sing the songs we wanted, but they didn't dream would ever be sung. . . . I kept softening down and 'working' them over, and finally they stood up and sang for us in and the sweet old way, the sweet old ballads." [62] In writing about ballad collectors Carl Sandburg and Randolph, May said, "If there is anything that riles them it is this whangdoodle, fake folk song whined over the radio." [63]

There was nothing whangdoodlish or fake about May, as far as her peers were concerned. She was selected for honorary membership in the Missouri Historical Society and first listed in *Who's Who in America* in 1943, selected "solely on prominence suggesting more than localized . . . interest in the public eye, and resulting from unique and meritorious achievement." [64] In 1950, the Golden Rule Foundation named May Missouri's Mother of the Year.

In 1975 the Greater Ozarks Hall of Fame was established by the Ralph Foster Museum at the School (now College) of the Ozarks in Point Lookout, Missouri. The first honorees were selected for their contribution to the retention of the cultural heritage of the Ozarks: May Kennedy McCord, Mary Elizabeth Mahnkey, Vance Randolph, Rose O'Neill, Thomas Hart Benton, and Harold Bell Wright.

Perhaps it was the simplicity of May's philosophy, motherly warmth, humor, and pride in being a hillbilly that made her loved in and beyond the hills. She said, "I've lived from the ox-cart to the Atomic Age. I've had the thrill of riding in the first rubber-tired buggy that came to town and I watched the first locomotive down through my country." Truly, her life's work was to share her love of the Ozarks and preserve the history of earlier times for future generations.

May died in Springfield, Missouri, on February 21, 1979. The *Springfield Leader and Press* announced her death under the headline "The Queen Is Dead":

> We called her "Queen of the Hillbillies." Not out of disrespect. Quite to the contrary, we called her the Queen of the Hillbillies because of affection that bordered on the downright worshipful, at times. She belonged to all of us in the Ozarks. . . . In an interview 10 years ago, in a message to all her friends in the Ozarks, she spoke her own epitaph: "Tell 'em I love 'em, and I always will." The Lord willin' and the creek don't rise, as she used to say in signing off her radio program, we'll see her in the "land beyond the river."[65]

CHAPTER 1

The Ozarks Country

*There is just something different, something peculiar to this
country which no one has ever found words to describe.*

Ozark Life, April 1931

. . . .

Even today, people living in the Ozarks may struggle with
the decision to embrace their hillbilly-ness or to seek a more
sophisticated identity. In 1937, May's readers explored this
dilemma through her Hillbilly Heartbeats columns. In addition to defining hillbillies, her columns explain the location,
land, and culture of the early Ozarks, including hill folks' curi-
ous ways, sense of humor, and dialect. As always May fiercely
defended her hillbillies and her beloved land: the Ozarks.

. . . .

Where Are the Ozarks?

Someone asked me in a recent letter: Please explain where on earth the
Ozarks really are? Well, here I look wise and stroke my chin and tell
you what authorities say—geologists and geographers and topographists

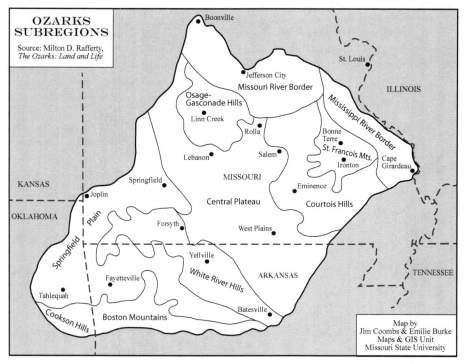

Subregions of the Ozark Uplift. *Map by Jim Coombs and Emilie Burke.*

and whatnot. They tell us this, and it is the easiest remembered: Broadly speaking, the Ozarks are bounded by four rivers—the Mississippi on the east, the Verdigris River in Oklahoma on the west, the Arkansas River on the south and the Saint Francis River on the north.[1] (*Dial,* September 1947)

As It Was in 1931

There is just a something here, preserved intact through the years, that cannot be portrayed by indulging in technicalities. That is the reason that we who love the Ozarks are fighting to preserve that something. . . .

I think Harold Bell Wright gave us such a beautiful name when he called us the land of the "trail that is nobody knows how old." Old trails are tramped away by the onward rush of restless feet in other places; here, they are the same old trails. I can take you to the trails I followed when a child, to find the shy pink columbine and the wild bluebell, and they look as though no foot had touched them since. There are no words to describe my feelings as I go over these still, dark, cool, woodsy little paths—smelling of cedar and mosses and the loamy earth. It just seems to me that civilization has stood still, and I cannot even remember that I have ever been harassed and hurried by the growing sweep and complexity of modern life, and the thundering boom of a gigantic civilization. (*Ozark Life*, April 1931)

Who Is a Hillbilly?

I have a communication from Arthur Galbraith, a young teacher and writer of this city:

> After some years of reading, I am beginning to wonder, and to find myself conjecturing on the somewhat hazy character known as the "Hillbilly." One story I read leaves me picturing the hillbilly character as lank, solemn people who almost never smile, and who live according to a code of morals that originated centuries ago. The next story destroys my previous image and I see wild, carefree rascals who would as lief pillage their neighbors' property as not, and who are notorious slayers of "revenooers" and other ordinary people. Now what or who or where are these so-called hillbillies?
>
> I am particularly interested in the Missouri Ozarks, and the problem of classifying myself as a resident of them is beginning to worry me. Are all people in the Missouri Ozarks hillbillies? . . . Am I a Hillbilly?
>
> . . . When I read some of the stories I find myself wanting to be a Hillbilly—the characters are so noble, pure and so

beautiful. Then again, I pick up another magazine and an author from another locality is presented to me through the printed page and I loathe his filthy hillbilly characters. I have fears, then, that I may be pointed out as a "native" of the Missouri Ozarks, hence a Hillbilly! . . .

Some of the chroniclers say that the hillbillies invariably go barefoot, wear one suspender and don't shave. But I don't go barefoot, I always try to maintain both suspenders and I own, free of all encumbrance, a very effective razor and I use it with a degree of regularity. So maybe I'm not a Hillbilly! I also have a number of neighbors, technically Ozarkians, who wear shoes and suspenders and shave.

Nothing, however, can buck up my fever for Hillbilly loyalty more than the mention that the Ozarkians are direct descendants of Elizabethan English; that our folksongs and dances show it. I always warm at that as a lover of good wine feels the warmth of rare liquors. I must be careful, however, that my alter ego doesn't get into a buff at the pessimistic thought that blood, no matter how dark blue and aristocratic it may be, can be thinned down to a robin's egg hue by repeated transfusions of turnip juice and springtime greens.

. . . Now comes the friction. Have I defined a Hillbilly? Would I know one if I should see him on a winding hill road? No, I have neither arrived at a conclusion nor built toward one. Why? Because there is no conclusion. There is no such thing as a definite Hillbilly. . . . To John Brown, I am a Hillbilly; to Jim Smith, I am not. So, I'll try to speed up my drawl, use less snuff and always wear both suspenders for John's sake. I'll cherish my heirlooms, learn some ballads and trace my genealogy for Jim's sake. (*SNL*, June 13, 1937)

I have communication from Bob Crow of Dillon, Missouri, answering Arthur Gilbraith:

The term "Hillbilly" was first an appellation of derision, very likely. And the term is much overused and misused. But there is a group of people in the Ozarks possessing a culture peculiarly their own and it doesn't take me long to recognize a fellow tribesman. There are certain characteristics common to the group which cannot be hidden. They have a kindly interest in the welfare of their fellow man. They like social conversation. Be it friend or foe, in distress they are ready to sacrifice comfort and face dangers to alleviate such distress.

There is a lank (not always) solemn class who almost never smile—at least when strangers are about, and who live according to a code of morals that originated centuries ago. There is a class of wild, carefree rascals who would as lief pillage their neighbors' property (but usually, in actual practice, limited to watermelon patches, peach orchards, and such). . . .

Mr. Galbraith, there is very definitely a Hillbilly. He may have a five-weeks' growth of whiskers decorated with tobacco juice, one suspender and binder twine shoestrings. In the same group may be a well-groomed gentleman dressed according to the latest standards of Fifth Avenue. But start a talking machine or radio on the street, see an accident involving life and death about to occur, or sound the old cow-horn for the hounds, and you'll find both tarred with the same stick, fellow tribesmen, Hillbillies if you please. (*SNL*, June 27, 1937)

Hillbillies' Curious Ways

There's something about living in the hills that makes you as independent as a tadpole's tail on its last wiggle. (*SDN*, February 5, 1941)

If an Ozarker tells you he will kill you—he will. If he tells you he is your friend—he is. (*SDN*, December 21, 1940)

We are a peculiar people in the Ozarks. This storied land which is a Pandora's box of strange tales, unfathomable superstitions, shouldering hatreds, fierce loyalties, simple religions and unshakable faiths. We absorb our own philosophy from the solitude of our hills, and of such spring the men who sometimes shake nations. We live along in our own way; we have not had to fight and conquer physically at the loss of our souls; therefore, we are an emotional people. We have our own credo and our own gospel of success. We are swaddled in traditions, but that is much to our credit. The world is too much forsaking tradition in the swing of the mad pendulum to the far side of the clock of destiny where we believe in nothing. (Speech in support of Dewey Short, McCord Personal Papers)

Independent, Honest, and Had Common Sense

I often think of the independence of our pioneer hillmen. Individualists to the heart's core, they couldn't be regimented or made to learn the goose-step. They tell a story about early Springfield, years ago when the city was just starting to grow pin feathers. Uncle Tuck Smith came from down on White River in my neck of the woods. Like the good individualist that he was, he just left his team right there on the public square and went into Jim Kirby's store to do a little trading. Jim had a little snort or two of "bug juice" on hand which he gave Uncle Tuck and he came out stepping a little higher. So, he just proceeded to unyoke his oxen and give them a good round of shock fodder right there on the square, muss and all.

A policeman came along and told him he couldn't do that. He said well, he didn't see why—the square was for the public. He said, "I jist come up from Bear Creek to trade a little bit in Springfield and help youen's out a little." The policeman said, "Uncle Tuck, I hate to do this, but I've got to fine you five dollars—that's my instructions."

So Uncle Tuck just walked right over to the judge's office right there on the square, and paid it. He gave the judge a ten-dollar bill, and as the judge started to give him back five dollars change, he said, "Jist keep that five. I'll want to feed 'em again in the mornin'!" (*Dial*, November 1951)

Paid His Parents' Maternity Debt

Down in the hills many years ago, a good old Hillbilly owed my father-in-law, Dr. McCord, a bill for many years. The bill was for delivering a baby boy in his home. Every time he ran on to the dad, for years after that, he would say, "Doc, I aim to pay you that. All I want is jist a little TIME!" Well, when the baby was eighteen years old, he came and worked out the debt of his own accord, plowing on the big thousand-acre farm in the valley near Crane. When he got it worked out, he said, "Doc, my pap always aimed to pay you. All pap wanted was jist a little time!" (*SNL*, February 28, 1937)

You Better Know Where You Are: The Locals Won't Tell You!

The funniest thing is to try to get a real Ozark Hillbilly to give you directions to a place. He'll probably tell you: "Take down that swag holler by Uncle Plumley's field—then you'll see a road a-slantin' off to the left. But don't go thataway! You jist foller the swag holler down to the draw below the Pickins Ford, then take up that draw and you'll come out in two whoops and a holler of the old Deadenin' Road and hit'll take you mighty nigh to the crossroads and youens can find your way on from there."

About four years ago a carload of us were going down into Arkansas to a lovely place called Blanchard Springs where they were having a folk festival. We got lost, of course. We knew we had to go to Leslie, Arkansas, so we stopped a woman carrying a baby up the road and asked her how far it was to Leslie. She looked a bit confused and said, "Jist about as far as it is to Timbo."

Then one of us got the courage to ask her how far it was to Timbo. And she said, "Well, it's a right smart piece up the road." So we drove on.

Vance Randolph, in one of his books, tells about asking an old chap, "Where does this road lead to?"

The man said, "Well, it goes a ways and then jist peters out." Randolph was a bit hot and tired and so he said rather bluntly, "What do you mean by 'peters out'?"

The old chap settled himself slowly and patiently as if talking to a smart-aleck kid, and said, "Well, sir, if you must ask questions, that road gits to be a bridle-path, then it gits to be a hog trail. Finally it's jist a squirrel track that runs up an ellum tree and ends up in a knot-hole."

The moral is—don't ever fool with an Ozark hillman You'll come out at the little end of the horn every time! (*Dial*, September 1947)

Mrs. Pearl L. Smith of Mammoth Spring, Arkansas, tells me a good story. She says when they came to the Ozarks in 1901, the country roads were marked by chips cut from trees. Indeed they were. We got that from the Indians who marked their trails that way. Here is her story of directions given them.

"Could you direct us to Mr. Jones's please?"

"Well, yes. Jist go down here a piece till you come to the three-chip road. Foller that till you come to the one-chip road. Foller hit to the end an' there you air."

Then they asked, "How far is it?"

"Oh, hit's a right smart chance fer a piece of a walk." (*SDN*, July 12, 1941)

Humor and Yarns

The old fellow went to a doctor because there seemed to be something the matter with his right leg. It ached and it didn't seem to track along like it "orter," he said.

The doctor looked him all over and finally he said, "Well, Grandpa, you know you are getting along down the hill—and it might be just the infirmities of old age."

"Old age, heck!" said the old man. "My left leg is jist as old as my right leg and they hain't nothin' the matter with HIT!" (*Dial*, June 1948)

A preacher was telling his congregation to be kind and tolerant, to love their neighbors—and he was particularly taking the women over the coals for crabbing and nagging at husbands. He said women were the sweet, brooding, charming mothers of the race. That God made them to mother everything. So he made a proposition. He said, "All you women who will go home now and mother your husbands—stand up."

One poor little deaf, dried up, sour, leathery, rooster-pecked woman arose. The only one. She stood there and the minister waited. Then rather let down, he said, "All right, sister. Will you mother your husband?" And she said, "I THOUGHT YOU SAID SMOTHER HIM!" and down she sat. (*SDN*, November 8, 1941)

These old tales were all more or less fun and banter and filled the lives of those old pioneers whose lives were on the drab side sometimes. . . . No harm meant at all. (*Dial*, September 1947)

Dialect of Native Ozarks Hill Folks

Lots of city people make fun of the Hillbilly because he talks differently than they do. (McCord quoted in " 'Queen of the Ozarks' Avers—," *Stars and Stripes*, September 1, 1944)

You see, the Ozarks were peopled by Anglo-Saxons. . . . Their forebears settled Virginia in the early days of colonization, later spread through the Carolinas, drifting through the southern Appalachians and into Tennessee and Kentucky. They moved on to the Ozarks, the largest wave of immigration being between 1820 and 1840.

Locked in the remoteness of the hills, these pioneers were not molested by the westward sweep of civilization. Consequently, their speech, habits, superstitions and mode of life changed little. If Shakespeare and Ben Jonson were living today they could converse freely with the older natives. Even Chaucer would recognize many of the words and expressions they use. . . .

When an Ozarker "gets his dander up" and threatens to "feather into" somebody, he means he will shoot the object of his anger. This expression goes back to the day of the longbow in England when to feather a man meant to shoot the arrow with such force that even the feather at the end of the projectile was buried in his body.[2] (*Rayburn's Ozark Guide*, January–February 1944)

There are two types . . . of dialect. One of the deep hills or hollers, where the inhabitants lived practically shut in from the outside world, and the other of the outer Ozarks, as one might say, which come in contact with the modern world to a greater extent. These two distinct phases of life and speech are, I think, responsible for the controversy as to what really constitutes the Ozark dialect. The ancient Anglo-Saxon speech is of the deep Ozarks. (*SNL*, February 11, 1934)

New Yorkers Heard about the Dialect Still Spoken in the Ozarks

It was a great experience to me to speak and sing Ozark early English ballads to the "English Speaking Union" of New York. And I have never yet had more enthusiastic listeners anywhere in the country. And they literally plied me with questions, so eager were they to hear all they could of this last seed bed of an old Shakespearian dialect. And the funny part was this: The people from England would say to me—"Why, we say those words in Cornwall!" Or in Devonshire, and so many places. Words like "reckon" as used in the King James Version. "Poke" for sack, "holp" for help, "clever and biddable" just as we use those terms here and as I heard them used last summer down at Jasper, Arkansas, by our hill-woman with whom we stayed all night. And there in New York they knew nothing of this old speech and couldn't understand it. So you see, New York, a melting pot, has lost the speech of the days of Bonnie Prince Charlie, and we who have had it here in our Ozark hills have kept it intact. (*SNL*, January 24, 1937)

We Have So Many Expressions in Our Hills

Did you ever hear the old expression "from kin see to kain't see"? That meant from daylight till dark. I always like to think of Aunt Matt Whaley and her "ornery" man, as she called him. And ornery he was.

Aunt Matt would sit and talk and you would rather hear her than go to a show, by far. She used to say, "Here I work jist like a gopher a diggin' a hole, from kin see to cain't see, and Clem, consarn his ol' hide, he ain't worth the patchin' on his britches! He's so stingy he'd skin a flea for its hide and taller—and he never give me one penny to rub ag'in another one in his whole life. And he ain't got brains to greaze a gimlet! He ain't got even mother wit! He gits down thar to the crossroads and gits with them horse swappers, and they're so slick you cain't even take your eyes offen' 'em long enough to spit. And they'll work some ol' wind broke horse off on him that you have to carry up hill, much less drive it.

"The last ol' critter he traded fer, why I had to bake cornbread fer it to eat! It didn't have no teeth, and it was spavined[3] besides. I tell you, Clem ain't got the sense Moses give little apples."

And just on and on she would go and it would take a native, born and bred, to understand her. The more she got worked up the thicker she'd lay it on. But Aunt Matt got old and a lot of the ginger and vinegar went out of her. And she got to liking Uncle Clem sort of better. Whether he improved or whether she just got used to him and attached to him, I don't know. That's one of nature's mysteries! (*Dial*, June 1947)

When a Gum Tree Goes Hollow

I had a card from our good friend Booth Campbell of Cane Hill, Arkansas. He told me why our people always say "bee gum" and "rabbit gum." He says that when a gum tree goes hollow it is the "hollerest" thing on earth. And they used to make soft-soap barrels of a hollow gum, also beehives and rabbit traps. You know our early people were extremely resourceful. So the name of "gum" for all these different things came into existence. And he made me recall something. I remember Aunt Hannah Barnes telling the youngsters to go to the smokehouse and get her some soft soap "out of the soap gum." So that must have been a gum tree. (*SDN*, April 25, 1942)

Examples of Dialect and Expressions

An old expression, so much used when I was a kid and acting up: "Quit your cutting a dido around them boys!" . . . In Grecian mythology there was an ancient queen Dido of Carthage. She did really cut didos around the men folks and didos in general. A very "for'ard" queen, as Aunt Susan might say. There is where the "dido" came from. But how did we keep it through the centuries away here in the Ozarks, bringing it from England? (*SDN*, May 23, 1942)

A "woods colt" is the only term of the hills ever known for an illegitimate child. It was considered a terrible harsh and unkind thing to use Noah Webster's word "bastard" and you would be more than likely to get shot if you did. No one ever used it except in the worst derision. They always spoke of "the pore little woods colt." It cast a sort of mysterious, unfathomable, kind-hearted silence over the whole affair, and was none of your business where the little fellow came from. Maybe out of the bleak dark woods or a holler log! (*SNL*, July 1, 1934)

"Hoe-down" refers to a break-down dance nowadays, it seems. But Mr. D. P. Dell of Springfield has given me some information. He says the expression originated nearly a century ago from an old Negro song or chant—"lay yo' hoe down." From that chant, which they sang in the fields on the day when they were going to have a big doin's at night, came the word hoe-down for a great big dance and joyful celebration. (*SNL*, September 19, 1937)

Having the "Buck Ager" comes from ague or chills, and the word "buck" comes from the buck deer. Often men had just that sort of nerve collapse when they got too close and too anxious during a hunt. That's what Uncle Sol said ailed him when he couldn't fiddle in the fiddlin' contest. He said he "tuk the buck ager, and couldn't hardly hold the bow." (*SNL*, March 11, 1934)

"Working by the dry month" was common in old days. It meant that a man was hired by the month, but paid only for the dry days when he worked. On the wet rainy days he had plenty of time to sit around and play the banjo and do nothing but the feeding. For that he got only his board on the wet days. Seventy-five cents a day and board used to hire a mighty good farm hand. (*Rayburn's Ozark Guide*, Spring 1947)

"Pack" was a great old-time word. It is yet. Away from here so many speech specialists ask me if we say "tote." They all seem to think our Ozarks said, "tote." Not at all. "Tote" is very southern and was never used in the Ozark country at all. You "packed" a sack of flour home, and you "fetched" your neighbor a load of wood. (*SDN*, July 14, 1942)

They used to say for pneumonia, "his light has riz." Not "riz" in the present tense. Also said: "he had a cold in the bronnikals." And then, "I'm powerful weak today." (*SDN*, April 22, 1941)

The Ozarkian speaks of his "womarn" for woman—the language is so full of "r's." (*SDN*, August 17, 1940)

Additional Examples of Ozarks Dialect

Posthumous Child—One that was born after the father died

The Nation—How early Ozarkians referred to Oklahoma

Level-lander—Resident of level farm "down there near the river bottom"

Ridge Runner—Resident of hills above the town and river (McCord Personal Papers)

Classic Shakespearian Words Still Used in the Ozarks

Whupped	for whipped
Clomb	for climbed
Nary	for ne'er a
Hit	for it
Hist	for hoist

J'ist	for joist
B'ile	for boil
Pint	for point
Spile	for spoil
Sallet	for salad
A-nigh	for near (McCord Personal Papers)

Dialect Must Be Used Correctly

There's one thing about the old Ozark dialect. It was used as technically as a Greek professor uses his verbs. I have so often called attention to the use of the word "hit" for "it" by inexperienced writers not born to the "feel" of our age-old dialect. An Ozarker uses "it" just as much as he uses "hit." . . . The Ozarker says, "Hit's a rainin', hain't it?" In that case he uses both "hit" and "it." He would never on earth say, "Hit's a rainin' hain't hit?" That would be not phonetic, it would designate no particular time or place or thing, and "hit" is rarely ever used at the end of a sentence. . . . Inexperienced writers make it their stock in trade and sign of all things Ozarkian! (*SDN*, April 22, 1941)

Dialect Not the Same as Old English or Bad Grammar

I was just thinking about an article by our friend A. M. Nesbitt of Hardenville, Missouri. He said his children got to saying "airy and nary" and "nestes" for nests, etc. Well, that was not dialect. Chaucer and all the writers of his period used "es" to make the plural instead of "s." That was the form of English then. I know an old saying of the Ozarks country—"wasp-es build nest-es in jist-es and post-es." In modern speech it is "wasps build nests in joists and posts." As for airy and nary, they are merely contractions of "e'er a" and "ne'er a"—such as, "I have ne'er a child to brighten my old age," and was perfectly good speech. It is of course now obsolete and out of date. As to "done went," Mr. Nesbitt mentions, or "done gone and went" that is simply poor grammar and you will find poor grammar in localities all over America and Europe too for that matter. (*SDN*, September 10, 1938)

Un-Lettered

CORAL ALMY WILSON[4]

What—a letter fer me?
Say, yer mistaken!
I don't git no letters,
Though my heart hit's a breakin'
To hear frum my boy—
You say hit's my name,
An' the town, hit's the same?
You open hit, Mister,
I cain't see to read—
An' I'm anxious indeed—
Ye say hit's from Bud?
O, Glory to God!
He's well an' a comin'?
Gin the letter to me!
How glad I'ud be
If I jest had the larnin'
To make these eyes see!

How that poem goes through me! For well I remember a few old friends of my childhood who wished so that they could read. And yet, I often wonder if I would have loved them as much. They might not have had the time to give to my childish play and questionings. They might not have sung me as many ballads or told me as many tales. (*SDN*, May 20, 1941)

Some hill people of the Ozarks are "unlettered" rather than "ignorant." There is such a vast difference. (*SNL*, December 5, 1937)

The Outside World Has Discovered the Ozarks

October in the Ozarks is known all over the country. Even the United Press will make a record of the "painted leaves" and the glorious colors in the hills. The whole outside world is interested in us. They want to know when we kill hogs, when we make soap, when we gather nuts and persimmons and paw-paws. (*Dial*, October 1947)

Old–Timers Not Happy with "Furriners"

The older natives resent the intrusion of the newcomers. Their feelings were portrayed by an irate hillman who tired of the antics of tourists traipsing over his land, and posted his notice:

> Trespassers will b persecuted to the full extent of 2 mungrel dogs which never was over sochible to strangers & 1 dubble brl shotgun which ain't loaded with sofa pillors. Dam if I ain't getting tired of this hell raisin on my place." (McCord quoted in *Jefferson City News*, May 19, 1942)

We Are Not Tobacco Road!

You know there's one thing that I am quite sick of. It is the constant calling of Ozarkians, "Tobacco Road." I expect that a great many of my readers over this Ozarks area have not read this unspeakable book. . . . It represents a people of sharecroppers known as "Georgia Crackers," a people such as were never even visualized in the Ozarks. A people so pitifully poor and anemic, so starved for food, vegetables, fruit and the necessities of life. When I was in Los Angeles the *Times* editors were very kind to me and one told me that I must see *Tobacco Road*, the "renowned hillbilly play," he called it. He was sincere. He actually thought it would represent my Ozarkian people and speak my language. And he called me after I had gone, to ask me my reactions. I will not attempt to tell you all I said!

But I told him: If we have ever known that condition in these Ozarks, this land of game and fish and dairying, of good river-bottom farms and extremely productive ridge-farm clearings, it has been negligible in very scattered places. The man in *Tobacco Road* was so starved that he was willing to sell his daughter's virtue for a peck of turnips. . . . We feed turnips to the hogs here in the Ozarks, and have for a hundred years. I told the editor that. He seemed amazed. (*SDN*, September 7, 1940)

If you think Ozark women are starving, *Tobacco Road* sharecroppers, as some western and eastern journalists like to sensationalize us, listen to what Mrs. Lillie B. Reid, of Buckhart, Missouri, writes me, and let your mouth water:

> May, I have spent a busy summer as usual. Canned everything on the farm. Jellies, jams, butters, pork, chicken, sausage, soup, tomatoes, corn, beans, peas, carrots, okra, squash, greens, pickles, relishes, beets, berries, peaches, apples, pears, plums, grapes and juices. As usual, I will give a lot of it away before spring. Each year I say I won't can so much, but when canning season comes again and the garden is ready I forget all my good resolutions and work as hard as ever. (*SDN*, October 10, 1940)

Woe to Him Who Criticizes a Hillbilly!

I'm of his tribe and his clan and I love every bone in his body. And if I or any contributor of mine ever misrepresent the Hillbilly may the blackness of the desert hide us, the sand fleas devour us and our bones bleach till the judgment day! (*SNL*, August 6, 1933)

How to Paint Barn Scarlet in New Style

"Hillbilly Queen" Learns That It Must Look Like a Turkey Gobbler
POOR HOMER AND WILBER
Their Mother Wanted Artist Arrested After She Saw Their Portraits!

[Newspaper] Ed's Note—Mrs. McCord—"Queen of the Hillbillies"—asked to be "assigned" to the Thomas Hart Benton lecture with permission "to say just what I think" about him. She was told to go to it. Mr. Benton himself dropped into the office a few minutes later and learned of the assignment. "Fine," he laughed. "Tell her to do her damndest." Here it is:

When a Hillbilly tries to go "arty" it's time something should be done. It was raining like pouring buttermilk out of a jug, but little did that matter—I had to see what it was all about. "Art for art's sake, you know."

Once I gazed upon a picture called "Ozark Musicians," and yesterday I gazed upon the perpetrator thereof. Now in all fairness, I am told that Mr. Thomas Benton is a great mural artist—that he is becoming very famous—that he is an Ozarkian (an awfully long time ago) and furthermore that he invites criticism and then doesn't like it. However, I like to see a man stick for his guns when he is put in a corner. And no man wants to be put in the position of seeming to have to "explain away" his pictures or apologize for them.

Furthermore, I realize that I don't know much art. In fact, what I know about art would be like Aunt Caldony said down home—"You could spit it into a Chigger's eye and he wouldn't bat it!" But while I don't know art I DO know Ozarks!

How to Paint a Red Barn

We'll just skip the point that most art now is a mess between cubist contraption, futuristic jumble, distortion and Gertrude Stein's poetry. If you start to make a red barn you don't make a red barn. You make an "impression" of a red barn, and it must resemble a turkey gobbler. Nevertheless, Raphael's Madonna and the Mona Lisa still live! Isn't that queer?

We'll also skip the point that I know the dear little boys from whom Mr. Benton painted the Ozark Musicians. That they are nice, clean, intelligent little boys, Homer and Wilber. They wash their faces and tie their ties correctly. Wilber slicks his hair with lard in the manner most prescribed. He carries his fiddle in a "poke" to keep it clean. Their cute little hillbilly "mammy" wouldn't let them even come up here in a car unless she came along, because "they never stayed a night away from their mammy and pappy in their lives." Homer has an enchanting little smile. I think the boys live up by Lebanon now, whereas they lived in my home-town and I knew them since they were "borned." We will also skip the fact that no artist has to stick exactly to the text, nor does a writer. But he ought to keep within smelling distance of the text. Poor little Homer and Wilber came out of the picture, after Mr. Benton had juggled the works, looking like a cross between horse thieves and "The Man with the Hoe." Poor Wilber! I could not gaze upon him without a sense of excruciating anguish! In direst tragedy the lines infested my brain:

> Whose was the hand that slanted back his brow?
> Whose breath blew out the light within this brain?
> . . . Is this the thing the Lord God made?
> . . . How will you ever straighten up this shape?
> Down all the stretch of hell to its last gulf
> There is no shape more terrible than this!

Wanted Artist Arrested

Now I'm not exaggerating—that poem must have been written for this especial occasion. I am told that "Mammy" wanted to have the artist arrested. No little self-respecting hillbilly mammy could wish to have her sons awaken to find themselves famous in quite this distressing fashion!

Seriously, I have lived in the Ozarks all my life, and longer than Thomas H. Benton. I will allow for his distortion. He says that your psychological patterns in life are very distorted, therefore art must be distortion, and you must take it and like it. But never have I seen faces and forms so benighted, so brutally distorted and witless in all the Ozarks as were those faces and shapes. It amounts to this—that the picture says

"Ozark" Musicians. If he had said merely "musicians," and left their habitat in the dark, I would have felt extremely grateful. The picture does not fairly represent us. Perhaps a few sophisticates whose "psychological patterns" have been distorted, might, with the wildest stretch of imagination understand. . . .

A lady tells me that I am not fair. That he is doing for the Ozarks with his brush what I am trying to preserve with my pen. Perhaps I should feel very flattered—but I don't. If that is what I am doing for the Ozarks, then someone take me to the creek and baptize me under three times and lift me out twice! I suggest that either Benton or I quit—and I'm willin'!

I have tried not to caricature the man of my native hills, above all things on earth. When I go away to other states to speak to audiences I am almost ill at ease for fear I will caricature him. I would not for all the world. He wears overalls and galluses and sometimes his haircut is not just up to sniffle; his back is bent with toil and his diploma is rugged honesty and frankness rather than sheepskin, but he was the advance guard of civilization in these hills, a true pioneer, and I would want him painted just as he is—with striking realism and fairness—leaving out the "distortion." Then if the picture won't sell—make soap-grease out of the oil in it!

When I objected to the fellow with the young boys sitting in the picture playing a modern accordion (for the typical Ozarkian never heard of a modern accordion until lately, when a few have traded two or three of their fiddles to some city slicker for some old worn-out accordion) Docia says, "But, May, there are all sorts of Ozark musicians!"

Yes, there are all sorts of Ozark musicians, but if you are going to paint a thing "to type" and tag it "Ozark," then make it so. Springfield is Ozark; we have musicians here playing piano, trombone, sax and cello, pipe organ and bagpipes. But they would never get painted as "Ozark musicians," would they? (*Springfield Leader and Press*, January 19, 1935)

MAY'S READERS RESPONDED TO HER ART CRITICISM

Well, I guess most of you saw my criticism of the pictures of the Missouri artist, Thomas H. Benton . . . I guess I had some cussin' for that article, but I'll say this: Never in my life have I written anything big or little that I got so much congratulation about. My folks said the neck rang off the phone that night when it came out, and they kept most of the names. Artists of the city, and real recognized connoisseurs that would surprise you. They said I said what they really wanted to. . . .

You know I meant no harm, and I'm for Missourians first and last. Above all the comments received, I value a letter yesterday from the mother of one of America's foremost artists—the mother of Rose O'Neill. A woman who in her eighties knows more art than perhaps a city full of us, and who is not "old fashioned," but so up-to-the-minute on art and artist that she keeps you jumping on your toes. This is her letter:

> We enjoyed your art criticism. I had intended to write you about the picture when we saw a print of it. I think all caricature is cruel, some of it very offensive to good taste. And in this case it amounts to positive libel as it gives the impression of all that is ugly and uncouth, while the hill people of the Ozark country are noted for their remarkable regularity of features and general good looks in the majority of them. At a "gathering" I met a lady from Kansas City who said she had never seen so many pretty girls anywhere. I told her to observe the men-folk too, and there were the fiddlers and guitar players, all handsome and skillful, and the dancers the same; perfectly graceful in their circling and promenading and swinging through the intricate figures, as they always are. There is a free grace in the composition of Benton's picture and the colors perhaps are beautiful, but it is a pity to have it spoiled by that tendency to caricature, which is so common just at the present.
>
> Hastily and Devotedly,
> Alice A. O'Neill, Bonniebrook (*SNL*, January 27, 1935)

May's Yearning: To Go Back to the Hills

I want to go back to the hills, tonight. I want to hob-nob and gas with some old weather-beaten Hillbilly, stout-hearted, rock-ribbed brother to toil. I want him to tell me again his simple story and throw in the howl of his coon dog for good measure. I'd love to climb to the top of old Piney and watch the mists as they rise from Sunken Hollow and listen to the wail of the fiddle as it weeps from the cabin of the tie-hacker over in the valley. (*SNL*, November 13, 1932)

I grew up in the hills and I love them with a bodily love. I keep tender memories for certain spots, certain springs, giving back the dreams long dreamed in the land of gray mists. The hills ever have a sensuous charm for me. (*SNL*, August 27, 1933)

Many a hillman lives on his little patch of ground on the side of the ridge. There isn't toe hol't for a mule. The ground is so rocky and flinty that they tell it on him that he has to shoot the corn into the hillsides with a muzzle-loader. My good friend Booth Campbell down at Cane Hill, Arkansas . . . recently told me that the ground was so hard he could hear his beans grunt for a mile tryin' to sprout. And you could look up his chimney and see the cows comin' home. (*Dial*, July 1949)

You May Travel Around in Circles, but Always Come Home

Just to Be in the Woods, Again

I am tired of man-made wonders,
Shafts of stone and bars of steel,
Ships that throb with mighty engines,
Wires that see and hear and feel;
I am tired, and sick, with longing
Just to hear the hoot owl call
In the woodsy, ghostly silence,

With the moonlight over all!
Where some cliff, whose shaggy cedars
Not a woodman ever mars, . . .
Dips its feet in dark blue waters,
And its head among the stars!
Let me share your star-lit cabin
On some rocky little knoll.
And let someone sit beside me
I am tired of man-made wonders,
Domes so vast, and towers so high,
Let me pitch my tent forever
'Neath the blue of God's own sky!
(*SNL*, November 20, 1932)

There's just a kinship, a something gets hold of you. Home! The dear old Ozarks! Where the drums of things primitive beat in your veins; where romance gets into your blood; where the lure of spring, the laziness of summer and the scent of dank, mossy glens steal into your senses. Where you lie on your stomach and drink from the springs and rivers, and forever you come back. Again and again. (*SNL*, March 12, 1933)

As Isabelle Alderman says,

"We Love Our Ozarks Best of All,"
So, "If you could have your 'druthers,"
A feller says to me—
"If you could have your 'druthers,
Where would you 'druther be?'
"Oh, if I could have my 'druthers,"
I says to him, says I,
"I'd 'druther live in the Ozarks,
Where the rugged cliffs run high!"
(*SDN*, July 30, 1938)

CHAPTER 2

The Good Old Days
in the Ozarks

They live by the Grace of God and hunting and fishing.[1]

. . . .

One key to May's popularity was her ability to tap the well-spring of nostalgia for the good old days. Ozarkers warmed to her reminiscences of beloved relics once kept in their parlors, men who spent their days sitting on barrels of salt at the general store, and her first trip to Springfield, Missouri, where as a child she believed "civilization began and ended." Her descriptions of the practices, characters, and philosophies she grew up with carried her readers back to their youthful days just as they reintroduce us to ways of life that are now beyond living memory.

. . . .

Simple Pleasures in the Good Old Days

No Man Forgets

No man ever forgets
The hills of his youth;
Stars may go down in darkness
And the winter gale
May open its talons
And beat its wings,
But the heart remembers
Its summers.
(*SDN*, January 10, 1942)

A woman signing her name "Mrs. N" from Springfield writes me:

Here are some of the things I can remember—living in a big log house with an old stick-and-mud chimney. The floor was of split logs turned flat side up. Part of our seats at school were split logs with legs. We churned in a cedar churn with a wooden lid and dasher. Every spring Mother would make soap from cracklings, bones and other meat scraps. We saved our ashes in a hopper and made lye to make the soap. In the winter we would bury apples and turnips, potatoes, onions, beets and green cabbage in the ground to keep them from freezing. In my early childhood my mother wove our blankets on an old-fashioned loom and I have worn dresses made from the cloth she made. I learned to knit my own stockings when I was nine years old.

We walked two miles to school every day, hot or cold. We didn't worry over the price of groceries for we butchered our own meat and always made a big barrel of kraut and one of molasses and we raised our own peanuts and popcorn and tobacco for Father. We had to go four miles to our nearest town for mail. We took corn to the mill and had it ground into meal, and such good cornbread as it made you never ate. When tax-paying time came, someone would ride fifteen miles on horseback to our county seat and pay them. Neighbors that lived within a mile would come on Saturday and visit till Sunday afternoon. We had candy pulls, spelling bees, singings, and in the winter a dance now and then. Everyone was happy and we didn't know we were poor for everyone lived the same way. (*SNL* June 21, 1936)

Remembering Aunt Polly Ann

Mrs. Alice Almy Gregory sent me this little sketch which is so typical of the dear pioneer women of the Ozarks:

How well I remember going over to Aunt Polly Ann Smith's house! We just followed the old deer-run up the hill behind our house until we came to the salt lick. There we found the dim, little-used road that wandered about the mountaintop until it found Aunt Polly Ann's house on a rocky clay farm.

Aunt Polly had once been a teacher. Soon after her marriage she was left a widow with her husband's family of children to raise. By nature a gentlewoman, Aunt Polly bent her back to the walking plow, to the loom and the spinning wheel, and fed and clothed these children until finally she was left alone.

Her face was tanned and lined with many years of outside work—I well remember that face. Naked of powder or rouge, a homely face but a pleasant, kindly face—a Christian face. And I always remember her homespun dress, white apron and sunbonnet. I hope you can see her as I picture her, for now she has passed beyond, and I don't think that even Saint Peter would ask her to change her white bonnet for a halo. Somehow it would not suit Aunt Polly Ann. (*SDN*, July 6, 1940)

Memory of a Parlor

I was telling a friend the other day about the old-time "parlor." They used to call the living room or sitting room the parlor, and many women kept it shut up like a shrine. The light might fade the carpet! Rarely did anyone ever get to peep into this musty and sacred sanctum sanctorum. It was like going into the catacombs or a funeral chapel.

I remember one little girl would have me go home from school and stay all night (that was our wildest recreation) and she would say, "Mama will let us look in the parlor." After supper, if we were good, we kids might go for a few minutes into the parlor. The curtains were all down. Usually there was a fine old walnut bed in there with a high back, for regardless of its being a parlor, you put a fine bed in it and if company came, great and distinguished company, they slept there.

The carpet was usually home-woven, bright and puffy, with straw under it. There was a stand table with a spotless worked cloth. The Bible was there always, and the plush album. And no kid could turn the leaves of that album; it must be done by a grown up. And there were all the ancestors with their mustaches, each looking like a cross between a pirate and an Oklahoma card slicker, and "Aunt Susan" with her prim braids and her "breast-pin," and the bride and groom, with the groom always seated in the chair and the bride standing behind him with her hand on his shoulder, scared half to death! (*Dial*, July 1948)

Pictures in the Parlor

We have a tenacious faculty down in the Ozarks of hanging on to our beloved relics like a heathen hangs to his fetish. There's the Old Enlarged Picture. We've all got 'em, and let's hang right to 'em even though the latest agony decrees that we must put them in the junk heap and hang up "The Dance of the Seven Veils" (with six of 'em gone to the laundry!).

These modern dog kennel bungalows won't permit any enlarged pictures, not even of Granpap, so I have mine stored in an attic where I weep over them, maybe laugh sometimes, and shivers of memories run down my spine.

But in the good old days, life was just all foolishness until we got Ma and Paw's picture enlarged and hung in the place of honor.

I can see the frisky agent coming now. And if a glib tongue counted for anything, success was assured at the outset. The party of the second part felt himself slipping, and the agent carried away some tin-type of a group from which he deftly plucked the member to be enlarged, as a brand from the burning. The candy besmeared youngster, the dear defunct husband of Aunt Polly on your Paw's side—the one with the wart on her nose. The wart being a matter of small moment, as it was removed with astounding magic in the process of enlargement.

If Paw had just an old work shirt on the day he "set fer his picter"— and Paw's poor old scraggly neck never had its virgin soil invaded by a collar—the artist juggled the works, put a high collar on him, a biled shirt, and turned poor old Paw out looking like a card slicker from Oklahoma!

Now it will take me many a day to forget the picture of Aunt Charity Beezeley's daughter Stelly. It occupied the station of high honor in the "settin' room." A massive frame tawny with gold leaf. Imposing and flamboyant! Encircled by this elegance were the sniveling features of Stelly. In the original, Stelly's apparel wouldn't have passed muster with the Smart Set, but the artist was a tactful soul and gifted by the gods, so he placed over her shoulders a wide profusion of lace, a string of glittering beads on her neck, her cheeks painted like a Piute squaw, ear bobs in her ears and frizzled side-bangs just above the ear bobs. Behold, a new and glorified Stelly!

When the agent brought the thing home, two dollars down and a chattel mortgage—no one recognized it. Even Tige barked at it as one outside the clan! But what did that matter? The agent merely told them they didn't understand art. It was a gorgeous thing to behold. A trifle low-necked for some of the persnickety neighbors, perhaps, but art was art and that settled it.

The picture hung just over the organ. A piece of pea-green mosquito netting placed securely over it to daunt the covetous fly! The netting served to cast a sort of mysterious glamor over the whole outlay, and gave to Stelly's features a sort of fascinating clairvoyance.

On the left of Stelly's picture hung the much-beflowered and hand-clasped marriage certificate of Josiah Beezeley and Charity Ellen Todd! You know it is a mighty skeptical world and it's better to hang up the proof of the puddin' on the wall. Besides, we didn't have courts, half the time, where they kept the records. On the left of this certificate hung the somber memorial of the death of Uncle Zeb Todd, a black gold-lettered affair with mating doves adorning the corners, notwithstanding the fact that Uncle Zeb had cashed in unwed, at the age of sixty and was as kind as a razor-backed hog. The fact is that they had got the frames mixed and the doves were intended to go on the marriage certificate which was framed in funeral black!

On the wall opposite, and entirely out of this virtuous aura, hung the picture of the chap Stelly married. In the original agony, Otho had been hatless, coatless, collarless and brainless. Not so, this thing of crayon and genius which returned in due time from the People's Portrait Co. Poor Otho! It was impossible to gaze upon it without a sense of excruciating anguish! A derby hat on the head, which God forbid, had never been really planned; a lemon-colored mustache, a clerical-looking collar, and a sort of cramped black broadcloth coat which gave you the sensation of walking slow behind him. However, the sensation was greatly mitigated by a "see-gar" stuck, with rakish tilt, in the corner of his mouth.

Aunt Charity was proud of this son-in-law who looked like a cross between a corpse and a horse thief! Verily do we become great in our epitaph, for she declared that he could "spit further'n airy man she ever seed, and he never struck Stelly a lick in his life!"

The mosquito netting had played out or run amuck before reaching Otho, so the flies reposed on the cool glassy surface of his elegance in the summer, as a change of pasture from the dried apples strung to the ceiling in the winter. O, well—what's the difference—Otho and Stelly lived their little day upon the stage of life, despite the dried apples, thereby mightily confounding an over-antiseptic generation which has lived to see the passing of the enlarged picture. (*SNL*, October 8, 1933[2])

Salt Barrel Sitters in the Hills

The Salt Barrel Sitter was parked on his favorite barrel when the storekeeper came to open up in the morning, and there when he closed at night. His record survived the acid test of endurance, and it stands today unchallenged.

There was Old Lum Skinner. He wasn't worth the powder and lead to blow him into the next dispensation, but he could sit longer, lie harder, and spit farther than any yokel who ever wore shoe leather. . . .

One of the chief amusements of the Salt Barrel Sitter was when the old cat emerged from her bed in the bin of loose prunes, with the five little sore-eyed kittens trailing, and one of them stuck its head around the coal oil barrel. . . .

The shanty stores circled the small square. At the foot of the little town of Galena, Missouri, ran the clear, blue River James. On the hill above, nestled in the trees, were the friendly little dwellings. When anything happened on the hill, and Paw was needed, Maw just went to the door and yelled at him. When Mrs. Beezeley dropped her false teeth in the well, little Blub just poked his head out and yelled: "Paw, run up here—Maw's lost her teeth!"

Now and then the spouse of an endurance sitter could get him sometime in the forenoon, long enough to bust up a little wood to cook dinner with. Not often.

Politics was discussed freely. "Say, Lum—are ye a scratchin' any this fall?"

"Nope, votin' 'er straight as a shimmy seam."

The Barrel Sitting didn't break up when the wintry winds blew. The sitter merely moved his barrel inside, by the stove, and the endurance was on anew. The drama of the survival of the fittest was enacted around an old box stove filled with hickory chunks, accompanied by windy yarns and the juice of the long green.

The sitters were short on facts and long on wind. The contest was a little hard on the seat of the pants; aside from this there was no over-head. (*Arcadian Magazine*, April 1931)

Plenty of Thrills Greeted Hillbillies Back When City of Springfield Was the "Great Mecca"

As the Muslim turned his face toward Mecca, so we of the hills turned our faces toward Springfield. It was the Rim of the World! Civilization began and ended there. When we dreamed of wonders beyond our sto-ried hills, we dreamed of Springfield. To me—a child of the Shepherd of the Hills Country—it seemed a faraway city of eternal Eden. My parents came to Springfield trading or on business at very rare intervals, but it was by far too inconvenient to bring the little brood.

I shall never forget my first visit. I had been promised this visit to the Great Mecca by some dear folks, former Springfieldians of our town, and my father's associates in business. I had been thrilled for months, with this promise. We came in a hack from Galena—a long, tedious journey, but I was promised all the way that we would dine at Culley's Cafe, which was then the fashionable feeding stall for the elite. I was all a quiver when we arrived and walked into the cafe, brilliant with lights and little white tables. I was there introduced to my first fresh, raw oys-ters, and I must have been a ritzy sort of kid, for they went down me like gum-drops down a newsboy—and they have ever since. . . . I remember dining again the next day at Culley's on delicious baked goose, cranber-ries and thick custard pie. Some joint!

With a grand flare we were registered at the Central Hotel. And that isn't half—the next day I was taken to see the stores and I emerged from one of them arrayed in a pea-green silk dress, all sleeves and ruffles, and high, tooth-pick tan shoes! Was ever a country gosling so adorned? Then came a hat—a leghorn—with very long wide streamers.

We went to the old Bald Theater. On Sunday we went to Calvary Presbyterian Church, and not long since, I sat in the very seat where I sat then, crumpled under the big hat like a toad in a storm, and filled my hungry ears with pipe organ, and it seemed to me beyond belief.

Well, time is the great leveler and I have since seen a great bit of the Land of the Free, and have lived a decade in the Great Mecca. It's a great burg, but I long for the hills. The call of nativity never dies from the bosom of a Hillbilly. When one gets one sniff of the jungle, he just has to go back. He hungers to hear the katydids—to see the cows coming home at eve, and the lazy goat munching the sprouts on the hillsides at noonday. He longs to climb the steeps with them. A Hillbilly naturally has one leg longer than the other for that express purpose anyway. (*SNL*, June 2, 1929)

Missouri Roads and Trails and the Rugged Teamsters Who Traveled Them

The old roads were laid out at first over the old Indian trails, the trails of fourteen tribes who once traveled over them. Many of them remain. At Eureka Springs, Arkansas, I can take you over twenty-eight miles of Indian trails without seeing a sign of modern civilization—there in the very heart of the Ozarks where beautiful highways are just across the way. We are being slowly choked by the grip of progress, and the very soul stamped out of us by the iron heel of a great civilization—but we die hard.

These old roads knew no such thing as a surveyor's instrument; they were merely "blazed." There was the "Old Wire Road" from St. Louis to Fort Smith, Arkansas. This road was used chiefly during the Civil War, and the government ran one single telegraph wire all along the long road. These roads followed the ridges, and were possible, of course, with very little work. But as the farms began to crowd in on the ridges, they pushed the roads into the hollows more and more, making them almost impassable in places.

Away before these roads, when there were only the narrow trails of the Osage, Kickapoo and Delaware Indians, freight was taken down the Mississippi by boat from St. Louis to Boonville, Missouri, and from there, freighted up into the Ozark country. This seems almost legendary to us now.

The most interesting road, and the one most freighted over through the Ozark mountain country, was the "Old Wilderness Trail." The greater part of it is used today, and it is a fine road, considering its ancient lineage.

From the little trading posts at the mouth of the great White River came the caravan of teamsters hauling freight to Springfield, Missouri, sometimes as many as thirty wagons in a caravan. They brought cotton from Arkansas, and from the little trading posts all along. They brought tobacco, ginseng, golden seal, wahoo, coonskins, cedar posts, possum hides, sorghum, poultry and "what have you." These they sold for provisions which they hauled back. Few of the teamsters could read or write. Very little money was exchanged. Some of the little trading posts did well to handle twenty-five dollars in an entire year, in currency. There were few ferries. Well do I remember the thrill when I espied the first ferry built across my home river, the beautiful "James." It seemed a sight beyond belief. The big cable, the clanking of the chains as we gathered up, and the old cumbersome, flat ferry moved slowly away from the bank.

The old teamsters were a jovial bunch. There was old Lige Blunt. Not only was he a teamster of the first water, but also he was "one o' the blue hen's chickens."[3] He was a "Hard-Shell," a predestinarian, and a believer in "signs." He could swear harder and spit farther than any yokel this side of Bald Knob, and, to use his own words, he could "drink red likker that'ed make a Tom cat spit in a bear's eyes."

He drove an old Lynch Pin wagon, greased with tar. Axle grease was an unknown quantity and on cold mornings the wheels of those old freight wagons would stick and slide until the tar got warmed up. Sometimes they would build fires around the wheels to warm up the tar.

Uncle Lige carried an old single action Colt. There was absolutely no robbery or holdups in those days, but the freighters carried guns just to liven things up a little for their own bunch. Uncle Lige used to cock his left eye, spit about four ounces of the long green, and say, "If them Springfield dudes gits to foolin' with yer uncle, I'll fill 'em so full o' cold lead that their own mammy won't know 'em—see?"

The freighters would drive in to their destination, and put up at the wagon yards. Free bunks, with the four-legged species thrown in. First come, first served. If the freighter were a real guy, a bunk and four walls were to him a prison cell, so he slept out under the stars—or if misty, he crawled under his wagon, tying old Sport to the hind wheels.

The bunks were sometimes of three tiers, and you put your bedding in when you arrived, thereby staking your claim. If you went up town to gape around at the bright lights, and some fellow pitched your truck out in the floor, and was snoozing peacefully in your bunk when you returned, then the law of the survival of the fittest went at once into effect.

The teamsters drove into the wagon yard, cooked their bacon, and scrambled their eggs with onions, ate, picked their teeth with their jack knife, and started up town to see the sights. Down by the old wagon yards, about every other door was a thirst emporium, and those so inclined imbibed freely. Those not so inclined went on and took in the sights—the chief joy being the eating of "chili." This was a new innovation in this country. It was a great luxury to the chap from the hills, in spite of the fact that he thrived on venison and wild turkey at home. The freighter brought his "old trusty" along and killed game a plenty.

Well the coming of the great iron horse into the storied hills began to ring the knell of the picturesque old freighter—then the gas wagon finished the job. Now the buses are trying to ring the knell of the railroads, and when I'm old and full of rheumatiz', the mighty monarchs of the air will have written the swan song for the bus. It's a funny world! (McCord Personal Papers)

The Iron Horse

In 1903 the Great Iron Horse threatened to plant his hoof within our peaceful little valley, and excitement ran high. We could almost feel the hot breath from his fiery nostrils, and it was the thrill that comes once in a lifetime. The railroad, long hoped for and dreamed of, was about to be built. It would open to us the great avenues of trade, touching the entire world. We could ship our cattle and the pelts of our wild animals, our tobacco and our grain.

In time the valleys resounded to the wild scream of the locomotives. They pushed their way along the beautiful river James, crossing it on a high bridge that was the gaping wonder of the natives. On down Stony Creek, past the little log schoolhouses whose lonely aloofness was now a thing forever past. Dashing by the lonesome Cedar Valley graveyard with a proud indifference to all things mortal. Plunging with a hollow roar on to dizzy, long legged trestles, so high that they looked in the moonlight like giant stilts; on and on to the beautiful White River, the cradle of a million pearls.

To us Hillbillies, they seemed human monsters fearfully and wonderfully made. You who have never seen a train come for the first time through your village, cannot even imagine what it is like. There were gatherings and wonderings and chawings and spittings galore. The thing that stands out most distinctly in my mind after all these years was the indifference of Aunt Eller Plumley. She wouldn't even talk about the "pester'n thing"—only she did make one remark: "She hoped t' God it run over old Joel Harp's ole sow and greased the track for forty miles!"

Joel Harp had an old sow. Nuf sed. She was the most exasperating free lance that ever parted the hoof. She was half hog and half devil. She belonged to the old original breed of razorbacks, and was proud of it. I think she was the mother of the whole litter. She had a snout on her like a coyote, and she could root up a forty-acre field or pick a lock. She lived from nine p.m. till five a.m. in the backyards of her neighbors, rooting up the gardens, pulling the wash off the line, and turning over the swill buckets on the back porches.

Well, we knew nothing about the New Psychology or the law of suggestion in those days, but Aunt Eller's wish did the work. The first locomotive that ever dashed into town aroused that old hazelsplitter's ire to the point of exasperation and she made one wild rush at it. There wasn't even a pigtail left to cook with the sauerkraut.

Verily, do we become great in our epitaph, for when the grief of Joel Harp subsided, he listed her as a purebred Chester White. That old sister had about as much Chester White blood to her credit as a snake has bunions. Some lawyer worked on Uncle Joel, for the old bewhiskered hill climber didn't know a Chester White from a ground hog. He didn't even know his own age, or where he was born. All he knew was that he was borned about cucumber time. Nevertheless, he received the sum of thirty dollars to assuage his grief. (*Rayburn's Ozark Guide*, May–June 1944)

Many an old Ozarker didn't like the idea of a railroad coming into his peaceful acres. It disturbed his hunting and fishing, his ideas and ways of life. Of course, the more progressive Ozarker knew that it would bring the outside world to us, more business and prosperity. But there was one old landmark who simply would not give the right-of-way through his land. He didn't mind the railroad so much; he said he "shore didn't have to ride 'em," but for some reason he hated the idea of the telegraph poles. "Those things a-straddlin' all around all over my land and a-sendin' readin' and writin' over 'em. They hain't any Bible fer it!" he would say. And by some queer process of reasoning, he got the idea that they would disrupt the morals of his family. He had six big, happy, corn-fed girls, all as pretty as speckled pups, and believe me, he took good care of them. (*Dial*, November 1948)

There was Uncle Lige who simply would not give the right-of-way. He told them he'd "stand right over his forty acres and fill 'em so full o' cold lead that their own mammy wouldn't know 'em!" Poor old Lige! You should have seen his forty acres of cockleburrs and oak sprouts. You couldn't raise a fuss on it. (*SNL*, October 30, 1932)

When a Wagon Went By

How many of you live yet to this day where every car passing and every rider or man on foot is an event—a real event in the day? When I was a kid we watched every wagon that went by, even in the little town, and every horseman. Out in the deep Ozarks, on lonely roads, the passing of a wagon was like the landing of a Graf Zeppelin is now.

It was second nature to go to the window or door and look out and see who it was. So would you, if you had little in your monotonous days, year after year, but the passing of a wagon. . . . Dear old Aunt Susan used to say, "Honey, run to the winder an' see whose waggin' is a goin' by. I've got my hands in the bread stuff!" I used to hate to stop my doll rags and go. (*SNL*, February 18, 1934)

Beds of Straw, Cold Winter Mornings, and Finally Springtime

Every now and then my friend "Hulda" get to settin' and thinkin' and jots it down, and here it is:

> Do you remember how much fun we used to have after we threshed the wheat going to the straw stack to fill the bed ticks with nice new clean straw? And how high it made the bed? So high we had to bring in the stepladder to get in bed—but oh, how fine that big bed felt. I remember we used to have such a time finding a nice flat button to sew on the bed tick. It had to be real flat so it wouldn't hurt our backs. And a good strong piece of muslin to line the buttonhole so it wouldn't tear out easily. And it was nice to have that clean straw to put under our rag carpets in the fall.
>
> Many is the time I have crawled out of bed and shook the snow off the bed, then tracked through the snow down the stair steps to the kitchen to find the water-frozen dipper in the old

cedar bucket. Then on to the living room, sit down by the fireplace to put on my shoes and a blamed old cat would reach its foot through a crack in the floor and untie my shoestrings fast as I could tie them.

I was always glad when spring came even if the March wind did blow the blaze out of the kitchen stove half way across the kitchen. I suppose the reason was that the flue to the old lean-to kitchen was so much lower than the rest of the house.

We always knew by this that it wouldn't be long until we could put a barrel under the house with its big wash board and catch a barrel of rainwater to pour over the ash hopper for our spring soap making.

We always tested the lye by putting a feather in it. When the lye was strong enough to skin the feather it was right to make good soap. Then, to the corn crib for new shucks, to put in the old shuck mop. With the barrel of rainwater and the home made soap you could scour the kitchen floor to a snowy whiteness. (*SDN*, May 2, 1940)

Wash Day for Clothes and Kids

I told a woman one time that my mother always bathed my brother and me in the rinse water after she finished the washin'—and the woman collapsed! I think she thought we were some sort of freaks or trash. You must remember that water was scarce, and my how clean we were after that good scrubbing and our hair nicely done and clean clothes on. I shall never forget it and I have never enjoyed any bath as much since. (*SDN*, February 28, 1942)

They used to wash with a battling stick. Beat and battle the clothes on a big board or sometimes on huge rocks down by the spring. This was before washboards, I suppose. Here is how the Reverend S. S. Pike, a pioneer Baptist preacher in Bolivar, described it:

In the pioneer days they chopped down a big tree, cut off a good length of it and hewed it down to a nice surface. Then they whittled out a paddle about two feet long and the right weight for a woman to handle on wash day. They scalded the clothes, soaped them well and then laid them on this flat surface of the big log and beat the dirt out. . . . On wash day when you went to a pioneer home the first thing you heard was the sound of the battling stick. (*SDN*, July 5, 1941)

Women Did Not "Take Baths"

A reader writes to me and tells about an old-time lady in the Ozarks who became indignant when her granddaughter mentioned that she was going to "take a bath." She said in her day no girl was so immodest to mention "bath." She said she was going to "wash off."

How well I remember that saying. And indeed, they did "wash off" only. We call it a "sponge bath" now. They did not think it modest to infer in public that you would take a bath which implied the nude! You simply do not have any idea of the inhibited modesty of the early Ozarks hillwoman. There is nothing on earth could have induced one of them to trust any doors or bars or keys enough to even have the remotest idea of stripping for a bath!

An old lady stayed with me for several weeks when one of my babies was small. She was awfully clean with her person—and one day I asked her if she did not want a tub bath, for we bathed in tubs then. I suggested to her that there were no "men folks" in a range of a mile, and none were coming. And the bedroom door had a key—and all that stuff. And personally, I would blindfold myself and tie myself to the bedpost in case I might accidentally wander in! But she told me she never did such a thing and would not even think of it. And she told me of a woman who was "washing off all over" and the house got on fire and her clothes were not in that room and they had to go in and get her just that way! She thought it was the most horrible thing she ever heard of! (*SDN*, May 16, 1942)

Lyle Caldwell, father of Kristene Sutliff, shot a wild cat that was eating his chickens. *Photo courtesy of the Caldwell family.*

Hunting and Our Household

Here is a fine piece of reminiscence from an old timer, J. F. Roberts, Van Buren, Arkansas:

> Household utilities consisted of spinning wheel and loom for the manufacture of clothes for the family. The larder of the average farmer was always well stocked with corn meal, bacon, dried pumpkin, dried beans and peas, to which was added sassafras tea and wild greens. Usually there was some wheat flour made from wheat grown on the farm and hauled ten or fifteen miles to a water mill.

In those days there were no game and fish laws. It was open season the year round. Men and boys with their muzzle loading rifles hunted and killed turkeys and squirrels in the daytime and at night hunted and trapped fur bearing animals which were even more plentiful than the day game. There were herds of deer for the hunter who was skillful enough to get within rifle range of them. Lack of skill was often taken advantage of by the hunter who would take salt into the dense wood and made a "deer-lick" and when the deer began using the "lick" the hunter would sit behind a blind and shoot them at night. If anyone had suggested at this time that a limit be placed on the hunting and fishing at any and all times, the country people would have thought their constitutional rights were being interfered with, and had a farmer "posted" his farm he would have been ostracized by all of his neighbors. (*SDN*, September 30, 1939)

Rabbit-Twisters, Squirrel-Knockers, and Hand Grenades

The chap who signs himself "Just Bolivar," writes me and gives me a real tribal history:

I am surprised that you who say you were "raised with a tick behind your ear," and yet know nothing of the society of Rabbit Twisters and Squirrel Knockers. These were the largest and most exclusive of all the hillbilly clans. Too poor to afford ammunition for the old rifle, they went forth and with a strong right arm and trusty rock they knocked the squirrels from the highest treetop. With an old tree dog they ran a rabbit in a hollow log. Their hillbilly genius turned the trick, and they twisted him out with a forked stick.

So there you are. But hold on, Bolivar—I knew what a squirrel-knocker was maybe before you were born. I always said the squirrel-knockers of my home country could kill more squirrels with a rock at long range than a yank could with a hand grenade; and they wouldn't have a gun if you made them a present of one. But I never could get anyone to believe it. I'm like Uncle Sol Hembree down at Galena—he just can't get anyone to believe what they did in the early days, he says.

We had a good old squirrel-knocker boy down in the hills who went to France in the world war, and they say he was the best hand grenade thrower in the whole American forces. They claimed it was his practice throwing at squirrels all his life. (*SNL*, December 25, 1932)

Kids Amused by the Threshing Machine

Nothing can ever equal to a child the coming of the thresher. Mae Traller[4] in Everton, Missouri, says,

> Do you remember how the threshing machine used to come chugging over the hill at this time of year, and we youngsters used to run down the road to watch for the first up thrust of the engine's nose above the row of sassafras as it came blowing great puffs of frightful smoke through its nostrils? Didn't we run to climb over the fence, and there with bare toes hooked over the rail, watch while the engineer manipulated the engine waveringly past and while the huge frightening old separator with its blow pipe turned crazily over its back like an elephant just about to take a bath, limped past?
>
> We would climb back over the fence after that and wait until the resounding water tank rumbled by—and then came the great thrill, the cook-shack jogged along with Aunt Mamie Shoke sitting in a split-bottom chair in the back door, her eyes lifted dreamily to the hills past which her destiny led her. We would scramble into the shack with her and have the thrill that can only come to an Ozark youngster who rides the last half mile of the way home in the cook-shack wagon!
>
> We went back to the threshing yard and there Aunt Mamie had already begun dinner. And we were permitted to help set the long board table under the oak trees for the men. Then too, Aunt Mamie gave us a saucer of blackberry cobbler to eat and

we took it out into the haven in the thicket to consume. And never before or since has there been anything half so deliciously good as that cobbler. (*SDN*, August 25, 1938)

The Country Doctor and the Granny

It was a great pleasure to talk to the ladies auxiliary to the Greene County Medical Association. . . . We talked about the early lore of the country doctor, among other things, and the old granny women of the hills, as Mrs. Mary Elizabeth Mahnkey[5] says,

> Who knew the cry
> When one came wailing from the dark to life,
> And did not shrink when death came stalking nigh!

You know these old women used to be omnipresent to help the sick and dying and give encouragement and hope, and often they were a standby to the country doctor who knew that Granny So-and-So would do all she could until he got there. Sometimes, however, they hated those doctors like sin. They thought it was positively indecent for women to have them about when the babies were born, and they didn't hesitate to say so. Old Granny Meeks used to tell me that no decent woman would have a "strange man-person a hangin' about the place in sich goin's on as that—an' they killed a heap more wimmin than they fetched thro!"

My dear old father-in-law Dr. McCord, who was one of the pioneer doctors of all this Ozark country with perhaps the largest practice of any one man, could tell stories until daybreak. He said old Granny Gore used to be everywhere he went no matter where he was, from Highlandville to Harrison, Arkansas, snow or sleet, hot or cold. And she hated a doctor. She would ignore him completely unless he took the case right out of her hands. He let her have her way a great deal, and now and then she would get out in the corner by the old clay chimney and "consult" with him. He said he vowed that someday he was going to know more than she did. So one time he went where a baby was coming and Granny Gore was having a terrible time of it, so she was rather glad to see the doctor and motioned him to the chimney corner.

"Doc, I've done everything I kin. I've wrung blankets of hot water and hung 'em around the bed. I've put the axe under the bed, and you know yourself, that never fails. I've even smoked her with cobs."

"Oh, you have?" said the doctor. "What kind of cobs did you use, red cobs or white cobs?"

"I used white cobs," said Granny.

"Well," Dr. McCord told her looking wise, "right there's where you made your mistake. You ought to have used RED cobs!"

Granny gave the case up with much chagrin, but to the day of her death she used red cobs, and she decided that young squirt of a doctor "knowed a little bit a sumpthin' after all!" (*SNL*, September 30, 1934)

Tincture of Iron

Do you remember when tincture of iron (which was about the only medicine ever given, aside from quinine) was just called "tinkter?" People used to fairly live on quinine, and now they don't seem to have chills down in the river bottoms. We kids shook from one holler to another in the fall with the chills. Well do I remember the burning fever afterward, and my brother staggering up to put a cold rag on my forehead, and after a bit, I staggered over and put one on his. Our mother, who was very tender, like all mothers paid little attention to the terrible chills and fever, but went on about her hard work. Chills were common as chiggers. Sometimes, however, a little spindly kid stood all he could, and he wilted over and died after about six seasons of them. (*SNL*, June 4, 1933)

The Blacksmith

How many of us loved the village blacksmith in days gone by! To me, the memories of watching the old smith in my childhood, the flaming forge and the bellows and the sparks—his skill, his strength, the red-hot horseshoe growing blue then gold—and shaping up beautifully. Then his fitting it to the horse's hoof after plunging it into a great hogshead of cold water—I can see it yet. Always there were kids standing around him. I guess the sight never grew old. What patience he must have had with the children, for he would always have to say when hitting a red hot piece on the anvil—"stand away back, children—the sparks might hit ye." (*SDN*, July 21, 1942)

Mrs. A. L. Zink, Aurora, Missouri, added,

> My father was a blacksmith, when I was born in Christian County near Clever, in 1888. The old trade of smithing was an honorable one. He used to use wood-coal which he burned in his own kiln, taking about three weeks to burn it ready for the forge. The bellows to furnish air for the forge was made of canvas and wooden staves and wooden lever, and what a flapping wheezing noise it would make! Father made parts for guns, bullets, and shot-molds, soldering pans which he melted solder in and poured it into molds making bullets and shot. He made powder horns . . . and he also made ring-mauls, fire shovels, plow-beams, dog-irons and most all of the necessary hardware which could be made at a home shop. (*SNL*, September 15, 1935)

The King Bee Hunter

I have a letter from Uncle Bill of Buford, Arkansas. He tells me about the king bee hunter of the country, John Smothers, who lives in Hog Waller Bend five miles from Buford. He says,

> Not long since, John was at the big spring at Buford Spur, and he saw a strange looking bee drinking water. It didn't look like an Arkansas bee, so he concluded it was from some other state,

and the thing to do was to follow it home. So he caught the bee, painted its wings white so he could course it, and then turned it loose. The bee rose in the air and flew due north. Smothers followed it for five days and nights, and never overtook that bee until it went into a post-oak tree in the town of Dogwood, Douglas County, Mo. The natives helped him saw down the tree and make a bee gum out of the butt cut, which was hollow. He then hived the bees, put the gum on his shoulder and went home. He was gone just ten days in all. My, but his folks were uneasy, thinking a swarm may have stung him to death, but he never got airy sting.

Well now, Uncle Bill, I'll swear to everything you say, for I have seen just such bee hunters as that in my day. (*SNL*, July 30, 1933)

Minerals and "Lost Mines" Were Legendary

Mrs. Elizabeth Stone, Calico Rock, Arkansas, sent me this story:

Back in the days not so long after the Civil War, farmers seldom raised enough feed to last through crop time, and there were no feed stores, so horses were turned out on the range at night and during the wet weather. Uncle Drew Southard was hunting his horse after such a spell and after finding it, started home across the woods.

Crossing a small stream he stopped to get a drink and, seeing a bright spot on a rock his horse had stepped on, he examined it and found it was lead. He would make secret trips to his lead mine to get his supply, and never filed on it for fear the government would take it from him. He took his small son with him one time to where he kept his tools hidden, but the boy was too small to remember where he went. Uncle Drew died without telling where his mine was. (*SDN*, May 26, 1942)

Angels Arrived on Bicycles

Here's a cute story shared by Mrs. A. A. Adams, Ava, Missouri:

> I am writing about an incident which took place some thirty
> years ago that happened down in the Ozarks. There lived a
> preacher and his wife and they had one son. They were unlet-
> tered people and made baskets and chairs for a living, and he
> preached, but they were good people. One day the wife and a
> relative woman had gone to the spring close by the roadside
> when two men passed riding bicycles. It scared the women
> almost to death. Well, they sat their water pails down and ran
> to the closest neighbor's house and asked if they had seen two
> angels flying by. They said they had seen two angels and they
> thought the world was coming to an end, and that the angels
> were sent to warn the people. (*SDN*, June 21, 1939)

Fall In with Progress

An old chap I used to know said he wanted his coffee "a hundr'd percent"
(never did find out what he meant!) and he wanted it "made in the same
biler and poured from the same spout into the same cup an' sasser" and
he "didn't want no newfangled perky-laters nor fumin' up sorta coffee
pots run by no electricity!" He said "there wasn't any Bible fer it." That
was always his objection to everything under the sun—there wasn't any
Bible fer it. He said he wanted to sleep in the same bed with his head
turned "to the risin' sun." He wanted his "ol' hick'ry che'r an' he wanted to
set in the same corner whar he could spit in the fa'r without a gettin' up
to do it!" He didn't like progress. He dreaded to see "them steam en-jines
a-cuttin' away the roads that grandpappy drove over, an' a-spreading con-
crete over 'em." He said "they run the wild turkeys all outen the hills and
they spiled the fishin' holes a-buildin' dams." He had his own coffin made
and sitting under the bed. He had his will made and had even carved

and fixed up his own tombstone out of a native rock. He didn't fraternize with progress nor make his bed with modern ideas. Well, he's gone to his reward and I expect his reward is just about as good as yours and mine will be, who knows?

I'll see you next month.

And with all my love, I am, faithfully yours—May. (*Dial*, March 1948)

CHAPTER 3

Crime and the Law

*One time they were rushing a man up in his preparation
for being hung. He said, "What in Sam Hill is the hurry!
There won't be any hanging till I get there!"*

SDN, October 15, 1938

. . . .

From Civil War bushwhackers to masked vigilantes, stories
of criminals and lawmen have enlivened long winter nights
in the Ozarks for generations. Though it was not as plentiful
as her stories of the good old days, May and her readers had a
healthy supply of tales of crime and violence. These accounts
of feuds and horse thieves, as well as accounts of real-life
characters such as the notorious Alf Bolin and the infamous
Bald Knobbers, reveal a darker side of May's Ozarks, but it is
one no less colored by romanticism.

. . . .

Bald Knobbers

I suppose the Ozarks will be known for untold years to come as the home of the Bald Knobbers, the daring, courageous vigilantes who organized about sixty or seventy years ago in the 1880s to preserve law and order in this pioneer, isolated country, but who retrograded, as bands of the kind nearly always do, into a mob—a lawless mob which had long ago been deserted by the upright men who organized it. Still, the story contains so much of vigor and color and romance—and is wrought into the very warp and woof of our hill history—that we have come to claim the Bald Knobbers with a sort of pride, perhaps. . . . Mrs. Mahnkey brings it to us in lyrics and grips us with the starkness of it, as she does everything of the kind:

The Tree Acurst

Whene'er I passed that grim old oak
I felt a sense of dread,
It spread its arms so wildly,
It tossed its blighted head.
The shade it cast was bleak and bare.
No flowers, no birds, no nestlings,
No sweet winds lingered there!

Then someone told the story
Of this piteous cursed tree;
And then, I went another way
For fear that I might see
The helpless wretches dying,
Swinging from that oak.
Victims of the savage mob
In sable hood and cloak!
(*SNL*, January 31, 1937)

A nice letter from Katie Waddle Clifton of Springfield, Missouri:

> One time Mamma drove from Highlandville to Springfield with my brother Willie and me. She finished her business early and decided at the last moment to go home. Uncle Jim Waddle was about 17 years old, so she took him along for company. She tucked us two kiddies down in the bottom of the buggy and out they started. By the time they reached James River it was about dark, but a beautiful moonlight night. They crossed the bridge and were driving through the tree-lined road, everything quiet as could be, when out of the darkness she was suddenly surrounded by masked horsemen. Not a word was spoken. One man looked close and said, "that's not him" and quietly as they came, they disappeared. She almost whipped her horses to death till she reached home. She always thought they were Bald Knobbers. This is a true story. Mamma didn't drive after dark with just children any more. (*SDN*, March 21, 1942)

Last summer I passed "the tree," where men were hung in the dark hours of the night, and I felt just as Mrs. Mahnkey does. . . . Some time ago I talked to a Mrs. Counts, who lives here, and her experience was interesting in the extreme. You remember, all of you, the famous hanging of the Walker Knobbers at Ozark, in 1889. They had killed Charley Green and Will Eden near Ozark. The killing has been gone over and over by Ozark historians and has been justified and condemned, but it was truly ruthless. . . . Mrs. Counts told it to me somewhat after this fashion:

> They lived all in one cabin, chinked and daubed with stick-and-clay chimney. They[1] came and told Green to come out. He said, "boys I ain't able." They fired, and one shot took off his wife's finger. She was holding his head in her lap. They shot again and shot his head all over her lap!

You remember that they had a trial, were convicted, and sentenced to death. They appealed to the governor for a penitentiary sentence but were denied. Zack Johnson was sheriff of Christian County and Mrs.

Counts was a pretty young girl working in the sheriff's family. The old jail was built onto the house, and they used to feed the young Walker (age twenty-five) and his father, who was to die with him, through iron bars which opened into the kitchen. . . . They had to offer $300 for the hangman, for no Ozarker wanted the job. Finally, Sheriff Johnson consented. Newt Howell and Jim Hurston built the scaffold right at the east end of the jail, and they took bricks out of the wall to let the prisoners walk out to the scaffold. Bill Miller, deputy sheriff, tied two of the ropes. Newt Howell tied the young Walker and sprung the trigger. The rope broke, and the boy . . . fell to the ground begging the sheriff to shoot him. His father had to witness all this. They picked him up very tenderly and sympathetically and hanged him over. Twelve minutes elapsed in the process. The father was hanged, then Matthews.[2] (*SNL*, January 31, 1937)

Story Became a Ballad

About five years ago I went to call on a Mrs. Crouch in this city. She worked as a maid in the family of the sheriff when William Walker and his son were hanged . . . Crouch was a young girl about seventeen, and she was I think, much taken with the young Walker boy who was good looking and very neat—she told me he always wore "such pretty, clean, white shirts" which she laundered while he was in prison. . . . She said she so often watched the young man walk the floor back and forth, and she said he "wrote ballets."

One day, she told me, he handed this song, "Gambling on the Sabbath Day," through the bars to her in a scrawly script and unfinished and told her he had written it. He finished it the next day. She will take oath to this. I have always believed it because I was about eight years old when this song came into our town and I imagine it came direct from Ozark. Everybody wanted a copy and wanted to learn the tune. This boy made the tune, so Mrs. Crouch says, and sang it over and over before he was hanged (about three months later). She learned it from his singing and it is the exact tune I learned. The boy may have plagiarized the old ballad, but I can find no one who knew the song before then and I have asked many an old timer. She says this boy told her that his mother never wanted him to gamble, especially on a Sunday when he used to go out with a crowd of fellows. . . .

That is the way folk songs come into existence. Out of the lives of the people. Unwritten and unpublished and often commemorating some tragic incident in their lives.

The words to the gambling song were sent to me by several readers. I am grateful for these songs. No two of the copies were the same, some differing quite a bit in wording. That always proves a folk song. (*SDN*, November 19, 1940)

Gambling on the Sabbath Day

Disobedient boy who dared
Turned away from his Father's care
Scorned his tender Sister dear
Nor listened to his Mother's prayer.

This wandering boy who fled away
Cards an' dice, began to play
For in prison he had to lay
For gambling on the sabbath day.

His father, sixty years of age
The best of counsel did engage
To see if somethin' could be done
Try to save his darling son.

Nothin could the counsel do,
The testimony was so true.
The bloody weapon that he drew
Pierced his comrade's body through.

The sheriff, he cut the slender cord
His soul has gone to meet his Lord.
Doctor said, the rich was dead
Spirit from his body had fled.
(McCord Personal Papers)

Old Alf Bolin, a Bushwhacker and Desperado

Much has been said about the death of Alf Bolin,[3] the old bushwhacker of early days who roamed these Ozarks and was such a terror.[4]

Like others, he was trapped by a woman! The soldiers had her husband a prisoner at Ozark, and she went to see him. Her husband had known all of Bolin's whereabouts as did she, and the authorities knew it. They told her if she would bring them Alf Bolin's head they would give her back her man. And she did it. She got him in from the woods by a false messenger who told Alf she had sent for him to come in because there was a man at her house who wanted to "jine him."[5] Bolin, shrewd as he was, came in unsuspectingly. After dinner, as he leaned over the fireplace to light his pipe, the other guest[6] knocked him in the head with the poker. She herself dragged him to a lean-to room and cut his head from his body. Women used to do a lot for "their men," didn't they? I have never run across anyone who knew him, but Uncle Sol Hembree down at Galena remembers seeing the head of Alf Bolin on a pole where it stuck for days at a little post which is now Ozark, Missouri. (*SNL*, December 2, 1934)

Mr. Thad Tunnel sent me a copy of a letter his mother, the late Nancy Pettijohn Tunnel, one of the earliest settlers of these Ozarks, wrote him at the time she had read about someone seeing the head of old Bolin on a pole. She and her brother were going to the first school in Ozark, Missouri. . . . She saw a man approach from the south with a big pine box. The children gathered in with horror and curiosity, and out rolled the head of Alf Bolin! That old terror of the hills with a huge head and great long hair! They never forgot it. The next morning as they went to school they passed the new mound where it was buried. It lay in Doctor Hansford's drugstore until burial. I think the story about its being displayed on a pole must have been a myth, and too barbarous a thing for our peaceful Ozarks. However, they were not peaceful at that time. (*SNL*, August 30, 1936; and *SNL*, September 6, 1936)

No Jailhouse in Our Little Town

Do you remember my telling you a while ago about their having no jailhouse in the little town when I was a child? We didn't need jails. Crazy people were about all we used jails for—poor souls. We had so little in the way of treatment then for mental cases. We did nothing but chain them and take them over hard roads in rough bumpy wagons, and they were wild, poor things, when after about three hard days the sheriff and other men got them to the state institution. These things break my heart yet! (*SNL*, October 28, 1934)

What the Sheriff Cannot Take

I read an article yesterday which entirely revolutionized my life. I'm now afraid of the sheriff! It says there is a very old law on the statute books, still in effect, which states that when the sheriff comes to take your possessions lock stock and barrel, that he can't take your church pew, your spinning wheel, your lettered gravestones, your loom, nor your spun yarn made into cloth. So I guess the sheriff would clean me out. He wouldn't want the precious gravestones of my loved ones, and my church pew is already taken, I'm afraid, the way I've been neglecting church the last year. I haven't any loom or spinning wheel and no spun cloth. So here go my earthly belongings when good lookin' Scott Curtis, sheriff, comes along. Maybe I could talk him out of it—but he's a Democrat and you know me—I'm one of those poor deserted Republicans! I'm the "other vote" they got last election! (*SNL*, September 15, 1935)

Feuds in the Ozarks

I get some good stories from Ozarkers. Here is a story from Patrick Adamson at the Devil's Washpan, Miller, Missouri:

> In the early days of southwest Missouri, the first mountaineers came in here from Kentucky and Tennessee bringing their portable distilleries, their rifles, their dogs, and their feuds.
>
> A rifle shot broke the stillness of the late afternoon of a summer day, and an unwary feudist lay dead on the hillside: The arm of the law reached out and got a hillman who was suspected. But the old ridge-runner was pretty smooth. He got a slick lawyer, kept his mouth shut and proved an alibi and was turned free. His lawyer knew he was guilty and asked him after it was over, to tell him all about it. The feudist shifted the long green 'tother side of his jaw and said,
>
> "Well, it wuz this way: I knowed that Blades would be erlong the trail that afternoon so I jist takes my gun and lopes over. I laid down behind a couple of little pines where the trail makes the bend above the crick. Elong about sundown shore enuf here he come. He had his gun in his right hand and wuz a packin' an ole rooster under his left arm. I tuck aim and got him square betwixt the eyes. He jist sunk down an' quivered a leetle. But, Curnel—I jist had to laff at the way thet durned ol' rooster went squawkin' off down the hill!" (*SNL*, November 13, 1932)

Horse Thieves

The horse thief used to be the most dreaded terror along the Ozark, Arkansas, and Oklahoma borders, thirty years ago. It was a sort of period between the rounding up of the nation's most daring outlaws—the James boys, the Youngers, the Dobins, and others. Horse stealing was an art practiced only by those who knew the ropes. A horse thief would sometimes enter a neighborhood and pose as a traveling preacher or good citizen, and learn the outlay of the country and all the good barns where fine horses were kept. He would do good things and win the respect of the people. He would steal the horses early in the night to get a good start and take them west and sell or trade them. Horse thieves were strung up in short order. (*SNL*, October 21, 1934)

CHAPTER 4

Ghost Stories

I begin a column of weird tales.

SNL, January 26, 1936

. . . .

Few things connect people around the world and across the ages like our fascination with stories of ghosts and monsters. The hill folks of the Ozarks are no exception; tales of the supernatural and unexplained are integral to the storytelling traditions of the region. Ghost stories are a popular subject both in May's writings and in the stories contributed by her readers.

. . . .

Visions and Spirits

I love life, and the supernatural has faint charm for me. It is not vivid and does not have clear red blood in its veins. I'm like my little brother. When Leslie was a very little tad, Mother was putting him to bed in the attic and he didn't want to go. He finally put up the cry that he was afraid as she covered him. Mother sprung the dear old story on him that I'm afraid the kids have come to look at with a weather eye, that the angels were there with him. "Aw, but I want somebody with skin faces!" he said. So that's me all over. I love those dear to me whom I can touch and know they are there. Sometimes a little boy will utter real wisdom. . . .

So now come these faithful readers of mine from over our picturesque Ozarks, so full of lore and legend and a child-like credulity which never dies. First, I have this from Mrs. A. L. Todd, Humansville, Missouri:

> There is a place right there in Springfield that was haunted some years ago. We tried to trade for it some nine years ago, but our deal didn't carry through or I could have "told you for shore!"
>
> When we were trying to deal for it, one of my friends living near said, "Surely you won't try to live there. Nobody can live there for that house is ha'nted!" I said I was not afraid of ha'nts, and I did think that would be a good place to invest in.
>
> I've been interested in watching that house since then, and believe it or not, it has been occupied only a few weeks a time or two since. So I've decided that people do believe in ha'nts, for that was a good house then. Lately it was moved back from the corner to build a modern filling station, for Highway Route 66 passes right by. Someone started to repair and modernize the house but suddenly stopped and I think it is vacant now.
>
> The poor old man that ha'nts that house carries a scalping knife!—That's what they say. I'm wondering how he remains so mysterious now with the bright lights of two filling stations and a grocery store so close by, but possibly the ravine and those dozens of tall trees at the back favor his activities. (*SNL*, January 26, 1936)

Was That Man a Ghost?

Mrs. Imogene Rice of Aurora, Missouri, writes me a real ghost story. It is spooky. It is one of the best I have ever had contributed, and Mrs. Rice is a splendid and reliable woman and I know she speaks the truth. I want you to figure this one out if you can. She writes,

> This happened in El Reno, Okla., where we were living at the time. My brother lived with us, and I kept a girl to help me. The two quite often sat on the porch and talked of evenings, when at nine o'clock a man would appear, seemingly out of nowhere and take up a beat walking, back and forth, back and forth.
>
> Brother would clear his throat at the fellow and make slighting remarks. But the fellow paid no attention. Occasionally he would stop and look up at the eaves, and then go on his pendulum beat again.
>
> They finally spoke to my husband and me about it and we thought it might be someone just a little demented. My brother said he "believed it was a ha'nt!"
>
> One evening the girl and I were alone and she stepped out on the back steps, to return with a scream, "That man, that man! He was looking around the corner of the house at me!" she managed to say.
>
> Just then the clock was striking nine. "Let's see if he is out in front," I said. We both went into the living room, where it was dark, and watched. Sure enough there he was, but he was climbing out of a buggy which had drawn up to the curb. The buggy disappeared down the street but the man took up his beat, walking.
>
> Our men returned directly, and when my brother saw him he brought forth an oath, saying, "Come on, let's get him this time." He and my husband flung wide the door and ran straight after the man. The girl and I, watching, saw the man go down, down, into the earth until he disappeared. The men folks ran all over that hillside and couldn't find a hole or any place where the man could hide. I noticed something strange—it was that I could see his form and features as plainly as if it was daylight.
>
> We moved soon to the first home north, and we did not see him there. But the people who moved into the vacated house were soon driven out. He frightened them so. He even peered

into the windows. Everyone was so convinced that it was a ghost that sending for the police wasn't even thought of. My brother-in-law met him once on the walk near the house and he noticed how phosphorous his face was, and he couldn't hear his footsteps. He bravely stood up under the ordeal but said he hoped it would never happen again. We did not learn of any reason for his haunting the place, but he certainly did!

There might be one explanation. A man might have been haunting or terrorizing that house as a matter of revenge. Maybe he lost it by someone's will or in some sort of deal. I know of a family who haunted a place down in the deep Ozarks for years so nobody would ever buy it, and very successfully they did it, too. (*SDN*, September 4, 1941)

B-r-r-r! Ghosts!

The True Story game we have now is coming. I have some this week:

I have a mystery story I would like you to hear. It happened when I was just a big gawky boy. We lived on my father's old home farm near Valley Springs, Ark. I had been for a stroll in the woods and thought it strange when I approached the house not to see some of the family in the yard. I went through the house and there on the front porch stood the whole bunch, father, mother, brothers, and sisters, gazing out across a large field of wheat about four inches high.

I inquired what the excitement was, so my mother pointed to the field and said, "See that big white bird in the wheat? It has been there a long time." I said, "I'm going to see what it is." But mother told me not to go for no telling what it might be. But I went and when I was getting near to it, the thing flew away and lit on a fence some hundred yards away. But I kept on going and when I was about the same distance away as the first time, it rose and flew straight toward me, just above my head, moving very slowly. I had picked up a stone to throw at it, but when the thing got close enough for me, it turned to the left and circled directly over my head with his big pleading eyes fixed on mine. It had a head, eyes, nose, mouth, chin and ears that were as natural as any baby's could have been. Its wings made no noise at all and when it passed over me it made a bee line straight across the prairie for the Holmes graveyard about two miles away.

I stood dumbfounded and gazed at it until its snowy white form vanished in the twilight haze. Some folks have told me it was a monkey-faced owl, but no one has ever convinced me it was anything other than a human being or spirit. I'd like to know the solution from anyone.—Pierce Wilson, Gassville, Arkansas. (*SNL*, February 6, 1938)

Spirits Speak from the Beyond

It is strange, amusing and to me perfectly fascinating how our superstitions cling to us in our Ozark hills and how sincere we are about them. . . . I have heard this same belief, from a reader in Hartville, Missouri:

> I read in your column about the ghost or spirit of the young lady walking into the pool. It made me think of what I heard my mother-in-law say. She heard her ancestors talk about seeing such things. They thought it was the spirit of someone who wanted to tell something which was worrying them and which they did not get to tell before they died. Especially when they went suddenly.
>
> They said if someone would just speak to the spirit and say, "In the name of the Lord Jesus Christ, what do you wish?" Then the spirit would talk and tell them what it was, and appear no more. (*SDN*, July 24, 1941)

Was That Ghost the Sad Mother?

I want to tell you a ghost story that Mrs. G. W. Kelley of Hartville, Missouri, tells me and she says it is a true story. It happened about four hundred miles from here in Holt County, so is not exactly an Ozark ghost story. But she can vouch for it and has always been so impressed by it.

Some people lived in a beautiful valley near her parents, and had two lovely daughters. The older daughter was betrayed by the man she loved and left to bear the shame alone, as were so many girls in that day and time. Her parents were heart broken and could not bring themselves to think kindly of the child. (I have known many sad cases like that, too.) The mother died at the child's birth and they hated the little child more than ever. But the younger daughter felt sorry for him and took his care upon herself and did the best she could by him.

The poor little fellow had a loveless, hard life and when he was four, he died of pneumonia. Two of the neighbor women went there to sit up, the old custom of sitting all night with the dead one in the home. (Many a night have I sat stiff and straight without one wink of sleep and five times I have sat stark alone.)

About midnight these women heard someone outside crying as if her heart would break. Thinking it was the child's aunt they went outside to try to get her to come in, as the night was chilly. But when they started to approach her she moved away and they ran after her, calling and trying to comfort her and beg her to come in. But she kept just ahead of them and started down the road. The women followed her in curiosity for over a mile; all the time the girl kept crying and walking on. Finally she came to the graveyard and turned and went into it. By this time the women got afraid and started back to the house, on the run. When they got back, there was the aunt in the house and she had not been outside at all and was wondering where the women had gone. (*SDN*, December 18, 1941)

About That Vacation Home

I want to ghost you up some more now. Mrs. A. D. Stealey, Route 4, Springfield, Missouri, writes me this, which knocks me cold:

> Some ten or perhaps twelve years ago, the family consisting of my husband, two daughters and myself, decided on a vacation where we could fish, rest and sleep. We caught some nice fish, but sleep just wasn't to be had in that house. I never did believe in ghosts, though now I often wonder. This is our experience.
>
> The nights were beautiful with a clear sky, full moon, and weather warm enough for ideal nights. The room in which we tried to sleep was well lighted by the moon; and while the ghost prowled around the room, scratching screechy on windows, bumping into bed, we could not see it. On examining the house inside and out we never could find anything to warrant these nerve-racking noises. But the last night we spent there my husband did see the "ghost" while not in the house. It was probably the same thing. He had gone to a pile of wood and sat down to enjoy the scenery and moonlight. My daughters and I had gone to get milk at the Turner home, some distance away, and when we got back he was still sitting there. We went into bed with the same experience as the night before. Next morning he told us what he had seen. There is a sort of ravine at this place and he saw a white object approaching. It kept coming toward him, and then within a few feet, it vanished completely. That settled it. When he told us this, we packed and left. (*SNL*, February 9, 1936)

A Vision by the Casket

Mrs. Virginia Lowe of Pierce City sends me the following, and I am sure it is true and sincere in every detail:

This incident occurred years ago when I was about fourteen years of age; while it is not a "ghost tale," it is the nearest approach to the supernatural of anything ever in my personal experience.

My grandmother who lived with us was stricken with pneumonia and died after a brief illness. On the following day I had occasion to go into the room where her casket stood, and in passing I paused a moment to view her face so peacefully reposing there and so dear to me. Suddenly I became aware of an illumination or light in the upper left hand corner of the room. This illumination or whatever one might choose to call it was in the form of a perfectly beautiful human eye, about 12 or 15 inches in length. I gazed at it in awe and admiration for perhaps a second, and then glanced at the casket. When I looked back up again the wonderful light had vanished instantaneously in the same manner as it had come. But the picture of that great human eye is as clear in my mind today as when it appeared, years ago. Perhaps some psychologist can explain it. I have never talked about this to people because you know some folks think one is off in the upper story when he tells experiences like that. Well, I believe the scientists tell us that no one is one-hundred-percent sane. (*SNL*, January 26, 1936)

A Ghost Greeted North Carolina Migrants to Arkansas

Thomas Elmore Lucy, Russellville, Arkansas, shared this bit of pioneering history:

It was the winter of 1883. A country home on Morristown Mountain, Pope County, Ark. A pilgrimage of half a dozen families had followed my father from North Carolina to this new Arkansas land where "flapjacks fell offin' the trees into puddles of molasses." Some of them had actually swallowed the glittering stories of the immigration agents, hook, line and sinker.

About fifty of us raw-boned farmers and our wives, scrawny hard working, snuff dipping, child-bearing mothers and aunts with their retinue of tousle-headed but pink-cheeked children, were crowded into the two-roomed house. Some slept in the barn and others in the kitchen. The half dozen families had all come in on the same train. But good old fashioned southern hospitality knew no such word as stuffy inconvenience. It was good to be alive and breathe the same air with the "kinfolks" whom we had not seen for two years. And the Ozark air was a panacea for those who had never seen a mountaintop.

White haired grandma and the youngest daughter had just stepped out the door into the darkness and the clouds hid moon and stars. There was a shriek as they came tumbling back in the door almost in a faint. "A big tall man with a white shirt front came right at us in the yard!"

After recovering a bit, they were still sure of the intruder. Grandma could almost describe his dress in detail, and he was giant in stature.

So there was an immediate posse formed. The men examined their muskets, after first carefully stalking around the house with lanterns and finding nothing. All night long they watched in relays while the women talked in whispers. Came daylight, the watchers peered from the doorway. A tall angular Arkansas cow with a white blaze-face stood contentedly chewing her cud near the doorstep! (*SDN*, April 26, 1941)

Hornet Spook Light[1]

We had some folks in to dinner and we got awfully worked up about this strange light that shines at night about twelve miles the other side of Joplin, near Hornet, Missouri.

About five years ago our *News and Leader* reporters went to see this light and it was discussed pro and con in the paper. I am sure you must all have heard of it. There are cars and cars every night in the summer anyway, watching the strange thing.

A certain young man who drives a truck saw it last week and he said the boys stopped and watched it a half-hour. And he said, "Believe me, it's the spookiest, craziest thing I ever saw, and if I had been alone I believe I would have taken out down the road afoot."

He said many cars were watching. I have heard it is around 1:30 to 2:00 a.m., and then I heard that it is any time after nine o'clock.

You park your car or get out and sit at a certain point. A large green-ish light, about as big as the steering wheel, is up the road and goes from place to place. Sometimes very near your car but you cannot run it down and you need not try. It stops before it gets to you. Usually is about one hundred yards away or more. It moves about strangely. I have talked with many people who have made trips to see it. Emma Galbraith went from Joplin out there with a group of Girl Scouts. They watched it a long while. This young truck driver gives what I think is a reasonable explanation. There are deserted mines and chat piles there. He thinks a sort of bituminous gas has formed on those old piles, or maybe a phosphorescent sort of mineral. And cars from away off reflect lights on it here and there. However, there are never any cars in actual sight when you see the light.

Many scientists have visited the place. People from Kansas City, Joplin, St. Louis and all about. And I am simply dying to go and always have been. But can never seem to get anyone who wants to go! (*SDN*, July 29, 1941)

Here's a good one from a contributor. . . I suppose this is at night. B-r-r-r-! Shiver my timbers:

> I feel that your group of Ozark mysteries would be incomplete without a description of the peculiar "ghost light" near my home. It can be seen about three or four miles west of Hornet, Mo., a small store located midway between Joplin and Seneca. Driving west on the graveled road one usually notices a whitish glow on the horizon. It becomes brighter and brighter, finally bursting

forth into a brilliant ball of fire. Sometimes it resembles the headlight of an approaching car; often it has the dull reddish glow of a lighted farm house window, and sometimes, it flickers brightly as an enormous jack o' lantern. On moist stormy nights it has been seen when it appeared as large as a washtub. Frequently it can be seen as two lights—one as a ball of fire rolling toward you while another hangs suspended in the air above the first. At times the light seems to remain stationary but usually it seems to be moving toward one, growing brighter as it comes near, then suddenly vanishing! Many people come to see this light, but none have satisfactorily explained it. Old settlers in the neighborhood have been familiar with this light for fifty years or more, and I have heard rumors of Indian legends woven about it.—Orpha Vaughan Haddock, Seneca, Missouri. (*SNL*, March 15, 1936)

A Real Graveyard Ghost Story

Here is a ghost story from a minister of the gospel:

> I read your ghost stories with interest, and I will add a modern daylight story. Two days before Christmas 1925, four of us were sitting in plain view of Little Creek Cemetery, and there appeared a pillar of fire about ten feet high with a flaming star at the top of it. It occurred at 4:15 p.m. and was there at the same time three days later. It appeared four times. I have lived here fourteen years and have lived in sight of other cemeteries and it is the first ghost I ever saw and I am 75 years old. I have been a preacher 55 years. A man went to the cemetery to watch for it and be there when it came; said he would throw his coat over it. Well, it came but he ran like a turkey. Yours in Jesus name,—A. J. Graves, Hartville, Missouri.

This story is interesting to me because I have heard that there have been like things in cemeteries seen by reliable people. It is said that there is sometimes in rare cases a sort of bituminous gas which escapes from decaying bodies which have not been buried deeply, and this produces a sort of blue fire. The gas gathers because the body is under ground where it cannot escape—just as any other gas. I do not know. But I do know that often in clay, hard, flinty little cemeteries the bodies were not buried very deeply. Not on account of lack of tenderness and respect, but because of such poor facilities for digging and no fine steel caskets and such things as more modern graves have. The coffins were crude and homemade and almost always they had to blast the rock. Often they had no dynamite and simply could not dig deeper. I have been to funerals in the little country churchyards long ago where the bodies were in pitifully shallow graves. What do the rest of you think? (*SNL*, February 2, 1936)

Graveyard Ghost

Parthenia G. Wilson, of Marionville, Missouri, described her neighbor's story, from Stone County, Missouri:

> There was a little graveyard not far from where they lived. People had been telling for several days about a ghost rising up out of a grave at night, always, when someone came along. This man did not believe in ghosts. One night he went by and sure enough there came up out of the grave something white, and it went down again. He said he could hardly keep his hat on! He stopped and watched and when it came up again he heard a noise. He decided to see what it was, and the closer he got the more scared he got. The thing came up and went back several times before he could get up nerve. Finally he got close enough and got his senses together and saw it was a horse's head. He went up and found an old white horse that had walked on to a grave, and it had caved in with him. He would rear up and try to get out then slip back and try again. So when the ghost is found it is always something alive.

All right, Parthenia, but aren't you ashamed to tear our stories down! I just love to believe somethin' is going to get me, because as I still declare—nothing wants me! Not even a ghost! (*SDN*, March 8, 1938)

"Ha'nted" Barn

Mrs. M. R. Smith of Marionville, Missouri, writes me . . . that when she was fourteen her brother married and moved to a place four miles away. All the neighbors told him the barn where he moved was "ha'nted." And he found it so. Even the horses would not stay in the barn at night. So an old man said if the father and brother and uncle would come, they would all make a night watch. As the sounds were always heard around two or three in the morning, they stationed themselves then, and waited. About three, they saw something climb a big tree close to the barn and leap into the hayloft! All the horses ran out into the lot, scared to death. Well, it was someone's pet racoon gone wild again and had a log chain fastened to its neck. The racoon always dragged the chain over the doorsill, which was covered with an iron strip, and it made a gruesome noise in the still of the dark hours.

Bang! goes another ghost story! (*SDN*, November 4, 1941)

Her Family Did Not Believe in Ghosts, nor Did She

And now another ghost tale from Parthenia G. Wilson, Marionville, Missouri:

> There are many of us Ozarkers who do not believe in ghosts and "ha'nts." My family before me did not, and taught me that way. When the truth has been found in every case, haunts and ghosts are something alive and not dead. I'm a coward, but not of something dead.
>
> Many years ago before I came to Lawrence County there was

a large white ghost out by the little cemetery here at Marionville. The road crosses the railroad track and curves around again on the north side of the graveyard. The road was narrow and had rail fences on either side and timber all along the north. For some weeks everyone who went by that side after dark was followed by a great white ghost that could stretch up, and then sink down. If the person ran, it ran. If they stopped, it stopped. Some people would not go that road after dark.

One moonlight night Dr. William Means was coming home on horseback after visiting a sick patient. He was riding along with the graveyard on one side and the timber on the other. Out of the fence corner came something white; it stretched up to most as tall as his horse, then it sank down. He started off in a trot and looked back and here it came. The nearer it came, the larger it got, but it was in the shadow of the timber. He stopped, and so did the ghost. When he started, so did the ghost.

He decided for once he would see what the thing was. He trotted on into the moonlight and kept looking back. When the ghost reached the moonlight spot, well, what do you think it was? A tame old white gander with a crippled foot that had in some way gotten through the rail fence around the timber and could not get back. He would follow everyone who came along, probably thinking he could get home. And he had to raise his wings with every step, to walk. Dr. Means' daughter told me this story, and I know it is true. (*SNL*, March 8, 1936)

Ghost Story of Dead Man's Pond
near Reeds Spring, Missouri

For some time I have been wanting to tell you about the ghost story of old Dead Man's Pond in my home county near Reeds Spring. . . . When a kid, I used to hear these tales. I am afraid to go there still now, especially by myself after night. Pioneer Will Sharp, of Reeds Spring, knows as much about this as anyone and I tell it to you as he wrote it to me:

It was in the spring of 1884 that my father, W. G. Sharp, came to Stone County and located two miles west of the old Reed's Spring with his family—a wife and six boys and three girls.

I was then sixteen, the oldest of the children and that was 57 years ago. I now live one mile south of Dead Man's pond, and will have lived within two miles of it for the whole 57 years. . . .

I have watched the deer lick in fifty yards of it, and killed deer and one wolf there, and have heard panthers scream many a time. But that is another story.

It was at the close of the Civil War that a band of robbers robbed a bank in Illinois and one in north Missouri of 67 thousand dollars, and pulled out for southwest Missouri and Arkansas. A band of soldiers chased them across Missouri and down what was then the old Wilderness Road, which is number 13 highway now.

The story is that they overtook them at the place we now call Dead Man's Pond on Highway 13, two miles south of Reeds Spring. There the soldiers followed them on to where the road crossed White River at the mouth of Bull Creek, two miles above the bridge which is now known far and wide as Kimberling Bridge.

There the soldiers killed two more of the party. And it is thought by lots of the remaining pioneer people that the seven buckskin bags with all that money in them, are in the hills of those Ozarks yet. I could show you dozens of places that have been dug for the money, and some think it has been found. I don't—and I will tell you why some day.

As I said, I was just a big wandering boy when we came here and one day I asked our nearest neighbor, Bill Pyatt, why they called this place the Dead Man's Pond, and the above is the story he told me and any of the old timers will tell you the same.

I asked him if he would go out there with me someday and he said he would. One day we went out to this little pond which was nothing more than a mud hole where the hogs wallowed, and mostly wild hogs then. There we found what we took to be the arm and leg bones of a man and the skull bone. The eye sockets were intact. We picked up a lot of those bones and put them in an old hollow stump that stands where the pond is now.

Now here is what my brother, Palmer L. Sharp, saw there one night: He had been to take his girl home, (his wife now) some thirty years ago. They had been to a party, riding a horse apiece, and he was leading her horse in the old fashioned way.

As he went back home it was a nice starry night and just as he was passing the pond, the horse he was leading slowed up and caused him to look around. He said he would have sworn there was a man in the saddle of the horse he was leading. The man just seemed to disappear right before his eyes, and he always tried to beat the dark after that. Now my brother was not afraid of any ghost, but what did he see?

Here is what Willie Webber saw there: In the late evening as he was coming home from Reeds Spring he was certainly not looking for any ghost. He is as truthful a man as I know. As he walked along the road just before he came to the pond, he found a small package tied up in brown paper in the road. He picked it up and after examining it found it to be a pair of stockings and a pair of shoestrings. He knew that the old man Osborne who lived out on the ridge beyond his place had gone ahead of him a short time before, and when he looked up the road there some forty yards off to one side where a path turned to go to his house and the Osborne house, he saw a woman coming down the path toward him. He thought it was Mrs. Osborne, with a black dress on and red apron and her hands rolled in the apron. She was looking down and he thought she was looking for the lost package. But when he came in line with her he could never see her anymore, though he looked all around and he could see for several hundred yards around the place but he never saw this strange woman again.

I could tell you others who saw this mysterious woman in black and many other unaccountable things all within a short distance of old Dead Man's Pond.[2] (*SDN*, May 14, 1942)

Another Ghost Story Happily Unsolved

I have another ghost story and a real and startling one from Mae Traller:

> I am a glutton for ghost scares, and I am going to tell you about the ghost that terrorized our countryside for a month when I first began teaching. The youngsters began coming into school with stories of how someone over by Payne's orchard had been frightened by a vague shape apparently composed of fog or gaseous substance. The thing would rise in front of someone riding or walking along the lonely woods front, float airily for a moment, and then drift off across the famous old orchard. Then older persons began seeing the ghost. . . . Of course by the end of the month that spirit creature had gained alarming proportions.
>
> One day another teacher and I compared notes, discovered we both loved ghosts and decided to beard[3] this one in its habitat. We hired two boys to drive us . . . and when the woodland grew violet with the weird hour of twilight, we loitered and waited. . . . Off to our left suddenly appeared a strange luminous object, something like a fog, but I shall always declare it had a human shape. The thing wavered and started toward us, then with a faint breath-like sigh, or maybe that was the pounding of our hearts, it drifted off above the orchard and away out of history. . . . It never was seen again so far as we could learn.
>
> But here is a secret which I'll bet anything that you, May McCord, can understand. I am glad that ghost mystery never was solved. So many of life's breathless wonders and mysteries have proved drab and disappointing when they were subjected to an analyzing process . . . and so I am glad the ghost escaped the cold eye of scientific explanation—to mix metaphors hopelessly—Why am I glad? Because at heart, I am a hill girl through and through. And no girl's life was ever complete without its bit of mystic lore to store away. (*SNL*, May 10, 1936)

CHAPTER 5

Politics and Religion

Candidates at our picnics . . .
they're thicker than ticks on a possum's tail.

SNL, July 8, 1934

. . . .

It is a testament to May's popularity and skill as a storyteller
that she was able to broach the topics of politics and religion with her readers and still be welcomed into their homes
week after week. Having grown up in one of the region's
most staunchly Republican counties, May shared most of her
readers' devotion to the Grand Old Party—though she did
admit to being a supporter of Democrat William Jennings
Bryan. She was an ally of fellow Galena native and long-
time Republican congressman Dewey Short who, like Bryan,
played up his common roots. May's reminiscences of religious life in the Ozarks, including river baptisms and brush
arbor revivals, were usually nondenominational enough that
they were relatable not only for fellow Methodists but also
for readers of other evangelical Protestant faiths. Like many
Ozarkers, however, she was fascinated with Pentecostalism,
and her use of the epithet "Holy Rollers" when describing

that movement reflects the comic disdain with which it was viewed by many mainline Christians.

. . . .

Family Politics Made Known

R. S. Doling told me he saw this printed on a barn door on highway between Cassville and Seligman the other day—"GOD BLESS OUR HOME. ALL DEMOCRATS." Then, in small letters was printed "and one republican." (*SNL*, March 15, 1936)

Story of an Old Politician from the Ozarks

If I were a politician, I wouldn't have any trouble about a speech. A politician always has just one, and when you've heard it, you're all washed up with him. He points with pride and he views with alarm. He consumes a lot of water from a pitcher during his speech. It looks important.

Let me tell you about an old chap down in my neck of the woods who ran for office perennially. And he never failed to get elected. His speech was just the same every time. It wasn't very long and he didn't drink any water. These were the main points of his speech and his sole claim to office. He said he was borned in that county and lived there all his life, and he had voted the same ticket his pappy had voted for nigh on to forty years.

He had been married three times and he defied anyone to prove that he ever struck airy one of his women a lick in his life. He said he had allus kep' the law. He never done no shootin' or cuttin' and he never done no stillin'. . . .

He's the one I told you about that they elected to the Missouri legislature and bless pat, he went to Little Rock, Arkansas. I guess all legislatures looked alike to him, and he lived about a hundred miles closer to Arkansas and a hundred miles meant a whole lot in those long ago days.

A few weeks later his brother-in-law had to go down into Arkansas with some cattle so he just went on to Little Rock and looked him up. He never had got connected up with the legislature but he was putting up in the wagon yard and still hunting where they were holding the thing. . . .

He was living on cheese and crackers and canned sardines which were a great luxury to him and he was having the time of his life.

Now this is all fact—I'm not kidding. They finally got him rounded up to Jefferson City and during the session he tried to introduce a bill in the legislature that there would never be any telegraph poles in his county. There wasn't a railroad in the county then. Someway he didn't have anything against the actual railroads, the engines and the cars, but he didn't aim to have them wires strung along over his land that you sent writin' over. He said there wasn't no Bible fer it and he didn't want 'em in the county.

Bless his old heart. He was a good chap. He didn't have much book learnin', and his diploma wasn't made of sheepskin and tied with a ribbon, but it was made of rugged honesty. He wove his own philosophy from the solitude of his own mountains and you know, sometimes there spring up men like that who shake nations. (McCord Personal Papers)

Yikes! May Kennedy McCord a Democrat?

Let me explain. You know in 1896 the whole wide world nearly went for William Jennings Bryan and Free Silver. My father was a "pizen" Republican who voted the ticket straighter than a shimmy seam from John C. Fremont on down! He went for Bryan with both feet, as did a million other Repubs. I don't blame him. I was for Bryan till he died, and for him yet!

Bryan was the most magnetic, the most fiery, the handsomest, most gorgeous young John the Baptist that ever sprung into the arena of America! He had uttered those immortal words—"You cannot place upon the brow of labor this crown of thorns—You cannot crucify mankind upon a Cross of Gold!" They rang 'round the world. I wondered if they were not prophetic. I am still wondering. (*SNL*, April 30, 1933)

Practical Politicians Knew How to Win

A prominent Democrat in Missouri told me that we ought to stop talking about everything which the country already knows about, and concentrate on one thing—get out the vote.

I often think of Charley Ferguson down at Willow Springs. He lives, breathes, and eats the Republican Party. It is his religion. He is well informed—but you folks who know Charley know that he knows what every Republican in his district wears for underwear or eats for breakfast. You know that you seldom hear him discussing ideals and fireside chats. He discusses ways and means! *Get out the vote!* Often when the biggest Republicans are speaking I have seen him stroll off to smoke a cigar. He doesn't care a hang what they say. He knows what he is and nothing on earth could change him. He knows exactly what he's going to do: He's going to get out the vote. Line them up. Get them to the polls. Account for them. See what each precinct and hill and holler ought to bring in for the party. And after all, that's all that ever counts. You know, it's votes that elect a president. (Speech by McCord, Greene County Republican Banquet, 1936. McCord Personal Papers)

A Campaign Speech for Dewey Short[1]

By far the most meteoric splash on the canvas of the Congressional scene in Washington is the youngish Dewey Jackson Short of Missouri, at least in the humble opinion of this reporter. An orator with the tongue of Demosthenes. A Hillbilly from the Ozark Mountains, with more degrees hanging to him than legs on a centipede. A Ridge-Runner in the king's court.

A sort of fire-eating give-me-liberty fellow who spits where he pleases regardless of where it hits. Often a rank iconoclast battling with the powers that be. A wisdom that out socks Socrates himself and a beguiling hemispheric smile that gets under your fifth rib.

This is not a sophisticated biography. It is a personal story without instigation, rhyme or reason written by one who knows him from clan days upward. For we are a clannish bunch in the Ozark Mountains. So, with all due apologies and with smokehouse technique, your reporter submits—Dewey Short!

Short is essentially Ozarkian and made of the red clay of the hills. We are a peculiar people in the Ozarks, anyway. Our storied land is a Pandora's box of strange tales, unfathomable superstitions, smoldering and fierce loyalties, simple religions and unshakable faiths. We live our own way. We have not had to fight any great frontier battles and conquer physically at the loss of our souls. We have a sort of "noble illiteracy." We have contemporary "ancestors" living right along with us. We have our own credo and our own gospel of success and are swaddled in tradition and individualism. If we tell you we love you—we do. If we promise to kill you, we pretty generally keep that promise. If we tell you we won't— we keep that too.

Out of this land came the young Short forty years ago, of rugged pioneers. His father was a Short and his mother a Long. In fact, three Short brothers married three Long sisters. The Shorts cut their way up from Tennessee, through the Cumberland Gap with a broad axe in front of an ox-drawn wagon. They planted their feet in the rocks in the Ozark country and nothing can remove them. A people with their roots in the soil.

This is the sort of stock that breeds a man who can never lose the common touch. For nine years this hillman of the Ozarks has represented his people in congress. And likely will for nine more for he can shoo more votes out of the rocky highlands of this last seed bed of Anglo-Saxonism on the American continent than Gideon used to blast the walls of Jericho.

He was the baby member of the Seventy-First Congress. He was for two years the lone Republican from the Midwest in Congress. He has held and does still, many prominent places on committees, and is rated one of the best orators in America. While he is a devout Republican, Dewey Short is an American first last and always and will stand by his country and its chief to the last ditch should troublous times come upon us.

That's the hillman in him. He has a passionate love for people and their problems. He is a politician but not very apt at learning the rather sub-rosa tricks of the trade. Usually he brings to his people an unbiased mind. Senators and congressmen are often like gangsters. We should shoot them when they get to know too much. Young Short has not yet come to that stage of the game. One time he said to this reporter who is many years his senior:

> Do you know, if I thought I should enter the world of scheming politicians and dehumanizing machines of civilization, and lose all the faith and honesty I have absorbed from my native hills, and be stripped to my foolish hide—I would rather live the rest of my days here at home in a one room tie-hacker's shanty down on Greazy Creek with a five-acre patch of 'lasses cane, a shot gun and houn' dog and a coon skin hung over the door with the bull frogs for philosophers.

And I know he meant it. Short comes from a strong partisan family because we are of the hills and generally feudally partisan down here. But he is strangely fair in his views. He seems to know no border breed or birth. The most flagrantly unconventional proletariat.

He will fret and fume over the pensions or farm problems or adenoids of a democrat friend and constituent, forgetting completely his politics, or that party lines ever existed. He cares not a fig. He loves his people. But no one can say that he is not a Republican by birth, by tradition, by practice and by all the seven gods of Rome. And he is a chap who gets from life all the gods have to give.

And we are that way down here. With a great capacity for contentment. Friendly as the simplest Acadians, happy as a band of nomadic gypsies. Our gates are never locked. Our fine saddle and our ham of meat hang in the smokehouse. We stir no strife. We have no foes. (McCord Personal Papers)

Religion Was Important
and Expressed in Many Ways

The simple faith of honest people, many who believed the Bible "kiver to kiver." (*SNL*, July 23, 1933)

Maybe Should Preach to Others

We like to hear the preacher preach while he is scoring somebody else, but when he gets on our toes, it's different. The old preacher was bearing down hard on the sins of drinking and dancing and general carousing. Snuff-dippin' Aunt Mandy in the audience was punctuating it all with amens and hallelujahs. Finally he mentioned snuff-dipping, and Aunt Mandy said, "Now he's done quit preachin' an gone to meddlin!" (*SDN*, June 3, 1941)

Fun at Revivals?

W. T. Moore of Cedar Valley, Missouri, tells me a story:

> In the days when the circuit riders used to come through the country they held camp meetings in the log schoolhouses and helped the resident preacher with his camp meetings. The young folks always enjoyed the meetings, as there was little in the way of "goings on."
>
> One particular meeting had gone on for a week or more without conversions or mourners. The tricky youngsters were afraid it would stop, so they decided to give it a little encouragement. They overdid the matter. About 12 couples, including Mr. Moore, then a young blade, went forward to the mourner's bench.[2] The circuit rider called on the local preacher to pray for them. This was very unfortunate, for he knew them only too well. So he prayed: "Lord, if you see fit, save these hell-deserving rascals, but remember, I know them better than you do!" (*SNL*, November 13, 1932)

Barefooted Baptists Did Not Sit with Their Male Family

A good Hillbilly writes me thus:

> At the old Wright's Creek Baptist Church I have seen grown
> ladies at church barefooted. However, I know them to be just as
> devout as any of the stylishly arrayed ladies of today. Then men
> sat on one side of the house and the women on the other. Now
> and then some daring fellow would bring his girl right in and sit
> down by her, but that always meant they were engaged. (*SDN*,
> July 26, 1941)

Old-Time Baptizings

The old-time baptizings will never pass, so long as people baptize by
immersion. Of course, they have them in the churches now in cities but
in the country they still have the old-time river and creek baptizings.
They are one of the outstanding things of my memory. Everybody would
gather on the river bank, or at Horse Creek, Railey Creek, Dry Creek or
Flat Creek or the James River.

I remember as a child the Primitive Baptists and dear old brother
Rickard. He went through a ritual. He would say to a man at the edge of
the water, "Brother do you wish baptism?" And the brother would say, "I
do." Then the preacher would say, "Friends, you have witnessed this man's
desire and willingness for holy baptism." "Amen," they would all murmur
in unison. Then he would lead the penitent into the water . . . often several penitents. He would wade out first and locate the depths. My, how
exciting to a child! Then when he located it, he would come back for the
penitents. All the time the crowd on the bank would be chanting, "O,
who will come and go with me, I am bound for the Promised Land!"

Then he would lead very gently the one to be baptized out into the
deep water and the crowd would sing, "Will the waters be chilly when I
am called to die."

Then he would take out his handkerchief and place it over the penitent's face, and many a time strong men were scared white . . . men who

could swim under water or who knew every foot of the river. But it was the intense drama and ritual of it.

Then when they were baptized, they would come out of the water and the crowd would break into happy songs, "Oh, Happy Day! When Jesus washed my sins away."

Always there were people on the bank with good warm shawls, reaching out to the baptized, and a good wagon or buggy to take them home. Everything was so kind and neighborly and very serious.

I remember one time when they baptized a widower, and a certain widow, who had her cap set for him, was there with her big soft shawl for his shoulders. And Aunt Phyla Powell said, "Well, they never was a widower baptized at a baptizing that they wazn't a widow there with a shawl!" (*Dial*, September 1946)

Modesty during Baptism

"Old Hillbilly" told me:

> When my dear mother was baptized in the Osage river, she fastened several pounds of lead to the bottom hem of her dress to ensure that it stayed down when she went under the water. (*SDN*, July 26, 1941)

Mrs. Mary Elizabeth Mahnkey Shares Her Memory of Revivals

A popular "fall festival" unsung and unheralded, is our old-time religious revivals. Little school houses out in quiet and peaceful woodlands, abandoned now, for the children are being conveyed afar to more progressive temples of learning—and the vacated places are given over to battles between the preachers and the powers of evil. One hears old hymns almost forgotten. There is shouting and weeping, brisk stepping and leaping, and in the Pentecostal congregations, a mystic ceremonial and strange weird tongue.

As a little girl, I attended a revival in a well-built brush arbor at Ponce de Leon, Mo., in the hills. Coal oil lanterns hung here and there from the ceiling of poles and dead leaves and stars. The preacher was a slight dark fiery minister of the Primitive Baptists. He possessed a wonderful eloquence, fluent and powerful—jeweled with the strong and beautiful scriptures from the Old Bible. I listened in trembling terror to the flaming destruction momentarily expected to descend upon us. One night when thin sheets of lightning waved in the southwest, and penitents had made their halting way to the altar mourning for their sins, kneeling and groveling, a woman began a song in a shrill rhythmic chant that I shall never forget.

> I've a long time heard that there will be a judgment,
> I've a long time heard that the stars will be falling,
> That the stars will be a falling.
> O' sinner, will you be there
> In that morning!

It went on and on, interrupted often by shouting and hallelujahs—and it foretold that "the moon would be a bleeding and the earth would be a rocking."

A beautiful girl and her beau were seated near me, and I had been amused and a little shocked at her flippant comments. With giggles, she had whispered loud enough for all to hear: "Look! A regular pigeon wing—see him knock that back-step! I wish I could dance that peart!"

Suddenly, at a certain line in the song, she sprang to her feet, her lovely head with the yellow curling hair thrown back, and she screamed in perfect agony. Immediately she was surrounded by a group of the sainted people working, and almost carried to the altar. Stricken, like Saul on that flowery way to Damascus!

Much the same emotional experiences are being nightly demonstrated near us. I would love to be one of that throng and join in that happy singing, and feel again the awe and wonder of that old-time camp meeting. There is much feasting, for there is often a visiting preacher and his family. And at the close of the meeting, there is the cheery, hearty, "You'ns come!" It is in a way a time of family reunions for the crops are all gathered in, 'lasses making time is about over with, and members of one family will go home with another clan or relations.

One neighbor said rather dryly when twitted with the fact that a certain well-known revivalist did not tarry long in his community, and the meeting "broke up" in a week or so, instead of being prolonged through weeks and weeks—"Well, you see, our chickens over on the ridge all died off with the flu this summer!" (*SNL*, October 24, 1937)

A Ridge-Runnin' Gospel[3]

The outside world hears a lot about the Ozarks, written by half-baked, cocky young writers who come down into these hinterlands to count the horns on a Hillbilly and write him up for the press. But you don't write us that way. You write us "by ear" or you fail utterly. Outsiders rarely get anything of any value from sketchy conversation with the hill people of the Ozarks. One reason is that the hillman is a silent individual and will not be exploited. He never subjects himself or his beliefs to any close scrutiny, and the most that a "furriner" gets is guess work and a rather wild guess at that.

But we have a natural aptitude down here for divorcing old Dame Reason, and the strangest among strange things is the Church of the Pentecostals, a people known generally as Holy Rollers. This gospel with its many variants is not confined to the Ozarks by any means, being very prolific in Tennessee and the Kentucky mountains, and sprinkled all over the south, over the Pacific coast and very widely spread in Europe. But here you may get versions of this particular religious phenomenon that you may perhaps get nowhere else.

Armoring myself with apology in the beginning, be it said that this writer has no intention whatsoever of scoffing, criticizing or even waxing profound. I am merely taking you to the scene and giving it to you as it exists and as I have seen the meetings and attended them for over forty years, in my own Ozarks.

Contrary to general belief, the Holy Roller, or Church of the Pentecostals, is rather a new denomination as denominations go. Baptists and Methodists made this Ozark country, religiously, but the Holy Rollers have taken it off their hands. The old Baptists and Methodists were more formal and stuck to ritual and tradition more. They sang the old modal songs of the Gregorian type and with no dance rhythm to them whatsoever. They discouraged the use of too many whanging instruments and too much free mingling of sexes. Some shouting was good, and lots of "amens," but an unseemly hysteria was frowned upon when it threatened to become noisy. The true Baptist and Methodist of the early Ozark hills was never one for a show of any sort and never submitted himself to exploitation either in his religious or social life.

The Meeting Begins

Without further discussion we are off for the "Holy Roller Meetin'" over in the Smackout Schoolhouse at the foot of Booger Mountain. The small building is crowded to capacity and great excitement prevails for the foot washin' is just over. The Holy Roller washes feet, but his Hardshell Baptist brother beat him to that ancient rite long before "Holiness" was ever thought of.

Brother Ward (and they used to call him "Jar-Bottle Ward") is preaching a very primitive sermon in a soul-sweating way. It is a mystic salvation. He intersperses it with the "unknown tongue," now and then going into a sort of "strange interlude." He mumbles in a kind of barbaric monotone for a moment, landing safely back at his regular routine. He tells you over and over the thing that baffled Nicodemus: "The wind bloweth where it listeth and thou hearest the sound thereof, but cannot tell whence it cometh, and whither it goeth. So is everyone that is born of the spirit!" With this rather confusing bit of Holy Writ, over and over, he finally leaves you quite flattened out.

The Testimony Meeting before the Main Sermon

The "testimony meeting" is on. This precedes the real sermon and lasts interminably. This is for the "saved" ones and they make the most of it. They have no terminal facilities whatsoever and each one preaches a small-sized sermon, screams, sings, dances unbelievably, weeps bitterly with eyes closed, pleads, and agonizes. When the time comes for the prayer, they get on their knees and each saved person in the building prays audibly. And audibly is rather a restrained word for the unspeakable din of it. During this praying many pass out and continue to lie on the floor perhaps for the rest of the service, stark, unconscious, white and rigid. Often or nearly always with the hands raised up, a favorite way with Holy Rollers, and they will lie with the hands raised straight up from the body for as long as two hours! They believe that the spirit "pours in the body" this way.

The sermon is often an anti-climax. In the Pentecostal religion, the sermon is quite the smallest part. A very few listen to it. The greater portion are exhausted or entirely wrapped up in their own prayers or moaning or perhaps dancing. The sermon is usually just of the exhorting type and well sprinkled with experiences.

Call for Seekers and "Getting the Power" to Speak in Tongues

After the sermon, the call for seekers is given, and they come to the mourners' bench in flocks, in a good meeting. With them come the "workers" who pray over the seekers, laugh, dance the "holy dance," rejoice and speak in tongues.

There are two different types of seekers. Those seeking salvation and forgiveness for their sins in the usual orthodox manner, and those seeking what they call the "baptism." This baptism of the Holy Ghost is a sort of second blessing that comes after conversion or "getting saved." Maybe months later, maybe never. They call it "the power," and on this sign hangs all their stock in trade. The sign of "getting the power" is that the recipient speaks in tongues. There is no other sign. It is often very hard to obtain, and when the seeker gets salvation and forgiveness for his cussedness he is just half way up the creek, so to speak. He must then harass himself in mind and body until he gets this "power," which is the sign or seal of an indwelling of the Holy Ghost. And as before stated, there is no other indication either to his own satisfaction or to the outside world, only that he suddenly and from apparently nowhere, begins to speak in tongues.

The seekers fall as dead men at the altar. It is now filled with those prostrate on the floor until the workers have difficulty in stepping around the bodies. Old and young, men, women and a few children.

The ordinary uninitiated onlooker finds himself a bit baffled in trying to distinguish those seeking salvation from those seeking "the power." Some on the floor writhe and weep convulsively and scream like the wail of a panther or a Comanche squaw. It freezes the marrow. Others have passed into unconsciousness, a sort of coma, and are very quiet and ghastly pallid. The quieter, the deeper the spell or self-hypnotism. Some kindly disposed soul usually throws wraps across their limbs, for often the floor is cold, but this is against the formula, for they are not to be touched while the power is "using" them. Only this small attention is ever indulged in; no attempt whatever at resuscitation.

These seekers lie on the floor perhaps an hour, maybe two, while prayer splits the heavens, all praying at once. The Holy Rollers never pray singly.

Then a strange change may take place! They may rise and dance rigidly and eccentrically in the most uncanny dance you ever beheld. Bending backward almost to the floor, a thing that could not be performed under any normal circumstances by that person, if his life depended on it. It isn't exactly a dance. It is usually a sort of rigid performance done in a somnambulistic manner with the eyes closed, the lips sometimes drawn and teeth set. They may throw their arms wildly and laugh or they may contort the body and scream beyond belief. I have seen them dance until they fell in a limp heap on the floor from exhaustion, but it is amazing how much it takes to exhaust one in this state. I know a little woman about seventy who dances for at least one hour like a queer jumping jack every night of a meeting lasting six weeks. And she is a servant and does her work with dispatch. It seems to be all in a day with them, and their purpose is to not notice the dancing and consider it just the most ordinary and natural performance of God's children. The fact is that it would lay great many of God's children in the nearest hospital if they didn't get themselves into a self-hypnotized state first.

Everything grows informal now. People stand around the altar and observe the goings on or walk about the congregation. The workers move about, praying, singing, crying, screaming, or rejoicing. They give the invitation to all in the audience both saint and sinner, to come to the altar for prayer. Often they fairly run. Many are reticent.

The Healings

At the "healings" they fall the instant the healer touches their foreheads —fall like a shot, perfectly unconscious, ninety percent of them. And often they fall quite hard. Members take the rugs from their homes and bring them to the pulpit for falling purposes, and other members assist in catching those who fall. For they fall almost quicker than the eye can work. Almost as if they were touched with a live electric wire!

Minervy Gets the Power

And now I want to tell you about my old friend Minervy who was a ridge runnin' Holy Roller after my own heart! I think you will like this story after so much reporting and explaining, because it is rich with a certain sincerity and side-splitting humor. Although, heaven help me, 'Nervy never intended it to be funny! But that the uninitiated among you may get the personal application of it all, I give you Minervy and myself!

I had known 'Nervy all my life. She had worked for my mother, my husband's mother and for me when my babies were born. She was a good soul and came of a good old pioneer family of sensible people. She carried a buckeye in her pocket to keep the rheumatiz' away and was very much a law unto herself.

She always took me into her confidence as a mother would. She knew I was not of her faith, but she knew I had wept and sung with Holy Rollers over many a grave.

Over a cup of coffee, for she visited me regularly, she told me about "gittin' the power." She said it "throwed her" now and then. But this time at the meetin' over at Smackout Holler, the power had seemed to wield the strong arm rather stiffer than usual.

"So it did, 'Nervy," I asked, for I was all ears.

"Yes, hit did. Hit throwed me right agin' the edge of the bench an' plum knocked me out a my head."

"Why, 'Nervy," I gasped. "Didn't they do anything for you?"

"Lands, No! I jist laid there till I come to. The brothers wouldn't let 'em tetch me. Pap come up and put some water on my face, but the brothers said the power had throwed me an' was a usin' me, an' fer Pap not to grieve the Spirit. I wouldn't want Pap to go agin' what the brothers say—no I sure wouldn't.

"Dreckly I come to. Seems like I jist cain't git the power. Brother Lafe got it long ago, and Caldony's got it, but I've tried might nigh a year now. You know the brothers say hit's on account of my teeth."

"Your teeth?" I gasped again.

"Yes, my store teeth. They say I'm jist a wearin' 'em fer proudness."

I remember how long 'Nervy had carried her old decayed teeth and the poor health that went with them. Then she had worked in the family of our little town dentist and earned a nice new set of shiny "store teeth." I recalled how proud she was of them and how her health improved. And now they were the great barriers to her getting the power because she was "jist a wearin' 'em fer proudness!"

She quoted to me that the brothers had said "thou shalt not make unto thee any graven image of anything that is in heaven above or the earth beneath. Thou shalt not bow down to them or worship them— etc." Verily, the brothers were always armed with the sword of the spirit.

But the store teeth were destined for a great adventure. A big meetin' was going on over on Little Greazy. Night after night as usual, 'Nevry had been at the mourner's bench praying and wrestling with her Maker for "the power"—the gift of the unknown tongue. She must have it at any cost. Like the poor Hindu woman she was cast on the funeral pyre of disgrace. The workers had prayed over her, beating her in the back and holding her hands straight up to the heavens until all were nearly prostrate with her, and perhaps inwardly a bit wearied.

It was getting quite late and 'Nervy on her knees wrestled with and yelled at Jehovah. Finally a great light dawned on her sister Caldony who was near by kneeling in an agony of prayer. She crawled across the straw and getting hold of 'Nervy she whispered in her ear:

"Take 'em out, 'Nervy—take 'em out!"

'Nervy slipped the teeth out and held them hidden in her hand. And this is the way she told me about it excitedly:

"I jist riz a shoutin'! The power came on me quick as I got 'em out, an I riz an' it danced me all over the floor! Hit used me a heap more than it used Caldony when she got it. An' I hain't wore 'em for four weeks. They're at home in the clock not a doin' nobody no good. An' they never was nuthin' but a tool of the devil! I can eat anybody's vittels that was ever cooked, an' I never aim to put 'em in my mouth again—God willin'!"

Words are often vain and foolish things and the flesh is weak. As time wore on, 'Nervy's penitence weakened. She had been so proud of the teeth. She was a widow and she told me once—"a widder needs all her enticements." 'Nervy had "spells" caused by some sort of indigestion, so on account of this fact and by some manner of twisting the Holy Writ leniently, and with some sort of kindly agreement, they got the church brothers together and she was permitted to wear the teeth again.

But the end is not yet. There came the time for her third baptism with water or rather in water. 'Nervy belongs to that particular branch of Pentecostals called the "One-ness" branch, which baptized under water, lock, stock, and barrel, for each member of the Trinity.[4]

A big crowd assembled on the banks of the Little Greasy. The candidates for baptism were being prepared for the chilly waters. All was silence when from the crowd some voice began a shrill treble:

> I've a long time heard there'll be a judgment.
> I've a long time heard the stars will be fallin'.
> I've a long time heard the moon will be a bleedin'.
> O, sinner will you meet me in that mornin'!

Like a saint of old, 'Nervy walked with her fellow penitents into the deep green waters of the Little Greazy. The preacher buried her in the clear hole. All was well until 'Nervy "riz a shoutin'" again. In her excitement the teeth fell out as her sins fell from her transformed soul! Not in the least did she mind. She started for the bank waving her thin hands to the tall sycamores, shouting:

"He's tuk 'em away, He's tuck 'em away! Glory Halleluyer! They never was nothin' but a tool of Satan, and the Lord's tuk 'em away!"

Two weeks later, her nephew, Orley, moved by pity for 'Nervy's soul-wracked condition between the flesh and the spirit, waded in the clear water of the Little Greazy and when he came to the deep baptizing hole, he dove down and got the teeth, nothing amiss! They were just as good as the day the Lord "tuk 'em away!"

The last I heard of 'Nervy—and I hope I never quite lose her—she was wearing the teeth and had "all her enticements." She had migrated for a while to "the Nation," as the Hillbilly still calls Oklahoma. (McCord Personal Papers)

CHAPTER 6

Death and Burial

I must go back to the hills again
And wash my lips with prayer.
And if the strange, white rider comes
He'll find me waiting there.

SDN, July 9, 1941

. . . .

Few human events are as shrouded in ritual and tradition as death and burial. May shared Ozarks superstitions (such as the venerated feather crown) and described burial practices in her writing. Some of her memories, such as hearing sawing and hammering during the night as men made a coffin for a neighbor, lie outside the experiences of modern Ozarkers while others can still be seen in country cemeteries, such as graves decorated with shells and pieces of broken glass: "silent expressions of love."[1]

. . . .

Reverence for the Dead

I've seen a lot of unlettered hill people, and even people with a certain crude callous exterior, but in the presence of death there was always respect and contrition and reverence and a sort of awe for that great abyss from whence no traveler returns. (*SNL*, September 1, 1935)

Do any of you remember when you used to see a man ride by on a horse with a hickory stick in his hand just the length of his neighbor, going to get a coffin made? And you knew, as you rode up to the cabin in the hills where sickness was, that death had entered, because the bed clothes of the departed one were on the line. And do you remember when they called the bier the "coolin' board?" And have you heard the sawing and hammering of coffin making all night long? Well, I have. Did you ever go into the little country graveyard and see the graves all covered with white shells and bits of pretty, broken glass and dishes—silent expressions of love, of grief, and a desire to "deck the hallowed mound" of the beloved dead. (*SNL*, January 22, 1933)

Funerals Preached a Year or So
After the Person Was Buried

Many people have wondered about this strange custom. There were certain iron-clad proprieties about the old-time funerals of the Ozarks and all the old Southern Mountains.

They called it "funernalizin'," and the sermon was called a "preachment." It was preached months after the burying and sometimes a year or more. That is easily explained. In the first half of the century, the settlements were so scattered and preachers and churches so few. There was no embalming, and when one died he had to be buried right away. There were no telephones. Only runners by horseback to tell of a death or a funeral. And often there would be a slim dozen or so of friends at the funeral, when there were worlds of friends who would go had they known of it. So, after some months when they could get the word out for weeks ahead and "norate it around," as they called it, they all met at some church and had this funeral preachment. And more than often, there sat a new wife or new husband taking in the ceremonies with great respect, and mourning for the dead loudly and dutifully. Most always, a man would marry in a very short while, and sometimes a widow did. They had to have someone to work—a man to farm and help raise bread for a widow's little ones, or a man had to have a cook and housekeeper for his little children. One woman in the old days described it this way:

> I loved my husband, but my children were small and I had to have someone to work my farm. So I married Mr. Butler in a year, lackin' a day. Pretty soon Brother Clemens came to preach my dead husband's funeral sermon. I had to go and take the chil'ern, but I just couldn't put on my crepe again. I studied and studied as to what would be respectful to both husbands, my livin' one and my dead one. So I made up my mind to wear my black sateen dress Mr. Butler gave me for our weddin' present and my purple bonnet, and felt it was nice and suitable.

So there's the way it went! Bless her heart, she meant well. (*Dial*, February 1947)

Old Beliefs and Superstitions

Some of the strongest superstitions in our Ozarks are those relating to religion, such as burying the dead with feet to the east so they may rise up and greet the "Star in the East." (*SDN*, September 28, 1939)

When someone died chairs used to be turned down and mirrors to the wall, and the clock stopped. (*SDN*, July 7, 1941)

Why do true hillbilly Ozarkers get an older person to set an evergreen tree? Because when the tree grows tall enough to cast a shadow it will shade the grave of the one who planted it. Therefore, the canny Hillbilly

. . . always got grandpap to set the tree because he would be dead anyway when it got big enough to cast a real shadow! (McCord Personal Papers)

When you feel shivers run over you, maybe on a warm day, or nervous "quivers," someone is walking over your grave! (*SDN*, July 9, 1938)

I see an old oak which is dying and for no reason. It is just dying. And I remember that there was an old story that if you walk straight one mile north of that tree there you will find where there will be a death before another year. There may be no one living there, but someone will die there just the same. (*SDN*, August 16, 1941)

Feather Crowns or Angel Wreaths— Mementos or Omens of Death

All of my life I had heard of this superstition, that a crown would form in the pillow of a dying person, especially if the person had lived a good and saintly life. I have always wanted to see one of the crowns. Some way, I had it into my head that they were very small, wispy bits of feathers that had got themselves into the shape of a crown, and you had to draw awfully hard on the imagination to make out a crown. I figured that this was possible in most any pillow, and that perhaps by opening up my own pillows I might find something that could pass for this strange superstition. But how greatly was I deceived! (*SDN*, October 15, 1941)

Last week my good friend and buddy, Mabel Gammill from Mountain Grove, and her mother, Mrs. Horner, were visiting me a while in the afternoon. We got to talking about different superstitions and the conversation fell to these crowns. Mrs. Horner said she had one from the pillow of her dead aunt and that she helped remove it with her own hands.

She said her aunt had complained of the "lump" which came in the pillow and they would not shake up the pillow or remove it, thinking it might be a crown forming, as she was such a sweet Christian woman.

Feather crown or angel wreath. *Photo courtesy of Patti McCord.*

When Mrs. Horner said, "lump" I fairly jumped. "You don't mean it is LARGE do you?" And she said, "Why of course."

Then she did a thing that I will appreciate always. She said she would mail it to me if I would take good care of it and return it before long. That it could be mailed and was not at all delicate.

I was amazed. I scarcely knew what to do with this crown. The news got out, and several friends came to my house to see this crown through the day. Being Ozarkians, all had heard the superstition and wanted to see it. Some had seen them before and said they all look alike. This one is especially perfect.

I was going to speak to the Kansas City Art Institute at their fireside dinner and I took the crown with me. For an hour, 250 guests examined it after dinner. Many would not touch it. One man suggested I turn it over to a scientist for he had a theory that high fever in the body would start the feather to swirling one way and perhaps packing firmly into this crown. Rather fantastic it seems to me, but perhaps could be. Another man said, "Mrs. McCord, let the scientists alone. Let's just leave it and believe it. Let's try to believe in SOMETHING in this old world. Something that our pioneer ancestors believed in and saw with their own eyes. And could not account for."

. . . One lady at the dinner said she saw one in Canada that was very much like this one. She said the superstition originated in England very early, and they were found there in pillows as long as two hundred years ago. The word "crown" is deceiving for it is more like a ball flattened out. It is compact and every feather sticks to shape without any glue or adhesion that the human eye can detect. I guess they called it a "crown" because the belief was that it was formed as a "crown" for the hereafter. (*SDN*, October 15, 1941)

May's Readers Wrote Her about Their Experience with Feather Crowns

I have two very interesting and sincere letters which I want to give you:

> The crown I have was removed from a pillow on which my 17-month-old baby passed away. I have had it 12 years and it is as perfect as the day I removed it. Your description is perfect, except for size and I understand they vary with the age of the person. The one I have is not a great deal larger than a silver dollar, but it is about an inch and a half thick. I have seen other crowns. Some larger, some smaller but each one too perfect to be made by human hands.—Mrs. Gretchen McKinley, Rocky Comfort, Missouri.

And here is a most remarkable letter about a chance acquaintance on the train:

> Last year I was on the train going to Tulsa and a lady got on going to Chelsea. She had been in Aurora taking care of her

husband's mother who had been sick for some time. The lady said to me, "and when she died there was a crown in the pillow." I just looked at her hoping she would tell me what she meant, for I had never heard of it. Instead of telling me she asked if I would like to see it.

She got out a round box, which had contained bath powder, and set down in this box was the crown, a most beautiful thing. It may be a superstition, but a thing as beautiful as that little crown of feathers—it just seems that God had to have a hand in its making, for no man could.

She told me to take it and hold it in my hand, for it would not come apart. I believe it was larger around than the one you have in your possession now. It was all clean, of the best white feathers. I am so glad I got to see it because one's imagination cannot picture one of these crowns in all its perfection and beauty.—Mrs. C. M. Steelsmith, Springfield, Missouri. (*SDN*, October 18, 1941)

A reader from Fordland, Missouri, writes me,

According to what my husband tells me, as I have no knowledge myself, these crowns are definitely of evil. In fact very evil. As you say they are never found in a finished state only after the death of the user of the pillow and if you'll take a fool's advice, you'll get rid of the specimens you have at once.

I was taught not to believe in superstitions, and this one I never heard of until I came to Missouri. My husband's people have lived in St. Louis since the days of Laclede and Choteau, and they firmly believe in this sort of thing. But they believe that if the pillow is burned if a sick person is using it, the hex will be removed and the sick one will recover. One of his nephews and his wife won't have a feather pillow in the home on this account. (*SDN*, January 15, 1942)

Then here is a very strange story, contributed by Mrs. H. L. from Lockwood, Missouri:

Thirty-eight years ago my oldest son was always sick. Some old ladies said for me to look in his pillow and see if there was a bunch of feathers. I did so and found one of those peculiar round crowns half formed. I showed it to one woman and she said for me to burn it. I asked her why and she said, "If you don't burn it, when that crown gets fully formed, the child will die." Believe me, I burned it. First I took a good look at it and tried to pull the feathers out, but couldn't. The boy got well.

Five years ago my husband was always sick and nobody knew what was wrong. We thought of the crown experience we had once before, so we examined the pillow and sure enough, there was a three-quarter crown in his pillow. I took and burned it, and he got well. How they got there I do not know. I sure watch my pillows now! (*SDN*, October 30, 1941)

A lady from Lebanon wrote me and said if nobody had died on the bed, that made no difference. The crown was forming because someone was going to die on it! (*SDN*, May 2, 1942)

Advice to a Reader to Balance Myth and Fact

I had a very strange and imperative letter with a stamped envelope enclosed for reply:

My sixteen-year-old daughter lately became ill. She is up now but not able to return to her studies. Just punying around. Well, last night as she was getting ready for bed, I picked up her pillow and found a "crown" not quite completed. It appears as if it had been started around a pink thread the like of which we do not have about the house and have not had that I ever know of.

Now these feathers were emptied out last spring, and the tick washed. And they have been sunned ever so often this winter. Please let me know whether I should burn this crown or not. It seems as if you had in your column from someone that they should be burned. Let me know by return mail, please. Should you care to print this please do not use my name or address.

Now, my dear woman with the anxious mother-heart, you put up a question to me, which puzzles. During all this discussion in my column, I found several who thought they should be burned at once. Even went so far as to say that their sick ones recovered when they were destroyed. When I went to the editors meeting in Kansas City there were two north Missouri editors there who said their people in that section always burned them. If I were you I would burn the phenomenon if for nothing else only to satisfy the mind of the girl, now that you have discussed it. The mind is a queer thing. It will not hurt anything to burn it and may do a lot of good. (*SDN*, April 11, 1942)

National Interest in This Phenomenon

The story of the feather crowns, which we discussed for months, certainly went far. Geer of the *Post-Dispatch* writes me yesterday that now *Newsweek Magazine* wants the picture and story and he is sending it on at once. The picture of that little feather crown from the pillow of a dying woman it seems will go all over America! As I say, people are always intensely interested in what we believe in the Ozarks.[2] (*SDN*, April 21, 1942)

Some Explanations

Now this is the possible explanation the *Post-Dispatch* writer offers. I want to give it to you from the story:

> A possible explanation lies in the physiological character of feathers. From the shaft of a feather, above the quill, are numerous vanes composed of barbs, as they are known to science. On these barbs are barbules with minute hooklets on the side toward the tip of the feather. These hooklets normally are caught in indentations on the side of the barbules toward the quill.
>
> In a pillow they are likely to become loose, ready to hook any other minute thing. When two feathers come into contact, they are held together by these hooklets. Other feathers join them

and a nucleus is formed. Just as feathers can be pushed through a small hole quill first with comparative ease, but tip first with difficulty, so feathers in a clump would tend to climb or move along each other toward the quill point. Such movement would continue until the quill points attained a common center and could go no farther. Since downy feathers are all curved, the tendency would be for the outward curve to fit into an inward curve and the feather clump would assume a spherical shape. (*SDN*, April 7, 1942)

Mrs. Hattie Shields of Bois D'Arc writes to tell me she thinks the superstition is ridiculous and that when picking young ducks or geese, other times you pull off a piece of the skin with the feathers and it dries. She thinks this is what starts and makes the crown. (*SDN*, October 30, 1941)

There might be some physical law, some capillary attraction evolved from this queer gathering of feathers in a pillow that might open up some discovery that would bless mankind. Even if we agree to leave out the supernatural, there is some physical or material reason for the formation of these feathers in the beautiful, symmetrical, and compact shape. Always round, always with the feathers going one way, always drawn toward a perfect center. I can readily see how an ordinary conglomerate lump could gather in feathers not stirred or aired or beaten well, but not these beautiful creations. And the fact that they do come is established beyond the shadow of a doubt by many honest people.

And so, I leave it with you. (*SDN*, January 15, 1942)

Poems of Mourning

To Cletus Parks
May E. Doms[3]

With a plane you played
In your homeland skies,

Adventure dancing
In steady eyes.
A tilt on the white clouds swinging high,
As the lilting days swept swiftly by.

With a plane you strayed
into far-flung skies,
Where the wheeling war birds
Sound their cries,
Awing where rolling war clouds lie
As the war-torn days slipped slowly by.

With a plane you paid
The price supreme,
That we be spared
The Nazi dream.
You made for your own dear homeland sod
A three-point landing at the feet of God.
(*SDN*, March 19, 1942)

A Family in Winona, Missouri, Chose May's Poem for the Obituary of Their Infant Child

A little light in the window,
Like a spot on a fevered cheek,
Where hopeless feet tread softly,
And helpless hands are weak.
And a little boy is choking—
White lips—quick fleeting breath;
And a woman sits in dumb despair,
And grapples the monster, Death!

A little grave on the hillside,
Out there in the bleakest night,
Where a woman's hopes lie buried
In a little robe of white.
O, God of the night of darkness,
O, God of a woman's tears,
Keep, keep my heart from breaking
Against the bitter years.
(*Current Local*,[4] November 30, 1933)

Rose O'Neill after the Death of Her Mother

I know how Rose O'Neill, the divine poet as well as the artist, felt when she lost her dear little mother, "Mimi," as they called her, last year. That sweet soul who looked like an ivory etching, a pearl cameo, but had the brain of Socrates and the kindness of a saint in heaven. Rose wrote a poem I shall never forget till I die:

Take all these other ladies if you must,
Scatter their sweet names and pretty dust.
Let the wind have them, and the sand—
Let Troy forget—but let THIS lady stand!
Let this one lady be what never dies,
Be history, Oh, heart! Oh, eyes!
Death is so cruel—and yet it is so kind . . .!
So cruel, and so kind (*SDN*, November 22, 1938)

The Buryin'—A Story[5]

There is a place where the fiddle waileth and the seed tick flourisheth. Where gaunt whang-leather madonnas still rock their babes to the terror of the hoot owl at night, and wean them "when the sign's a goin' down past the middlin's." There is a place where yet the dank smell of the good earth is sweet to the nostrils. . . .

Away back beyond Nubbin Ridge, just at the foot of Sunken Holler, stood the rough log cabin of a timber squatter. Two rooms and a lean-to, a puncheon floor and the walls chinked and daubed.

Looking from the point of old Nubbin into the Holler, all was quiet, for Bud McCager's boy had died at noon. The lights from the cabins of the squatters specked the darkness like tapers for the dead. The hounds howled mournfully.

Rarely are there less than a good half dozen hounds around the shack of the tie-hacker of the Ozark Mountains, and these sneakingly wise four-footed critters know instinctively when someone is "sottin' up with a corpse," and they tune their dirge accordingly. And for harrowing up the very soul for the Day of Judgment, this ungodly wail holds the trump card.

This Anglo-Saxon hillman of the Ozarks traces his lineage back to the blood of Cavaliers, and in his veins is that wine of almost tragic sympathy which is neither bought nor sold. He rallies to the call of distress, gathering himself into the house of mourning to comfort and "sot up." And because there is little excitement in his round of days, he loves to relate stories of death and sickness and blood curdling disasters which are always hauled out and gone over for the comfort of the bereaved.

At the unseemly hour of four in the morning, Aunt Susan Plumley was leaving. She untied her mule from the line of tired, pot-bellied animals hitched to the fence, and her face wore a look of determination. She was shaking the dust of that breed off her feet forever.

"I never see'd sich a set, anyway. Right there I've bin since eight o'clock last night, an' they hain't even made a biler o' coffee! Some folks is so pester'n little thet you could spit 'em into a chigger's eye an' he wouldn't even bat it!" With this, Aunt Susan mounted furiously and was off up the Holler.

Shortly the light dawned, and the hot July sun began to paint a suspicious tinge over old Piney. The mourning family and kin and the "sotters" stirred about, while the odor from the tardy "biler o' coffee" tantalized. One by one the youngsters crawled out and went to the creek to wash. The morning came on and the sun waxed hot. The settlement folks gathered in; some on horseback, some in wagons, bringing the children, the dogs, the old, the lame and the blind. All turning out to the buryin'.

Inside the cabin two or three good women fanned the flies off the coolin' board where lay poor overworked and under-fed Gippy McCager, his hands crossed on his breast, with the dirt, gathered in his sixteen years of grapple for bread, still under his fingernails.

They had fixed him up in store-bought clothes. A gray, half cotton, checked suit which was plainly rueing the day it was born. Too big in the shoulders, too long in the sleeves and the coat half way to his knees, the pants lapped over in the waistline behind till the pockets struck him almost in the small of the back. On the boy's thin neck was an article seldom found either in life or death on a timber hacker—a collar! Stiff, celluloid and shiny, with a four-in-hand tie which every mother's son in the bunch had tried his hand at tying, and the round ended by lapping it in a cross down the front of the striped shirt.

Someone, may God forgive him, had put tan shoes on the lad. New, and two sizes too small. Laced as far as they would, and left gaping the rest of the way. A cloth, saturated with camphor and home-steeped wahoo bark, covered his face, refreshed now and then by the women folks in the unreplenished solution in the washbasin. A worn sheet covered all.

The coffin was finished, and the hammering, every blow of which jarred the marrow, ceased. It was brought in. A rude ox box, shaped at the foot, covered with cheap black cotton cloth and sporting a pitiful attempt at decoration—shiny tin buttons, used for putting building paper on walls, ran over it in rows and rows as pleased the capricious fancy of the decorator. The receptacle was in gala dress.

Now the very climax of tragedy ensued. The coffin was too short! Lacking even a rule, the long elm measuring stick had been inaccurate, and the poor boy was squeezed in until he bulged up in the middle. Someone suggested the removal of the tan shoes, softening the suggestion by a promise to bury them in the coffin with him, but his mammy did not want them removed. He had longed for them in life, and she was there to see that they were his in death. Even Solomon knew not the ways of a mother!

All was now in readiness and still they came. The big pot and the little one were put on. Kindly donations of white-faced pies and home-cured meat were added to the noonday spread. More kin folks gathered in; the men in their work clothes and a number of the boys smelling loudly of pole-cat aroma which played mercilessly upon the olfactories of those present!

Minty Snell took her two big boys around behind the smoke house for a going over. "Hain't you abashed of yerself, Otho? You a goin' and gittin' all stunk up with that varmint right when we was nearly ready to start to the buryin'! I tole you boys how it would be last night. We're pore, an' they hain't no disgrace to that, but we don't have to be ornery an' triflin'!"

"Maw, it hain't us. The Beezeley boys is bin a huntin' an they ketched a skunk fer they said they did. Me an' Otho didn't ketch none. An' besides, Maw, hit hain't ornery nor triflin', and hit don't bother nobody as long as we're out in the open."

After a general handshaking, weeping and embracing, the funeral procession started toward the graveyard over on Big Pine Ridge; a hard, rocky, clay-baked bit of godforsaken land, too unyielding to farm, and almost impossible to even scar. Old Brother Rickard presided. He never fraternized with progress, neither did he make his bed with modern-ism of any sort. He was the flintiest most ante-diluvian old Hardshell Baptist that ever "argyed scripter." He knew the doctrine from the orig-inal Sanskrit on down. He was full of his subject, and chafed like a war-horse at anything which might delay the delivery of his message.

His listeners were by far more interested in seeing how those most concerned "took on" at the last rites, for be it known here and now that if there were not some sort of wild hysteria or fainting or some uncanny strokes of catalepsy, they had not done full justice to the departed, and such folks were the talk of the settlement henceforth and forever.

Old Brother Rickard believed that we're predestined to be saved or damned as a good God chose. If it were fore-ordered, so be it, and the gates of hell could not prevail against it. His gospel was not a cheering one. The rock upon which the faith of this primitive Ozarkian was built was a rugged one, and it gave no shelter in a weary land.

He lined the hymn, possessing, ex officio, with great rite and ritual, the only hymn book present—the old shape-note *Christian Harmony*, still in use in our back hills.

> Hark, from the tomb a doleful sound,
> Mine ears attend the cry;
> Ye living men come view the ground
> Where ye may shortly lie!
> E'en though I walk the mountain height,
> My body low must lie,
> And in some lonesome place must rot,
> And by the living be forgot!

These lines, one at a time, were sung in a straggling falsetto, with many stanzas, and there was handshaking and weeping and trembling and moving about amongst the mourners. The preacher then reached for his sturdy leather saddlebags which he had placed across the foot of the coffin, and took from them his small Bible. The primitive Ozarkian preacher refers invariably to the Old and New Testaments as the "Hind Sights" and "Fore Sights."

He read the text: "He that hardeneth his heart and stiffeneth his neck, he shall suddenly be destroyed, and that without remedy!"

He roared, he warned and threatened and thundered from Mount Sinai. He took his unoffending hearers by the scruff of the neck and fairly shook them over the fiery pit. He was flaying the living who were caught like a rat in a trap. He held up the death of the anemic lad like a flaming cross. An uninformed bystander would have thought the subject under discussion had met death by the hand of justice while robbing the bank at Lizzard Gulch!

Brother Rickard then stepped to the shallow hole in the ground, and standing perilously near it, repeated in his righteous wrath, "Ye living men come view the ground where ye may shortly lie!"

All eyes were upon him, and tears of repentance flowed freely. This was no time for mourning for the dead; this was a shaking up of dry bones! The mute figure in the coffin was forgotten. The sun beat down upon him, the insects possessed him. The only human attention paid him was the fixed gaze of a small nearby group of little girls intent upon seeing whether the two flies which threatened to crawl into his nostrils, were going to do so. One poor heat-tortured hound came and laid himself down contentedly under the sawhorses which supported the coffin, in the only bit of shade available. There he yawned and scratched in bored indifference to all things of the spheres or of the earth.

Still the gospel truths thundered on. "Before mornin'," declared the now perspiring brother Rickard, "the whole hit an' bile of ye may be on the coolin' board! No wonder yer a weepin' an' a snivellin'. Hit's high time before the Lord. I like to preach to sinners when ther' meller. That's the time. The biggest passel of the time yer hearts is as hard as a water-soaked back log. Yer on the broad road thet leads to the regions of the damned. The Lord foreordains thet we have fallin's by the way an' buryin's to meller up yer hearts. Any of ye kin be tuck down with a turrible fever, ye kin git yer innards busted loose'ith a gun in the hands of a tool o' Satan. Ye kin pine away an' no medicine take a-holt of ye or holp ye. But the truth of the Word kain't be got around er straddled to suit yer own capers!" And not once did he forget to nail the facts with numerous quotations from the Hind or Fore Sights.

Finally after renewed weeping and singing of hymns and calling for penitents, the long drawn onslaught was ended and the coffin lowered into the ground. As the last of the big flint stones were shoveled upon it, the preacher dismissed with a final prayer for conviction and mercy, and the people moved slowly homeward. Only the mother and the pathetic looking little children remained to place upon the clay-red mound some bits of prized colored glass and broken dishes and some polished mussel-shells gathered from the bed of the White River. In the center of all, they placed a tin tomato can filled with water and holding a bouquet of scarlet Indian Berries and the wild Bluebell.

"Come on mammy, pap's done been in the wagon a waitin' fer ye a long while. He says fer ye to come on and quit a hangin' back that-a-way. Hurry up mammy, pap says ol' Pide has done got to her calf right now, he's shore an' done sucked her dry. Come on mammy!"

Climbing sorrowfully into the waiting wagon, they rattled away over the Old Wilderness Road to the cabin in Sunken Holler. (McCord Personal Papers)

May at age five. *Photo courtesy of Patti McCord.*

May in costume for *The Gypsy's Daughter*. Her involvement in
the play caused her minister to fear she would become an actress.
Photo courtesy of Patti McCord.

May at age sixteen. *Photo courtesy of Patti McCord.*

May as a teenager. *Photo courtesy of Patti McCord.*

May and Charles as newlyweds. *Photo courtesy of Patti McCord.*

May with her first child, Charles Jr. *Photo courtesy of Patti McCord.*

May with her brother, Leslie, and their mother, Delia. *Photo courtesy of Patti McCord.*

May riding her horse in Galena, Missouri, 1933. *Photo courtesy of Patti McCord.*

May at age sixty-eight, 1948. *Photo courtesy of Patti McCord.*

May with two of her grandchildren, Patti and Jim McCord. *Photo courtesy of Patti McCord.*

May with actress Judy Canova at RKO Pictures studio in Hollywood, 1940.
Photo courtesy of Patti McCord.

The best-known personalities on radio in St. Louis, 1943. May took first place. *Courtesy of Patti McCord.*

CHAPTER 7

We Had Fun!

*Just nothing on earth equals a good Ozarks
gatherin'. And nothing ever will.*

SDN, January 1, 1941

. . . .

No one was more qualified to write about the many forms
of frolic in the Ozarks than May, who seemed to have fun
wherever she went. She described reunions, fish fries, square
dances, shooting matches, play-party games, saplin' rides,
husking bees, and river fishing, and could hold her own with
any of her readers when it came to telling big-fish tales.[1]

. . . .

Hospitality in the Hills

Mrs. Elizabeth Mahnkey and I are good old Hillbillies who are not
ashamed of it. She asks me if I remember the hard winters when the
neighborhood had just one piece of meat and they loaned it around to
"bile" the vegetables with. (*SNL*, December 4, 1932)

I have been thinking of the ways of our gray hills—thinking of the old-time hospitality. People who come here seem to sense it more than any place else they visit, so surely we still have the old spirit left.

There is so much said about going into meatless days again and eggless days, it brings to my mind the old-time spirit of hospitality—give and give. They used to butcher hogs and scatter the fresh meat out among the neighbors, spare ribs and backbone and sausage. They made hominy and took the neighbors some. They cut into a big ham and sent the nearest neighbor a piece to boil with his beans.

Neighbors had these old, old greetings and sayings when you'd drive up, "Come on in! We hain't got much, but it will hold you up till you can get somewhere." And the "much" they had would be just about everything you could think of. A table groaning with food!

Sometimes they would say, "Come on in and eat a dirty bite." That's the oldest saying I can remember, away back when I was a child; a saying of humility.

They used to say, "Well, you come over and stay as long as you can. We're poor folks but we hain't scrapin' the flour barrel yet." In the old days they used to have flour milled and bring home a whole barrel full. A good provider always kept his well filled, and never let it get low. If it got down to where the women folks had to take a saucer and scrape to get flour to make biscuits, that was considered "mighty ornery," and there was liable to be neighborhood talk. "Why, them folks are always a scrapin' the flour barrel!"

You never went anywhere but they wanted you to "stay all night." The house or cabin might be mighty small, but they meant it. The least 'uns would sleep on pallets and maybe the men go out to the barn with quilts and blankets and sleep on the hay, but they made you a good bed and don't ever doubt it. And you were welcome to stay just as long as you wished.

That was the way of the gray hills. Whether invited or just a surprise guest, you got the best. They put on "the big pot and the little one." You warmed by their fire, you ate their "vittles," and you basked in their hospitality. (*Dial*, November 1947)

We Have Plenty of Food, Even during Wartime

Ruth Tyler[2] takes time off and I wonder what has happened to her, then here she comes with something hot from the hills. This time she sends me a record from down in her part of the highlands, and believe me, I'm tickled to know what's goin' on. Here it is:

> War time spells sugar rationing and a scarcity of sweets, but down in the hill country the native hill people are planning to grow a sight of sorghum cane and make a "right smart o' lasses," come Fall. Sorghum (long sweetnin') is always in high favor in the backcountry, along with homemade apple butter made with cider. And if a body knows how to hunt and rob a bee tree, there's scads of wild honey for the taking.
>
> What with black walnuts, "hickernuts," paw-paws, persimmons, wild huckleberries, game and fish in season! Then there's wild greens, cornbread, hawg-meat, turnips, punkins, taters, cabbage, onions, and "all sich as thet!"
>
> We can drink fine spring water, buttermilk, spicewood, or sassafras tea in the springtime. We even know how to run off a batch of homemade ash lye and with it make up a sizeable batch of hominy. Nothing better than old ash-lye hominy. We aim to dry apples and gather wild herbs and work to raise and store our next winter's "vittles!"

Yes, the hillfolks always manage to eat and are willin' to share. So "youn's come!" (*SDN*, June 25, 1942)

The Reunion and Fish Fry

Well, I told you I was going down to the Old Settler's Reunion and Fish Fry at the old Kimberling Ferry, now called Kimberling Bridge, and I went! Just myself and my son and his sweet new bride. And did we enjoy it! We took our cots and our skillet and camped out under the stars, on the banks of White River. The wind sang to us in the trees, the bullfrogs croaked and the dancers swung to the old-time tunes while the fiddle wailed till early morning. That's the picnic for me! None of your carnivals and confetti and snake charmers. And there were the old timers. Many I had not seen since a kid, and we talked and sat around and swapped old-time memories all day long. Thirty-five boats came in that night off the float. They had a hundred and fifty pounds of fish, and everybody fried fish. Great giant catfish weighing forty-two pounds, and red horse, and bass galore. Bill Bilyeu was fiddler supreme. I never heard a better one. The boys were wound up right, and yelling "bear down on 'er Shorty," "Take a chaw of terbaccer an' spit on the wall—four hands 'round and balance all!" (*SNL*, July 9, 1933)

Corn Husking Bees

I was husking roasting ears today and I remembered with a start that I had gone to a few husking bees when I was a youngster. Many of you who read this wouldn't know what a husking bee was. You husked corn (or "shucked" it as they called it) with a boy, and if he found a red ear he could kiss you! (*Dial*, September 1948)

Puncheon Floors

The young one may not know what puncheons are. . . . They are logs split in two and laid close to make a floor. . . . Sometimes they worked for weeks on the other side, smoothing and polishing the puncheons for dancing. Then when they had a dance, they turned the puncheons over and danced on this fine slick side, then turned them back to keep the floor nice and slick for the next dance. I have heard it said that rather slovenly folks, when they were going to have company, "turned the puncheons over" rather than scrub the floor! (*SDN*, July 29, 1941)

The Square Dance

Fannabelle Ford writes me about the square dance of the hills. She says I am neglecting the dance. Well, I don't neglect one when I can get to one! Fannabelle writes,

> The endurance of Ozark hillfolks is terrific, and backed up by a will to "carry on." They begin early and last all night, with no refreshments for the ladies and only a nip of "corn" for the men. Oh yes—I've ridden fifteen miles on a cold clear night when the snow squeaked under the horses' feet, to see the dust tromped from the sagging floor of some hill home. They don't roll back the rug, they "cleared the room!" Often it's the only room they have, and they must move back in from the yard before break-fast. I've seen tired little tots lined up on a pallet against the wall of the dancing floor, oblivious of stamping hob nails, and—
>
> > Once an' a half, an' a half around,
> > Hawg in the tater patch rootin' up the ground.
>
> There are no wallflowers at a square dance. Any old tow-headed cross-eyed Annie will do. What is a partner anyhow? The noise is the thing. There is no evidence of ballroom etiquette at a square dance, but no rudeness either. Not because it isn't permitted, but because it isn't even thought of. They are having too good a time, and too busy. You have to step lively at a square dance.

Yes, Fannabelle, you're right. No more fun anywhere on earth. But the trouble is that nip of "corn" wasn't always a nip. If you had been to the court murder trials that I have, over a nip of corn at a square dance where that nip kept the chip on the shoulder over some gal, and just dying for someone to knock it off, you would conclude that was the thing that always spoiled the picture of the good old "square dance." Yes, they always said—"come on over everybody—we're goin' to move out the safe and have a dance." They always "norated" it around. I went to one not more than six years ago where we danced all night, everybody brought the kids and babies, and one family brought the pet goat and the sleepy kids that had to be aroused, and departed. (*SNL*, September 10, 1933)

An Old-Time Square Dance Call

Salute your partner, lady on the left,
Eight join hands and circle left:
Once and a half as you come round,
Make them big feet hit the ground!
Swing or cheat, cheat or swing,
How can you cheat that pretty little thing?
Alaman' left and do-se-do,
You'll never get to heaven till you do just so.

Swing them gals and swing them hard,
If the house hain't room enough,
Swing 'em in the yard.
Swing the one that stole the sheep
Then the one that et the meat,
Then the one that gnawed the bone,
Then the purty gal all your own.

These old calls are so interesting. I know many of them myself. There are hundreds of them and many forms of the square dances. (*SDN*, August 31, 1940)

The Leghorn lays a milk-white egg,
The Plymouth Rock's egg is brown;
So drag a wing to a leghorn hen,
And swing her round and round.
The Banty is a cocky bird,

The Leghorn he is gay,
So sashay out to the fellow on the right,
And take his gal away!—"An Old Square Dancer"
(*SNL*, June 25, 1933)

Right foot up and the left foot down,
Eight join hands and circle round,
Holler in your heel, knock a hole in the ground!
Swing your honey with a good big swing,
Grand right and left all around the ring.
First couple dance with the couple on the right.
Lady round the lady and gent round the gent,
Lady round the lady and the gent go behind.
Lady round the lady and the gent cut a shine!
—Mrs. Lyda Wilson Pyles, Pocahontas, Arkansas.
(*SDN*, September 10, 1940)

Civil War Army Reunion in Taney County Included a Square Dance

My old friend Judge J. W. Keithley, down at Chestnut Ridge in Taney County, wrote me a story which I will give:

I will have to tell you the story of the first reunion that was ever held in Taney County. It was held where the campground is now at Rockaway Beach, in October 1885. It was the J. N. Hilton Army Post No. 254 (Grand Army of the Republic) of Taney County. There were several hundred old soldiers there, most of them came in Springfield wagons loaded with corn and blade fodder. There were three days of it. Charles Weinstine, a veteran, had the dancing platform, and a man who ran a store at Kirbyville by the name of Watson ran the stand. Clint Abbot and myself made the music for the dancers at night. There were big campfires all over the hills, and ten or fifteen of the old soldiers would sit around each fire and tell the old war stories. It was so interesting to me that I would stay around the campfires until late at night. Somehow they took a liking to me, and I would go and get cigars for them and help them about feeding their teams. When you would throw the big ears of corn into the feed boxes and the big mules and horses went to eating them it sounded almost like a freight train.

Well, the last day some of the old fellows wanted me to play for them to dance a set. The first set was Judge W. D. Hubbard, of Springfield, Congressman; W. W. Wade of Greene County; Capt. Nat M. Kinney of Kirbyville; Col. A. S. Prather, father of our Mary Elizabeth Mahnkey. Capt. Kinney was marshal of the day. He walked over to the fiddler's stand and unbuckled his revolver and said to me, "I want to lay my corset here on the bench till I get through." Well, it didn't seem to me that I could do the matter justice. Seemed like the fiddle bow was about a foot too short. I tell you, them boys went high, wide, and handsome, and that's not all, they swung the girls with the waist swing, something if us boys had undertaken would have been as dangerous as fooling with dynamite. But the girls were as glad to have the pleasure of dancing with these four remarkable characters as I was of playing for them. (*SDN*, September 20, 1938)

Shooting Matches

Now a fine old gentleman and good friend, J. A. Dethrow of Springfield, Missouri, answers my request about how the old shooting matches were conducted.

I am going to do my best to write you a description of how the old settlers managed the shooting matches back in the 70's and

80's. I have been to many, and have acted as judge. They had 3 judges.

Most times they would shoot for a beef—generally a two-year-old heifer. Sometimes they would have several matches the same day—some for mutton. The owner would price the beef reasonable—say twelve dollars for a two-year-old. That was a fair price in them days. They would set the price to the shooter at fifty cents a shot or $2 for 5 shots. When they sold enough tickets to make $12, the shooting would begin.

Anyone who bought $2 worth could sell one or more shots to someone else. I have known men to sell all but one and then win. But most times they would rule out what they called experts from the free for all match. And the experts would often have a match on the side. Many called that gambling and very few would have anything to do with the shooting matches. . . .

The first one that "drove center" got first choice. This is the way the beef was divided: There was six choices. The first and second choice being the same—the hindquarters. The third and fourth were the same—the forequarters. The fifth choice was the hide and tallow. And the sixth choice was the lead in the tree. They always set the targets against a big tree. (*SDN*, July 23, 1940)

A Rich Imagination and Folk Games Kept the Kids Occupied

I was talking to my sweet friend "Emmy" the other day . . . about old games and what grand times the kids had. She said she played all the time and the games were original and unsupervised. They brought back memories to me—her old games.

They played funerals and baptizings. Buried the dead in piles of leaves. We did too, and held funerals. They baptized in creeks. They played wood tag, stink-base, hopscotch and hide-and-seek. A bushel of wheat and a bushel of rye—all not hid, holler "I."

They played on cornstalk fiddles which they made. They made whistles and rode stick horses. And they made pokeberry ink. (That used to be my greatest fun.) They made slippery elm bridles for their stick horses. They tied June bugs to a string and got down over a doodlebug hole and played doodlebug. They played jail and sheriff and they rode flat rocks, imagining they were trains. And they played the old

> Jiggety, jiggety windy cup
> How many fingers do I hold up?

And they played "thumbs up" and pussy wants a corner. All of these things the rest of you played, or else you simply didn't have any childhood. . . . I used to ride stick horses "sideways" or get a spanking. No little girl rode astride. We threw our skirts across the stick on one side and just galloped away like mad. And it seemed to me, and does yet, that I was really riding! And I remember how the boys' horses would buck and caper and whinny and take a wild fit. (The little boys doing it all, of course.) But it seemed to me it was real. A good boy rider of a stick horse who could caper and buck elegantly was a hero the same as Tom Mix is to the modern little kid. (*SDN*, July 14, 1942)

I know all these old games and played them. Our Rabbit Twister, W. S. White of Bolivar, Missouri, writes me,

> I really think we take all the initiative out of the present day games by hovering over the youngsters and supervising them too much. I think they ought to be let go barefooted and stub their toes, and it would not kill them any more than it did us. There was a lot of virtue in being brought up the hard way. (*SDN*, June 15, 1942)

A Saplin' Ride

Several times lately someone has asked me why I never wrote about the olden-time sports of girls and boys, the riding of "saplin' horses." Rose Lines Hirlie says she recalls that thrill as no other. I myself remember how I used to mount the bent down saplin' out behind the schoolhouse. Sometime the tree would be so stout the boys had to bend it over. Then with a lot of leaping and tight holding I would mount the saplin' and a way up in the air it would go and back down again—and I imagined I was riding a fast wild pony around a great racetrack as I had seen in pictures. Sometimes I thought I was a great lady with long green sweeping velvet riding habit and a big Gainsborough hat with gorgeous plumes. Sometimes I didn't imagine anything but trying for dear life to stick on. Sometimes I fell off and my dress flew over my head and left me rather al fresco! Which was an awful situation in those days. (*SNL* October 31, 1937)

Rode Her Pony

I shall not forget to my dying day the first time I ever "loped a horse." You who have not had the sensation cannot imagine it. I was about ten. I was a bit scared, but there was a rocking sort of wild hilarity about it—new, and a bit foolish as one feels after taking some sort of anesthetic. I seemed to be in the clouds going on and on and never ending and riding down the road from Galena to Crane on my pony who would do nothing but gallop. She wouldn't trot or pace and it was either the slowest walk or a wild gallop. She had no compromise. So for the four years I owned her, she galloped. And she shied mud puddles so long as she lived, quick as a cat, and literally dozens of times dumped me and the saddle right in the puddle. She broke the girth sometimes with the quick movement of her muscles. She was a Texas mustang. What ever kept me from being killed, maybe the fatalists know, for I swam the James River with her several times when it was swift and muddy. (*SNL*, September 27, 1936)

Play-Party Games[3]

These things sound awfully foolish . . . but they mean much to folklore and the history of the games of our civilization. (*SDN*, November 1, 1940)

How to Play Miller Boy, an Old Folk Play-Party Game

> Happy is the miller boy that lives by the mill.
> Every time the mill turns it turns to his will.
> Wheat in the hopper and flour in the sack,
> The ladies step forward and the gents fall back.

When the gents fall back, then the "Miller" who is in the center while they are marching around and singing, grabs a girl. And the fellow who was left without a girl has to be the miller. And so on and on. Lots of fun. (*SDN*, February 6, 1941)

Weevly Wheat

I pick up a letter from my dear old friend now silent in death, the Reverend A. M. Haswell of Joplin. He was writing about the old play song, "Weevly Wheat" which is the great classic standby of our Ozark play days:

> We used to call it "Presbyterian waltzing" because even those shut out from dancing by ironclad church edicts could swing into Weevly Wheat because "it's only a little singing game." For all its bad grammar, it went this way:
>
> > We don't want none of your weevly wheat,
> > And we don't want none of your barley,
> > We want some flour in half an hour
> > To bake a cake for Charley!

Charley he's a fine young man,

Charley he's a dandy,

Charley he's the very lad that stole my apple brandy.

You think I'd marry the likes of you?

You think I'd marry my cousin?

When I can buy such lads as you

For fifteen cents a dozen!

(*SNL*, October 11, 1936)

King William

I had a very interesting letter from Mrs. A. V. Hair of Mountain Grove, Missouri. She said she played "King William" the old play party game when she was a girl, but it was not a kissing game. . . . In my old game of "King William," we said,

Down on this carpet you must kneel

  as sure as the grass grows in the field;

Salute your bride and kiss her sweet,

  and then you may rise upon your feet.

In her[4] old game . . . they marched round and sang this:

Say, young lady, won't you list and go,

Say, young lady, won't you list and go,

This old slouch hat you must put on,

To follow the man with the fife and drum.

Then a young lady would step from the ring and place a hat on her favorite young man's head, and he would again join the ring of marchers. And so on. Well, I'll say this—they missed a lot!

Then she tells me of another old game she played which is indeed interesting:

We all are marching through Quebec,
The drums are loudly beating,
The Americans they have gained the day,
And the British are retreating.
The war is o'er and we'll turn back,
Turn back from whence we started,
Arise to the ring, go bring one in
For I know they're broken hearted.

Now if you ever doubt that we have early English ancestry in the Ozarks—where did we get that song? (*SDN*, June 24, 1939)

Candy Breakin' Game

All the players are paired off into opposite-sex couples and the woman selects a colored gum drop from a sack and the man, his eyes turned so he cannot see into the sack, picks out a gum drop. If the color of the gum drop he draws from the sack matches the color of the one which his partner has drawn he is permitted to kiss the loser—through a veil. No game of post office ever proved to be a more successful ice-breaker. (*Rayburn's Ozark Guide*, n.d.)

Club Fist!

Mrs. George Roebuck, Morrison, Missouri, brought back to me the old game of "Club Fist!" My! How many years since I thought of it. You have all played it—you older ones. Winter evenings round the fireplace. You remember how each player stacks up his fists on top of the others, catching the thumb just below. Then the owner of the first fist says to the next fist "What you got there?" And he replies "club fist." "Take it off or knock it off?" says the first one. So he may decide either. I used to get smart aleck and brave and always say "knock it off." And many an old stout rough boy has knocked my fist into kingdom come. Then the last fist to be knocked off would answer to "What you got there?" "Bread and cheese." Then this ritual would follow:

> Where's my share? In the woods.
> Where's the woods? Fire burnt it.
> Where's the fire? Water quenched it.
> Where's the water? Ox drank it.
> Where's the ox? Butcher killed him.
> Where's the butcher? Rope hung him.
> Where's the rope? Rat gnawed it.
> Where's the rat? Cat killed it.
> Where's the cat? Hammer killed it.
> Where's the Hammer?
> Dead and buried, behind the Church door.

And the first one that laughs, grins or shows his teeth will get a little red box with ten nails in it! The little red box was a box on the ears and the ten nails were ten slaps or ten hard pinches. Then an endurance of a Spartan nature set in to keep from laughing! For if the big old rough boys gave the box and nails, they left the marks even on the girls. My—my! Will I ever forget it! (*SDN*, December 7, 1940)

Occasionally, a Circus Came to Town!

Well, there was a circus here last week, and it took a mule team to keep me away. I always get the jitters when a circus poster is pasted up: It brings back the old days when posters around on the barns and black-smith shops just drove me wild. We got only the smaller ones down our way, but they didn't look small to me. Everybody went, even if we had to live on paw-paws and persimmons through the following winter.

Well do I remember when a family came to town all loaded in the wagon with the cook stove! Bringing it to sell to go to the show! What was a cook stove to stand in the way? "Hell's farr!" said Buzz. "We kin cook on the farr'place!" (*SNL*, August 6, 1933)

Beware the Brass Band

Flora Elsey always brings something back to me with a keen memory, a roar of laughter or a poignant sadness. This time she asks me if I remember how afraid the kids were of the first brass band that ever came to the little town of Galena. She says she remembers being scared to death. I remember how it burst out in the small courthouse with a march and the kids scattered every way, running and falling down the old outdoor steps! It just doubles me up yet. But if you could only know how that band sounded to kids who had never heard more than a fiddle or an organ now and then, or a French harp. . . . To this day I get scared when I'm with a band in a small auditorium, thinking of that panic we had that day. (*SNL*, February 7, 1937)

God at a Foxhunt

"Makes no difference if he is a houn'
They gotta quit kickin' my dawg aroun'!"

The pure-strain fox hunter in this great Ozark uplift—dubbed "The Bible Belt" by the H. L. Mencken crowd—believes that he can take his God with him to a fox hunt, and that God is very definitely a member of the Association.

Fox hunting is as old as these hills and as deeply ingrained in the life and traditions of an Ozark hillman as his politics and his religion.

So God Almighty took his seat on the official board of the annual Wright County Fox Hunters Association for three great days—August 18, 19, and 20 at Hartville. And his servant, the Reverend Self Jones of Aldrich, opened the meet with a sermon.

He took for his text, "Man's Three Terrible Responsibilities": To find out that they are men, to find God, and to find their fellow man.

Courtesy of the Springfield News and Leader, *August 31, 1947.*

Mr. Jones said, "The finest people and the best Christians I have ever known are in and around Wright County. Plenty of fox hunters among them, and not one fox hunter has ever double crossed me or played me false."

"Fox hunting is a clean sport," he said. "And it's a funny thing that a fox hunter will contribute more of his possessions to good works and to the poor than the man who owns the finest herd of Herefords in the state."

Like an Annual Reunion

Three thousand people were seated and standing in the lovely valley by Lake Casadora. The Gasconade River flowed nearby, and back in the shadows where the tents were pitched, and the small lights specked the darkness, the hounds, some 150 of them, whimpered and complained restlessly as a girls' quartette from Odin sang "Where You Goin' to Hide on That Great Day?"

In the natural amphitheater, some five hundred people were seated on wooden benches, and hundreds stood and listened while hundreds milled about eating hamburgers and drinking pop. And indeed the concessions did a rushing business. Everybody was happy. People visited and met old friends and neighbors they see only once a year at "the meet" as they call it.

The weather was terrific, but at night it was cool down in the Casadora Valley. People came from far and near, one great caravan of automobiles coming 'round the highway, their lights looking like fireflies as we sat and watched them make the turn. The Wright County Fox Hunters Association has over two hundred members comprising farmers, merchants, bankers, preachers and teachers, and anyone else interested in this old sport of kings.

There was a large stage of rough lumber and a piano and electric lights and a loud speaker that certainly told the world. Howell County's popular speaker, Will H. Green, came on and made a memorable speech. He gave some fine tributes to the dog as a friend of man, including the immortal tribute of Missouri's own late senator George Vest. He kept the crowd in an uproar between laughter and tears.

The Hounds Join In

Then the fiddlers started in. My, the fiddlers! And the guitars and the banjos and mandolins—and as the music got higher and louder the hounds joined in occasionally at high and mournful pitch, away from the glare of the lights, in their kennels.

Finally, at exactly eleven they announced that the pack would be turned loose for the hunt, and then there was a scramble for cars. It seems a bit odd, "riding to the hounds" in an automobile. A sort of feeling of let down as if we had betrayed our old ancestors sleeping in their graves. Men of the mountains who knew no such soft life as a rubber-tired gas wagon! . . .

Suddenly the dogs were turned loose and the music of the long bugle calls of their voices! They seemed to speed miles in just a few minutes. In no time they had the scent and hit a real trail. Long deep bass voices and high clear ones—"silver mouths" some of them had. High keen cries almost like a woman. All in one great chorus. Away on the bluff by the river.

A man standing by me would say, "My dog hasn't hit the trail yet . . ." Men know their dogs' "mouths" for miles and miles just as you know a certain tune you hear. The yelps would be far away, then closer. One time they seemed to come almost at our feet below us. We could see nothing but the blackness of the wonderful night.

Hindered by Dryness

The next night this was done all over. Hundreds of people gathered, more fiddlers, more singers, quartets, solos, sacred music and the old fiddle tunes mixed right in. "Billy in the Low Ground," "Arkansas Traveler," "Blue Mule," "Soldier's Joy," and "Fisherman's Hornpipe," with the "The Cacklin' Hen" and "The Drunken Hiccoughs" thrown in for good measure.

Old men played and young boys. Little shavers sang, and men with their own sons and daughters. Pretty young girls singing and yodeling and a Mr. Atkinson who gave as fine imitation of a fox hunt as I ever heard on any stage or in any place. A one-man show.

Something to Remember

The finest regiment that ever went to war was the Houn' Dawg Regiment of Missouri. You may look down your nose at the houn' dawg, but you better not in Missouri. He is here to stay, along with the mule, ready to carry the name of Missouri throughout the world. Take him how you will, tired and exhausted, or with muddy feet, or bounding with affection, but remember to do him honor. He's not to be trifled with.

In the late war, a houn' dog took up with the 203rd Regiment which was the Missouri Houn' Dawg Regiment, and went all through the blood and mud with them, and they gave him the chevrons of a sergeant.

As for me, it was a thrilling experience, this Wright County fox hunt, to which I was invited to speak and to meet all the clan. I was never quite so familiar with the fox hunt—what I remember so well was coon dogs. I remember old Gip's dogs and how he loved them. He said, "My dawgs has got more sense than a woman, and mighty nigh as much sense as a man. They're the best darn coon dogs that ever follored a branch. They never bark up the wrong tree, and whenever my dogs do bark up a tree, there's meat up thar!"

He said they was the best, the huntin'est, the fightenest and snake-killin'est dogs on Little Straddle Creek. They were not fine registered hounds of the "Walker" strain like these at the Hartville hunt. They were a mixture of everything that ran on four legs between the Devil's Soap Kettle and the Arkansas Line. But Gip loved them and greased them with coal oil for the ticks and with lard and sulphur for the mange, and sat up all night with them when they were sick. Old Jerry and Jupe and Steamboat and Lady and Spot, and a whole kit and bile of others not so important.

And so, fox huntings is one of the traditions that will never pass in the Ozark hills within the life span of you and me—and there may never be a time when these valleys and low green mountains will not ring with the clear clarion call of the hunting horn and the answering silver-mouthed cry of the Missouri Houn' Dawg. And "it makes no difference if he is a houn'—you gotta quit kickin' my dog aroun'." (*SNL*, August 31, 1947)

The Society of Hillcrofters: Guardians of the Ozarks[5]

The date of the Hillcroft picnic is Sunday, June 1 at Galena, Missouri, (me hometown it happens to be) at the lovely Camp Clark. It is not used as a camp now but is private ground and one of the loveliest cool retreats in the Ozark country. It overlooks the river like a silver ribbon below— you can walk down to the river. And you look on the river bottom farms below like an etching in green and silver. And the little town of Galena like some Swiss Alps picture. Bring your basket and "eatin' tools." Bring your friends. Bring your fiddle and your guitar and "banjer." Bring your dog and your kids. Bring your old shoes (and your fried chicken!). If you have a campstool bring it. If you have a sweetie, bring her! Or a grandpa or a grandma. Bring the fellow you owe money because he will forget it and forgive you at that lovely place! (*SDN*, May 22, 1941)

By the light of the blazing log fires, beside the tall trees, amid the whispering leaves the stories of the past years are retold with all their picturesque details. Where in the twinkling starlight, as rippling waters flow, they talk of old legends, and songs of dawning days, then gracefully and gently they slowly fade away.

Old-time fiddlers with one-string fiddles greet the rising moon with such old ballads as "The Mocking Bird," "Red River Valley," "Comin' Round the Mountain" and "Turkey in the Straw." Poets and writers of all the varying degrees of sanity rub elbows with fisted sons of toil. Plain ordinary Hillbillies in blue shirts and overalls mingle with the city sheiks, flappers and flapperettes—1935 models—in one rollicking, friendly throng around the festive board, laden with everything in the culinary line, including possum and trimmings, forgetting for a while about the drab and humdrum routine of their own days, and recalling the hallowed memories of the saintly days of yore. (*SNL*, January 20, 1935)

We will celebrate our Festival of the Painted Leaves next Saturday and Sunday. This celebration is the Hillcrofters of Missouri, Arkansas and Oklahoma. Invitations are out and you must make your plans. Others who would like to become Hillcrofters may do so for the small sum of fifty cents a year. . . . We plan a pilgrimage which will be very little expense indeed. Listen closely. We will go first to Marvel Cave Lodge Saturday noon and have a steak fry. If you get your name in the pot so we will know the amount to buy, it will be just a few cents apiece, maybe ten or at the most fifteen. Have a basket lunch of sandwiches, cake or salad or something along with you.

We will drive on down to the Maxey cabin "Happy Days" at the Shepherd of the Hills estates near Forsyth. There we will spread our supper and have a fish fry also, but bring something along because we don't always have enough fish for our mob! We have a bonfire, and Indian

Pow-Wow around the fire in commemoration of the Indians, the first Hillcrofters and whose Moon of Painted Leaves we are celebrating. . . . Then we will stay overnight at the small sum of thirty-five cents each in the cabins and at the El Bonito Inn there for the same price, special only to us. Next day (Sunday) we drive over to Harrison, Arkansas, (sixty miles I believe) where we have a fine noon luncheon for fifty cents, special also only to us, at the beautiful Spanish Hotel Seville. Then back home.

    We will have a great moon! Oh Boy! A good appetite and a guitar is all I want, and some old shoes to tramp in! Better bring your blankets, the president says—not much sleeping done, but we make a stagger at it. Then Sunday is our "dignified" day where we have a splendid program and well-known speakers on folklore, literature, etc. (*SNL*, October 6, 1935)

River Fishing in the Ozarks

Down where men were men . . . An' fishermen were liars. (*SNL*, February 19, 1933)

You know, Fishing Is Not a Recreation—It's a Serfdom.

It may be fine to sleep "pillered in silk an' scented down," as the poet says—"pulse nigh to pulse," an' all that junk—but there's no bed so sweet in the world as an old quilt on the gravel bar with the trotline set an' the stars overhead an' the catfish a bitin'. (McCord Personal Papers)
I was reared in the little town of Galena, Missouri, on the James River. . . . When the first warm spring days came, the bank of the James was lined, especially down at the old slough where the big perch hid. You put on the worm, spit on the bait, threw her in, and sat back and waited on the Lord. . . . Here I am the mother of two boys who began digging worms before they cut their stomach teeth. I spent so many years running up and down the river hunting for the older one, yelling and threatening and scared to death, that I have wished a thousand times the bottom would drop

May's son, Charles McCord Jr., catching a bass on the James River. *Photo courtesy of Patti McCord.*

out of the whole blooming river. . . . I have dried pants, shaken sand out of socks, untangled hooks from the bedclothes, picked up rubber boots and burned fish heads until my country ought to award me a medal for distinguished service. (*Field and Stream,* June 1936[6])

Fishermen Knew the Direction the Wind Blows

> The wind in the south
> Blows the hook in the mouth,
> When the wind's in the west

The fish bite best.

When the wind is in the east

The fish bite the least.

Now the fish know nothing about the wind. But they know that they get hungry. Insects and their eggs and many forms of vegetable matter which furnish feeding ground for the fishes blow from the willow and weeds along the shore into the water. These immediately attract the fish. If the wind is in the right direction from a given point where these growths are found, the fish will gather there for the feast. (*SDN*, December 11, 1941)

Town Fish Fry Was Fun for All during the Depression

I would give my bridge work to go down to Kimberling Park this "Fourth" on White River, twelve miles south of Reeds Spring. They are staging a fish fry and home picnic and each family brings the frying pan, and men are going to be busy weeks before catching plenty of fish to supply the crowd. O, boy! Gravel beach a mile long, dance platform where you can "swing 'em around" all night and all day, swim and fish! Hillbillies and town lounge-lizards all welcome! A depression good time, where ninety-eight cents will just about do the work. A dollar at an old-time picnic used to be a small fortune. (*SNL*, June 25, 1933)

Jumping Fish?

I have a letter from a young man on the USS Battleship *West Virginia* who says I must help him out, because his friends have no confidence in him as long as he tells them that we "jump" fish in the boat back home. Well, Tom, that story has the worst sailing of any story on earth, and is as true as gospel. When I was a girl in Arizona visiting, I told it innocently one day and they nearly mobbed me. Even back here, some people don't know it. Vance Randolph, the writer, says they nearly rode him on a rail in the east for writing it.

Most surely, in the months of July and August, when the water is a bit murky, we go "jumping." Everyone is excited because the old river rats know it's a good night for "gossin''em in!" We take a lantern or fish light these modern days, and paddle slowly along holding the light down near the water at the edge of the boat. It seems to scare the fish, and they jump. Nine times out of ten they land in the boat. Sometimes they go over. In an hour we often jump in ten big bass. One time a three-pounder hit me in the back, scared me to death, and nearly knocked a lung out of me.

My hard-boiled, practical, conservative husband has come in and I have referred the fish jumpin' story to him as a veteran who put the "f" in fishin'. He dampens my ardor a bit by saying that instead of nine times out of ten they jumped in the boat, as I state, nine times out of ten they miss it or jump over. Oh, well, why be technical and split hairs! He doesn't deny that we jumped nine in one night when they were jumping good! And when they raft logs down the river, often they jump a whole army of them on the raft. I'm quitting before this fish story gets any bigger! Fish stories have just a slight tendency in that direction. In fact—I was going to tell you that down on the "Jeems," my home river, the fish bite so good you have to get behind a tree to bait your hook! (*SNL*, April 16, 1933)

If You Don't Believe Fish Jump into the Boat, Try This Fishing-Worm Story

Now this is the way I get treated about my fish-worm story:

> Dear Mrs. McCord: When I was a boy I used to go down on the creek and take with me two fishing poles and lines and hooks and hunt me up a fish-worm bed right on the bank of the creek. I'd take a board and beat on the ground just over the worms. They would come out and then I would lay the hooks on the ground among them and they would swallow the hooks. Then I'd drop the hooks in the water and throw out a fish. Then I'd

place the hook back among the worms and take the other pole and put it in the water. By the time I had caught another fish the worms would have the first hook swallowed, and I would change back and forth that way and soon have all the fish I wanted. I would never have to touch a worm or bait a hook, egad! Now don't let anyone tell you that fish-worm story of yours isn't true!—"Rabbit Twister," Boliver, Missouri. (*SDN*, April 23, 1938)

Speaking of Fish Stories

I heard a tale the other day about a fisherman who said he felt something bite and he gave a heave and tugged and tussled at the line, and lo and behold, he pulled out a twenty-four-inch bass! A fellow listening said: "That's nothing. I had the same experience the other day and pulled and tugged at the line and drew out a lighted lantern!"

"Now, look here," said the first fisherman, "nobody ever pulled a lighted lantern out of the river!" "Well," said the second one—"If you'll take twelve inches off that bass, I'll blow out my lantern." (*SDN*, September 14, 1939)

CHAPTER 8

Music of the Ozarks

*Folk music is unwritten music, handed down
from parents to children for generations.*

Dial, October 7, 1949

. . . .

The Ozarks may be more associated with its traditional music than any other region of the United States; many visitors once assumed Ozarkers possessed a genetic predisposition to musicality. As a talented musician and singer, May certainly fit that image. She wrote about fiddle playing, singing schools, and shape-note gospel conventions, but more than anything May loved old ballads handed down from generation to generation in oral tradition. They were part of her soul, and she lamented their passing in an age of radio and moving pictures. She believed the songs of the Ozarks should be sung with simplicity and sincerity and were sometimes hard and bitter, like life in the hills. May shared her research on ballads and their background and declared "The Missouri Houn' Dog Song" the "unofficial song of Missouri, the cry of the real Missouri."

. . . .

Yes . . . an Old Ballad before They Pass Forever!

No wonder we are trying to record them and keep them for posterity. For with them go the days of the buffalo grass before the plow and the windmill took the plains . . . and the storms came and the dust shattered even our memories. With them go the days of the mountain lover when he told his secrets to the trees and bladed the grass with his dreams! When his true love pined in the holler and shook like a willow, from root to crest, when she heard him coming through the leafy dusk. The days when men tried to carve a blameless name on malleable hearts; when emotion was older than reason; when they spoke the one language that endures—the simple, unlettered language of the heart. (*SNL*, October 11, 1936)

An Old Ballad

Sing me an old, old ballad, dear,
While I lie here and rest;
And I shall remember the tracery of lace
Against a sweet old breast.

I'm tired of songs with labored themes,
With motif stiff and strained.
Sing me a mournful mountain tune,
And I'll find my heart again!

Sing of the plains and the buffalo herds
That Granny tells about,
While I lay my arm across my eyes,
And shut the mad world out.

Sing an old "come all ye" ballad, dear,
With notes so strange and wild,

The Gipsy's Warning, dark with pain,
The grave, where sleeps her child!

Sing an old tale of love, my dear,
With death-bells in the telling,
Like crying winds that can't forget
The love of Barbara Ellen.

For love is a dim, gray laughter, dear,
And life is a crimson pain—
So sing me an old, old ballad,
And I'll find my heart again.
(*SNL*, October 11, 1936)

In many of our hill homes you may hear ballads sung that were sung in the Mermaid Tavern in London three hundred years ago. You may hear ballads from the Scotch border which were sung long before the Stuart kings of England. You may hear English idioms and sayings which Shakespeare gathered up and put in the mouth of Falstaff. (*SNL*, October 10, 1937)

Folk songs are usually ladened with tragedy, a broken heart, a forsaken love, or a murder. Sometimes they are a bit tarnished—keepsakes of ancestral days. In the songs of the Ozark hills there are many hard, bitter notes because life in the hills in pioneer times was hard and bitter. Unlike the songs with literary tradition, they have no technique, style, elaboration or theme, and they are completely ruined by any attempt at polish. (*SNL*, November 13, 1932)

Nothing in all my childhood ever went through the heart of me like this tragic old song, as were all old hill songs we used to sing—I can hear Aunt Caldony now, rocking her little boy across her lap, an emaciated skeleton for years from scarlet fever. Back and forth she moved her knees softly and sang:

May playing guitar. She often said to "pitch it shaller, because the Lord's in shaller music." *McCord Personal Papers.*

No home, no home! Cried an orphan child
At the door of the rich man's hall,
As she trembling stood on the pearly step
And leaned on the marble wall.

They were descendants of the pioneers who came from the Southern Appalachians more than a century ago and brought their songs with them, many from the British Isles. (*SNL*, December 30, 1934)

"The Blind Child"

This is an old mournful folk song which was sung in our Ozarks more than any other and still is, with the exception of "Barbara Ellen," and "The Little Rosewood Casket." The blind child says,

They say, Dear Father, that tonight
You'll wed another bride,
That you will clasp her in your arms,
Where my dear mother died.
That she will lean her graceful head
Upon your manly breast,
Where my own darling mother, too,
In life's last hours did rest.

They say her name is "Mary," too,
The name my mother bore,
But father, is she kind and true,
Like the one you loved before?

And is her hair so silken soft,
Her voice so meek and mild?
And father, do you think she'll love
Your blind and helpless child?

There is nothing on earth that ever takes hold of the heart like the old ballads of the people of the hills, who sang with such untrained simplicity, but such tender sincerity! There I sat, a child of ten, living with such intensity that whole drama which Aunt Polly sang with so little knowledge of what was going on inside me. She was singing an old tender ballad of her people. I was living a tragedy as the story unrolled before me. No wonder I love folk songs.[1] (*SDN*, February 8, 1940)

"Barbara Allen" or "Barbara Ellen"

This ballad is often sung "Barbara Allen." However, I have always declared it to be Barbara Ellen. I have seen an old book of 1718, and the ballad was originally "Barbara Ellene," in the old English. And I heard it "Ellen" in my very earlier singings, always. It rhymes with "and death was on him dwellin'," don't you see. Also, in the old ballads they often omitted last names. They would just say, Mary, or Lady Nancy, and leave that mysterious quality around the old tale. They assumed that you knew the name, because the ballad would be about some incident in the immediate vicinity. You will note that in Barbara Ellen, the young hero was "Sweet William." They never gave him a last name. (*SDN*, February 5, 1941)

"Lie Low, the Lily of Arkansaw"

I got to trying to recall the tune to the old, old ballad, "Lie Low, the Lily of Arkansaw." I sang it when I was a very young girl. Such a strange, mysterious old song—with a cry in it. I never have known just what it was about or what it meant. You know folk songs and hillbilly songs are not the same at all.

It's one of those ballads, a strange mix-up that is surely the hangover of a British ballad, like all our old Ozark ballads, for the "four and twenty seamen" have nothing to do with the state of Arkansas. A hangover from the sea songs of the Colonists who trekked westward across the

Mississippi a half century before the Civil War, and settled this highland region of the Missouri and Arkansas Ozarks.

> My father built the bow,
> The ship that sailed the sea.
> With four and twenty seamen to keep him company.
> The waves and winds are beating while sailing on the sea.
> Lie low—the Lily of Arkansaw has parted you and me.
>
> I fear my love's been drown-ded,
> I fear my love's been slain,
> I fear my love's been drown-ded on his way to France and Spain.
> The waves and winds are beating while he sails on the sea.
> Lie low—the Lily of Arkansaw has parted you and me.
>
> There's girls enough in Texas,
> I know there's one for me.
> But my own dear and lonely one is far away from me.
> The waves and winds are beating while sailing on the sea.
> Lie low—the Lily of Arkansaw.
> (*Dial*, November 1946)

"Cheeries Are Ripe"

I want to talk about the fine response I had about the little song, "Cheeries Are Ripe." I found that so many knew it as their mother sang it. None of the letters were from those who know anything of it in the present day. It is very old. And the last two lines especially come to me. I remember Mother said, "My dear little child," making it personal.

> Cherries are ripe, cherries are ripe,
> Oh, give the baby none.

Cherries are ripe, cherries are ripe,
The baby can have none.
Cherries are too sour to use
Babies are too young to chew,
But by and by, baked in a pie
The baby may have some.

A robin I see, up in the tree
Picking them one by one.
Eating his fill and shaking his bill,
As down his throat they run.
Robin eats no cherry pie.
Quick he'll eat then away he'll fly.
Dear little child so gentle and mild
Surely will not cry.
(McCord Personal Papers)

"The Whistling Song"

This ballad dates back at least one hundred years, maybe more because my mother remembered her mother singing it.

Whistle, daughter, whistle, and you shall have a cow,
I cannot whistle, Mother, you never showed me how.
Oh I would have a husband to love and live with me,
For I am dreary, and oh I am weary with single-ar-ity.
(*SNL*, July 5, 1936)

May Kennedy McCord taught this song to her granddaughter, Patti McCord, who provided this notation of the music, in May's handwriting. *Courtesy of Patti McCord.*

The Old Ballads Have No Copyright

I'll tell you, I never saw anything so funny as this scrap they are having all over the US now about the American Society of Composers and Publishers, commonly known as "ASCAP." They insist that all songs or copyright music of any sort be tied up and a fee be placed on the use of them over the air or anywhere else. So they called me twice about the Los Angeles Breakfast Club program I am to sing on. They want to know the names of the songs and who owns them and who has a copyright. I get to have the laugh on them. I tell them that the people who wrote my songs have been dead maybe two hundred years or more! That if they know any way of getting in communication with them and getting their consent, just do that very thing at once! And I think it rather tickles the Breakfast Club people. Yes, sir—the ASCAP has met its waterloo when it comes to folk songs. You can collect no royalty off

of anybody. For instance, who wrote Barbara Ellen? It was written in
the sixteenth century—rather it was compiled or just grew out of an old
love tale, or nobody knows how it grew! So that has the ASCAP by the
ear! Or the old folly ballad, Risselty-Rosselty. Or the Jesse James song.
Nobody on this earth knows who wrote our "ballets"! And the singing
of them is free! (*SDN*, January 25, 1941)

Musical Instruments: The Fiddle

I often tell folks who want to know about the early Ozarks music, that
our ancestors believed that "the Devil was in the fiddle." You old folks
will recall that this was true. That is, the religious people, and I believe
that at least eighty percent were religious. I ran across the most interesting article in an old book . . . giving the history of Brother Hicks, a very
noted preacher of his day. . . . This is from the article:

> He would often, after his conversion, amuse his family in pri-
> vate by playing on the violin as an accompaniment to the sing-
> ing of the sweet songs of Zion. But be it said to his everlasting
> credit, he was discreet in that he never carried his violin into the
> pulpit where the word of God was preached.

I should say not! You have no idea how these dear old primitive
saints abhorred an instrument of any sort in church! When the railroad came to our little town of Galena in 1903, there was such a flood
of bridge builders, workmen, saw-filers, engineers, etc., that everyone
rented rooms. My mother took in a good old "anti" man to room. That
night he heard my mother playing and singing at her little cottage organ,
and the next morning he moved out bag and baggage! He was a saw-
filer from Tennessee, about seventy-five, who was a good workman and
a good man and followed the railroad camps. Mamma told him that he
must have forgotten about the good book telling him to praise the Lord
with the harp and the timbrel and the dulcimer and sound the trumpet and goodness knows what other instruments. A long list! He said

that was the Old Bible and he didn't give much houseroom to it. Funny world isn't it—and yet such a lot of good but "sot" folks in it. Maybe you and I are "sot," who knows? (*SDN*, December 6, 1938)

Hill Music Played on the Jawbone of an Ass

I have a letter from Mr. Kermit Shelby of Star Route, Reeds Spring, Missouri. He writes interestingly to tell me of Albert Smith in Reeds Spring. He says that recently he heard Albert play hill music "on the jawbone of an ass." Albert, who is forty-three and crippled, is a wonder, Mr. Shelby says.

> He holds the jawbone on his left knee with his left hand. He holds its small end up, the teeth turned outward. In his right hand he holds a plain old Barlow knife, blades closed, so that either end knocks against the inside of the jawbone from underneath. He beats a rhythmic double-time tattoo. It sounds something like Cuban rhumba players shaking their dried seed gourds. And it sounds something like bone-knockers, only more violent.
>
> . . . He follows this up with a vigorous slap-slap along the smooth side of the jaw-bone in the manner of the hidy-ho boys who slap a bull fiddle. This makes the loose teeth vibrate in an unearthly fashion like skeletons dancing up and down. You shiver. And if you've got a hollow tooth you feel it there. But it gets you. Make no mistake, this Albert fellow has got rhythm. (*SDN*, October 8, 1940)

Shape-Note Singers[2]

In her broadcast on KWK in St. Louis, January 1, 1942, May McCord described the "shape-note singers" of the Missouri and Kentucky mountain regions who are also known as the "fa sol la" singers. "These singers,

Shape-note music. *From* The Missouri Harmony: Or a Collection of Psalm and Hymn Tunes, and Anthems, from Eminent Authors: With an Introduction to the Grounds and Rudiments of Music to Which Is Added a Supplement, by Allen D. Cardin, an Amateur, *published by Morgan and Sons, 1837.*

some of them ninety years old and older, . . . recognize the notes by their shapes . . . These shaped notes are arranged for part-singing with unusual intervals."[3] (*St. Louis Post-Dispatch*, December 27, 1942)

I have an awfully nice letter from a woman who tells some history about the famous old shape-notes:

> I want to thank you for your mention of the shape notes, for these shape notes have made it possible for a great many hill-billies to learn new songs and enjoy singing them that we could never have learned without the help of this simplified method afforded us.—Mrs. Annie H. Bauer, Houston, Missouri. (*SDN*, August 23, 1938)

Singing Schools and Conventions

The singing school of the Ozarks enters into her musical history more than anything else. You know they came in about fifty years ago and came with a rush. And it was this singing school which began to run out the old British ballads. They thought that these up-to-date songs which they actually went to a school and learned by note, were the only thing, and that they must not fool with the old "ballets" that grandpappy and grandmammy knew, any longer. Thereby throwing away the most priceless heritage of folk music which is now being sought with a vengeance. The old singing school songs are also being preserved. (*SDN*, July 22, 1939)

Sunday last I fulfilled a long desire and went to the Wright County Singing Convention at Hartville. It was a great day. Hotter than anything I ever experienced in my life, but the good times went right on. About three thousand people attend these singings, sometimes around five, I am told. I thought of the words, "I Hear America Singing." Yes, classes from all over the Ozarks, choirs, solos, young folks, old folks—and the thought came to me that while Europe is building bomb-proof dens to crawl into to protect them from the black belching of death and hell overhead, America is singing—at least in the Ozarks! At this convention Sunday, there were people from Oklahoma, Nebraska, Colorado, Kansas and some from California who come every year to attend. . . . By eleven o'clock the crowd had drunk the town pump dry and almost all the water in town. The old historic courthouse was the place of the singing. It was jammed and packed, and there was a loud speaker which carried the program out on the lawn where literally hundreds milled around or sat in the shade and listened. (*SDN*, July 7, 1938)

Ballads Grew Out of Events of the Day

The Missouri Houn' Dog Song

> Ever time I go to town
> The boys keep kickin' my dog aroun'.
> Makes no difference if he is a houn'
> They gotta quit a kickin' my dog aroun'!

This is the unofficial song of Missouri, and the cry of the real Missouri, to which the hound has always been provider, companion, leader in the fox chase, the keynote sounder in the misty nights of coon hunts, the garnisher forth of breakfast tables with brown, crisp, juicy squirrel. And this is the defiance of the greater Missouri to the lesser. It is the heart throb of thousands who in these late days of urban presumption have found the dogs which trot into town under the tall ends of their wagons insulted and mistreated by half-baked people without enough of sporting blood in their veins to love a hound—and with the vague notion that the poodle has become the canine badge of aristocracy. It is the real aristocracy which voices this song. The aristocracy of hospitality and good cheer. (*SNL*, February 28, 1937)

And from an old *Springfield Republican*, Mrs. Stewart of Battlefield, Missouri, sends me a very informative letter dated December 28, 1911:

> I saw by the papers that a whole lot of talk is going around about a booster song. The paper says this houn' dog song was written by some land agent. It ain't no such thing at all. I heard this song long before the Civil War. I was living three miles from Forsyth and my paw and Grandpa Sinter was freighting goods from Forsyth to Springfield. In them days, there was no railroad and they brought the goods by boat down the Mississippi from St. Louis, then up the White River to Forsyth on a little stern wheel boat named the Rosie Bell. When the goods were unloaded, Paw and Grandpaw Slater took them to Springfield.

Another freighter was Pursley Parrish and he had a boy named Zeke who used to help him freight. Zeke was a right smart of a hunter and always had a houn' dog. Every time Zeke and his paw come to Forsyth he brought his dog. He was a good hound all right, but Zeke only fed him when he thought about it, and that was about once a week. When the houn' come along he was a rustling grub ever minute and he wasn't very particular whose grub it was. So everybody knowed this houn', back doors and stores alike, and they got such a grudge agin him that they would kick him every time they saw him. One day a big feller about 18 kicked the houn' and Zeke saw him, and he lit into him and sure changed his looks some. The sheriff come along and arrested both the boys and Zeke, being a country boy, was skeered and blubbering. Just when the sheriff was taking the boys into Squire Johnson's office Zeke's paw saw him and hollered to Zeke to ask him what was the matter. Zeke was crying and he hollered back to his paw—"Every time I come to town the boys all kick my dog around. I don't care if he is a houn', they gotta quit kickin' my dog around!" It sounded just like a song, and all the fellers around Forsyth made a song out of just them words and started singing it till the war broke out and there wasn't time to sing. That's when that song started, for I was there and knew Zeke and his paw and the houn'.

So that letter is a great relic from Uncle Aaron Weatherman, a fine old pioneer of Taney County who has been dead several years. (*SNL*, February 28, 1937)

Ballad of the Meeks Murder[A]

Maybe a lot of you remember about the Meeks Murder song. . . . Many versions in many places have been un-earthed of this old ballad.

So, fitting right into my story—here comes a letter this week from Mrs. M. R. Smith at Marionville, Missouri, telling me a very startling and fearful story of this crime. It is true because she saw some of the incidents photographed. . . .

Here are a few things about the Meeks murder you may not have heard. Those fellows, Bill and George Taylor, were mean men. They went to the Meeks home one morning and told Meeks they wanted him to go help with a piece of work. Just bring your wife and children they said, and we will make a picnic of it. So they started.

Well, they got a ways from the Meeks house and pulled into a field by a straw-stack, to put in more straw, they said, so it would ride easier for the children.

They all got out of the wagon and one of the Taylors killed Mr. Meeks and his wife while the other one killed the children. They killed four of the children but they only stunned Nellie. She was eight. When they drove away she came to and crawled a half mile and told a neighbor.

Mrs. Meeks was expecting another child in a month. Those fiends also killed the unborn baby. Then they covered their bodies with straw and left. A young man working on a farm close by was one of the first to get to the scene. He afterwards became my husband's brother-in-law. He with his own hands lifted the unborn baby to a woman in a wagon. So he is the one who told us all about it. I was at that time a young girl living a mile southeast of Brookfield, Mo. Well, I saw the pictures of them, even the unborn baby, laying on some boards as they were all dressed for burial.

So by that, you see just how authentic Mrs. Smith's experience is! I wish I had space to print this old ballad but it is long. One version is the story of the crime and another is little Nellie's story. Nellie's song winds up with a rather simple, childlike and striking end:

> I saw them kill poor papa,
> Dear mama and sisters, too.
> And then they tried to kill me,
> And that was all I knew
> Until we reached the straw-yard,

Our burial to prepare,
And God was there before me,
And God was with me there.
Kind friends and neighbor people,
Who in this world are poor,
Be kind and even honest,
For honesty is sure.

And so you understand how ballads are made. It is no wonder they interest the world in general. The reactions of a race. The life and dreams and tragedies and tears and joys of a people recorded in the simplest thing they know—poetry and song. Crude but real. Sincere and unlettered. Honest and eternal. (*SDN*, March 25, 1941)

"The Sad Song," Also Known as "The Palace Grand" and "Lady Mary"

He came from his palace grand,
An' he came t' my cottage door.
His words, they were few, but his looks
They will linger forever more.
Th' smile an' his sad dark eyes
More tender than words could be;
But I was nothing to him,
Tho' he was the world to me.

An' there in his garden strolled,
All robed in satins an' lace,
Lady Mary so strange an' cold,
Who held in his heart no place.
Fer I would've been his bride
With a kiss for a lifetime fee,

```
                                    Harbert, Mich.,
                                    July 10, 1931.


Dear Mrs. McCord:-

          Thank you for so thoughtfully letter-
with such breadths and airs from the foothills of the Ozark.
It is good to have the second verse of the Sad Song; More
verses after these two would be too heavy a weight of
melancholy.  I shall expect that Charlie Hiatt's Paper of
Pins song- and shall also hope for the Blind Girl song.
You were also kind to me that I feel human magnets pulling
me back to your corner of Missouri.  A copy of the
American Song Bag is being sent to you from my publishers
with my compliments, and when in Springfield again I shall
write in it when you are old and cannot see put on your
specks and think of me.  Or else, something about how when
you get into Christian County the hills don't get any
higher, but the hollers get deeper and d-e-e-p-e-r.

                    Faithfully yours,

                    Carl Sandburg
```

Letter from Carl Sandburg to May Kennedy McCord, July 10, 1931.
McCord Personal Papers.

But I was nothing to him,
Tho' he was the world to me.

Today in his palace grand
On a flower strewn bed he lies,
With 'is beautiful lids fast closed
O, his beautiful sad dark eyes.
Among the mourners who mourned,
Why should I a mourner be?
For I was nothing to him,
Tho' he was the world to me.

How will it be with our souls
When we meet in that spirit land?
What the mortal heart ne'r knows
To the spirit then understand?
Or in some celestial form
Will our sorrows repeated be?
Will I still be nothing to him,
Tho' he is the world to me.
(*Ozark Folksongs*, 1982[5])

Ballads Called "Folly Songs"

You know the old folly ballads they used to call them. Those with the funny refrains like whack-fol-loddy, etc. They are among the oldest in existence. (*SDN*, October 5, 1940)

"Rolly Trudum"

So here is an old folly ballad so popular with your grandmothers. So jolly, and considered by them a bit flippant and none too serious-minded for a young lady. It is a great favorite. Whenever I go away singing ballads, Rolly Trudum makes the hit and I wish I could strum the guitar and dash it off for everyone of you. I love to sing it. I get more fun than you would. . . .

When I was out a walking.
To breathe the pleasant air,
I saw a lady talking
To her daughter fair.
Rolly trudum, trudum, trudum, rolly day!

"Now hush up dear daughter,
And stop your rapid tongue,
You're talking about marrying,
And you know you are too young—"
Rolly trudum, trudum, trudum, rolly day! . . .

"They've gone for the parson.
The license for to fetch.
And I'm going to marry
Before the sun sets—"
Rolly trudum, trudum, trudum, rolly day!

"Oh, now my daughter's married,
And well for to do,
So hop along my jolly boys
I think I'll marry too."
Rolly trudum, trudum, trudum, rolly day!
(*SDN*, November 12, 1940)

CHAPTER 9

Critters in the Hills

Here's an old superstition: To Cure a Cold, Kiss a Mule!
I don't suppose many women kissed a mule, but a lot
of them kissed a man who was stubborn as a mule!

Dial, May 1949

. . . .

Until the mid-twentieth century, most Ozarkers lived close
to the land. They interacted daily with a menagerie of animals, both domesticated and wild. Naturally, more than a few
regional stories emerged from this proximity. May's columns,
typically a communal effort drawing on the collective memory of her rural readers, covered everything from the gentlest
saddle horses and milk cows to the fiercest razorback hogs
and mountain lions. From her self-deprecating discussion of
a gargantuan turkey to her witty analysis of the importance
of the Missouri Mule, May described critters as essential ele-
ments of her Ozarks.

. . . .

The Missouri Mule

A recent article in the magazine published by the Missouri Historical Society gives the history of the Missouri Mule and the part he has played in the life of Missourians. For instance, the Santé Fe trail in the 1820s brought the first mules to Missouri. A small Mexican breed which soon became as good as money in trade. The first European jacks known to enter Missouri were brown Maltese jacks brought up the river to New Franklin in 1838. By the 1850s the Missouri mule was known around the world. This marvelous beast fought our wars for us—we owe much to him as a civilized people. (*SDN*, May 30, 1942)

This Mule Gave Us Music!

Missouri, already famous for her fine mules, now lays claim to a most outstanding critter of that hybrid population—one "Jerry" of Benton County, property of Uncle Joe Henderson, noted fiddle-maker in them parts.

It seems that Uncle Joe has been making violins since he was a boy, and has turned out two every year. He is now seventy-nine. For the past thirty years, the tail of old Jerry, his mule, has furnished hairs for all the bowstrings. It takes one hundred for each bow made. We neglected to find out if this mule is a special pet who doesn't mind having his tail yanked out, OR—if all this tricky business was transacted at great risk of life and limb!

. . . The strange part of it is that we do really have some fine fiddle makers in the Ozarks. Where is this Uncle Joe Henderson? I wish I could hear one of his fiddles and hear him play:

> I had a piece of pie,
> An' I had a piece of puddin'
> I give it all away
> Fer to hug Sally Goodin'.
> Went upon the hill

To see my Sal a comin'
And I thought to my soul
I'd kill myself a runnin'.
(*SDN*, June 25, 1942)

Hawgs

You don't know the Ozark country until you have seen a Razorback hog. Lean and "whangleathery," he used to run wild on the range. It's said that "his head was as heavy as his hams" and when you fried him the meat was so tough you couldn't even "stick your fork in the gravy." (Program notes for *The Wilderness Road and Jimmie Driftwood*, RCA Victor LPM-1994, 1959)

A Tusk of a Wild Ozark Boar

Mary Elizabeth Mahnkey sends me a great relic. The tusk of a wild Ozark boar!

. . . This tusk is about eight inches long (broken off at that). This is the history she gives me:

> Here is the verification of your wild hog story. This tusk came from a wild boar shot September 1928. He did not kill a man, but he killed two mighty fine dogs. Nor was he hunted down in the Old World manner . . . but after he had been chased from Long Creek corn fields and killed the valuable faithful dogs that chased him, Dutch Barnett vowed vengeance. He went out along the cornfield fence and watched for him all night. Along toward morning he came and tore into the field just like we read about the elephants. So Dutch up and shot him. Our Reggie boy later went over there, broke off the tusks and brought them home, broken off as they were, probably not the real length. But you see these things are still in our Ozarks, although hidden and unspoken of.

This tusk is worth coming to see. It is a barbarous-looking cruel thing. It curves upward at an acute angle, and has the sharp razorback that Bob Burns speaks of. But I still believe the common razorback hog got his name from the thin line of bristles that stood upon his wild back like a razor blade. These hogs show what "going wild" can do. Once they were gentle domestic animals brought here by our early ancestors. Mr. White (Rabbit Twister) and I were talking yesterday. He says the dogs used to jump up a herd of wild hogs sometimes, but most dogs were afraid of them, and hunters and boys climbed trees like scared monkeys. (*SNL*, July 25, 1937)

Old Time Ozark Hogs Knew No Law but Own[1]

[Newspaper] Editor's Note—The imminent opening of the Ozark Empire District Free Fair next week has set our inimitable May McCord to reminiscing, with results both diverting and enlightening, as you will find by perusing her hilarious narrative. Here is a story of the origins of the Ozarks fair and show stock that you will find in no prospectus of the Ozark Empire Free Fair or Chamber of Commerce—and more's the pity, say we. . . .

Docia[2] doesn't know how I'm laughing yet because she said, "May, why don't you write about the kind of livestock they used to take to fairs in your earlier Ozarks?" Docia, you know, is a very sincere and credulous little person—

The livestock we used to take to fairs—yes! Hold my side! The four-footed critters!

In the first place we didn't have any fairs. We had picnics and reunions and gatherin's but we didn't know anything about "fairs." And the four-footed critters! I walk around now and look at the sleek stock displayed at our Ozark Free Fair, and I seem to have lived somewhere before the Mexican wars. I have to pinch myself.

Yoked Hog. *Hall Photo Co., #860.*

Snout Was Versatile

For instance, did any of you ever see the old hazel splitter hog or the Arkansas razorback? His head was as heavy as his hams. He had a snout on him like a desert coyote. With this versatile appendage he could drink buttermilk out of a jug through the cracks of a worm-rail fence or crack hickory nuts through it. He had a long lonesome tail which hung down to the ground. My friend Bair Inman says he has seen their tails drag. A hog couldn't curl this apparatus up over his back with any snap and zip even if he wanted to. And he didn't want to. His hams looked like the drumstick of a turkey. You couldn't fatten him if you stalled him in the grillroom of the Ritz Carlton. He was wild as a wolf and he ran everything off of himself that might be called fat, by the wildest stretch of the imagination. His meat was rangy, stringy and whangleathery.

But there is one thing you could say for that hog of the deep Ozark hills of south Missouri and north Arkansas—he took care of himself! He was able to earn his own bed and board at any time, and preferred it. In fact, in those days, fifty years ago or seventy-five, the hog took care of the man—now the man takes care of the hog. The independent wild razorback lived and fattened all winter by digging acorns out of the snow. He went two feet or more into the ground and dug up roots to eat while the old man went fishing and hunting. That's the plain truth of the whole matter. He kept meat and lard in the house and his "middlin's" were good as gold for barter which kept the coffee and sweetnin' on the table. Now the man keeps the hog. He spends his days plowing and raising corn to pour into the animal just to take him to market and lose money on him (providing we don't have war!).

Standard Is Reversed

We used to always judge a good hog by the length of his snout. Now we judge him by the shortness of it. It mustn't be more than a button nowadays. It used to look like a quart funnel.

We used to have the yoked hogs. So many folks think that is funny and must be one of our tales we razz the outside world with. . . . We yoked them to keep them from going through fences. We used to yoke geese, too. . . . We used to put bells on hogs. Dr. Elkins and I were talking about that recently. He said he never happened to see the belling process, but he was always told that it was some picnic! I can readily imagine. We used to have the "balance hog." You could put a hook in his nose and weigh your meat and lard on the end of the tail!

In the earlier days we had no stock law and the cows and hogs roamed the streets and the fields and ranges at will. The hogs were especially distressingly familiar. They roamed your backyards if you didn't have fences, and so few did. They haunted the back ends of the little stores, turning over goods boxes, eating the melon rinds and even investigating the coal-oil barrels. They walked right in the stores unless you kept a pocket full of rocks and yelled "S-o-oey!" and whaled them with the rocks. If the devil Beelzebub himself ever came back to earth in any physical form it was in an Arkansas razorback sow.

She Could Pick a Lock

I can never forget one old sow that took my little village of Galena over, soul and body for about three or four years. She belonged to Uncle Joe Melton. He was a gentle, kindly soul, but his old sow wasn't. The wrath of the whole community went up in one great invocation against that old she-devil. In the first place, she was smarter than a corporation lawyer. She knew all the answers. As for locking against her that was out. She could pick a Yale lock if she had to. When the good people of my town got up in the morning their first thought was to look and see what Uncle Joe's old sow had done. There wasn't a fence built that she couldn't get through, go over, or root under. There wasn't a gate she couldn't someway wangle open. She could root up every garden in town if you would just go on to bed and give her from about 9 p.m. until 4 a.m., and give her the gardens. She would turn over every slop bucket on the back porches. She would drag whole washing off the line and tear them into giblets. Women liked to leave their washings out all night for the dews to make them snowy white. She would eat enough frying chickens to set the feast of Belshazzar, and setting hens' nests were her especial tidbit. She loved the little tender roots of flower beds and had a snout that could bore down into the earth and dig up the bodies of your ancestors.

Sometimes when she got enough of your trying to discipline her, she would give you a fight. If she ran at you once with a wild "woof" and her teeth bared, you didn't try it anymore without a good dog to back you up. When she had young pigs—and she had litter after litter of no less than fifteen at a time—she could stand off a German tank. As soon as the pigs got big enough to waddle and squeal she brought them right along and began showing them the ropes early.

I remember she used to always flop right down at the end of Old Man Carson's little store porch and give the whole fifteen a square meal, just as my beau and I would come along and have to nearly step across her. This was the only time she ever seemed at peace with the world. . . .

We built fences up a little higher and stopped holes with boards and home-wrought spike rails, and weathered through until she was sold down on White River.

It may be that the citizens finally waited on Uncle Joe with an indignation committee, but I doubt it. You know it was a funny thing in those days—a good man who would give you the last bite, would come to you and wait on your sick and help bury your dead, would pay you the last farthing he owed you—that same man would see you in the bottomless pit before he would put his animal away to keep it from destroying your property.

It was considered an insult to ask it. A sort of feeling akin to the feeling if you would ask him to put his children in jail so you might have peace and quiet. It was a strange thing that I can scarcely explain on paper. I think after all, that it was pure Americanism! An individualistic something which reigned in the hearts of us Ozarkers and was an unspoken and unwritten law. That's the only way I can figure it out. But this particular phase of it was hard to take. (*SDN*, September 12 1939)

Blooded Hogs, Cattle Unknown in Old Days[3]

The first blooded hog that ever came into the Ozark country was the red Duroc or Jersey. They seemed to be more able to stand it. I remember my father bought a Chester white boar. He was the sensation of the neighborhood, but my father worked him off on somebody else. The lazy old fool would lay right under the trees and starve to death before he would get up and eat the acorns! And the same with the Poland China.

But they began breeding those hogs to the wild range hog and bringing up the stock. A hog simply had to make a living, and this cross breed made a critter that would have at least a semblance of fat and at the same time had some get-up-and-go to himself. They had to have that rangy blood to stand the rough country. Then it began to get fashionable to breed hogs, and farmers began buying the blooded breeds and the country was slowly being cleared off more and more so that we might keep that gentleman in his required luxurious laziness.

Back in the olden days, nobody kept hogs. A man went out in the fall and shot his meat or trapped it. They used a sort of pen with a trap door, and when they got one trapped it was some sport. He had to be shot then and there of course. He fought to the death. Some of the boars had tusks that could rip a man open. Those wild boars were a terror. My father once had the theory that he could tame a wild hog—so he and my uncle built a pen like the tower of Babel and got a man on White River to trap one and manage to get him there in a boarded-up wagon. They gave it up in about three days. Men have had theories before!

Short of Milk

As for the cattle, we just had "cows." That's about all there was to it. We called them old "Roan" or "Reddy" or if the horns were a bit short we called her "Muley."[4] I have never understood that, because there's nothing short about a mule's ears. They had no blooded cattle. They saved the best-looking bull calf for breeding.

None of the cows gave much milk. But we were not a dairy country then as we are now. The cows roamed the streets peacefully as do the cows in India where they are sacred. If you were roasting-ear eaters they soon found it out and were waiting at your backyard fence each morning for the green husks. Also the apple cores when you dried apples or canned them. They drew flies and they outraged your sense of cleanliness, but as I say, if you ever dared to cheep a "stock-up" law, even a village ordinance, you had more trouble than the AFL and the CIO combined ever dreamed of. Out on the ranges it was treason and a shootin' matter entirely.

Dual-Purpose Breed

Our cattle were really an offshoot of the Texas longhorns. Many pioneers had brought cows all the way from Tennessee when they came through in wagons and cleared the way with their broadaxes; then someone was always going to the "Indian Nation" and bringing back the longhorns that mixed in the breed. A lot of cows were pretty vicious and awfully mean with children. Even in the bringing up of my children I always had to go out when they were coming home from school and stand off an old red cow who always stood by the blacksmith shop (I gather that she was mechanical). And one time I had the terror of seeing her take Leslie, the baby one, between her horns and throw him in the air about fifteen feet. I shall never forget it because I was looking straight at the tragedy and I thought sure one horn, long and pointed, went straight through his body. Thank God I was mistaken. But it wasn't her fault. It was her miss.

The first blooded cattle that came into the Ozarks many years ago were the dual shorthorn from north Missouri and Iowa. They edged their way in through the far-sightedness of some progressive ruralists. This was a dual sort of animal, good milker and good beef. And rather durable. Cattle had to make most of their living also. And the rocks simply ruined the feet of the blooded breeds. Later came the red Poles, then a long time afterward, the black Angus—and lastly white-faced Herefords.

I shall never forget the first herd of black Angus I saw roaming the fertile valley of the old McCord farm three miles east of Crane, Missouri, brought there by Grant Ashcraft of Webb City, who bought the farm and was a wealthy mining man. Later he stocked it with Herefords and called the lovely old place "Hereford Hall." I don't think he ever made any money. Perhaps didn't want to. Play-farmers with a lot of money and impractical ideas can't come into the Ozarks and make anything. Ask the man who knows. They have to be born here and know their onions. Now many farmers who read this article will doubtless find differences of opinions but I am only telling you the small bit that I know and have seen.

Good Saddle Horses

Now as to horses, it was a bit different. Even in the days of the ox for fieldwork, and the mule for all work, we had very good saddle horses.

A man loved his saddle animal and it was all the horse he had any need for. The roads were fierce and the uncleared fields broke a horse down if you put him to a plow. All going was done on horseback. Judge Charley Henson's grandfather used to take the county funds once a year to Jefferson City on horseback. And when my father-in-law came into the county and was treasurer for a term, they kept the county funds in a gourd and he carried the gourd home every night! (How's that for you "gourd raisers"?)

We didn't have fairs but we had just a sort of jack-leg hoss race now and then if we could find a stretch of field level or straight enough to get up into a loop. I remember going to one when I was about five, down in what we now call "Uncle George Short's Bottom" down on the bank of the James River.

But at these gatherin's and picnics we had the hoss traders. They didn't bring horses so much to show them, they brought them to swap. It was a great old business and the excitement of every get-together. Even the women tried to look on, though it wasn't considered very ladylike for a woman to be at a hoss swappin', though now and then at great intervals you found a woman hoss swapper who could cheat the ears off of you. But she did it at home and rather quietly. Sometimes she came out into the lot and helped her pap or her man. And the trader usually quaked in his boots and it was no time to even turn your head to spit. You had to watch your corners.

Slickers from the City

They used to often get taken to a cleaning by the slick hoss traders from the city of Springfield! Joe Meredith, popular police officer here, recalls old Uncle Andy Ray from Springfield, and another good swapper was Charley Armour down near Reeds Spring. A horse swapper always had what was known as a "snide." This was an animal which he fixed up and patched up (like a lot of us women "make-up") and he passed for what he wasn't. Not all hoss traders were smooth, tradition to the contrary. Uncle Andy's snide was a fine-looking mule. This mule was up-standing and slick as grease and curried and ready to go. But there was one little discrepancy. The mule was badly ruptured! But Uncle Andy would put a fine saddle on him and a very wide, good looking girth, which held up the protuberance, and he would tempt the heart of any hoss trader who would get him at a fair swap. He would be so busy looking in the mule's mouth that he would neglect all other parts of his anatomy. The mouth was, and seems to be yet, the sum total of all hoss trading.

The victim would take his mule home and unsaddle him, or maybe to the edge of the picnic grounds and discover this bad rupture of the animal. Then he would come back spitting froth of anger and demand to trade back. Uncle Andy would hum and haw and apologize and take back the mule and return five or ten dollars to the gullible one. He would work this gag maybe ten times during a three-days reunion or picnic and net a good sum!

Made Him Pay

But Joe recalls that one time he got hold of Uncle John Plummer of Reeds Spring and put the snide off on him. Uncle John was kind and good and looked as harmless as a house cat, but there was a nest of owls back in his thinking process somewhere. He took the fine mule home and unsaddled him. He saw it all but he kept the mule. Time went on—and the next day as he expected, out came Uncle Andy to Plummer's farm to get back his snide, and Uncle John made him pay him twenty-five dollars for it!

Horse traders used to go through the country trading with the farmers, making a racket of it. And sometimes they carried women with them of unsavory stripe who did the cooking and kept the camps. These women they carried behind them in a light spring wagon, and left them hidden in camp while they went out to trade with the farmers. I asked in my column awhile back if anyone knew what a "cat-wagon" was. Nobody seemed to know. This wagon in which the women traveled was called the cat-wagon.

But the funny part was that now and then a hoss trader from unknown parts got up against a good old Hillbilly who never "talked when he o'rt to be listenin'" and got taken to such a fleecing as has never been seen before or since, in the marts of trade! Leave it to the Hillbilly! But that Hillbilly was a marked man after that, as the news was usually passed around among the breed to "look out fer that feller Ransler" or some such. (*SDN*, September 13, 1939)

Cattle and Oxen

Help a Cow Who Loses Her Cud

You know a cow chews her cud continuously. All ruminating animals must have this cud. Now and then a cow used to lose her cud and was very sick. Mary Elizabeth Mahnkey told me one time that they used to make a yarn ball and fry it in grease—a soft small ball, and give it to the cow. This established a cud until her stomach got back to normal. I used to hear that they used a piece of greasy dishrag, too. (*Dial*, February 1948)

Cows Will Give Bloody Milk If You Kill a Toad

Mrs. Maud Lindsay of Halfway, Missouri, writes me interestingly:

> One time when I was a child, while playing with other children, we accidentally killed a toad. Their mother insisted that the cows would give bloody milk, even though it was an accident. And sure enough, next day one of their cows gave bloody milk! She said, "Now you kids killed that toad, so you each get seven pebbles and at sundown throw them over your left shoulder into an open well." We did, and the old cow gave good milk again. (*SDN*, May 17, 1941)

Want to Know How to Shoe an Ox?

And now some ox tails (I mean tales) because this is stuff you all had better be learning for it will never return so long as time lasts . . . Why not learn something about the long serfdom of the noble ox who so

patiently helped us beat a path to civilization. Thanks Mr. Hackett—
a lot of young buds didn't know this:

> I came into possession recently of an ancient relic, an ox shoe.
> It reminded me of pioneer days. The ox refuses to hold his foot
> up for shoeing as the horse does, and has to be thrown down
> or swung up to be shod. So a stall is built having a windlass
> attachment. The ox is tied within, and a strong bandage or belt
> is passed under him and attached to the windlass. Soon Mr.
> Ox finds himself suspended between earth and sky and is then
> quite easily shod.—S. M. Hackett of Thayer, Missouri. (*SNL*,
> August 9, 1936)

The Lead Steer and Off Steer in a Three- or Four-Ox Team

My good friend Rabbit Twister, W. S. White, Esquire, Ozarkian deluxe,
tells me some things:

> In a two-, three-, or four-ox team they tied a rope around the
> horns of the left-hand steer on the front team, and he was
> the one that guided the group. They called him the lead steer
> because he was the leader and the one next to the driver. The
> driver walked on the left-hand side. The lead steer's yoke mate
> on the right side was the "off steer" because he had to be reached
> across the lead steer, with the whip, in driving them. They very
> seldom used the lead line in driving, which they called a jerk-
> line, because the leader knew "gee" and "haw" so well that they
> guided them mostly by saying "gee" and "haw" when they
> wanted to turn to the left or right. (*SDN*, July 5, 1941)

How the Oxen (and God) Got Them across the Swollen River

This is Mrs. Angie Brown's story about oxen. She is eighty-two and lives
in Carthage, Missouri.

> Grandpa was six-feet-four. He and I and a young aunt of 15
> were coming from camp meeting and hurrying our old Buck

and Bright oxen with a long stick and a bit of plaited leather on it to sting em a bit. It had rained very hard the night before and rivers were rising fast. We crossed old muddy Crooked Creek twice and then had a real shady fairyland for miles. I saw squirrels flitting about and an occasional rabbit would sit up in the road and dare us to the limit. Crows were cawing and blackbirds holdin' camp meetin's. I saw Grandpa as he climbed out in a narrow rut, to find the high water mark on a tree at the water's edge. He stepped out on a rock and measured with his stout whip stick nearly six feet. So he came back and put the feather bed up on a deal table and roped it and the table fast to the wagon and set me upon it and told Aunt to tie us together with her apron, put the end of a rope around and hold tight to it. She was to brace her feet and hold me no matter what happened. Grandpa said, "We've got to take a jolt over that boulder. Now, Sis, don't you get scared and cry, cause God will guide me, and the oxen can swim."

We drew up and into the water slowly, but one broad rock we had always crossed on was gone, and we rocked nearly over. He waded out until the water was to his shoulders and put one arm around Bright's neck, and lifted his nose out of the water. He snorted and began to swim. The wagon went head down and water splashed us and ran through under the table. Grandpap gee'd Buck up stream and practically carried Bright's load and had to tread water himself between the two swimming oxen past the middle of the swift current. He stooped to push a floating log and I screamed for I was scared, I could only see his head. But he was singing, "Arise, my soul arise—Shake off thy guilty fears!" We were nearing the ford, the usual sand bar was gone and no chance for even a breathing spell as the oxen gained foothold once more, and a steep muddy slippery hill the only way out! Again he went to Bright's head and talked, and straddled the tongue and pulled his best.

As soon as my aunt could jump out and get a big stone she scotched the back wheel and unhooked the chains from the oxen. They fell to their knees and laid down and Grandpap said,

"Let's rest and thank God!" So he prayed there in the woods, and that's my only memory of his face as I was so small—talking to God! The Doctor said he strained himself and he died a few months later. (*SNL*, August 23, 1936)

Turkeys

Did You Ever "Honey-Dew" a Turkey?

What do you folks know about honey-dew? When I tell about honey-dew to people in the cities, they just don't believe it. I wonder if this was a honey-dew year. Honey-dew is a sort of sticky, mysterious substance that comes on the under part of foliage in the fields and hills and dales of the Ozarks. They say that the botanists have never been able to tell what it is or what causes it. But in a real honey-dew year it is fearfully sticky. They used to go out and honey-dew a young turkey whenever they wanted one. . . . When the honey-dew was heavy of mornings, the young turkeys would flop around and get it on their wings and it would stick their wings together and you could just walk right to them and pick them up. (*Dial*, November 1950)

I've Lost All Hope of Ever Again Eating Wild Turkey

One time the "mighty hunter" of this household killed a forty-eight pounder. Now believe that or not. It's a mighty fishy tale, but I'm going to tell it. It was about twenty-eight years ago (1909). He was hunting down near the White River . . . before Lake Taneycomo, even. And they used to kill turkeys, MY! When the husband threw this gobbler over his shoulder his feet dragged the ground (the gobbler's feet). I can remember what a job it was to scald and pick the gentleman (I mean the gobbler again) and in those days we did our own work. Nobody brought us "dressed" fowls and stemmed gooseberries, and predigested vitamins!

We put on the wash boiler and got it hot and dumped this old bird in. We cut off the breast, (he was young, believe that or not) and we sliced that breast in steaks and fried it—my, will I ever forget it. It melted in your mouth. We had all we could eat for three meals. We gave two of our neighbors all they could fry, just of the steaks off that breast. Then we baked the rest and for days and days until we could hardly endure the sight of turkey, we had turkey! We fairly forced it upon everyone who came in. . . . Anyway, that's my turkey story and I don't ever expect to have another. (*SNL*, November 21, 1937)

How Big Was May's Turkey?

Everything is going hotsy-totsy with me, only I'm starting out by telling you that I told a lie about that turkey!

My, maybe you don't think I've had razzing about the poor gobbler! And I didn't tell it on purpose. I actually thought it. I wonder where I got forty-eight pounds in my mind and held it all these years. The turkey weighed thirty-two pounds, and was the largest gobbler ever killed in that country in recent times excepting one killed by Emery Boyd down in Swift Shoal Hollow, which weighed thirty-two pounds. (Must have been a twin brother to this one!)

Now I got forty-eight in my mind and you know I am a person who slings figures around. What about a little difference of sixteen pounds of turkey? True, here in Springfield at thirty-two cents a pound, it comes to $5.12. (Figure it up. I may be wrong about that!) But don't you love me enough to forgive me five dollars' worth? Now I'll tell you, I distinctly remember hearing that old Uncle Gip Bowman once killed a forty-eight-pound gobbler. Maybe that's what I had in mind. Some member of the family says that was a catfish! And a friend of mine says that I may have it mixed up with a cow! No sir, it was a gobbler! (*SNL*, November 28, 1937)

Friends to May's Rescue with Tales of Big Turkeys!

Mrs. Elizabeth Mahnkey writes me about the "phantom gobbler" of the hills once upon a time.

> Just you ask Frank Rice, Mrs. Una Keltner's brother (Nixa, Mo.) of the big gobblers they used to kill in these hills. He was a master huntsman. And the big birds were so plentiful and fine and fat that turkey meat went begging and only the breast was used, fried like steak. . . . In the year 1932 Earl Box killed a big gobbler that weighed forty pounds in the Long Creek hills. This was called the phantom gobbler and had been hunted every season. The old turkey bore honorable scars of many glorious escapes. (*SNL,* January 2, 1938)

Turkeys Roosted in Trees

Mrs. Clara Bradley Drummond of El Dorado Springs, Missouri, seems quite an interesting alert person of many wise summers.

> In those days, farmers drove their turkeys to Ste. Genevieve. It was 25 miles, so they had to camp and let the turkeys fly up in trees to roost. Next morning they would come down and start on their journey. They had a good road to travel, as the longest plank road in the world is from Iron Mountain to Ste. Genevieve, Mo. (*SDN,* October 25, 1938)

Skunks as Pets?

A splendid contributor sends me some good information:

> The odoriferous liquid which was put there as the animal's chief means of defense is contained in a little pouch which is very easily removed with a sharp blade. And the little fellow is thus

rendered completely odorless. Treated in this way, they become nice pets and will remain about the place. They do not seem to become accustomed to handling, however, and they will spend most of the daytime in seclusion. But one pet skunk will completely rid your premises of rats, mice, moles, snakes, roaches, frogs, lizards. (*SDN*, December 11, 1941)

Panthers

This panther story was thrilling . . . I have heard of many in the early Ozarks during my childhood:

> When my father was eight years old, my grandfather had to go several miles to mill. They lived in the edge of the pine forests in Texas County. One time Grandpa had gone to mill with the understanding as usual that he might be home that evening and it might be late the next day. Late in the afternoon, as Grandmother was doing evening chores, she thought she heard Grandpa calling from the barn. They listened and heard him again, so she started the eight-year-old boy to see what he was wanting. But soon she saw a big panther come around the barn. She and the son began at once piling indoors all the pine knots they had time to bring before the panther was too close to them. A panther is afraid of a bright light, but the tallow candle didn't bother him. Their one-room house had no loft: a board removed might admit the panther from the roof. He climbed and clawed, and each break was watched and jabbed with a pine torch while the pine knots burned brightly in the open fireplace. They had to burn two chairs because the pine knots gave out. The panther must have been very hungry for he spent the night on the roof trying to enter. Guns were high priced and a family generally had but one, and a man always took his gun when he left the house.—Mrs. Mattie Todd, Humansville, Missouri. (*SNL*, November 29, 1936)

Animal Behavior Predicts the Future

Animals and insects, as you know, have a very strong instinct which goes far beyond human intelligence. Mr. George Clinton Arthur of Rolla tells me that his old father, who is still living and one of the grand old pioneers of the Ozarks and a real man of these gray hills, knows many things. He says,

> When it is going to be a hard winter the hornets build their nests low. They are built very low this year.
>
> And the kingfisher, that bird that flies along the water looking for fish, will build low on the banks of the streams if we are going to have low water. If the water is going to be high, and flood a great deal, the kingfisher will build high.
>
> When a deer lies down on a snow there will be another snow real soon. But if it paws out a place for a bed, the snow is over for a while.
>
> When the katydid hollers in summer there will be frost in 90 days.
>
> Fishing is no good when there is an east wind. They won't bite.
>
> When a crane flies up stream there will be high water.
>
> When chickens feed out in the rain there will be more rain.
>
> A sow will start to carry leaves for her bed for her little ones 24 hours before a blizzard, and long before you know it is coming.

These are valuable signs and beliefs of this fine old pioneer. He has known their value through the years. As I once said, things are proved when they happen so often they cease to be coincidence. (*SDN*, November 4, 1941)

Roosters and Hens

This is an interesting item. A woman says,

> Pa had planted some peas. I guess the rooster must have been looking through the paling, for as soon as they were planted and Pa left the garden, that rooster came flying over and took the rows one by one, eating all the peas. I never had killed a chicken, but I went in and got him and cut his head off and got the peas out of his "craw" and planted them over! I dressed Mr. Rooster, cooked him, and he was good. He never ate any more peas. But we did. We always called them "rooster peas."—Clara Bradley Drummond, El Dorado Springs, Missouri. (*SDN*, July 12, 1938)

Signs and Roosters

Did you ever hear the many signs about roosters? If the rooster crows on going to bed, he'll wake up next morning with rain on his head. And if the rooster stands right in the doorway and crows, company is coming to stay and eat, so you might as well get ready. If two roosters fight, the girl always names one for her lover. If he won the fight, her lover is much in love with her. If he lost, then she would lose her lover.

> I love to watch the rooster crow,
> He's like so many men I know
> Who brag and bluster, rave and shout
> Without one thing to crow about! (*Dial*, April 1951)

If you have a crowing hen, kill her at once because she will bring bad luck. I have helped eat a crowing hen many a time. The old timers would kill her at once. From that comes the very old saying—"A whistling girl and a crowing hen, always come to a sad end." And when I was a child, no real lady whistled. (*SDN*, December 6, 1941)

It was a sign of death for a rooster to turn his back to the door and crow, or from the roof of the house.

We used to hear if you set a hen on Sunday, the chicks would all be roosters, but if you carried them to the nest in a woman's bonnet they would all hatch pullets. (*Dial*, November 1948)

Keep a round smooth rock in the firebox of the cookstove, to keep the hawks away from the chickens. (*SDN*, September 7, 1939)

Superstition

Orpha Vaughn Haddock

I've cleaned and swept and dusted all morn;
Fer company's comin' as sure as yu're born—
How do I know? Why the rooster crowed
On the big front porch—that's how I knowed.
An' jest last night I dropped a knife
It'll be a woman, ye bet yer life.
I think it'll be Aunt Sadie West,
For the rooster's tail wuz p'inted west.
(*SNL*, March 22, 1936)

Dogs

How to Keep Your Dog at Home

Here's how you keep your dog at home: You cut a little hair off his tail and bury it under the corner of the house. Or you cut a green stick the length of the dog's tail, rub grease on it and bury it under the corner of the house. Anybody want to try it? As I heard one hillman say, "My ole houn' ain't worth the bother!" (*Dial*, May 1950)

My Smart Dog

Two old hillbillies were arguing about which had the smartest dog. One said, "Well sir, I've got the smartest dog in the world."

"How do you know you've got the smartest dog?" said the other one.

"Well sir—I've got three guns. A deer gun, a turkey gun and a squirrel gun. When I take my deer gun down, my dog won't hunt nothin' but deer that day. When I take my squirrel gun he won't hunt nuthin' but squirrel. And so on.

"T'other day I thought I'd jist fool my dog so I got my fishin' pole down to go fishin'. I lays my fishin' pole down in the yard to go back after my pocketknife I'd forgot—and when I came back my dog was gone. I couldn't git him to come. I hollered and whistled. Finally I went around behind the barn to look for him, and I'll be durned if that dog wasn't a diggin' fishin' worms!" (*Dial*, May 1947)

CHAPTER 10

Superstitions
and Granny Cures

*The whole thing is not what we BELIEVE—that's not what
I have been bringing out—but it is what superstitions or
traditions or perhaps actual facts went into the making
of our early culture. That is what I love to bring out.*

SDN, July 1, 1941

. . . .

Among the most fascinating aspects of the backwoods
Ozarks to many visitors in the first half of the twentieth century was the survival of superstitions and the widespread use
of home remedies. May recalled many beliefs, granny remedies, and practices she experienced during her childhood
that may strike modern readers as superstitious or humorous.
Pioneers brought many of these beliefs when they came into
the Ozarks and had to face life's challenges on their own: how
to cure the sick, how to ward off serious maladies, and how to
interpret natural phenomena they did not understand. May
was no granny woman in the Ozarks sense of the label, but
her columns dispensed a great deal of traditional advice.[1]

. . . .

A friend of mine recently told me that he questioned whether I should tell Ozarks superstitions and talk about them on the air and so on. He thought it might make people think I believed in them and might lead to harm, or harm my Ozarks, or something of the sort. At least, that was the idea he was getting at.

I explained to him that I told superstitions merely as a record, as a history of the race, that the whole country was interested in superstitions. They are part of the background of our racial childhood. Often they are told just for fun because many of them are too ridiculous for words. But they are recorded and preserved and carried along the same as any other history, lore or tradition.

I am frank to tell you that many superstitions I do actually believe in and cannot tell you just why. (*Dial*, September 1949)

Superstitions are merely a record. . . . They are part of the background of our interesting childhood. Often they are told just for fun because many of them are too ridiculous for words. But they are recorded and preserved and carried along the same as any other history, lore or tradition.

. . . My great granny wouldn't start a garment on Friday, wouldn't button a garment before it was tried on, wouldn't plant a cedar tree, wouldn't cut a baby's fingernails before it was one year old. All of these were supposed to bring on some calamity. (*Dial*, September 1949)

Hair cut in the dark of the moon produces baldness.

To get rid of freckles, smear the blood of a white hen on your face, count to fifty, then wash it off and the freckles will come with it; or get up before sun-up on May Day and wash your face in dew.

Don't comb your hair in the morning before you dress your feet or you will be an old maid. (*SDN*, June 7, 1941)

Don't throw hair combings in the yard. If a bird finds them and weaves them in her nest you will lose your mind.

It was considered bad luck for friends to go on different sides when passing a tree, to step over a broom, or allow anyone to sweep under your feet. (*SDN*, October 7, 1939, and June 1, 1940)

Locusts: A Sign of War

You all know it is a locust year. Some say the seventeen-year locust, and some the thirteen-year. People say you can't sleep for them out in the country, howling like little tree-frogs. . . . Fannabelle Ford Nickel writes me about the locusts, and she tells me something interesting which has escaped most observers. They have "W" in their wings this year, which means war, as any good old Ozarker will tell you. Well, whether or not, let's pray till we split the heavens, that it be not fulfilled—but well I remember the big locust year of the Spanish–American War. They had the "W" in their wings, and I haven't seen one since.[2] (*SNL*, June 4, 1933)

Many Are Interested in Our Superstitions and Granny Remedies

So many of my readers, and people who come into the Ozarks to tour or to live, ask me about Ozark superstitions or "granny remedies." These things are old; they have tenacious roots in the soil of our age-old civilization; and they are interesting. . . . So I will give some of the old remedies.

Now you all know that we think soot or cobwebs stop bleeding. A bag of "fiddity"[3] as we call it, hung around the neck prevents measles, mumps, etc. Amber necklaces cure or prevent goiter. They used to call it "big-neck," and you will find it listed in very old doctor books by that name. Rubbing a greasy dishrag over the baby's face stops convulsions. Piercing the ears aids weak eyes, and they used to make them intentionally sore for weeks by putting in a black thread and turning the thread around every morning. What kept a lot of folks from dying of infection puzzles me, only that you do not die of things as easily as you think, unless you are scared.

Nutmeg worn around the neck prevented colic in babies and indigestion in adults. A coin held under the upper lip and a cold key dropped down the back of the neck stopped nosebleed. Hiccoughs were cured by taking nine sips of water. People everywhere do that to this day. Putting on the baby's clothes feet first always, to make him grow; and cutting his fingernails makes him a thief! Wearing the kneecap of a sheep on the calf of the leg prevented terrible leg cramps. A pan of water under the bed stopped night sweats. My father tried that faithfully when he had TB. It didn't work!

Wearing a rattlesnake belt prevented lumbago. Snake oil or fish-worm oil or skunk fat rubbed into the joints for inflammation. That is good yet. A warm woolen sock or stocking round the throat for sore throat. I've suffered that as a kid. . . .

There are a thousand others, but I don't recall them now. That is enough to start you out as a good granny doctor, and at that, you may have a lot of success! If you fail, console yourself that the dear MDs and the X-rays and the rubbin' doctors fail now and then also! (*SNL*, March 1, 1936)

Granny Signs
Carl B. Ike[4]

> Grandma says, when the fire won't burn,
> Or butter won't come in the old dash-churn,
> When the wind blows shrill down the ol' rain spout,
> You better be good, for there's a spook about!
>
> My Grandma says, when her j'ints git sore,
> Till she can't get about like she did 'afore,
> But hobbles along on her ol' bent cane,
> "You can jist look out, for hit's gonna rain!"
>
> My Gran'ma, shucks—she can cure more ills
> With her skunk grease ile, an' her home made pills,
> Than the doctor can stop in a week, I'll bet—
> Fer she doctors me, an' I hain't dead yet!
> (*SDN*, June 7, 1941)

Treated with Granny Remedies

Born in 1871, Mrs. A. S. Johnson, West Plains, Missouri, shared her stories:

> There were six of us "youngens." . . . We lived in a big chinked and daubed log house with a dirt floor. We had to be doctored with granny remedies. When a kid had colic, maw would take a teaspoon of her own breast milk and paw would fill his old pipe and smoke in the milk and put it down us. I guess it helped for the sick baby would go to sleep. . . .
>
> When we had a stone bruise paw would go out and peel the outside bark from a big black oak—take the inside and boil it down then thicken it with wheat bran and put that on hot. Then the swelling would go just like nothing in one day. Chewing gum was unheard of. We always had plenty of rich pine in the yard and we would clean off the outside of a piece, stand it in front of the fireplace and let the wax run out on a dish or something. And the good old turpentine we chewed and swallowed left us free of stomach worms.
>
> We all had the measles at once and never had a doctor. All just drank spring water out of a gourd and hot mullein tea. (*SDN*, April 11, 1942)

Stopping Bleeding

A druggist in this city says this about stopping nosebleed:

> An old lady told me when I was a young man, "When your nose gets to bleedin' jest drop as many drops of blood into a bottle as you are years old. Cork the bottle up tight and hang it in the chimney. Your nose will stop bleedin' and will never bleed any more as long as the bottle hangs there." (*SDN*, March 11, 1941)

Many Believed Bleeding Could Be
Stopped by Reciting Scripture and Charms

Here is the charm: walk to the setting sun; draw a circle in your hand and make a cross in the middle; then repeat the Bible verse 6, from Ezekiel 16, "When I passed by thee, and saw thee polluted in thy own blood, I said unto thee when thou was in thy blood, Live." A woman may tell the charm to a man, and a man may tell the charm to a woman, but never to one of the same gender. (McCord Personal Papers[5])

People Who Had "the Power"

Today a West Plains reader writes this in regard to the charm for stopping blood—one of the oldest charms in the Ozarks.

> I'm backing you up in your statement that some people have that power to stop bleeding. My grandmother had it; at least three other people (she never told me their names) had it. I remember asking her once years ago about it, but all she told me was that she had the power to pass it on to three other people. I can remember the phone ringing—someone who was bleeding profusely. And I can see her yet very clearly walking out the path to the barn, to be alone, with her Bible under her arm. She would be gone for perhaps fifteen minutes and in a few minutes someone would call and report the bleeding stopped. Your statement is true, May. I know, for I've seen! (*SDN*, July 23, 1940)

Otto Rayburn Saw the Charm's Cure

Otto Rayburn, the editor and wizard of *Arcadian Life*, comes across with a mighty interesting communication:

> Now about the blood-letting charm. It really works. We have a neighbor here who can do it. Our 11-year-old son had a severe case of bleeding recently and we were unable to stop it by ordi-

nary methods. We told our neighbor and he asked the boy's full name, went out into the yard and repeated a few words (we couldn't hear them). And lo and behold the bleeding stopped. I do not know how to explain such things but they DO happen. (*SDN*, July 23, 1940)

Was It Faith Healing?

The remedies and lore still come in. They do not come from hearsay, but from the people themselves who have actually known and experienced strange things. We speak of these old things as silly and imaginary and cuckoo and ignorant. . . . But I am telling you that we are dealing with forces we know not of, and maybe our old ancestors, unlettered but sincere, searching for physical help, touched forces that you and I know not of. Mrs. A. V. Hair of Mountain Grove, Missouri, writes,

> My sister lifted a pan of fat from the oven and tipped it and was badly burned on the wrist and frantic with pain. She went at once to a neighbor lady who "used" for it, and she got relief immediately. I have seen cataract and erysipelas[6] cured, and I had quite a goiter cured about 40 years ago. All these things are done in the name of God. These faith healers were very common when I was a child and nobody thought anything of it.

I am glad you brought out that word "using." That was what they called it when I was a child. I remember Mag Burke. . . . She would always say, "I used for Mr. So-and-So and the lump went away right off." (*SDN*, August 10, 1940)

Hieroscopy

Mary Elizabeth Mahnkey writes me a very interesting thing which puts me to thinking:

The charm and "conjure" stories have been pretty grand. Here's something else—a word I chanced upon: "hieroscopy." It meant fortune telling by entrails of animals and may have given foundation to many old remedies, as a mole's skin against your breast to prevent swelling and like troubles. So many chilled and suffered when nursing babies. A mouse's head tied around the baby's neck prevented certain ills. Angleworms placed in a bottle, set in the sun soon liquefied, and this was a sure cure for rheumatism.

This angle worm oil, Mrs. Mahnkey, was used for runners, prize fighters, etc., in my girlhood, in all training. Maybe yet, for all I know. And what about carrying a rabbit's foot? And the old remedy of shooting a hoot owl and binding it on the sick one's breast for pneumonia or "lung fever" as it was called.

The Indians killed a buffalo or other large animal and stripped it clean as a whistle and immediately put anyone dying of chills or lung fever inside the animal for days. Often saved them. Very vital blood warmth coming from natural life sources. It is all very strange. (*SDN*, August 13, 1940)

Blood Cured Her Shingles

My correspondent, Anna Munro, Rosedale Farm, Imboden, Arkansas, writes,

> I had the shingles years ago. All remedies failed to give relief until we tried the blood of a chicken. We were told to use a black cat, but a neighbor said to use a black chicken. We could not find an all black chicken at the time, anywhere, so we used a black one somewhat speckled.
>
> They laid me on a bunch of newspapers spread out to catch the surplus blood. Then they chopped off the chicken's head and let the blood run on the eruption. It was from the small of my back and down one leg to a little below the knee—very painful,

swollen, and a solid eruption all around my leg. They spread the warm blood to cover it all.

This was one night at bedtime. I slept restfully and awoke next morning to find the soreness, swelling and inflammation all gone. The skin of my leg peeled off and came clean. There were faint spots for a while, but I never suffered any after the hot blood was applied. This is true in the smallest detail. But I have never seen anyone with shingles who would try it. (*SDN*, March 11, 1941)

Mad Stones[7]

Mrs. Mahnkey suggests that I have you folks write and tell me all you know about the mad stone and its use. This is passing, and we must preserve this great old remedy or superstition or what you may call it. As for me, when I was a child I saw too much done by old Mr. Carney's mad stone over on Flat Creek to call it a superstition! . . . This belongs to our folklore and tradition and is very important. (*SNL*, February 17, 1935)

The medical fraternity laughs at the mad stone and considers it in the line of superstition, along with carrying a buckeye for rheumatism and stump-water to remove warts. But this is a matter which may be argued with some degree of pathological truth, I firmly believe. We have the great discovery of Pasteur now for the treatment of hydrophobia,[8] and we do not need the faithful old mad stone; but you must remember that our forefathers did not have those things.

Parthenia G. Wilson of Marionville, a pioneer daughter, writes me about her little brown dog and a beautiful white cat in the winter of '88. She was devoted to them and they to her:

> One morning Bulger, the dog, was shivering and slobbering and father thought he was choked on a bone. He pried his mouth open and one of his teeth sank into my father's thumb, making a small, round, deep hole that bled freely. When I came home

from school, Bulger was killed, and neighbors were advising my father to go to the mad stone. We were in great grief.

Before we went to bed that night, Mr. Heady of Brighton in Polk County was there with his mad stone, and it was sticking to my father's thumb as if it had been glued there. In a day or two my white cat took sick and was instantly killed, and I was a miserable child. The stone stuck to father's thumb eight days and nights. When it was sticking, it could not be pulled loose. I saw it with my own eyes. When it filled with the green poison, it dropped off of its own accord. It was then boiled in sweet milk and put back. The stone came from the intestines of a white deer. The milk where the stone was boiled was a muddy green. When the stone would come off, it looked a bit dirty, and under a magnifying glass, which we had, there seemed to be green smoke or vapor moving in it. It looked like a small smooth white rock, but under the glass was very porous. People went to that stone for miles on horseback and in farm wagons, and if the stone stuck, they stayed till it would not stick to the wound. Our M.D.'s today laugh at the mad stone, but the doctors then knew the stone would do what they could not do. . . .

One of my father's neighbors, Alvin Killingsworth, lost most of his cattle, hogs, and most of his horses from hydrophobia after the raid of a mad dog before he knew what the disease was. He got an infection in his hand from trying to give them medicine. When they found it was hydrophobia, he went to the same mad stone my father did. Mr. Killingsworth lived several years after, and my father lived to be an old man.

So you see, these Ozarkers know what they are talking about. Cora Pinkley Call[9] of Eureka Springs belongs to a very old pioneer family of the Ozarks. She is exceptionally authoritative in matters of the early ways of Ozarkians. She writes me,

Seeing you are wanting stories concerning the mad stone, I'll give you one—and I can prove it by fifty or more people that

I am telling the plain truth and that it all occurred. About thirty-six years ago when I was a small child, a mad dog came through our part of the country, nine miles south east of Eureka. My sister's father-in-law, known to his neighbors as Uncle Billy Hull, was an old man in his eighties, and almost blind. Early one morning he went to his son's crib to shuck corn. A dog was lying by the crib door, and when he started to enter, it bit him on the hand. The dog then crossed Kings River near by, and went into the Fanning community below, biting stock, dogs and most everything it came to. It went on down into the Walker community several miles below, and bit a man by the name of Moody. It was killed later near there.

Relatives and friends of Uncle Billy tried to get him to let them take him to the mad stone—one of old Mr. Carney's on Flat Creek. He would not hear to it, saying, "I'm an old man and do not have much longer to live—I'd just as leave die that way as any." He had his way. Everything in the country that the dog bit began to take hydrophobia—mules, horses, cows, and hogs. Mr. Moody went to the Carney mad stone. It stuck nine times. He came back home and is living today and his hands bear the mark of the dog's teeth. Uncle Billy died within a half mile of my home. My mother and brothers and father helped nurse him, and everyone who saw him said he died the most horrible death they ever witnessed. It was three months before he went mad. He was fearful to hold and take care of, and during a fit he spat on a sore on the bridge of his son Jim's nose. After his father's death Jim went to the Carney mad stone, but it would not stick. Carney told him it would not bother him, and it never did. Moody is living today on his farm near Kings River, Mo. No, the mad stone is not superstition. If so, how did this happen? Perhaps the world will say "co-incidence," but you will never make the participants in the horrible tragedy believe that. (*SNL*, February 24, 1935)

Caring for the Babies and Children

Lida Wilson Pyles of Pocahontas, Arkansas, sends me some interesting things:

> My mother raised eight children and during the teething period she always made a string of burdock beads for us to wear around our neck. These beads were made by cutting the root of the burdock in small pieces and stringing them on a twine string. This was worn around the baby's neck until the painful process of teething was over, and the little wearer of the beads was always free of teething pains. When the little ones suffer from croup, try pouring some hot water over pokeberries and giving the child about a spoonful of the water. It is well to gather some of these berries when they ripen in the fall and lay them in the sun until they are dry. They can be kept all winter.
>
> The old timers always gave the children sage tea for worms, and it was also used to reduce fever. No one thought of calling a doctor every time a member of the family had an ache or pain. Every family had its own home remedies.
>
> I've heard mother tell many times about me having whooping cough when my baby sister was born. She took it when she was ten days old, and no one thought she could possibly live. A neighbor woman who was a dear old soul and always present in time of need walked away up in Dead Man's Hollow and brought back a little piece of Indian turnip.[10] This was soon grated and mixed with sugar and boiled into syrup and given to the baby. They still say she owes her life to that little piece of Indian turnip.

I can well imagine that it would kill or cure. Did any of you ever try biting into the root of Indian turnip? Hot! (*SDN*, September 6, 1941)

Never make a baby's cap before the baby arrives or you'll have bad luck with the baby. (*SDN*, July 25, 1940)

Be very careful who carries a baby from the house for the first time, for she will be like that person.—Marshall Jones, Marionville, Missouri.[11] (McCord Personal Papers)

The left hind foot of a mole fastened to a yarn string and tied around a baby's neck will cure teething sickness. (*SDN*, October 1, 1940)

Thrush in Children

I had in the column recently about letting a child with the "thrash" (sore mouth) drink water out of a shoe belonging to someone no kin to the child. That was often done, but the chief remedy was to let a posthumous person breathe in the baby's mouth.[12]

I was in Jefferson City recently and ran plump into my friend Forest Smith, state auditor, who never tires of hearing the ways of his boyhood. . . . He told me his father was a posthumous child and all his life he breathed in babies' mouths to cure the "thrash." He said he remembered how he used to hate to crawl out of bed on a cold night and hitch the horse for his daddy to go to some sufferer. He used to wish they had never heard of such a remedy. But his father was kind, and like all early Ozarkian people, rallied at once to any neighbor in distress. You cannot realize the kindness of the people in sickness. They had almost no doctors and they took care of one another. (*SDN*, March 11, 1941)

"Bowel Trouble" and "Summer Complaint" in a Child

A little slice of strong old smokehouse bacon or "middling," as they said, was held in the blue flame from a saucer of burning whiskey. And directly, when the flame died out and the brew had slightly cooled, it was drunk—meat drippings, whiskey and all.

I remember when my oldest child was a baby and had what we called summer complaint. I had tried everything. My father-in-law, Dr. McCord, was a physician. I had fed the child every cereal and was so careful with his diet. An old lady said to me, "Quit them sop feeds! You are ruining that child with sop!" She told me to cut off pure raw bacon, a bit salty, well smoked, and let him suck it and live on it. I did and he got well at once. Then she told me as he recovered to fry chickens in butter and give him the legs only, for the glucose in them. After that I reared my small babies on fried chicken legs! You know, the doctors don't know it all! (*SDN*, August 4, 1938)

Babies Born with a Veil over Their Face

Many people are studying, among superstitions, this interesting one of a "veil over the face." The person was supposed to have supernatural powers. You know the Gypsies carry this superstition to the extreme limit. The supernatural powers may be a fluke, but the "veil" is real, I am told by a physician. It is simply a small extra membrane that sometimes covers the face of a newly born infant and is peeled off with little trouble. It is very thin and lacy looking. Hence it got the name "veil." (*SDN*, January 11, 1942)

Della Dee of West Plains wrote me a grand letter. . . . She tells me that her mother was born with a veil or caul over her face. She could see and know things that we of the common herd pass by.

> Whatever it was, I never knew her to be wrong in her judgment of things and of human character. We spent a few years in the dry southwest and she always told us a few days before when the rain would come. Once we traveled two days without water and mother told us on the morning of the third day that we would come to a stream of water on our left about ten o'clock. Believe it or not, we did that very thing! Father always had some alibi for her uncanny insight—guess work, good luck or something. But I often wonder what this gift might have developed into had it not been ridiculed by him.

I am grateful for that very interesting letter and it is one among many that has told of strange clairvoyant powers or insight of those born with a veil over the face. (*SDN*, June 14, 1941)

Wild Artichoke for "Summer Complaint"

Mrs. Mary Elizabeth Mahnkey told me a story, one of those stories which happen every day in our hills, and out of which she always weaves a flower. A young native, absent in Oklahoma, just recently made a furious drive back to his old home on the ridge in the White River region to dig up wild artichoke to take back and steep the roots into a tea for his sick baby, almost dying with summer complaint. The baby got well. This is the remarkable poem in which Mrs. Mahnkey tells the story of wild artichoke, one of the great old healing herbs of my childhood days in the hills:

Wild Artichoke

The ugly weed—yet, from the bitter root
The old crone brewed a tea that healed a child.
Mystic lore—to vanish with that race
Of ancient wives who understood the wild.
Who knew all weeds and seeds and fragrant soothing herbs,
These granny women of the hills, who knew the cry
When one came wailing through the dark to life,
And did not shrink, when death came stalking high.
Her back is bent with burdens bravely borne,
Her eyes are dim from serving other's need—
Her frail old hands no longer point the way—
Wild Artichoke is but a useless weed!
(*SNL*, August 20, 1933)

Did you ever hear of sleeping with crawdad pinchers in bed with you for stomach trouble? (*SDN*, April 21, 1942)

The Rheumatism

Now here is a very strange letter from C. A. Dickenson of Houston, Missouri, about the "potato."

> I notice in your column today you mention the old superstition of carrying a potato in your pocket for the rheumatism, and I would like to relate my experience. I spent forty years teaching school, and something like twenty years ago I was attending Teachers' Institute and had a severe attack of rheumatism in my shoulder and could not put my coat on without help from someone. One night several of us were sitting in the lobby of the hotel where we were boarding and my rheumatism was discussed and an old man sitting there said, "There is no need to have rheumatism if you will just carry a small Irish potato in your pocket." We all laughed but I said I would try it. I selected a potato about the size of a small hen egg and placed it in my pocket. The next morning I dressed without help and in a very few days it was entirely gone and in twenty years it has not returned. I carried that potato for about four years and it never rotted but became as hard as wood. I have told a number of persons of my experience and they have tried the cure with the same results. Of course I cannot believe in the cure but these are the facts. I am almost 72.

So there you are! How are you going to get around that? I have always heard that if the cure works the potato will become hard and dry up. If not, the potato will rot. (*SDN*, January 17, 1942)

How to Assure Strong Teeth

I think this one would be worth trying:

> My grandmother, Aunt Polly Hively, lived until almost ninety. She had all her teeth but one. When she died, all sound as could

be. She said she had the toothache when young just once. An old lady told her to go to the woods and find the jawbone of a horse, hold her hands behind her, get down on her knees and pick the jawbone up with her teeth, get up and walk backwards with the bone in her mouth, keeping her hands behind her, and she would never have the toothache again. She said she did this and it worked, for she never had the toothache again, or a bad tooth.—Elizabeth Stone, Calico Rock, Arkansas. (*SDN*, August 20, 1940)

Didn't Know about Appendicitis

There's a disease they didn't have in the old days, or at least they didn't know what to call it: Appendicitis. They called it "information of the innords"—and sometimes they just called it "information." And they didn't operate for it—they didn't know about it. Reminds me of a story: A man called the doctor frantically over the phone and told him to hurry to his wife; she had appendicitis and would have to be operated on right away! The doctor said, "See here now, let's understand this, I operated on your wife two years ago for appendicitis! We don't operate for appendicitis twice!" And the fellow said, "Yes, but a man can marry twice, can't he?" (*Dial*, January 1947)

The Chills

My, how we used to chill all winter down on the James River! Will I ever forget the chills? Horrible things—I would be running rings around the doctors now if I should have even one of the things. And we paid little attention to them! One good thing was that we got to go home from school when the shaking set in. I had to just run down the hill to home and Mother put me to bed with a good warm tea. Do you remember "Grove's Chill Tonic?" And "Smith's Cure" and quinine and the old wahoo tea, and then arsenic for chills came around and everybody took that, and it made you so pretty and white, but you almost folded up! (*SDN*, March 11, 1941)

Aunt Tabitha says to cure chills you tie knots in a silk thread. A knot for every chill you had, then bury the thread under the eaves of the house or barn. By the time it rots, the chills will be no more. It works on children over a year old, only. And someone must do the tying who is not related by blood or marriage to the patient. (*SDN*, July 9, 1942)

Many Strange Old Remedies

Now here are some old-time remedies that go in our folklore:

> Saffron tea used to be a common remedy to "break out" the measles. Also they used "sheep tea." Gather a quart of fresh sheep droppings, boil in water, strain, sweeten with molasses and drink.
>
> Whiskey mixed with strong sassafras tea boiled almost to jelly was given for chills. For itch, they took pokeroot boiled in water, making a strong tea in which they bathed. For croup, mix kerosene with sorghum molasses and give a teaspoon at a dose, at intervals.—"The son of one of the original Bald Knobbers."

I have known of all the remedies you state. The "sheep-nanny tea" as they called it has always been a joke with "outsiders" or "furriners," and they did not believe we Ozarkians ever used it. Well I should say we did! (*SDN*, June 21, 1941)

E. R. Kildow of Lebanon, Missouri, sends me some interesting superstitions:

> A crust of bread carried in the pocket was considered a safe-guard against danger. Two sneezes were considered wholesome, and three signified that a convalescent was fit to be turned out of the bed. To get rid of jaundice, eat nine lice on a piece of

bread and butter. To destroy a wen,[13] touch the place with a dead man's hand. Goiter or "neck swelling" as our pioneers called it was believed to be destroyed the same way. To live long let your house be filled with spiders.

Now that one about eating nine lice on bread—I heard that almost forty years ago when a young girl, and I remember how it revolted me. I have had it sent into the column about a dozen times, but always hesitated to print it. But it was actually an old belief. I do not know any instance of its ever being tried. It was chicken lice "the way I heer'd it," and that wouldn't be quite so bad! B-r-r-r-r-! Anyone want to try?

I never see anyone with the jaundice any more. You remember they used to call it "yaller janders." Isn't it queer how many old ailments that were once common have almost disappeared? I remember an old saloon keeper in our town had the "yaller janders" from whiskey and died a horrible death. "Hobnail liver" I think they called it. They used to have slight "janders" from chilling so much—kids and adults. But that would clear up. (*SDN*, September 9, 1941)

Mrs. Magie Kreitzer, Mountain Grove, Missouri, writes me some of the most intriguing old remedies yet. She says they were handed down from her grandmother and an old neighbor that knew every herb and its use, although she could not read or write:

> For measles to break out, they made tea from sheep manure. To keep mumps from falling into the lower body, a red yarn string was saturated in the manure of swine and tied around the neck like a strand of beads. For jaundice (they called it the "yaller janders") angle worms were dug and fried in their own grease and this given to the sick.
>
> Skunk oil rendered from the fat of a skunk would cure the croup. (It doesn't have an odor and is the most penetrating oil known.) Sage tea and honey was the remedy this old lady used for sore throat. Onions roasted and the juice extracted and honey added would cure babies' colds and act as a laxative. (I used to do that, too, Mrs. Krietzer.)

Salve to cure any kind of a sore was made from bittersweet and tallow. Onion poultice was used on the breast to break up pneumonia. A buckeye with a hole bored through it and tied around the neck so it will rest in the hollow of the stomach will cure boils and carbuncles. An Irish potato carried in one's pocket will cure "ketch in the back." (*SDN*, September 17, 1940)

Mrs. P. J. G. of Aurora, Missouri, sent me a letter with old remedies she remembered:

A yarn string tied around the toe when the under-skin is cracked. (Ouch! How it still hurts!) Dried puff-balls (a kind of toad stool) powdered into a cut to stop bleeding. I saw that used once when my father cut his foot badly with an axe. Red stemmed smart-weed tea for diarrhea. (It works, too.) Tea made from the dried inner lining of a chicken's gizzard to stop vomiting.

Peach bark tea, always scraping UP the limb, to check the bowels. Scraped down the limb to loosen them. Soot in a cut to stop bleeding. Red clay on a sting to draw out swelling. (*SDN*, June 7, 1941)

Mr. Harry N. Force says he gathered old cures while in the drug business at Gainesville, Missouri:

To cure neuralgia, dress the left foot every morning first. For ringworm: Go to a teakettle of boiling water; rub your thumb in a circle the size of the ringworm on the inside of the lid of the teakettle. And then around the ringworm. Do the same with the forefinger, then the thumb again. Do this with all the fingers on that hand, alternating with the thumb every time. When finished, go away and do not look back at the teakettle. (*SDN*, October 1, 1940)

And More . . .

I'll never find out why Ozark superstitions interest people more than anything else. But that follows me wherever I go . . . so I dug out a list of some very, very strange ones. . . .

The old belief that no snake dies until the sun goes down. That isn't true, of course, and yet so many people will believe it to their dying day. That dogs' tails and walnut trees draw lightning. Both of those could be possible. That thunder sours milk and kills the chickens in setting eggs. That teeth should never be pulled when the sign of the zodiac is in the "head." Too much danger of bleeding. That the best whetstone rock is always found on the north side of a mountain at an angle of forty-five degrees. That transplanted trees should always be set in exactly the same position, side for side, as they were taken up. That one always works, and of course, has reasons. That the seventh son of the seventh son has miraculous powers. And can anyone tell me of a seventh son of a seventh son?

That snakes will not enter a garden where gourds grow. That hens will not lay in a field where there are potatoes. That to sleep with the moon in your face will induce insanity. That scrambled owl eggs will cure drunkenness. That hair cut in the dark of the moon produces baldness. (*Dial*, August 1946)

Old Herb and Granny Teas

Mrs. Mahnkey writes to ask me if I have ever discussed the old herb and granny teas. How many do you know? There was wahoo teas for chills. The chewing of a bit of yellow pocoon (or golden seal) root constantly in the mouth for a year will cure almost any stomach trouble that is curable. Then there was mullein tea for colds and asthma. There was senna tea for laxative and all around grand medicine. They used to call it "senny" tea . . . There was white oak bark tea for stomach trouble—white oak bark (tannin) is used in drug stores now. And there was red pepper tea to relieve all sorts of cramps. (Never use black pepper. It is a spice, not a pepper.)

There was slippery elm tea for bowel inflammations (they used to call it "informations"). Horehound tea mixed with honey was excellent for coughs. Drink sassafras tea to purify and thin the blood in the spring after the winter's meat eating and lack of exercise. (*SDN*, December 3, 1940; and *SDN*, August 16, 1941)

Skillet Bark Tea

Granny knows about "skillet bark tea." Just scrape the bottom of her old skillet and tie the scrapings up in a rag and bile 'em. It will cure fainting spells. (*SNL*, November 5, 1932)

Axe under the Bed to Promote Healing

Dear old Aunt Susan Meeks down home—peace be to her soul—used to visit me. . . . One time I was ill and suffering quite a bit. Unknown to me, she had gone out to the woodpile and slipped the axe under my bed. (If the sick one knows about the axe, it will not work.) Every hour or so she would step up to the bed and say, "Are you airy bit better?" I wasn't and I would say, "No, Aunt Susan, I don't believe I am." She would seem puzzled and sort of whipped. I wondered about it. Finally, she gave it up and walked into my room and dragged an axe from under the bed. "Well," she said, "I put this axe under here. If it hain't a doin' you airy bit of good I'll take it back out to the woodpile. Charley might need it to bust up kindlin." So ended the axe deal! (*SDN*, June 23, 1938)

Warts

Mrs. Christiana Robertson, of Springfield, writes,

> My daughter-in-law had a number of warts taken from her hand by an old man who rubbed them with a piece of meat, saying some words. They disappeared. He told her to bury the meat where no dog could get it. (*SDN*, April 26, 1941)

Orpha Vaughan Haddock of Seneca, Missouri, sends me another interesting bit on . . . the hillbilly methods of charming warts away:

> Rub the wart with a small piece of onion, throw the onion over your right shoulder and walk away without looking back to see where it lit.
>
> Wipe warts well with a greasy dishrag, then hide the rag under a rock, being careful to replace the rock in the exact position you found it.
>
> Tie a woolen string around the wart. Spit on wart and rub the spit in well. Remove string and burn it when no one is looking.
>
> Kill a toad and take out the entrails. Rub the entrails on the wart, and then place them under a rock. When removing warts by any of these methods be sure not to let anyone know about it or the charm will fail. There used to be a "wart witch" in our community. She would tie a string around the wart, mumble a few magic words, remove the string and tell you to bury it where no one would find it. If the string were not disturbed for nine days, the wart would disappear. She once used her magic on a wart on my little finger.

Well, Orpha, you forgot to wash warts in stump water, or to have someone kiss the wart and "wish" it off. Another thing is to let a child who was born after its father died (a posthumous child, you know) rub a ring three times around the wart with his finger and walk backwards out of your presence, saying nothing. This is also said to remove tumors, wens and all sorts of lumps. (*SNL*, October 25, 1936)

Another cure was to cut as many notches in a stick as there were warts and bury the stick. When it rotted, the warts would disappear. (*SDN*, August 20, 1940)

Take three grains of corn, go to a place where the road forks into three roads. Put a grain of corn in each road and place a little rock over each. The warts will leave you and go to the first person knocking those rocks off the grains. (*SDN*, October 1, 1940)

Pierce each wart enough to make it bleed. Rub a grain of corn in the blood and feed to a goose! The warts will disappear. (*SDN*, December 7, 1940)

Cures from "Aunt Tabitha"

Harry N. Force, veteran druggist of this city, says Old Aunt Tabitha, whom he used to know, was a real hill character. Here are some of her cures:

To Cure a Burn, or "Take Out Fire"

Repeat to yourself: "Two little angels came from Heaven. One brought fire and the other frost. Go out fire and come in frost" and blow on the burn just as you say the last word. A man must not teach a man how this is done, nor women teach a woman, or they will lose the charm. But it is all right to teach one of the opposite sex.

To Cure a Bunion

Go to a dusty place in a road. Find a flat stone, take off your shoe and rub the stone on the bunion three times and say, "bunion, bunion, if you be one, leave my foot and take this stone." Then cover the stone in the dust in the road and by the time the stone is uncovered the bunion will be gone.

To Cure a Boil or "Risin"

In the words of the party who told me this: "You jest run your finger round the edge of the risin' and then make a cross with the end of your finger right in the middle of it. Then put your finger in the dust on the ground and touch the center of the cross with the end of your dusty finger. If the risin' ain't too fur gone it will go away inside of twelve hours, and iffin it is too fur gone, it'll come to a head right away and the core will come out plum easy like. You've got to believe in it though or it won't work." And by the way, that "you've got to believe in it" was always attached to all these "cures."

If You Stick a Nail in Your Foot

Pull the nail out and stick it into a piece of tallow just as far as it had been stuck into your foot and the foot will heal right away.

To Cure a Sore Throat

Get the refuse in the nest from a mockingbird that is setting on three eggs (no more, no less). Dissolve it in a glass of lukewarm water and gargle it.

To Cure a Sty

You go to the forks of a road and say, "Sty, sty, leave my eye and catch the next one passing by." (This is rather a selfish treatment, but after you have had twenty-one on one eye as a girl did I went to school with, you might be willing for somebody else to take them a while!)

So now I have given you all this good medical advice today, and it hasn't cost you a penny. And nobody gets more fun out of this than my physician friends. And they do not prosecute me at all for practicing medicine. In fact, they are threatening to take me into the medical society and give me a diploma! (*SDN*, July 9, 1942)

Beliefs about Cures Were Often from Scripture

Religion ruled in the hearts of the superstitious—a looking to a higher power, a mysterious one. So many old cures were done by making the cross, you will notice.

During my grand visit with Mrs. Mahnkey, we got to talking about how the cross came into so many superstitions, probably from our Catholic colonists who are indeed very faithful to the cross. And I love that symbol.

For instance, from childhood we all have said "cross my heart" when we want to utter a truth. Cross our fingers if we have to consent to something we are not quite conscience-free about. If you leave home and have to turn back for something, you make a cross in the road with your foot. After the scrubbing and mopping was done, our old folks used to cross the mop and broom to keep out witches. Mrs. Mahnkey says one old woman who used to clean for her mother did this until it made her shiver.

And there are hundreds of things in which the cross is involved. Peculiar symbolic beliefs of our pioneer ancestors.

In many superstitions, I note that the person must "not look back." I wonder if Lot's wife's calamity had anything to do with that? (*SDN*, October 1, 1940; and *SDN*, July 9, 1942)

Tansy Leaves

A dear old lady reader out at Dunnegan wants to know if anyone has an old-fashioned tansy bed. If so, she wants a root this fall to start herself a bed. She says that some of your tansy leaves in the cupboard will keep red ants away.

In the old days no one was without a tansy bed. It smelled so spicy and the leaves were so beautiful and always green and it was used for more things than most any herb. (*SDN*, August 30, 1941)

Now about Abortions

Girls used to use tansy leaves soaked in buttermilk to whiten their skin. But quietly, when they went to Grandma Melton's to get the tansy (for she had the finest bed in town) they were very particular to tell her what it was for. (*SDN*, December 3, 1940)

I recall that no woman ever drank cedar berry tea without being "talked about!" Men might take it for chills—but never women! (*SDN*, August 16, 1941)

Chaw of Tobacco on Bee, Wasp or Bumblebee Sting

One time when I was about ten, I was out at Aunt Jane Crouch's on Dry Creek. A wasp stung me over the right eye and there was no one there to chew the tobacco (as they didn't think it effective unless chewed). So Aunt Jane chewed it up herself and she had never done such a thing. It stopped the pain instantly. Of course, tobacco is an "anti-spasmodic," chemists say. And nicotine kills some sorts of poison, although it is itself a poison. (*SDN*, October 12, 1940)

Catarrh

They used to have an old remedy for catarrh when I was a kid. (Now called sinus trouble. Like a lot of other things, it has gone to college too.) They would go out to the very shady side of the house and find the mouldiest ground they could. They took a hoe and dug a little, and then they knelt down on the ground and made a cross in the middle of each palm. Then they inhaled that dirt, or rather just smelled it nine times with each nostril. They did this nine mornings, then skipped three mornings, then another nine mornings and so on until they had done it twenty-seven mornings. They were supposed by then to be well of catarrh. And if you only knew the old people who said they were cured! I don't suppose they were liars, were they? (*Dial*, October 1947)

Typhoid Fever, Epilepsy and Asthma

Dr. Whit Burnes of Buckhart, Missouri, gives me his experiences with Ozarkian superstitions.

> Many years ago I was called to see two sisters who had typhoid fever. While I was making the diagnosis, an old lady came in and told me she hated to do anything against my treatment, but

if I would go to a dogwood tree and peel the bark off and make a tea of it they would be cured. And she told me, "Be sure you peel the bark up. It raises your patients. If you peel it down, they will go right down to the grave."

A neighbor woman here told me that her brother was cured completely of epilepsy by feeding him a colt's tongue.

A man claimed to have cured himself of a very bad case of asthma by tying a live frog on his throat and leaving it there till it died. "It completely absorbed the disease." (*SDN*, August 24, 1940)

How to Overcome Sleep Problems

Just stuff cloth into the keyhole to stop unpleasant dreams. Can't sleep? Get up and turn your shoes around. This drives away the witches. Also be sure you sleep with your head toward the north so your body moves with the rotation of the earth. (McCord Personal Papers)

A Little Fun with These Cures

I hear that Engineer Reed at St. John's Hospital had the hiccoughs and he said, "Fire the doctors and let May McCord give me a granny remedy!" He didn't know I would get the word! So here it is, engineer-man:

Drop three grains of corn into a glass of water and name each for the best friends you have (what say you name one for me?). Set the glass on a shelf or where it will be over your head. Let alone and you'll get well of the hiccoughs! (*SDN*, March 19, 1942)

Doctors Were Interested in Granny Cures

In 1944 I spoke to a doctors' post-graduate class at a university on Ozark granny remedies. I never saw any group of people so interested as those doctors! They wanted this background as a history of medicine. "Primitive materia medica," they called it. . . .

I told the doctors about the old remedy for child asthma. In the old days they called it "phthisic" (pronounced tizzic). You took the child out to a hickory tree and you bored a hole in the tree with an auger, at exactly the height of the child. Then you cut a lock of the child's hair and poked it in the hole, made a cork of hickory wood, drove it in and stopped up that lock of hair. When the child grew two or three inches taller than the hole, the asthma or "tizzic" would be gone. And usually it was! When I used to write my column of Hillbilly Heartbeats for the Springfield paper, several people wrote me that they were cured that way.

When I told this to the physicians in the university, a doctor got up and explained it this way. He said the whole procedure was dramatic to the child and enlisted his complete faith, and faith was ninety percent of the cure of disease anyway. . . . He said the child so fully expected to be cured, as they took him out every few weeks and measured him up to that tree, that the cure was worked by mental suggestion. (*Dial*, December 1947)

If All Else Failed, We Bought Tonic at the Old Medicine Show

I do wish we had a good old medicine show. Uncle Allen Oliver (who got himself married lately) is my soul mate on the medicine show question. He wishes, too, that life were just one long medicine show.

I wish we had that grand old show of old "Kickapoo Indian Sagwa!" Everybody in the whole Ozarks remembers that. I was talking to Dr. Hammon recently whose father is a fine Ozark pioneer, and he said his daddy used to buy "sagwa." Many's the bottle we have taken internally ("infernally" as the old woman said), rubbed on, smelled and gargled.

Every year the medicine man used to come to our little town and hold a show. He brought with him old Chief Sagwa of the Kickapoos, who was supposed to have made the medicine. Old Sagwa danced in all his feathers and war paint and shook a gourd or horn or something. He grunted and wouldn't talk. . . . Yes, I'll be pinin' for the good old medicine shows! (*SDN*, September 14, 1939)

CHAPTER 11

Signs and Gardens

How's the Spring Fever? Got the Garden Itch yet?

Dial, March 1950

. . . .

For generations rural Ozarkers planted gardens sowed crops, and tended livestock according to moon phases and zodiac signs. Even those whose religious faith would ordinarily cause them to dismiss other superstitions as the devil's work could put great stock in planting potatoes in the dark of the moon or weaning a calf when the sign was in the knees. One family's dry moon might be another family's wet moon, but it was inherited knowledge passed down through the generations and thus not to be taken lightly. May appreciated that many of her readers still held firmly to the old ways, and she was able to mine the topic's mystery and occasional humor in her inimitable way.

. . . .

Planting

A good old Hillbilly planted his things by the moon, and you couldn't change me on that—if the moon controls the tides (and nobody denies that) why couldn't it control planting? The way the scientist tests a fact is to prove it so many times in the laboratory that it leaves not a shadow of a doubt. Just so have our old pioneers tested and proven moon planting. (*Dial*, February 1947)

This is where you are going to get wised up and it isn't going to cost you a penny. . . . Maybe some laughs with it: Planting superstitions!

As for me, I'm a "moon planter" and you couldn't change me. What the hillman calls the "dark of the moon" is the period from the full moon to the new, the decrease or waning of the moon. The other half of the lunar season, from the new moon to the full, when the moon is waxing or increasing in size, is known as the light of the moon. So says that wizard authority, Vance Randolph. And I was "fetched up" to believe all of it.

Vegetables that grow underground, such as potatoes, turnips, beets, onions and the like, our Ozark ancestors planted in the dark of the moon. Otherwise they "all went to tops." Beans, peas, tomatoes and such that bear their edible crop above ground were planted in the light of the moon.

You used to get calendars and almanacs everywhere, and they always had all the "signs." You planted potatoes "when the sign's in the feet"[1] . . . and all farmers were agreed that potatoes should be dug in the light of the moon or they would rot.

March 17, Saint Patrick's Day, was a great day to plant potatoes, and is yet. February is too soon. You remember that they didn't plant potatoes and onions close together because they said, "an onion makes a 'tater cry its eyes out!" And truly, there is something queer about planting onions and potatoes too close together. They never do as well.

My folks planted beans when the sign was "in the arms."[2] Many people won't plant beans until "after the first whippoorwill hollers."

Plant them in Virgo and you will get fine large plants but no beans or blooms at all. And I think I told you before that you simply must plant your beans in the morning and not in the afternoon. I was planting a row of beans in the afternoon one time and a good friend came by and, I'll declare, she nearly had to go to bed sick over my planting. And I scarcely raised a bean! I told Miss Ada that she "hexed" my beans. Bunch beans should be sowed on Good Friday. Many think, however, that this day is too early in our Ozarks, but it didn't used to be. The seasons have changed so.

Folks used to have a horror of burning seed bean hulls or pea hulls, because you wouldn't get a crop if you did. Perhaps that comes from the old idea we were all brought up on, that you mustn't destroy anything that could be eaten by man or beast. We would never throw an apple core or peeling in the fireplace. They said you were "feeding the devil."

Cucumbers had to be planted May first, before sunup, to protect the vines against insects. Also, cucumbers planted by a woman never amounted to anything. "Don't let your old womarn plant the pickles!"

Prune fruit trees in the light of the moon, without fail. There is an old belief that sprouts cut on the ninth and tenth of May will never come back. Try it. To deaden trees, do it between the first and twentieth of August.

They said it took a fool to raise gourds and a jealous person to raise onions, a high-tempered person to raise peppers, and radishes had to be planted, my father said, kneeling on the ground.

Many old timers said that watermelons should be planted May 10, Sunday or not, and before sunrise. People stick to February 14 for planting lettuce, to this day. Vance Randolph said that one time, when Valentine's Day fell on Sunday, the people at Kingston, Arkansas, got up before daylight to plant their lettuce so as not be seen "breaking the Sabbath!" Valentine's Day is a wonderful day to plant peas for food and sweet peas for flowering. There was an old rhyme, "Sow your turnips the 25th of July and you'll make a crop, wet or dry." One time Booth Campbell of Cane Hill, Arkansas, was discussing turnips with some of us. "Poor man's grub," we were saying, and Booth said, "Well, turnips beats nothin'!" As for me, I am very fond of turnips but they have to be good turnips or they don't even "beat nothin'"!

You know they always say that corn must be planted when the oak leaves are as big as a squirrel's ears. Some planted corn right after the first doves cooed in the spring. An old belief handed down to us in these Ozarks by the Indians was to plant six grains of corn in each hill.

> One for the cut-worm, one for the crow,
> One for the blackbird and three to grow.

A good farmer never had his hair cut during the oats growing season. It ruined the crop! Never laugh while planting corn or the kernels will be irregular.

Lots of folks buried old shoes at the roots of peach trees, and they often drove nails into peach trees. Randolph said he could never find out the reason. (Ozarkians didn't tell everything they knew.) He said he tried to find out the reason from one old man and he growled, "Them's family matters!"

They used to say that a season that was good for tomatoes was bad for walnuts. And there is a belief in southern Missouri that if a season is good for a big yield of peaches, then corn, wheat and oats will be scabby.

Otto Rayburn found many old timers who believed if it rained on June 20, the grapes would fall off the vines.

And so, on and on I could go. These strange superstitions—they must have come about someway, maybe from much experimenting, the most reasonable of them, just as facts are discovered in the test tubes of laboratories. As Rayburn says, "We have no apologies for them." You may take them or leave them. Anyway, they go along with the history of civilization and the traditions of a race.

So plant your garden, go fishin' by the signs, and good luck to you!

With heaps and oodles of love—May. (*Dial*, March 1949; *Dial*, March 1950; and *Dial*, February 1948)

How to Predict a Good Crop

I had a chap help with my garden the other day. He was a real fellow from the "boot-heel" of Missouri down swamp-east where they grow cotton. He was full of lore. He told me I must break open a persimmon seed left over from last year and if we are going to have a good crop year, there will be a perfect spoon in the seed. If not, there will be a knife and fork. He found a seed while gardening but it was too decayed to tell. (*SDN*, April 21, 1942)

Mrs. Sarah Michael of Lebanon, Missouri, sent me a seed split open. There in its bed, looking as if it were laid in dark velvet is as beautiful a small white spoon as any artist could paint! There is a frosted film over it and it looks as if you were looking at the little spoon through some lovely glass. The whole mechanism and the beauty of the thing simply got me. . . . And so this means a great crop year! (*SDN*, April 30, 1942)

Frighten Away Potato Bugs
for a Great Crop of 'Taters

Mrs. Julia Armour of Harrisburg, Pennsylvania, sends a tale which happened while she was in the Ozarks, and says it's true, whether any of you believe it or not. It is a potato bug story. Now I have often heard that great noises would run off potato bugs. In the olden days they often set off a few gunpowder caps in the garden. I have heard that many people go out in the evening and beat on pans and ring a bell and clap two thin boards together in their potato patches—anything to make a concussion and a loud noise. And I have heard it works. Anyway, Mrs. Armor says,

> While down on our campsite we planted potatoes. Soon we began to find that the leaves were being all eaten but no insects were visible through the day. The farmers, thinking to get a laugh on us city folks, told us at the break of day to be on hand with any sort of noise maker we could find, out in the patch, and

scare them away. Lo and behold bugs came out of their holes around the potato stock and took to the woods or someplace else and never came back, and we had a fine crop of potatoes, and so we had the laugh on them!

Year before last I was dying to try that stunt on a little garden patch of "taters" we had—but was a little afraid. Can you see me out in the garden with firecrackers and ringing a bell and beating on a dishpan? About six families would get on their phones at the same time and call the police station! (*SDN*, June 4, 1938)

Weather

Weather superstitions are not always superstitions, as many of them are now recognized as authentic. Even our Charley Williford[3] takes a great interest in them and is broadminded enough to give all credit that is coming to the "goosebone" prophets of weather. You know what the goosebone prophets are, don't you? They will tell you whether it is going to be a very cold or very mild winter, by the thickness of the goose's breast bone.

These old weather rhymes and signs are very interesting because they were handed down from a long, long past era. And they were thoroughly believed. Often these old goosebone weather prophets wouldn't miss it more than five out of fifty times. It is a sort of instinct with these people who have lived in the hills, also on the prairies. They studied the sky, and their prolonged experiences often beat all the dictums of the meteorologists.

They used to say, "Evening gray and morning red, sends the shepherd wet to bed." And then you have all heard the old rhyme, "Rain before seven, clear before eleven." Weather meant a lot to the English people and most of these beliefs came from England, handed down to us.

They said, "If grass grows in January it is bad luck for crops the whole year, and a fair February is a curse." A very old one using the old

Chaucer dialect was "As many mistises in March, that many frostises in May."

Another old saying was: "A cold April a barn will fill." That one nearly always panned out. And this one: "When April blows his foggy horn, 'tis good for both the hay and corn." "Mist in May and heat in June, makes the harvest come right soon." "A dripping June brings all things in tune."

Another old saying I remember always was "A dry March never begs its bread." You know you can begin to have too much rain in March and then the floods start. Another old one is, "The oak should leaf before the ash." Another one: "Ash before oak, there'll be a smoke." The "smoke" meant drought. "Oak before ash, there'll be a splash." That meant rain. Here is an interesting old weather rhyme that the collectors will like:

> The west wind always brings wet weather,
> The east wind, wet and cold together,
> The south wind surely brings us rain,
> The north wind blows it back again.

I remember our old doctors used to go out and shake their heads at an east wind, in a case of pneumonia or croup. My mother knew a very old doctor who used to tell her that he rarely saved a child with croup when the wind shifted to the east—not in all his practice. So the early sages had their superstitions about the weather. (*Dial*, September 1951)

Vance Randolph in his book *Ozark Superstitions* records and files in such a plain and deeply fascinating way the weather superstitions of our Ozarks. He has collected them for many years, and when you read them they all come back to you. I have heard almost every one of the hundreds of them.... One belief is that for every hundred-degree day in July there will be a twenty-below day in the following February.

Well, we've had nothing but rain this summer. They say "all signs fail in dry weather." So, I suppose that all signs also fail in wet weather.

There is also a belief that if November 1 is clear and cool, it means that big rains or snowstorms are coming soon. One sign so often makes good, and that is that "a warm winter makes a fat graveyard." Lots of flu and pneumonia and colds. Nowadays, science is so far advanced that the graveyard doesn't "fatten" from colds and pneumonia like it used to when I was a kid.

So many old timers believed that the first twelve days in January ruled the weather for the entire year. Randolph says that he found many old timers who believed that the "ruling days" are the last six days in December. Anyway, there are literally hundreds of these weather superstitions, and if anyone just had presence of mind enough to watch them and make a record of them they might find out whether they worked out.

Time flies and I get the fidgets about it. Like the old woman who always yelled upstairs, "Get up, gals! Here it is a Monday mornin', tomorrer's Tuesday, the next day's a Wednesday and the week half gone and nothin' done! Git outen that bed!"

Well, we have our funny old ways—but bless Pat, it isn't always the new, shiny things that are the most durable. Old pioneers knew what they were about. (*Dial*, August 1948)

May Loved Her Garden!

I always need a flower garden in my life. We all do. A garden is a place where we learn strength—the strength of bulbs against a hard and bitter winter. Where we learn faith—the faith of a crocus in the spring. Where we learn persistence—the persistence of a weed. And healing—the healing of rains. And infinity—the infinity of a seed. (*Dial*, October 1949)

> I think the greatest peace is found
> By those who live near to the ground,
> Who find their work and play and rest
> Close to the kind earth's warm brown breast:
> Who work with flowers and trees and grain,
> Who feel the summer sun and rain—
> Who read with understanding eyes

The changing message of the skies:
And see in earth, from sky to clod
The open, living book of God.
(*Dial*, July 1949)

Bless your hearts, here I am again! Bad pennies will bob up, you know. By the time you read this, spring will have "busted out all over!" This is the lovely month of May—the month for which I was named. . . .

I wonder how your new gardens are coming along? Aunt Tabithy used to say, "Law me! To raise garden truck you've got to outdo the weeds, out-smart the bugs, and get up before the sun. The bugs and worms hain't on no forty-hour week and they never take a vacation. It's jist like when you cut firewood: It warms you twice—Once when you cut it an' once when you burn it!" (*Dial*, May 1949)

Spouses Don't Always Agree

I am beset with the woes of a backyard gardener, and I'm mad as a wet hen. In the first place, it's that man of mine! He shore "done me wrong!" If ever there is a time when I want to swap him off for a spavined mule, it's in the spring of the year. He has an arson complex, if you know what that is. He wants to burn weeds. In spite of all these years of my going into different varieties of fits, preaching and yelling, he crawls out some spring morning when all honest people ought to be asleep, and goes and burns off my garden, flowers and all. He doesn't know a jimpson weed from an orchid. (Last year he planted marigold plants for tomato plants, and I spent a half day hunting my marigolds, finally calling up the florist and he sent me another dozen. There I discovered them the next day, planted by this 10-karat husband, in the tomatoes!)

Nevertheless, he gets this spurt of energetic pertness and is consumed with the urge to burn something, and out he goes. A few hours later I go out and there is my lavender burned up, all the young tender sprouts of my mint bed black and desolate, half of the blooming jonquils lopped over like a sick dishrag, and he has dug fish worms in the middle of the larkspur bed and gone fishing! I stand there and very silently grapple with a desire to murder, and he's gone and there's nobody to take it out on! . . .

Well, there's nothing to be done. I have threatened everything but a poison pill in his coffee, and next spring he will crawl out the first lovely morning when the world ought to be at peace, and stalk into my tender little flower beds like a Frankenstein monster and burn them to a meat rind again! Does anyone want a six-foot, 185-pound husband to keep for odd chores around the house next spring during the weed-burning season? If so, apply at 817 North Jefferson. Or has anybody a seven-hundred-acre plot where a man could spread himself and burn weeds till he got a sick stomach?

Then that isn't the half of it. He goes out and gets a man to work in the garden. I suppose I shouldn't lay the shortcomings of this hired individual on to him because I concluded that person was born wrong from the beginning. The man worked an hour before I knew he was there, solely under the straw bossing of the better-half, then the better-half deserted the ship and I went out to be the man's helpmeet! Well! Words fail me! He had dug up my phlox and Sweet Williams! He was planting potatoes over my hollyhocks and verbenas. And not only had he dug up the mint, but he had for some reason hung the roots on the iron fence to dry. Threw them at the fence it seemed. I began to salvage and replant and weep and swear inwardly.

This chap . . . informed me that he didn't know much about gardenin'. He made some radish rows and just poured the seed in, sort of wheat and tares all at once in a general broadcast. It looked as if somebody had jabbed him in the ribs and he had spilled the whole package. He planted away from himself, down on his all-fours, then crawled over each row and wallowed it as he went. I suggested that he get his planting end around the other way and plant toward himself. "Well!" he said—"I never did think of that!" Then he started in on the Bermuda onions and set them about a foot or more apart. I never saw such a crooked looking mess of a row; it looked like a coon dog's hind leg. I told him to plant them thicker. (Of course, I meant closer together.) But he took me at my word and bunched them up in bouquets and planted them in wads! I asked him what he was doing, and he said, "You said plant 'em thicker!"

Well, when I went away and left him, then came back and found that he had not only planted them upside down, in bouquets, but had covered them under, soul and body—I gave it up. Fortunately, there is a law of the Creator that a thing planted upside down will finally, through struggles, work its right end up to the light. So when I realized that God was on my side, I put down my hoe and silently walked into the house! I turned on the radio and flattened out on the couch. A man's voice came over the air from Iowa. He was delivering a speech on the subject "Get Back to the Soil!" After that, I know nothing. I think I became unconscious. The husband returned about then and I gasped, "Can you get that man out of my garden!" . . . The last I remember was the poor goof walking away with two dollars in his jeans, which was worse than thrown to the chicken hawks, and a very meek-looking husband read the magazines the rest of the day. You never get too old to learn. (*SNL*, April 18, 1937)

My Mother's Garden

Oh, how she loved her garden!
She whose passion was blossoms,
And leaves and roots and soil,
And tender little orphan plants,
Their names, their loves, their needs!

She nursed them, watered them,
And talked to them.
Transplanted them and moved them
To the sunny window, to the blessed rain,
To the soft loamy beds.

And when they grew for her,
And stretched their strong young arms,
And decked themselves in tawny garb,
She gave them to the sick, the poor,
To sacred altars and to happy girls.

She gave them with a wantonness,
And when a loved one asked her for a rose
She stripped with joy the well beloved bush!
She laid them on a little grave,
She placed them in a waxen hand.

And I do not grieve, for well I know
She lives—somewhere, in a garden.
(*SDN*, August 16, 1938)

CHAPTER 12

Time for School

Did you ever have a dear old school teacher who chewed
long-green and spit half way across the little schoolhouse?
I did, bless his heart, he has gone to his reward.

SNL, January 22, 1933

. . . .

There may be nothing more central to our notion of
Americana than the little one-room schoolhouse, an institution that would have been vital to the childhood of many of
May's readers and listeners. She recognized the limitations of
an education system that could pay teachers ("soldiers of progress," as May called them) as little as twenty dollars a month
for supervising a room in which all the students recited their
lessons aloud simultaneously, the old blab school. But May
tapped into her readers' nostalgia with her own memories of
school days: being tormented by little boys on the first day of
school, people coming from miles around for spelling bees,
making ink from poke berries and pens from goose feathers,
and the oddity of her mother voting in school elections when
the family lived in Arizona from 1891 to 1892—something

that would not have been possible back home in the Ozarks at the time.

. . . .

May's First Day of School

I think I'll never forget one thing about my first day at school. They played "Froggie in the Meadow," and they put me in for the frog. And when they put me in the middle of that ring, I broke and ran home like a wildcat. It took a little hickory oil and persuasion to get me to go back. The kids meant well, I suppose, but that's a poor stunt to spring on a kid the first day of school, with all the little boys around. I was scared of the little boys—I'm not scared anymore! . . .

I think of the great contribution the little rural schools of a bygone day have made to America. Poorly supplied schools they were—almost no equipment, scarcely warmth and shelter, but from the hills of the little rural wayside schools have come men who have moved nations to their foundations. The little *Blue-Backed Speller*, an old painted blackboard, some worn-out erasers, benches for desks, puncheon floors—ragged, dog-eared books. (*Dial*, September 1948)

Dr. Traw at Lebanon wrote me about his old school days and how they had to run the sheep out the doors and windows of the little schoolhouse of mornings, and sweep the room out with buck-brush brooms. (*Dial*, January 1951)

The *Blue-Backed Speller*

I have been reading the *Blue-Backed Speller* again, and I am always carried away with that fine old classic, for that's what it is. Perhaps many of you do not know that many a pupil went to school and carried that little book and it was his sole education and all he ever got.

It contained fables; it had sentences which brought up geography, science, religion, astronomy, mathematics, and everything known to the textbook world. The good old school master then aired his limited education as these topics came up.

The interesting thing and the thing which shows how far we have departed from the ways of our rock-ribbed forebears was this: There was the long list of words for spelling. Then, to their meaning there would be sentences on the next page using the words. And they never failed to score a hit on morals, religion, honesty, and conduct in general. This was a magnificent psychology, for as long as the pupil lived, whenever he ran across that word, he associated it with that maxim.

I am going to give you a sample of the sentences which defined the following words in the spelling lesson—injurious, embellish, expedient, manifest, love:

> Do nothing that is INJURIOUS to religion or morals.
> The most refined education does not EMBELLISH the character like piety.
> Many things are lawful which are not EXPEDIENT.
> Blushes often MANIFEST modesty.
> The LOVE of whiskey has brought many a good man to ruin.
> (*SNL*, October 7, 1934)

My edition of the *Blue-Blacked Speller* was printed in 1857, and is called "The latest revised edition, by Noah Webster." There is an older edition, whose aim, so it states, is to "impart general knowledge and to teach children the true pronunciation of words."

Then along came primer lessons thrown in, "She fed the hen. The hen was fed by her." Then the lessons became harder and harder until came such staggering sentences as this: "The world turns around in a day!" I shall never forget the last words—"Prodigious, egregious, rhinoceros," etc.—all with elaborate syllabication. Now and then there were stories and fables—all with a moral. Every one is burned in my memory. "The Bear and Two Friends," "The Impartial Judge," and many others. All were in such stilted language that the poor little kid was next door to unconsciousness the whole time the thing was being read to him. The story of the milkmaid and her milk pail starts out thus:

> When men suffer their imagination to amuse them with the prospect of distant or uncertain improvements of their condition, they frequently sustain real losses by their inattention to those affairs in which they are immediately concerned.

Laugh that off! Imagine your little sleepy, tousled pioneer boy with a stone bruise on his heel, and his head full of adenoids, digesting that lofty hypothesis!

Then I must give you some of the many, many axioms scattered through it. The biggest "passel" of them sound like a Chinese proverb gone wrong:

> The children will submit to the will of their parents.
> The neck connects the head with the body.
> All mankind take their origin from Adam.
> The body is material and will return to dust, but our souls
>   are immaterial and will not die.
> Ladies should know how to manage a kitchen.
> A relict is a woman whose husband is dead. (I never knew
>   THAT before!)
> Boys love to make a great racket.
> The doctor sometimes bleeds his patients with a lancet. . . .

Go on and on—hundreds of them: Philosophy, facts, axioms, and religion and temperance almost every other one. (*SNL*, April 9, 1933)

Spelling Bees

From J. F. Roberts of Van Buren, Arkansas, came a letter about spelling bees:

> Spelling was considered the foundation of an education and spelling matches were a regular feature of the schools. Friday afternoons were often devoted to spelling matches for the whole school. After choosing up, the teacher opened a book. The two chosen as leaders guessed at the number of the page at which the book was open, and the one who guessed the closest to the page had first choice of spellers. They lined up on the side of their respective leaders.
>
> When all were chosen the teacher began pronouncing the words for them to spell, beginning with the leaders and alternating. Those missing it were out and had to leave the line.
>
> So interesting were the matches that they were often held at night as an entertainment, the older people frequently coming and taking part and encouraging the practice. Frequently one district school would challenge a neighbor school to a spelling match. People went for miles to attend. So exciting were they that often sporting-minded men and boys would bet on their respective schools. No book but the old Blue Back was ever used. (*SNL*, March 28, 1937)

And Speaking of Spelling . . . Old Rhymes

Bumble Bee

> B, U, umble, umble E.
> B, U, umble, bumble bee.
> (This one said with a deep nasal sound,
> trying to imitate a bumble bee.)
> (*SDN*, March 5, 1940)

Bull Frog

B. U. hippity,
L. L. croak and crunk,
F. R. splash,
And O. G. sunk!
(*SDN*, March 5, 1940)

Tennessee

One, I see, two I see, three I see,
Four I see, five I see, six I see,
Seven I see, eight I see,
Nine I see, Tennessee.
(*SDN*, April 9, 1940)

Constantinople

Can you count, can you stand,
Can you count standy-I,
Can you nople, can you bople,
Constantinople!
(*SDN*, March 12, 1940)

Learned the Succession of Presidents by Singing

In the old days they sang the alphabets and the presidents and the multiplication table, etc. This old president song I am going to give was sung to the tune of Yankee Doodle.

George Washington, first president,
By Adams was succeeded,
Thomas Jefferson was next choice,
For the people's cause he pleaded.
Madison was then called forth,
To give John Bull a peeling,
James Monroe had all the go,
The era of good feeling . . .
(*SDN*, February 17, 1940)

"Literary" Debates

We used to have "literary" debates when I was a kid, like, "which is the more useful, the broom or the dish-rag?" Or "the cow or the horse?" Or "which is mightier, the pen or the sword?" And I distinctly remember that used to bring up the war question, and we knew practically nothing about any war but the Civil War—then the fur would fly. We would forget all about the "pen," and turn the thing into a free-for-all about the Civil War.

I remember how we used to debate about "should women vote?" And the fact that women might someday vote was perfectly laughable. Nobody had even the remotest thought of such a thing.

But when I was eleven and twelve we had lived in Arizona with our invalid father, and women voted there in school elections away back then. I distinctly remembered that a man came to get my mother to take her to vote, as my father was ill abed. And it seemed so funny that my mother was going to vote! So when we had our debates after that, I would tell them my mother voted and it didn't make a "bad woman" out of her! They always argued, on the negative side, that no woman would ever think of voting who was "any account"! (*SDN*, February 5, 1941)

Country School Teachers Boarded Around

I wonder if we really are grateful enough to those faithful teachers of old, those soldiers of progress who held the torch aloft under every difficulty and handicap of pioneer days. God bless these dear women and men who paved the way for a higher education. Ten dollars a month, sometimes five, and "boardin' roun'." One week they stayed with the Higgins and the next they trundled up their scant little bag of clothing and went to stay at Goodalls and get their board and keep. No privacy. No place to study or rest or relax. The little Goodall children crowded around "teacher" and ate apples in her ears and snuffled their little noses, and Mr. Goodall entertained her poor tired soul with his ideas of how a school ought to be run. Finally she sneaked to bed when the men folks weren't looking, and up at daylight in the cold to trudge with the little Goodalls maybe four miles to the crude schoolhouse. This was the rural school. Swept out her own room and dusted, and if there was an awfully good big boy who was work-brittle, or if she were young and fetchin', the big boy built the fire before her arrival. If she was aging and weary and wore specks and was a bit stern and sour, she was out of luck about the fires. God bless these dear women and men who paved the way for higher education. (*SNL*, November 15, 1936)

D. L. Massie of Fremont, Missouri, shared her story of boardin' roun' in 1878:

> Fifty-nine years ago I taught a country school where Winona, Mo., is now located. That was before the branch railroad was built from Willow Springs in Howell County to Grandin in Carter County. I received twenty dollars a month and boarded round. I usually stayed a week with each family living in the district. Then I would start in again and make another round. The community was made up entirely of farmers. The year 1878 was very dry and the farmers did not raise much grain and very few vegetables. The eats that year were rather meager. I remember at one place the only meat they had was chicken. So we had chicken fried,

roasted or chicken and dumplings almost every day. While I am very fond of chicken that was one time I got fed up.

Another farmer threshed a few bushels of wheat that year. He needed money to pay his taxes, so he took the wheat to mill and had it ground and sold the flour and brought home the shorts, which were very coarse and dark. The good wife made bread out of the shorts. While the food I had to eat that fall may have been shy on some vitamins necessary for a balanced diet, I lived over it. (*SNL*, March 28, 1937)

Here is Mr. Guy Howard's experience with proof that the old ways of the people have not passed.

During the school years of 1933 and 1934 I had the privilege of boarding around in an isolated rural school district. There were no funds to pay a teacher and all funds were used to rebuild and equip a new building after the old one was burned. My salary was my board and room, but it was worth it. The people who live in such rural communities in God's Ozarks are the salt of the earth. A number of homes were log cabins, the others were the small cabins built entirely of native oak—that characteristic kind that dot the Ozark hills.

Each week as I moved to another home brought a wealth of new experiences, concerns and friends. Never have I enjoyed a year's work more. The last day of school brought tears as good-byes were said.

One mother paid me one of the highest compliments possible when she said, "We all shore hate to see you leave, teacher, for we all know our youngens has been getting' the right kind o' fetchin' up." (*SNL*, April 11, 1937)

Blab Schools

Some friends at a party the other evening were talking about the old "blab schools." A gentleman from Texas said he had no idea there was ever a blab school other than those of our Pilgrim ancestors of New England. But I told him I had heard of blab schools in the early Ozarks. It was said there was a teacher who taught a blab school once near Oto, down in my home country. Also schools near Eureka, Arkansas. They were schools where all the pupils studied out loud you know. (*SDN,* September 6, 1941)

Well, all things come to him who asks—sometimes. I asked about the "blab schools.". . . I insisted that we used to have them in the Ozarks. . . . I had a letter from none other than Walter Coon of the Union National Bank telling me of his mother's experience.

> When I read your article about blab schools and your urgent request for information concerning them. I was reminded that my mother had told me again and again about them. She called them "loud" schools, and she attended them.
>
> Loud schools were where the pupils (they called them "scholars") studied out loud. Especially did they bear down on the reading and spelling, and what a commotion it was!
>
> My mother used to tell about a boy when he was getting his spelling lesson. For instance the word "proportion." He would spell the old way and sing, "p-r-o, pro, p-o-r por, propor, t-i-o-n shun, proportion!"
>
> And by the time he got to the last syllable and going back to repeat the previous syllables, he would be singing in a loud nasal whine. In fact these loud schools made so much noise that they often called them "yelling" schools.
>
> Uncle Elijah Yeager was one of the pioneer teachers and taught a great many schools in Hickory County just west of Urbana. They were all of them "loud schools." That was in the period preceding the Civil War. Uncle Elijah was a very capable teacher. He would have his scholars memorize those classic readings in McGuffey's Readers and then recite them Friday afternoons. Loud schools began to disappear at the close of the Civil War.
>
> My father, William Benton Coon, who is 97 years old[1] . . .

says he went to a loud school. He has taught many schools but never taught a loud school. Immediately following the Civil War he was superintendent of schools in Dallas County and one of his big problems was to convert these loud schools into silent schools. He thinks loud schools helped the children to read aloud and learn to spell. But it was very hard on a teacher to hear a class recite with everybody talking out loud and whining. (*SDN*, September 13, 1941)

And now here is Judge (Uncle Billy) Keithley's letter about his blab school experience. This blab school history is just like a lot of others. We never knew we had it until we dug it out. So it is with our great unworked mine of lore and legend here in the Ozarks.

. . . The first school I ever attended was a blab school on Bear Creek across from where the Day post office is now. It was a log house about 12 by 14 and had no chinkin' or dobbin' in it. We had split log seats and a clapboard table in the center to lay the books on.

The teacher walked constantly backwards and forwards through the house with a hick'ry about four feet long, and if he caught anyone looking off the book or not studying out loud, he would raise the hick'ry and it would hit the ridge-pole in the ceiling as he would come down on the table. And you would almost jump clear off the log seat.

I was hardly of school age, but my mother sent me just the same. I can remember most of them who went to that school. . . . They would all stand up in reciting and the big boys would spell as loud as they could and drown out us little boys. We thought that was the reason we didn't make as good grades. The teacher couldn't hear us. But if we didn't have a good lesson nobody was any the wiser about it.

Our teacher was a young man and had the misfortune to be cross-eyed and it made it mighty bad on paper wad throwers. It seemed to me he could see everyone in the house at the same time.

The school was on the old Springfield and Harrison freight road, and when a train of cattle wagons would pass with sleigh bells ringing on the harness and neck yoke, I was bound to look out through a crack and wonder if ever I would be able to get one of them. Just then I would get a crack on the head.

It makes you feel sad when your mind just will pop full of things that happened then. And to think that I am the last one to tell the story of that blab school. A leaf has balanced, and the book has closed never to open again. I am going to give you a copy of the contract of that school. My dad, Ambrose L. Keithley, was a judge of the county court at that time, and he made a record of most of his transactions. And in a little book he left this contract:

> This contract between Fim Keithley, a school teacher of Taney County, Mo., A. L. Keithley, John O. McKee and N. E. Smith as directors of said district number 3 of township number 24 in the county of Taney, State of Mo.
>
> I witnesseth that the said Fim Keithley agrees to teach the publick school in said school district for the term of four months, commencing on the 17th day of July, 1871. And to faithfully perform the duties of said teacher in said school according to law and the rules legally established, for the government thereof.
>
> In consideration of said services, the said A. L. Keithley, John McKee and N. E. Smith as directors aforesaid, on behalf of said school district agree to pay the said Fim Keithley the sum of $20 a month at the close of the term, and to perform all the duties required by law as such directors.
>
> Witness our hands this the 15th day of July, A. D. 1871.
>
> Fim Keithley.
> A. L. Keithley.
> John O. M'gee.
> N. E. Smith (*SDN*, September 18, 1941)

No Supplies in Blab Schools

I've received lots more interesting correspondence about the much discussed and interesting "Blab Schools" of ye olden time and it begins to assume the proportions of a nice bit of history which should be recorded and preserved as folk history.

> Lihu Norris is my grandfather. He is seventy years old[2]. He told me the following about a blab school he attended:
>
> It was in Ozark County where I have lived all my life. This school was a mile and a quarter from my home. It was built up a long hollow with tall wooded hills on either side. A cool sparkling spring flowed out of one hill and a springhouse was built in the branch.
>
> The schoolhouse was a small unpainted one-room building. In one end was a huge seven-foot fireplace where they burned large logs for fire. There were no desks, and our seats were made of rough oak lumber. We had no tables. The paper we used was a large white sheet of paper folded together like a newspaper. We made our ink from ripe pokeberries and the "ink balls" that grew on post-oak trees. We had no pens. We split a goose feather in two and sharpened one end for a pen. We sat on the benches in front of the fireplace and studied out loud.—Miss Lois Barnes, Foil, Missouri. (*SDN*, September 16, 1941)

The Little Candle

MARY ELIZABETH MAHNKEY

Little red mittens
And Blue Back Speller,
Trudging through the woods—
A lonely little feller.

To a little log school house
With a puncheon floor,

And a big brown hound
Asleep by the door.

But someone was there
With a smile true and sweet,
To pat little hands,
To warm little feet.

To teach forty youngsters
To write and to read
And to add and multiply
To parse with skill and speed.

Someone with a vision,
With joy in her task;
Oh God, make me as faithful,
This is all I ask.
(*SNL*, November 15, 1936)

I think of the great contribution the little rural schools of a bygone day have made to America. Poorly supplied schools they were—almost no equipment, scarcely warmth and shelter, but from the hills of the little rural wayside schools have come men who have moved nations to their foundations. The little *Blue-Backed Speller*, an old painted blackboard, some worn-out erasers, benches for desks, puncheon floors—ragged, dog-eared books. (*Dial*, September 1948)

CHAPTER 13

How We Did Things

And few things are more pleasant than to recall the things
intimately connected with a peaceful, delightful, happy past.

SDN, July 9, 1942

. . . .

Some of May's most effective "conversations" with readers
and listeners involved little more than reminiscing about the
way we did things back when. Her fans were always ready to
swap recipes with the accomplished cook—the more obscure
and backwoodsy the better, from entrées of possum to poke
sallet and paw-paw pie. Many readers likely shared May's
disdain for shoes—she claimed to have gone barefoot into
her teenage years—and humble Ozarkers knew she was not
exaggerating when she described a time when women had (at
best) one dress and one hat for summer and one for winter,
one pair of shoes for Sunday and one for everyday.

. . . .

How to Find Water

I have seen the power of water witching run in families, the girls and all. And really, believe me sincerely, there is NO FAKE to the stick moving violently sometimes in the hands! (*SDN*, April 28, 1938)

University President Was a Water Witch

I went to Columbia, Missouri, to talk to the Missouri Historical Society at their annual banquet. At first I was really scared at all those professors and educators and historians from over the state and from the university there.... Then Vance Randolph spoke of water witching and I stuck up for that. I told them it was no less a science than the present radiology which located metals. That it was no less a science than the recently developed "corpuscular philosophy" which was mere water witching with a thousand-dollar name to it. I was afraid they would really run me out of town, but bless pat, when I finished, here came no less personage than Dr. Middlebush, the president of the university. His eyes were big and wide and he said excitedly, "I'm a dowser!" At first he had me, for I had forgotten that a dowser is a water witch. I thought he was joking—"You are?" I said. "Yes, I am, you bet. I'll come down to Springfield and show you. I can locate water anywhere." Well, I didn't doubt it because I have seen it located too many times with the ash stick. Dr. Middlebush said he used a peach stick.... Don Wright, who is editor of the morning sheet there, wrote it up on the front page and by morning it was on the Associated Press wire that Dr. Middlebush was a water witch! (*SDN*, April 23, 1938)

Otto Rayburn's Experience as a Water Witch

Now the thing is settled with me once and for all. Our Otto Rayburn at Caddo Gap, author, voice in the wilderness and editor of *Arcadian Life*, writes me that he has tried it and it works.

I am a water witch? I didn't find it out until recently. It came about this way: A neighbor who lives across the road was showing some friends how to do the stunt. I called him into my yard to try to locate a vein of water for me. With his forked willow stick held firmly in both hands, fork upward, he started walking across the yard. After a few steps the fork or stick turned downward. That indicates a good location for a well. I asked my neighbor if he could tell how far it was to the water. That was an easy matter. He began walking away from the spot, counting steps. It took seven steps for the forked stick to regain its upright position. He explained to me that each step meant three feet and if I dug at that point I would find water in 21 feet. I then took the twig, grasped it firmly with both hands and started walking. At the exact spot where it had turned for my neighbor, it began turning for me! I was surprised and delighted.

There is something mysterious about this thing, May. The stick actually turned very strong in my hands. I had always thought it might be some kind of a trick but this experience has made a believer out of me.

I have been told that only one person in a family had the power to witch for water. Henceforth, I am the water witch of the Rayburn clan. (*SDN*, September 12, 1940)

A Devil's Lane:
Sometimes Our Folks Did Not Get Along

A devil's lane was a strip of ground between farms where the owners had quarreled over the property line, or maybe they quarreled over cattle or a dog or politics or the Civil War or religion or family troubles, in-laws, or a lot of things. So they wouldn't even let their fences join, they hated each other so badly. Each fellow would move his joining fence back a little way, and they would create a small, narrow lane running between. Nobody owned it. It grew up in weeds. Nobody could give a title to it

so they called it the devil's land. And believe me, it was! I know of two
sisters who married and lived on adjoining farms and wouldn't speak to
each other and each set back the fence line and made a devil's lane in
between. Think of people letting a situation come up in life like that!
(*Dial*, April 1949)

What We Wore

Do you oldsters remember when we had just one dress for good, winter,
Sunday-Go-To-Meetin' dress, and one for summer? Also a hat for summer and one for winter, and no in-betweens? We had what we called
"fine shoes" for Sunday and "coarse shoes" for school and sturdy wear.
The fine shoes were made of really fine glove kid and they were high, and
buttoned, and fit like a glove. I shall never forget those shoes. And few
people will ever forget the little copper-toed shoes the young children
wore long ago in the Ozarks. . . .

I remember one thing my mother did, however, that I question until
now. You remember the little dresses with the set-in velvet fronts? One
time the front wore out of a little dress of mine and my mother wanted
something to set in just to make it do until the end of school. Having
nothing else, she put in some real black crepe. Mourning crepe they
had in those days! Well, every time the boys looked at me they sniffed
and snubbed and wiped their noses and said, "Who's dead?" I took it as
long as I could and then I lit in, and such fighting and scratching you
never saw! But after several bawlings my mother did away with the dress.
She made me wear it a few times just to make me know that I must
rise above such small obstacles (I suppose), but mothers are kinder than
fathers, and she took the dress off of me to remain off. (*Dial*, June 1950)

Grapevine Hoops

Does anyone remember when the girls used to make their hoops out
of young grapevines? My husband told me that. He used to go to the

old Blackjack school in Stone County and remembers when the girls came to school with grapevine hoops because they couldn't afford "store" hoops. (*SDN*, July 25, 1939)

Corsets and a Small Waist

I missed the chemise period for young girls, but my mother wore them. But I certainly did the corset cover subject up brown. Then came the camisoles. We were talking the other day—can anyone tell why young girls had smaller waists then? We weighed about like girls now, but a waist over twenty-four inches was a disgrace only to be repeated in the family—and the ordinary waist was twenty-two. I had a twenty-two, and my sister who was tall and beautifully rounded and still larger than I had a nineteen-inch waist! And perfectly healthy! Was it because we began to wear corsets at age twelve? So much was said about "lacing" and the magazines —even the pulpits preached agin' it—it was talked of all over the country. But I don't remember any girl who "laced." Can anyone explain it? Is there a young girl of nineteen with a nineteen-inch waist now? A girl who weighs about 126 like my sister? (*SDN*, January 29, 1942)

String of Buttons

A Hillcrofter sends me some information:

> A beautiful memory of my childhood is the old-fashioned charm string of my mother's girlhood. She said girls all had to see who could collect the most charming string of buttons. They were principally shank-buttons, made in many beautiful colors to match elegant dress materials. Used both for trimming and for fastening all the way down the front of "basque-waists." You were supposed to exchange charm buttons with your friends and get them in different ways. They were strung through the shank with cord or narrow ribbon and tied with a bow and worn around the neck like modern beads. I believe a charm string now would be better looking than some of the monstrosities

worn today.—Katherine Butler Friar, Springfield, Missouri. (*SDN*, June 1, 1940)

Hillbillies and Their Shoes

I went barefoot until I was fourteen years old, from choice. And if I had my way I would go barefooted yet. I used to get to go barefooted and take off my flannels on the first day of May and not one wink sooner no matter what came. And from then till November I never knew where a shoe was. And I never kept shoes on all summer until I was sixteen. And they were a prison. Shoes will always be a prison to a youngster. . . . No child is ever quite the same who has missed going barefoot. (*SNL*, February 12, 1933; and *SDN*, March 6, 1941)

I never think of shoes to wear but I think of how in the outside world they are always making fun of Ozarkers and Arkansas folks about going barefooted. That old gag wore out long ago but they don't know it. When I used to speak in the city to big groups they never failed, in introducing me, to get off something about my being fourteen years old before I ever saw a pair of shoes—and all such, thinking it funny. Rev. Johnson of the Grand Avenue Baptist Church, St. Louis, just about the most popular preacher in the city, introduced me to a large audience, just this way: "Well, here's May—and she's got shoes on!"

I always took it in good nature, of course—you know nothing ever makes me mad. I came right back at them and owned up to the corn. I told them we didn't wear shoes in the Ozarks because our feet were so tough we wore the shoes out on the inside. I told them the reason I didn't like to wear shoes was because I had jaybird heels.

I even told them that old chestnut that the late O. O. McIntyre perpetrated about the old woman standing barefooted on a coal of fire and her son drawling—"Maw—you're standin' on a coal of fire." And without moving, she said, "Which foot, honey . . . ?"

Yes—I told those city folks that they had missed half of their lives if they had never felt the plowed ground under their feet, soft and warm. Or never felt the dew on the clover as it bathed their feet when they went out after cows. Or never felt the mud oozing up between their toes in the meadow, or dug their bare feet in the sands in the shoals of the creek at the foot of a cool hollow on a hot summer afternoon. And I quoted to them, sometimes:

> Here's to the gal from Arkansaw,
>
> She can saw more wood than
>
> Her maw can saw,
>
> She can chaw more terbaccer
>
> Than her paw can chaw—
>
> That purty little gal from
>
> Arkansaw!

I told them that we Ozarkians and Arkansawyers had no wild urge to push the collar, chasing industrial phantoms—and no particular quest for a veneered culture only skin deep. That a Hillman was a feller "who hain't yet learned to be what he hain't." That whether the early Hillman wore shoes or not, he had within him a something not nurtured on brick sidewalks, or in tight dude shoes. He had a virility added to a native intelligence which made for men, not mice! Sure as shootin'! (*Rayburn's Ozark Guide*, Spring 1947)

Copper-Toed Shoes

"Do any of you remember the old copper-toed shoes?" asked Virginia Lowe of Pierce City, Missouri.

> Perhaps they made such a lasting impression upon my mind because my sister was the proud possessor of a leather pair while I failed to get any. Of course, we went barefooted in the summer time except on Sunday, when with much pulling and sore pain, we managed to crowd all our sore toes into our shoes and go limping down the country lanes to Sunday school. But we came

home carrying a pretty Golden Text card in one hand and our shoes and stockings in the other and a fine pair of blisters on our heels. These blisters had to be coaxed all week to grow a new hide for the coming Sunday. . . .

They still walk barefooted in the Ozarks, as in the olden days and carry their shoes and put them on before arriving. When a young reporter and I went down to Bryant's Mill Church this summer, we saw the children sitting by the roadside squeezing into their shoes and lacing them, as we approached the meeting house. (*SDN*, December 8, 1938)

"Fittums"

When a storekeeper asked a man what size shoes he wanted, he replied "fittums." That was an old expression meaning try till you fit the foot. People knew so little about shoe sizes. They bought few shoes. There was another old reply to the storekeeper which said—"Fittum, big as you can—Gittum, then maybe have to split-em." (*SDN*, June 6, 1942)

How They Used To Cobble Shoes

A dear old person writes me in reply to my request about early shoemaking.

When I was a child all our shoes were homemade. We had one pair a year. We always got them for Christmas. The hides were tanned by using oak ooze. There was a regular tannery in the community. They had a pattern to cut the leather by. The lasts were of wood, and wooden pegs were used instead of shoe-nails or tacks. These pegs were made of maple. Little blocks of maple were sawed off just the depths they wanted the pegs to be, then they were split into pegs and sharpened with a pocket knife.

They had two awls, a peggin' awl and a sewin' awl. Holes were punched with the awls. The thread was waxed by using a ball of shoe wax. This was fastened on to two hog bristles and double-sewed, starting in the middle of the thread with a bristle on each end and sewing with both hands.—Mrs. Lillian Smith, Willow Springs, Missouri. (*SDN*, May 30, 1939)

Hats! Hats! Hats!

Be kind and not judge what is in a woman's head by what is on it. (*Dial*, April 1947)

Down town the other day, in the store watching women buy fall hats, I had to laugh when I thought of the old days when I was a kid. Do you remember, any of you, when a woman always bought a hat to please her husband? He went along with her to buy it, if it took all day. Hats were not bought very often and this was a day of days. Often a woman wore her summer hat and her winter hat as much as five or six years. I had a dignified father, but I remember distinctly that he went with my mother to buy a hat. Someway it was a sort of unspoken law that a man had to be pleased with his wife's hat, and she was just a sort of poor dumb bunny dragged along to park the hats up on her head and let her man look at them. Can you beat it?

I have watched that process many a time in the little stores and I wonder how it ever got started. It's certainly gone out of date nowadays —but it was funny. I remember it took almost all afternoon for my mother to buy a hat and my father laid off and went along and made a day of it. When mother would get home after this hat-buying ordeal, she would look as meek as Moses—hating the hat as usual. For it never turned out to be the hat that she really wanted. In those days a woman wore the hat her husband thought she OUGHT to wear, so long as she bore his name and was his property! And he could either "point with pride or view with alarm" this hat.

I can imagine a lot of things—jumping off a flagpole or eating pucker persimmons . . . but for me ever to have dreamed of taking a husband along to buy a hat! I would rather have taken the Supreme Court! And not even a team of Texas mules could have dragged him! That's one crime he would have no part in—a woman's hat! (*Dial*, October 1951)

The Old Slat Bonnet

Ruth Tyler

They's an ol' slat bonnet hangin by the door,
Since Granny died hit's never bin wore.
Pa's sister Liddy said "give it to me,"
But Grandad told 'er—"jest leave it be."

So the ol' slat bonnet hangs by the door,
Limp an' faded—dusty an' tore.
I've an idy hit'll hang thar still
When they lug pore Grandad over the hill.
(*SDN*, June 1, 1940)

A Hat Could Help Her Looks!

One time there was a good soul lived across the river from our little
town. He had a whole family of children and a rundown, overworked,
faded little wife, but he loved her—he certainly did. One day he came
into our little millinery store to buy her a hat. He said he wanted to buy
a hat that would make Minty look like she did before she was so "pore
and run down." He had all the faith in the world that a hat would do
the trick. They sold him one all covered with pansies, and he went away
happy. (*Dial*, April 1950)

Who Took My Hat?

And now comes the saddest of all. You've heard of men going away on a
bender and getting their hat stolen? But did you ever hear of a woman?
Well, I did! I put my hat in the rack on the bus and then I moved across
the aisle because the sun was hitting me, and just left my hat! The bus-
man searched high and low—especially low, under everybody's feet, with
a flashlight—no hat! And how I did love that hat better than any I have

May loved her hats!
McCord Personal Papers.

had in years. A lovely little blue feather hat—new and becoming and just what I had wanted. I was mad as a March hare and my family and friends seem to see nothing but a chuckle in it. Now don't lay that on to a man. No man on this earth ever wanted a woman's hat! They sit up nights to hate these modern little flub-dub hats. Some sister walked off with that lovely hat and I hope she chokes! (*SDN*, February 7, 1942)

What We Ate

We're plain and simple. We'd have to be, for half our blood is sorghum and the other half's turnip juice. (McCord quoted in *St. Louis Star and Times*, May 1, 1934)

Not Very Good Cooks

Well, I seem to have stirred up a fuss. Ain't we got fun? In a little interview about the doings of the early Ozark pioneer, I stated that the hillbilly women of olden days were not very good cooks. Did I stir up a hornet's nest! Well, I stick to my point. They did not make cooking an institution like the women of New England or the mammies of the Southland. One reason was the early pioneer settler had a lot of hardship and privation and he had little enough to cook. If one is going to cook well he must have something to cook with. They simply had to eat to live, rather than live to eat. (*SNL*, November 20, 1932)

How to Cook a Possum

Well, I got a recipe for cooking a possum! All I need now is the possum! You boil your possum an hour in weak, red-pepper tea, then roast in a pan slowly with peeled, quartered sweet 'taters, two or three hours. . . . The boiling is to get out the excessive grease in the possum, and the pepper tea I am sure, is to pep it up and take away that pervading sweet taste. Possum when cooked tastes like you had spilled the sugar bowl into it. And it is about the tenderest meat known. (*SNL*, December 11, 1932)

How to Cook a Rabbit

Mrs. E. H. of Springfield writes,

> I prepare my rabbit, salt and pepper it to taste and roll it heavy in flour. Put it in a baking pan, "kivver" it with hot water, then take another baking pan and put over the top. Put it in a hot oven and let it cook till done, then remove the top pan and let it brown; frequently dipping the gravy up over it till it is cooked low and brown, and that leaves the finest gravy and brown crust. I take this up all together on a big platter. (*SNL*, December 25, 1932)

Want Chicken for Dinner? Here's How to Wring a Chicken's Neck

I shall never forget my experience as a bride in wringing a chicken's neck. I had a mother-in-law who was disgusted with any sort of fol-der-rol about killing a chicken, and she just made me wade right in and kill my own, and I am thankful now to her for it. She told me just to go after it. I grabbed the big old Domineck rooster and shut my eyes and swung him around and around and I fell down and got up in the process, and he made an awful sort of squawking noise and I wrung again. Finally I put him down and he was just a bit addled and dizzy but not dead at all! He started off sorta "anty-goggling" down the slope of the backyard (if you know what that good old Ozark word is). I ran after him and chased the poor thing under a barn with him trying to give up and die in the meantime. Then I went at it again and after about a half hour I got his head off. I don't think I shall ever forget that. The trouble was I had tackled an old gentleman. Now I can wring them young or old just as fast as you can bring them to me. (*SNL*, November 17, 1935)

Grease Gravy

My correspondent, "Mossback," writes me interestingly. She says to make the "grease gravy" or spotted or pided or "black-eyed" gravy with ham as a lot of folks call it, if it is not dark enough, pour a little coffee into the skillet when making it. And it makes the gravy better. She says,

> An old lady used to come to our house years ago and say to Mother, "Now I tell you what I want for dinner—cornbread with eggs in it, fried ham, then make some of that good ol' thickenin' gravy to whollupin' my bread in." A young lady visiting our house for the first time, said, "please pass that stuff you all are whollopin' your dodger in." (*SDN*, September 23, 1939)

Milk Gravy

Our Ozarkian ancestors were brought up on milk gravy; and I don't know what would have become of the little shavers if they had not had their milk gravy. They grew up on it, plowed the fields, laid waste the timber and went to the front to fight our wars . . . on milk gravy. (*Dial*, November 1947)

Tackey-Whack

Hot off the griddle as they say, came a recipe for old sorghum, as I asked, from Mrs. C. L. Davis, Aurora. She says it was called "Tackey-Whack."

Take good meat grease and make it hot. Pour in sorghum, boil for a few minutes, stir occasionally. Pour up in a bowl and serve with hot biscuits and butter. "And it makes my mouth water," says Mrs. Davis.

A lot of you might think that is "tackey" for sure, but you just try it. Especially if it's ham gravy! (*SDN*, October 24, 1939)

Paw-Paw Pie

Here comes a recipe for the much-discussed paw-paw pie: Mrs. Anna Robinson, Fordland, Missouri, says, "I am just an old woman 87 years old, sending this to you." (Thanks, my dear, eighty-seven isn't old!)

> Two large paw paws; 3 eggs; one half cup sugar; one half cup milk; tablespoon sweet cream; juice and pulp of one lemon. Bake with only bottom crust. When cold, ice over and let to harden. Fine, just try it. (*SNL*, January 24, 1937)

Pot Likker

I daresay that over half of you don't know what pot likker is. The late Huey Long of Louisiana was famed for his filibusters about pot likker. It has nothing to do with alcoholic likker. Pot likker is the juice left in the pot after cooking wild greens with a big ham bone. And you dunk your corn pone in that, and it's rich with every vitamin known to science, believe me! Nothing better than pot likker! (*Dial*, April 1949)

Poor Man's Dumplings

Right here, I have to stop and tell you how to make "Poor Man's Dumplings," the best dumplings ever put in your mouth. That's the kind they made in early days and the kind I make to this day. I know that hundreds of people have asked me for the recipe on my radio program in the last few years.

You have plenty of good rich soup or "pot likker" with your fat hen. Take out a large cupful of the juice, hot. Mix in all the flour it will possibly take—nothing else only a very little salt. Then dump it on a breadboard and keep on kneading in flour until it is stiff as you can make it. Remember, you make it up HOT. I always have to start with a fork, as it is too hot to knead. Then you pinch off some of your dough and roll it just as thin as you can get it, using plenty of flour to dredge. Roll very thin. Then shake off any extra flour and cut in thin strips and drop in the boiling "hen soup" and cook ten minutes, slowly.

If you don't say these are the best dumplings you ever ate, then tell me about it. Some say they are just a glorified noodle, but whatever they are, I can eat my weight in them. (*Dial*, July 1948)

Sleep with Your Bread Dough?

There was nothing like that old-time salt-rising bread, the loud-smelling kind. They said if it didn't smell like "old sock feet" it wasn't made right. It had to send that old cheese odor all over the house and the yard while it was baking. And my, it was wonderful bread!

I'll have to tell you something funny. In the old days they made lots of it, and it has to be kept warm from the moment it is started. If it gets cold once, it is ruined. We had no steam-heated houses, hot water, electricity or anything of the sort. The process of making took all day and all night. So the women would wrap their dough in several thicknesses of paper, then in thick wool blankets and take it to bed with them! Many a man slept with the dough at his back while the woman had the baby on her side of the bed. Sometimes they put the bread down at the foot! Just so it kept warm from body heat. Did you know that?

My mother used to get up as early as four o'clock and start her bread. We kept fire all night in a big old cast-iron box heater. At night she would wrap the bread in paper and blankets and put it in the cradle that had rocked us all, pillows underneath it and over it. Nowadays they shorten the process someway, but the bread doesn't even start to taste like salt-rising.

Some few years ago I made some salt-rising of a sort to take to a big dinner where everyone was supposed to bring an old-time dish. A certain lawyer here in town who knew the old ways slipped up to me and said, "May, did you sleep with this bread?" I told him no, I was very modern. I kept it in warm water from the time it started, and while it "riz." (*Dial*, August 1950)

Cracklin' Bread

So many have asked me about "crackling bread" and what it is. Well, it's one thing—it's delicious! There are places where you may buy nice clean, well-rendered and "squeezed" cracklin's[1] from people at butchering time. Mrs. Mahnkey at Mincy can make it and sends me her recipe. . . . You know the old song, "Shortnin' Bread."

> Pour about two teacups of boiling water over one teacup of cracklin's. Stir until it has softened, then add a little salt and sifted corn meal to make about as thick as ordinary cornbread batter. Bake quite a while. No soda, but just as I've said. (*SDN*, October 5, 1940)

Stack of Pies

Do any of you readers know what a "stack of pies" were? They always baked a stack. One pie would have been an insult. You cut clear through the stack. Lemon pie was considered "stylish," and was always in great demand, probably because of the scarcity of fresh lemons in the Ozarks in early days. (*SNL*, September 15, 1935)

Jeff Davis Pie

We are indebted to Jewel Mayes, Missouri commissioner of agriculture, for this recipe. While I used to be taught a little song which ran, "We'll hang Jeff Davis on a sour apple tree," you can bet I'll eat and like any Jeff Davis Pie. . . .

> Jeff Davis Pie was originally compounded by Mary Ann, the slave cook of George B. Warren, a merchant of Dover, Mo. She first made and served it at an affair after church, midday Sunday dinner, at the Warren home in the early days of the Civil War.
>
> At the conclusion of the meal, the guests flocked to the outdoor kitchen to make inquiry of "Aunt Ms. Ann" and to the delicious dessert. In a spirit of loyalty to her master and his political bias, she informed the inquirers that they had eaten a "Jeff Davis Pie" and told them it was concocted of:
>
> One cup of butter, two cups sugar, one cup cream and six eggs. Mix well. In a pastry crust bake 45 minutes in a slow oven. Serve cold. The foregoing will make two pies.

I know that would be delicious. It sounds like a custard pie gone to college—but the full cup of butter and the very slow cooking would make it a sort of caramel. Let's try it. Then maybe nobody will want to "hang Jeff Davis on a sour apple tree!" (*SDN*, May 2, 1940).

Blurps of Molasses

Mrs. Emma Lloyd wrote to me from Collinsville, Illinois, and asked me if I knew what "four blurps of molasses are." She said when she was a kid someone sent her to borrow four blurps of molasses. Well, you know how the molasses blurps when it goes to pour on a cold day out of a barrel. . . . It "breathes" and blurps. I guess four blurps would be about a half pint. Then I asked Emma if she knew what "Two whoops and a holler" meant—How far is it? Well it's a "good fur piece, believe me." (*Dial*, December 1950)

Greens

Now did you know that there is the greatest art imaginable in gathering greens? It takes years to learn just the right mixture, and of course, no greens or spinach, mustard or stuff equals wild greens. You can't have too much dock, plantain or wild lettuce or they will be bitter. Too much poke is too "slick" like spinach, which the Hillbilly detests! I don't blame him. Only Popeye would eat spinach. If the blackberry leaves are a speck too old they will scratch your gizzard! Too much mustard makes them strong. Every Ozark woman knows different greens. . . . Wool Britches, Old Maid, Mouse Ear, Tongue Grass and radish tops. My, I wonder if I will ever get to gather a mess of wild greens again! Maybe my "wild" days are over. Maybe only wild wimmen gather wild greens. Maybe if you gather wild greens you have to sow wild greens! (*SNL*, April 25, 1937)

Hill Folks Not Always Open to Sharing Information

Mrs. Lillie Revels of Arcola, Missouri, writes me that my talking about the Ozark Hillbilly being mysterious about his "information" reminds her of asking an old lady who was famous for her white cake, how to bake it. Aunt Molly said, "Oh, a pinch of this and a cupful of that and a smidgen of this and four eggs." Finally it dawned on her that Aunt Molly didn't want anyone to know! (*SDN*, August 28, 1941)

Ruth Tyler's "Pinch and Taste" Punkin' Pie

This Neosho, Missouri, woman who has made herself famous from coast to coast in ordinary papers and big New York papers, with her grand old "receets," sends this to me and says it is an old way to make pumpkin pie, older than time:

> Le's talk about makin' a punkin' pie!
> Hyar's my Aunt Betty's old receet;
> Older'n time an' quicker'n scat!
> Hit simply kain't be beat!
>
> Greeze yer pie-pan with good hawg lard,
> Then with corn meal—strew hit thick!

Dust out the extra—now that's that!
A pie crust! Hain't that slick?

Now—take some punkin', yeller an' nice,
Add cream and sugar an' pinches o' spice,
Cinnamon, ginger—jest season hit high!
(An' I like sorghum in punkin' pie.)
A smidgen o' salt—two aigs beat right smart,
Jest stir an' taste an' mix by heart!

When yer fillin's ready, jest dump it in,
Bake kinda slow—so's hit won't burn!
Ye tell by the looks when yer pie's all done,
Hit's thick as yer foot an' a nice deep brown!

Then whup some cream till hit stands alone.
Add honey er sugar an' heap on each one,
A dash o' cinnamon (on the sly)
Some walnut goodies—That's Punkin' Pie!
(*SDN*, December 4, 1941)

And If the Food Didn't Turn Out Right

Some people can always find alibis. I am that sort; I can fix up an alibi on short notice. I made some soup the other day and they said, "May, you got too much salt in your soup." And I said, "O, no I didn't—there's just not enough soup for the salt!" Like the old woman when the preacher came to dinner. She was apologizing for her biscuits. She said, "Well, my biscuits hain't any good this morning. They squat before they riz' and then browned in the squattin." I've had biscuits to do that way many a time, and that describes them exactly. (*Dial*, May 1949)

CHAPTER 14

Seasons and Celebrations

*If we don't glean a bit of precious heritages of the past
and record them, they are going to forever disappear.*

SNL, February 7, 1937

· ·

Despite her unwavering devotion to her beloved Ozarks,
May's writings were inclusive. Her columns and radio programs highlighted events that brought people together in
common understanding, no matter where they were from or
how they got to the Ozarks. The characteristics of the changing seasons interested her rural readers and listeners as much
as they interested May. Her stories of seasonal celebrations in
the old days brought everyone's mind back to specific events
and people from years past. May's childhood memories suggest the true value of a good swimming hole and faithfully
depict the solemnity of Decoration Day, the raucousness
of Independence Day, and the understated and communal
Christmas celebrations of more than a century ago.

· ·

Spring

Of a Spring Morning
Ruth Tyler

Granny flung her windows wide
And propped the door with an "arn" inside,
With an old shuck broom she tore around
Cleaning and sweeping the cobwebs down.
Her "warshin'" billowed like snowy sails,
And she aired the beddin' upon the rails.
She lugged out ashes, scrubbed the floor
And shooed the chickens from the door.
"Howdy, Granmaw!" I yelled with a grin,
"Tryin' to let the springtime in?"
Shading her eyes, she turned about,
"NO . . . I'm aimin' to let the winter OUT!"
(*SNL*, April 1, 1934)

May Day

Today is May Day. I wonder if the old May-basket custom is still kept in the little towns. One of the sweetest customs of early days and next to Christmas, the gayest and most thrilling.

It all comes back to me now. Waiting at home for the sly knocks on the door then feet scampering away. And running to the door to see the lovely basket and who it was from! The boys hung baskets for their girls, and their sisters made them. I remember now how we girls gathered at someone's home the day before and worked hard all day. I can just feel the cramp in my legs right now as I sat all day long on the floor working. We took tissue paper and cut yards and endless yards of fringe and crimped it with a knife or scissors. Then we pasted it on, row after row. Always the very best one got much care and work, and was for the very best beloved. The most popular girl got more May-baskets than she could carry. There was always one awful hitch in affairs, because we wanted to go out and hang baskets of course, and we wanted to stay at home and see who hung for us. But our mothers usually stayed in to gather up the baskets. Mothers were always kind. They waited a few moments after the knock to give the sly sweetheart time to get away and hide in the shrubbery.

Then sometimes we hung weeds and cabbage heads and old bones of a dead horse. One time a girl and I hung a real dead cat on a boy's door. But we were crazy about that very boy, nevertheless—just trying to do something cute. . . .

Never did I enjoy anything so much—if I just could quit thinking and remembering how happy I was and how long ago it was and how many tears have gone under the bridge since I trudged those same spots with my brother and all of those happy-hearted dear ones of my youth. (*SDN*, May 2, 1939)

Decoration Day

Every Memorial Day I think of the striking lines I once printed written by Whit Burnet of Seymour: "The hardest task God ever gave is trusting Him beside a grave." (*SDN*, May 30, 1942)

And so I felt as I stood in the little graveyard yesterday—Never never bring them back again! But as King David said of the beautiful baby that he lost, "He cannot come again to me, but I can go to him."

There is something so sweet about Decoration Day in the country and little village graveyards that just simply is not there in the formality and ceremony of the larger cities. Friends gather early in the morning and decorate and maybe just sit with their dead. Clear away the weeds and old leaves. Place their bouquets so they will look the prettiest. Then they go to other graves and visit with neighbors and friends. It is a general coming home and we see friends that we see only once a year, come from afar, some of them. We know where everyone is buried and when they were buried. We know all their people—we know the circumstances of their death. We know whom they married and maybe whom they secretly worshipped all their lives. We know romances and tragedies and great griefs. We visit and recall old days. We divide flowers and there is such a sweetness of spirit and such a tenderness and sense of peace out on the sun-bathed hill!

And finally, we come to the place that we have more friends laid there than we have left here—then we begin to know that it is just such a little while—and we do not seem to care so much. Many have already selected the spot where they are to wait for the resurrection morning. Some of them have had the spot elected for them by having their mate cross over before them and there is the double tombstone with mother on one side and father on the other. The date of their births but only one date of their deaths! One old fellow said he never looked on that double stone at the head of his good wife but what he wondered what date his side would bear and he didn't care how soon they carved it.

After the graves were flowered there was dinner on the ground and the afternoon devoted to talks and singing and visiting. Then as the shadows lengthened one by one they turn homeward each wondering somehow if next year they would decorate graves or have theirs decorated. (*SDN*, May 31, 1938)

FAMILY VISIT TO GALENA GRAVEYARD WITH GRANDMA, BORN IN 1854

Yesterday was Decoration Day and we drove downhome into the hills. And we took my little ninety-year-old mother-in-law out to the graveyard, bless her heart. Living yet, frail little soul. We took her out to see her graves. The day was beautiful. We seemed so far from wars—and yet, they were fighting and dying at that moment in a far away and savage country. It didn't mean much to the little mother for she didn't realize it. She lived with a child's mind, in the past and with her memories. She was in the car with her children and her children's children's children! She had lived beyond wars. She lived in the country of the heart. She read the inscriptions on her graves as if they were new and picked a tulip from them. And the little great-grandson was gathering bluetts and bringing them to her and she was cackling a merry laugh. What were wars and injustice and death and terror and wrong and grief to her? (McCord Personal Papers, 1945)

Mother's Day

Home again—home for Mother's Day. To me, the saddest day in the world—always. I wish it were not so. If I could wear a red flower—it would be all joy. But I must wear a white one. I would give many worlds to be able to do the things I left undone and say the things I could not say then when I had the chance!

I expect to spend the first thousand years of eternity, not playing on a golden harp, but with my head in Mother's lap telling her all about it. So you, my friends, who expect to be there too—for it is but a thin vale—please just leave me off your program for things celestial for the first thousand years, for I shall not be open for engagements!

I am thinking of mothers today. Mothers of Europe who have nowhere to lay their heads. Mothers who have no place to still the wailings of the little ones in their arms. Mothers whose sons face the forces of hell in battle and the screeching bombs overhead. They who know the deepest suffering—for it is a gamble that goes with our great joy. Mothers who carry the dove of peace in their bosoms and hate war instinctively, biologically, fundamentally! God knows they hate it! (*SDN*, May 10, 1941)

Her Things

Dearer to me than the wealth of the world,
Or treasure the pirates hid,
Is the little blue teapot she left on the shelf—
Little pot, with the broken lid!
Sweeter to me than the thrush at eve,

Or the wood-dove's throaty call,
Is this poignant peace that drapes the night,
And the tick of her clock on the wall.
(*Golden Age Companion*, May 1939)

A WOMAN'S TOIL-WORN HANDS

Some dear woman writes me this:

> When I have cooked the Sunday dinner, washed the dishes and swept the kitchen, I put on my Sunday attire and timidly sidle into the front room where the young folks are holding forth. I sit uneasily, trying to cover the knobby fingers of first one hand and then the other; meanwhile, endeavoring to arrange my feet so that the bunions are not so dreadfully prominent. I feel that I am the target of a dozen or so pairs of bright and appraising eyes, and while I know they are willing to make allowances, I feel that they are secretly thinking how much better I would look in the kitchen. . . .
>
> —Signed, "Toil Worn Hands," Springfield, Missouri

I wish you would not take that view, because you are feeling something which perhaps does not exist. Any hands which can write so beautifully as the above are lovely hands. . . . I have ugly hands; that can't be denied. They are the hands that the lord and master around here used to think were long and tapering and white—but they have rocked the cradle and dressed the dead and carried poultices to the sick and hot water bottles and ice water. They have helped a neighbor scrub and sew. They have fondled babes and spanked them a plenty to keep them out of the reform school when they grew up. They have mended socks and washed and ironed and made jelly and flapjacks and curried a pony and rowed a boat on the James River when they were strong and young. They have played soft hymns for funerals and prayers, made a truckload of biscuits and washed enough dishes to set a banquet for the courts of Israel for a dozen years. And they are still never quiet, only when I am asleep. Now if any set of young people doesn't like these hands, they know what they can do. (*SNL*, September 27, 1935; and *Dial*, November 1949)

Mothers All
Mary Elizabeth Mahnkey

My black hen talks to me of many things,
Cuddling her brood beneath her ragged wings.
Of winged death, and things in the dark wood,
Of love and fear that throb with Motherhood.
(*SNL*, July 25, 1937)

MOTHER'S LOVE

This month of May is a month of love, both for the living and the dead. Mother's love—that one great mystery, that passion which no man has yet understood, or even been given the language to explain. That love which buries itself in a grave "between the crosses, row on row" or on a lonely battle-scarred hill or in the depths of ocean with a sunken submarine. That love which sits and grapples with death, fighting over a white little face on a pillow. That love that sometimes watches and walks the corridor on the night of the death watch before the dawn, when the flesh will walk the long last mile to a hissing dynamo or a noose in a rope. That love which believes that he was innocent, that just knows her boy couldn't have done it, that someone led him into it. That love that excuses and alibis and pitifully covers up, which never sees a wayward daughter as a woman, but always as a young, gay thing whose ribbons she tied and whose ruffles she stood over the ironing board to make lovely.

About ten years ago I used to get the paper published in the penitentiary at Columbus, Ohio. . . . I remember that "Convict 4000," a lifer, wrote this about his mother:

Forever is a long time, the life of a moon or star.
Forever knows no judges or prison chains or bar
And I shall love you forever, forever and a day—
Till beauty turns to ashes and stone walls melt away!
(*Dial,* May 1948)

Summer

It's Hot as a Ground Hog's Hole: Must Be Summer!

Summer is here again—right upon us. It never comes early enough or stays long enough to suit me. To a woman who was a country kid, it brings memories which can never pass away . . . the long lazy hazy days . . . the sort of alkalescent, fugitive days that got away from us all too soon.

You know, we have an old Ozark superstition that when the first whippoorwill sings in the spring, the wife has to get up and make the fires from then until fall when the whippoorwill is gone. I don't know how many lived by this, but many's the time I have heard it. Yes, the wife was supposed to "git the fa'r wood, and bust up the kindling." Those were the days of peace and neighborliness and no worry. . . .

In summer came the picnics and the reunions and the family get-togethers and big dinners and the Sunday-school conventions and the baptizings, and out in the little crossroads brush arbors they had meetings and sat out in the cool of the arbor. And sometimes they had foot washings—and now and then an all-day log-rolling and house-raising where neighbors came and helped a neighbor to build his house and get it up quick. The women came along and cooked enormous feasts for the working men. . . .

And then "the ol' swimmin' hole." Men and women didn't go bathing or swimming together when I was a young girl. I was a young mother when I remember my first "gregarious" swimming. Then we simply made a fiesta of it. I lived on the bank of the James River and we swam every day from May until October. When the weather got so cold it would freeze the egg on your Uncle Snazzy's whiskers you quit swimming in the river, and not until then. The beach would be just lined with big, little, old and young. I had learned to swim quite early, back with the "gal swimming." It's a wonder more of us were not drowned in those treacherous currents. We must have had some guardian angels hiding around the corners somewhere. (*Dial*, June 1948)

Brides and Marriage: Who Will I Marry?

After a summer shower, look under a rock and you will find a hair of the color of your true love's.

On May Day, throw a mirror's light into a well and you will see your true love's reflection. (Some have done that and claimed they saw a coffin!) Also on May Day, watch in a mirror as you come down stairs and you will see somewhere the reflection of your future mate.

Name the corners of a room (four boys) the first time you sleep in that room, and when you waken, the one you look at first you will marry. (We used to do that always when I was a gal.)

Eat a half teaspoon of salt slowly, go to bed without a drink, and you will dream that your future mate comes to bring you a drink of water. (*SDN*, June 7, 1941)

DON'T MARRY CROSSWAYS OF THE BOARDS

In the old days a couple would not marry crossways of the boards in the floor. They believed they would separate before the year ended. They married lengthways of the floor always. One old woman neighbor of ours once said she married crossways of the boards and she believed that was why her man died in a year. But little did she care. She said, "He never died soon enough!" She had five husbands before her days ended and she used to say, "Well, I cain't help my men a dyin'. I reckon if the good Lord is willin' to take 'em I ort to be willin' to keep a furnishin'' em. Someone asked her if she was just going to keep on marrying. She said, "Yes, I reckon I'll jist keep on now—I've spiled myself for anything else." (*Dial*, July 1946)

THE "INFARE" PARTY LASTED ALL NIGHT

An infare is a "second day dinner" given by the groom's folks to all. The wedding dinner was at the bride's, then the infare at the groom's.

I went to an infare I remember well, in a big four-room log cabin, chinked and daubed and clean as a whistle. Two of the rooms were connected by a dogtrot—you know what that was. A gangway. In bad weather, the dogs slept in this gangway to keep out of the rain and snow. So it was called the dog trot. The table was piled high and everybody was there. Ham meat, turkey, chicken and dumplings, wild honey, cakes and pies and all sorts of jellies and jams. There was roast venison because the father had killed a big buck that week. The floors were scoured white with suds and sand. They danced till morning. I'll never forget it. Everything was left on the table and we ate all night.

Yes, the infare was one of the old American traditions and I'm sorry it has passed out of existence. (*Dial*, September 1946)

HUMOR IS ONE OF THE GREAT EMOTIONS OF LIFE

My advice to a young woman about to select her dear ball and chain for life is to have him carefully examined by competent inspectors as to his sense of humor! Forget all about his bank account, his car, his fraternity and the grease he rubs on his hair. I'd rather marry the fool in the king's court than the undertaker. Don't ever, ever pick a tragedian for a husband! Better take the comedian—or even the simpleton! (*SNL*, November 11, 1934)

HOW TO ASSURE A FINE MARRIAGE AND GOOD HEALTH

I read where an old mountaineer from North Carolina was undergoing a physical examination by a city doctor, and the doctor was amazed to find the old man in such fine condition. Better than men ten or even twenty years young than he. And the doctor asked, as they always do—"To what do you attribute such good health and long life?"

"Well, I'll tell you, Doc," he said, "when my wife and me got married we agreed on something. Whenever I got to arguing to her or quarreling at her she was to say nothing at all, but just go back in the kitchen and sit down. And when she got mad at me, I was to walk right out the door and stay in the backyard till she got over it."

"I see," said the doctor, "but what has that got to do with it?"

"Well, Doc, as the result of that—I reckon I've led what you might call somewhat of an outdoor life!" (*Dial*, August 1946)

REPLACE HIM?

One time there was an old woman we all knew and liked, but she was plenty "quare" as we might say. Her ol' man died and she was true to his memory. No new-fangled husband for her. She really should have had a second try at the game for the first one was "mighty pore per-taters, and few in the hill!"

We used to tease her about getting married again to some good old plug, but she would say, in her kind, whiney voice—"Now folks, don't twit me about marryin'! The name I've got right now will be cyarved on my tombstone!" And believe me, it was. (*Dial*, March 1948)

Myra's Big White Hens
Mary Elizabeth Mahnkey

Myra, gentle one who loved her home,
Her husband, her little grandchildren

And her big white hens,
Died in October.

I was glad it was October
When her yellow chrysanthemums
Were blooming.
And the walnut tree was covering
The blue grass with gold.

I reckon, William, Myra's man,
Was lonesome.
Anyhow, he married again
Almost too soon.

It made us all sad
When Mrs. Number Two
Caught up Myra's big white hens
And sold them
To pay for her permanent.
(*SDN*, November 13, 1941)

Now Comes July!

Hit's a Fur Piece Back . . .[1]

It's a "fur piece" as Uncle Bud used to say, from the old gatherings and picnics of fifty years ago in the Ozarks, even forty years and less, to the up-to-date and spiffy "Ozark Free Fair" we are having here this month. Yes. It's a "fur piece," and whether we have gone forward or backward in the matter of "gatherin's" all lies in your point of view. . . .

. . . We had our "Fourth" picnics and our August reunions and they were the great thrill of the summers to which we anxiously looked forward. Galena is an old town, very old. We held the great "Fourth" (that's

Hit's a Fur Piece Back.....
TO THE FIRST FAIR WITH HAMBURGERS and POP

Courtesy of the Springfield News-Leader.

all it was ever called) down in the "slough bottom" by the river. Damp and cool and plenty of water for the horses and mules. Girls fixed ruffles and furbelows for weeks. They picked berries very often to get their Fourth finery. The boys wore their gay shirts and the sleeve bands on their arms of gay colors. Celluloid boutonnieres or "button-bouquets" were in their prime. The hats were generally of the ten-gallon variety. Every girl had a beau there if she never had one any place else. Boys were just going to waste in those days—now it is just the opposite—they are at a premium. The reason for that I have often tried to figure out.

Spurred Dancers

The real celebration started on the third of July. The dance platforms were up and they danced all night. In the early days many girls danced with sunbonnets on but they always let them fall back on their shoulders as they swung. They were really pretty and dashing looking. The boys always with their hats and spurs on. It was sissy for a fellow to take off his hat to dance. There was no place to put it, for one thing. The girls sitting around didn't want to hold a ten-gallon felt hat and those standing up back of the "settin' bench" and just watching wouldn't hold the hats, of course. The boys danced in spurs and they jangled as they knocked the backstep. And a fellow wasn't a dancer if he couldn't knock the backstep all the time. Many girls did also. I remember the McCracken girls, and so does everyone else, as the loveliest square dancers in all our country. . . . The river boys from Cape Fair and farther down on White River were excellent dancers.

Somebody always started the day by reading the Declaration of Independence. If some girl was especially good in "elocution" she was asked to read it. Most of the crowd listened intently.

We had nothing but these three things: The "circle swing" which you might call a merry-go-round, but we knew no such word. We had the dance platform, and the lemonade stands. No carnival stuff, no amusements of other sorts like throwing at dolls, gambling devices, eat stands, Ferris wheels, and all the hundred other things which came in later years to the country down in those parts. The lemonade was made in big tubs and was invariably colored red with some sort of fruit coloring. The coloring was not government inspected in those days and was usually "aniline" which is poisonous if you get enough. No ice cream. That came much later, and it was homemade.

Ice had to be hauled at a terrific waste from Springfield. Imagine hauling it on hot days clear down in the Ozarks, and camping on the way! But they did always get some for the lemonade. It ran out about the heat of the day. Some men got to putting up ice along about 1899. My father did, for one, to sell in the summer. He built a room and cut out the ice from the river, sometimes sixteen inches thick, and it was packed very deep in sawdust tight in the "icehouse." They didn't open it until July because it wasted then terribly. Strange to say, the rivers never freeze over now.

First Phonograph

One of the funniest things Mrs. Nellie Tromly of Galena (wife of the editor) tells me which she recalled (I had almost forgotten it) was when small attractions began to come in and one was an Edison phonograph. It was a little squeaky cylinder thing with long tubes to hear through just like a doctor's stethoscope. You put the things in your ears and listened dizzily! Just the faintest squeak of the old "Kiss Waltz" or a band playing. At least, if you bore down hard on your imagination you might imagine it was a band. It really sounded more like somebody tearing a rag. You paid a nickel. Nellie says she recalls her mother taking her up and paying the nickel and sticking the things in her ears and she didn't know what it was for and never did know until years later that she was supposed to hear anything.

Circle Swings

The circle swings were the great attraction. Those who were not riding were standing around looking on, wishing they had another nickel. They were run by a mule in the center that was hooked to a sort of tug or something and around and around the poor critter went in a small circle all day long. No music, only a fiddler who sat all day long and swung and fiddled. He got free riding and free lemonade. I don't know whether he got pay or not. Many times they had a banjo picker who picked and sang. I remember Virgil Breeden and shall remember him always. He had an eye for me and I got to ride all day if he was the music. He always sang "The Railroader." A railroad was a great thing in those days—to even get to see one, to ride on a train, to hear one toot! People lived to be near the century mark and never saw a railroad. I can hear Virgil singing now—

I would not marry a farmer
He's always in the dirt,

The circle swings were the treat attraction. *Courtesy of the* Springfield News-Leader.

But I would marry a railroader
Who wears a striped shirt.
I would not marry a blacksmith
He's always in the black,
But I would marry an engineer
Who pulls the throttle back!
A railroader, mother, a railroader
A rail-ro-der fer me.
If ever I marry in all my life
A railroader's wife I'll be.[2]

Pop

I recall when "pop" came into existence at our picnics. They hit a wire in the top of the bottle and if the pop was warm (and it usually was) it shot three feet in the air and when it got through fizzing you had about a tablespoonful left! But boy, it was good! It was swanky to have a boy collar you and lead you up to the stand and get pop for you. Everybody, all the hillbilly kids, stood around and looked on at us green eyed with envy. Then some of us down home the other day were recalling the popcorn and fan, which came on as small stands began to come in, with candy and little extras like that. A flat stick or red candy popcorn about an inch thick and a folding-fan fastened to it with a rubber band. Popcorn and fan for a nickel! Then the "rubber return balls" which you threw at your sweetie as a sweetie passed milling around, and the ball returned to you!

Hamburgers and a Poke o' Goobers

And how very well I remember when hamburgers came to the picnics. A man came along with a little flat oil stove of a thing and this hamburger meat on his own ice in a box. He stood right there before our wondering eyes and ground the meat in an old sausage grinder. He did a land-office business.

About 1894 a hot peanut stand came to the slough-bottom Fourth picnics, along with the first great attraction "Bosco the snake-eater!" For

They hit a wire in the top of the bottle and if the pop was warm it shot three feet in the air. *Courtesy of the* Springfield News-Leader.

five or six years Bosco did a rushing business. He was the talk of the country. But about the peanuts—the man "barked" which was also very new. The Ozarker is timid and restrained. He stood and yelled, "Peanuts, double-jointed, knock-kneed, fresh-roasted peanuts!" A fellow went up and bought a sack of the things and looked in and said, "Aw, the devil—just a poke o' goobers!" A peanut was a "goober." We planted and raised them and the word peanut was a misleading proposition. A poke o' goobers was very popular after that.

Then after the "lover's tub" came into the country, we began to get very urban. We were goners! That was the sensation. The tubs where the lovers go in and they twisted and spun and lurched—My! People came to Galena from miles around to see the lover's tub which had come down from Springfield. For many years these things came only to Galena, the county seat, then they got to coming to the smaller picnics and down to Forsyth and on down in the Arkansas towns.

Anvils Boom

I must tell you about the firing of "anvils" on the morning of the Fourth. Very early—about four o'clock, we were awakened by these mighty roars. That is one thing that has passed and gone but will never be forgotten by little Ozarks kiddies. This was usually done down at Frank Acree's black-smith shop. They put a round iron ring on a huge smithing anvil. They filled this with gunpowder, leaving a little trailing outside the ring. Then they set another anvil right on that, several men and boys helping lift it. Then someone touched off this powder with a torch or something, and ran. The anvils flew up in the air and such an explosion you never heard. It was like a mighty cannon reverberated up and down the old James River and woke the little hamlet all in a jump. Over and over they would fire about twenty of these anvils. A very dangerous job, but the nearest approach to fireworks we had. And believe me it was some doin's!

The days are gone! . . . Nothing is left of the old picnic of the Ozarks. I wonder if we are happier now or were we happier then? Yes, as Uncle Bud says—"Hit's a fur piece!" (*SDN*, September 11, 1938)

MAY'S FOURTH OF JULY PICNIC
WHEN SHE WAS THIRTEEN

Well do I remember my first picnic for it was my first beau! I was about thirteen—started early to avoid the rush. Dear old Lou came and got me, a timid little freckled boy, and he informed me on the way out to the picnic on the hill west of the little town, that he had seventy-five cents! It seemed to me like a bankroll! I had a white dress with a long bow sash, a pair of slippers, we held hands as we walked and we had seventy-five cents! No other boy had that. My brother Leslie had a quarter and Elsie Clark. That was a whole world.

Lou and I began to plan how we should make that money last. We wouldn't swing until the day wore on a bit and they got to giving two swings for a nickel. We bought lemonade made in a big tub with a few lemons to start. The ice was hauled from Marionville, Missouri, twenty-five miles packed in a wagon in sheets the best they could. It took all day, and looked like an eighty-five-cent steak on a Hollywood café platter when it got there. Early in the morning we had ice in the lemonade. Later in the day we had flies. Lou and I bought one orange and went out and sat on a log and ate it, then carried the peeling around and munched on it all day. Then be bought A COCONUT! He put it under his coat lapel at my suggestion so the kids wouldn't follow us out to the log to eat it. Some of the kids saw him buy it, and it was a sensation! Twenty-five cents gone right there, but it was an event he had long promised me. We bored a hole in the end of it with a nail, and first drank the milk. MY! But we had a time! Then he went and borrowed his father's knife, which was also an event for him. He cracked the coconut, peeled it by bits—we ate till we were choked then carried that around all day also in his pocket with the orange peel. Then we swung some more. Never such a picnic and never will be. Just milling around, full of coconut and orange peel and fried chicken and lukewarm lemonade, and he was the only fifteen-year-old on the grounds with a watch and chain, and I was as conscious of it as if he were a Wall Street broker. But in spite of me, all day I had a sicky sort of feeling from sneaking off from the girls I loved with that coconut. And the dizzy swing driven or pulled by a constantly prodded mule around and around didn't help the sicky feeling. Will I ever forget it! No fireworks, no confetti, or pop or gambling things . . . just a lemonade stand, a dance platform and a mule circle swing and a basket dinner and a "speech." The smell of new lumber in the making of benches, fresh huckleberry pies, little fires around where we made coffee, babies eating candy and running around, and lovers holding hands. How little it took to please those who were not jaded by the mad world! (*SNL*, June 3, 1934)

I have a letter full of fun and fact from Flora Elsey at Marionville, Missouri. . . . I knew Flora in my youth, and I was "present in the body" at most of the stuff she is telling about.

> Recently I read your mention of the farmer bringing his cook stove to town to sell so the family could all go to the circus, and at first I wondered if that wasn't my daddy. . . . The picnics were the one place my father would go if it took a cow to raise the money to get shoes and duds for us six kids. Two days and one night we always stayed, for the "night afore the Fourth" was as big as the Fourth. I didn't shy so much at the fiddling because

my dad always kept one and could fiddle any tune he would
hear play once or twice. I remember a song he would play and
sister and I always stood by his side and sung it—

> The big bee sucks the blossom
> The little bee makes the honey,
> The poor man hoes the cotton and the corn
> And the rich man gets the money.
> (*SNL*, September 3, 1933)

But She Wasn't on the Program:
Woman Riding a Sow Featured Galena Fair

I must tell you about the first fair ever held in the county of Stone at
Galena. It was in 1905. It was a pretty good fair. They had two or three
more but the enterprise died out. The women had nice quilts and canned
goods and it was a great time.

The carnivals came for the first time. Up to that we had seen no
doll-rack or bobbing heads to throw at. They just had an old sheet or
cloth stretched and a fellow stuck his head through a small hole in the
sheet and they threw eggs at him while he dodged them. Twice as much
fun as a doll rack, for those old boys who were trained to knock squirrels out of a tree at long range, could spat that chap in the eye with an
egg and splatter it over him nine times out of ten. That's one reason the
enterprise annihilated itself down among us. No profit.

It was a very good three-day fair. But one thing stands out in memory if nothing else lives. Somebody tried to get the "city council" to put
the hogs and cows up just for the fair, but nothing doing. So they kept
some little "feist" dogs around the streets to run them off. An old sow is
worse scared of a "feist" than of a herd of bloodhounds.

A big woman weighing about two hundred pounds was going down
the middle of the little square wearing what we wore then, a loose flowing
mother-hubbard with about ten yards in the skirt down to the ground. A
big old razorback sow was nosing around. She was about four feet high,

and six inches through. Lean and muscular. A little yelping "feist" took in after her. She ran down the street and right between this woman's legs from the back, and got caught and wound up in that mother-hubbard. She couldn't get through the front widths. The woman went kerflop and down and square on the old sow and rode her for nearly a block at high speed. Such screams of laughter you never heard and if you don't believe it, just ask some who remember it to this day and will never forget it so long as they live. . . .

The fair leaders were a bit chagrined especially as some of them had tried to have the hogs penned up during the fair and it wasn't a laughing matter. But if you could only have seen it! And so we showed off our hogs at our fairs to some advantage, believe me!

I remember the medicine man selling soap. He always made a lather of the soap and ate it then blew bubbles! This was to show it was mild. I bought a bar of it and found it would eat the face off a bronze monument. (*SDN*, September 14, 1939)

August

Well, August is here! We have so many blessings. We don't appreciate them until they are about to be taken away from us in some way, by war or internal strife or the many things that threaten our good old boat here in America. We're like the old chap who had an awfully ornery little farm of sprouts and cockleburrs and he couldn't even raise a fuss on it, so he made up his mind to sell it. He went to a real estate man in town to get him to put his farm on the market. This real estate feller was one of these up an' comin' boys, so he put an ad in the Sunday paper that read like this:

> For sale: beautiful home, forty acres of rich bottom land, with ten acres of rich virgin timber on the picturesque hillside. A crystal stream runs across the property with a rustic, romantic old farm cabin half hidden by fragrant honeysuckle and old fashioned roses. Why not come out here where you can enjoy

life and be your own boss with no alarm clock to awaken you but the sweet songs of birds? Here you can enjoy the sunshine and fresh air and live off of the fat of the land.

Well sir—the old chap read the ad through once, then he read it clear through again. "That must be my place," he says. "And if it is, by cracky, it's too good to part with!" So he called the sale off.

We have so much to be thankful for. The old things. . . . The true and substantial and never-failing things. . . .

> We get the sweetest comfort when we
>   wear the oldest shoe,
> We love the old friends better than we'll
>   ever love the new,
> Old songs are more appealing, to the wearied
>   heart—and so,
> We find the sweetest music in the tunes of
>   long ago.
> There's a kind of mellow sweetness in a
>   good thing growing old,
> Each year that rolls around it leaves an
>   added touch of gold.
> (*Dial*, August 1949)

Fall

Soon it will be time to go possum hunting. (*SDN*, September 2, 1939)

Goodbye Summer

> O, the summer is never long enough
> For me!

I hate the wild wind's icy breath,
While winter stalks to the drums of death—
O, the summer is never long enough
For me!
(*SNL*, September 27, 1935)

Beauty and Bounty

September is here! Autumn is upon us. . . . Autumn, the troubadour of seasons. . . . Bittersweet and the muskiness of paw-paws and the tang of puckery persimmons and buttery nuts. Corn shocks standing at attention near fields of golden pumpkins. (*Dial*, September 1950)

The old hills are flinging away their summer garments with no tears or dirges and decking themselves in flaming seductiveness for the coming of another lover! . . . Nothing on this earth is more beautiful than the colors that are being stirred just now by the great Alchemist in the Ozarks. (*SNL*, October 22, 1933)

You know—there's so much to do out in the hills! Possums are ripe now, and there are rabbits to track and nuts to crack, corn to shuck, camp meetin's are going to be in their prime right away—Oh, there's such a lot to do. (*SNL*, November 20, 1932)

Winter

It's cold as a setter pup's nose. (*SNL*, September 1935)

Christmas

And soon, Christmas will come sifting down upon us like a homing pigeon—and O, how I love it! (*Dial*, December 1946)

The joy of living—the joy of giving! Bells, holly, packages, smiles, joys, memories—this is Christmas! The day of love and peace and forgiveness, the birth of the Christ, the great Norse Yule Feast. Screams of joy from the children, love gifts for sweethearts, youth and happiness again for Mother—and a noble enduring patience and a stack of bills for Dad!

You know, you can't go wrong in the Ozarks—you just can't; but I'm afraid we don't have the Christmas we used to. Now don't go and accuse me again of being in my dotage and living in the past. Believe me, it was some past to live in! (*Ozark Life*, December 1929)

THE CHRISTMAS CELEBRATION
WAS THE TOWN'S SHARED EVENT

People know what's going on now at Christmas, but a lot of folks don't know what they did in the bygone days. We didn't have trees in our homes very much. I never knew just why that was, but maybe it was because we always had them in the church—a big community tree—or in the little rural schoolhouses. And never will I forget the smell of cedar—the excitement when Mother was on the "committee" to go down and help decorate, and we kids would try our best to peep all day. But the door was kept locked.

Then the great Christmas Eve came! The huge cedar tree, the popcorn and cranberries strung on it—the little candles (and why there were not more fires I don't know). The program and the singing of carols by the children. Then Santa came in! I can see him coming down the aisle of the church. He arrived outside in a sleigh when I was little. Coming from nowhere—from the great land of snow and ice. . . .

I remember when John Butler and several other men always went out into the woods and cut the tree and hauled it in with a team of horses. It was a huge tree. And I think the most holy incense in the memory of a hill child is cedar at Christmas.

Before we had a church in our little hometown of Galena, we had the tree and celebration in the courthouse. And it was awfully small and crowded. Your most personal presents were put on it. Even your mittens and knit striped stockings and your wearing things. Your candy and dolls and the sled and your cake and cookies, in a nice box. . . .

Happy as a June bug in a gay and peaceful world! No wars, no bombs, no grief past understanding, warm and cozy with the wind howling outside and the merry party going inside. . . . The snow glistening on the lovely landscape and icicles hanging from the eves—"A world of cold shut out and a world of love shut in."[3] (*Dial*, December 1946)

Only the drugstore ordered the gifts and we would look at them all for weeks ahead. How well I remember the wild anxiety we went through wondering when the gifts were coming and would be opened. It was the great event of the year. Then we would begin to hang around the store and look longingly, not allowed to handle things. We would wager that So-and-So gave his girl this fine velvet lined toilet set, and Mr. So-and-So would get this big blue plush album for his wife. And before I was thirteen, one of the small plush autograph albums was what I was sure I would get, and I wondered and wondered which one, and we girls would pick out in our minds just which one Bert or Louis or Harold would get for us. Then when we got older, we might (O, heavenly thought!) be the favored miss to get that fine silver puff box or toilet set. A big bulky comb and brush which we set upon a favored spot and never, O, never dared to comb our hair with it until its gorgeous velvet faded and its trimmings tarnished. It was the center of all romance on the dresser.

And a bottle of perfume! I remember Hoyt's German Cologne, and before Christmas the merchant gave out cards scented with it until we were tempted almost to die for a bottle of it! I have wondered so many times if that old cologne of my childhood is still made. No exotic perfume from oriental harems could ever smell so sweet to me.

Then that present was put on the Christmas tree by our lover, and our name called out, and maybe some cute remarks by Santa and craning of necks when it was delivered to us and we blushed and burned—yet feeling very much the pride and distinction of being singled out to get "that big box of candy" or the like. Then every little child got a small bag of candy made of netting, and an orange or apple from the community and church fund. And gifts. My! The call of them lasted for hours. And jokes were played. Perhaps the town's most popular young gent got a corset hung on the tree for him—Santa took it out of the wrapping and displayed it with a twinkle (pretending a mistake) and the audience roared. The young man blushed but felt secretly very important. . . .

Then we hied home to bed. Maybe the young folks serenaded some and rode the huge bobsleds in the moonlight. But by midnight all were in and the little sleepy, white town was ivory-etched and still and glistening in the moonlight! Then Santa brought candy and nuts to the stockings and often some toys again to the more favored ones. (*SNL*, December 20, 1936)

MAY STILL REMEMBERS HER CHILDHOOD GIFTS

When taking down my Christmas tree—always there pours over me such a strange sadness to take down a gay tree—I could see, and I always can, the first doll I ever got on a Christmas tree. . . . That doll! A "wax" doll with rather bold, stationery blue eyes and awfully false "jute" hair they called it then—red shoes, and a stiff red and white tulle dress—that doll looking down at me—and the smell of cedar right out of the woods—the strung pop-corn, and the small candles which had to be watched like hawks—all the loads of hanging mittens and scarfs and hankies and bags of candy—and the warm church and the excitement—and my waking up just like I had ether or chloroform, sort of like an opium smoker—on air—hypnotized!

I know that many of you women who read this have the same sensation. Then tell me that childhood forgets? Never! If I live to be ninety that will never leave me, one iota! (*SDN*, January 1, 1942)

The gift I remember most of all was that I got a little thimble when I was nine years old! I loved to sew. And who could ever believe that such a thing as a thimble for a child could be in existence? My aunt sent it to me from Colorado. I slept with it on for many nights. Never can I forget that thimble, though many Christmases have gone under the bridge since then. (May McCord quoted in *Springfield Leader and Press*, December 18, 1963)

MAY'S HOLIDAY WISH

Above all, let us be happy this year. Let's revive old sleeping fires—let's renew our youth and play with the kids. Let's remember again that the greatest institution on the face of the earth is the home and that a front-line trench or a fox hole never made a home and is a poor place for a homesick boy to be on Christmas day!

And so, I wish for you a very merry Christmas. I wish you "a little meat for the pot and a little cheer for the soul."

Goodbye and God keep you and "May the peace of Heaven abide with you wherever you go, wherever you stray, on holy, blessed Christmas Day!" (*Dial*, December 1948)

"Goodbye, My Time's Up"

Goodbye, my time's up. Just go right on and be good. Remember that the world is still hungry for the great simplicities—the sweet commonplace things of life. Keep your faith. Stick to the God of your fathers—and—chins up in this worried old world. And I'll be seein' you, Lord willin' and the creek don't rise. (Undated radio script. McCord Personal Papers)

NOTES

EDITORS' NOTE

1. Although ownership of the newspapers cited in this book changed during this period, their names did not. Name changes in later years has caused confusion in the archiving of these papers by some sources. For example, papers referenced in this book by the internet site newspapers.com filed *Springfield News and Leader* (*SNL*) under *Springfield Leader and Press*; and the *Springfield Daily News* (*SDN*) under *Springfield News-Leader*. We have cited the names that appeared on the mastheads at the time of their publication.

INTRODUCTION

1. "Christmas Gift Instead of Merry Christmas Deep in the Ozarks, Says May Kennedy McCord," *St. Louis Globe-Democrat*, December 25, 1942.
2. F. A. Behymer, "She's Filled with the Lore of Ozark Hill People," *St. Louis Post-Dispatch*, July 26, 1942, 52.
3. "'First Lady of the Ozarks' to Sing at Folk Festival," *St. Louis Globe-Democrat*, March 30, 1953, 9B.
4. Unless otherwise noted, all biographical information on May Kennedy McCord and her family comes from the McCord Personal Papers in the possession of Patti McCord.
5. Robert K. Gilmore, *Ozark Baptizings, Hangings, and Other Diversions: Theatrical Folkways of Rural Missouri, 1885–1910* (Norman: University of Oklahoma Press, 1984), 17.
6. Diogenes, "The Spotlight on Missouri Mother May Kennedy McCord," *Dial*, June 1950, 5.
7. "France's Greatest Composer Writing an Opera for a St. Louis Girl," *St. Louis Globe-Democrat*, August 30, 1903, 49.
8. Washington Township, Stone County, Missouri, 1900 United States Federal Census.

9. Letter from Delia Yocum to Leslie Kennedy, November 1, 1902, McCord Personal Papers.

10. Hillbilly Heartbeats, *Springfield News and Leader,* September 23, 1934.

11. Hillbilly Heartbeats, *Springfield News and Leader,* February 26, 1933.

12. May Kennedy McCord, "The Buryin'," *The Sample Case,* December 1925.

13. Hillbilly Heartbeats, *Springfield News and Leader,* October 23, 1932.

14. Hillbilly Heartbeats, *Springfield Daily News,* November 25, 1940.

15. "Historical Notes and Comments," *Missouri Historical Review* 35, no. 3 (April 1941): 473. Also see "Missouri History Not Found in Textbooks," *Missouri Historical Review* 37, no. 1 (October 1942): 110.

16. May Kennedy McCord, "Speakin' of Fishin,'" *Field and Stream,* June 1936, 16–17.

17. Letter from George Horace Lorimer (editor of the *Saturday Evening Post*) to McCord, May 22, 1935, McCord Personal Papers.

18. Vance Randolph, *Ozark Folksongs,* 4 vols. (Columbia: State Historical Society of Missouri, 1946–1950).

19. Jane Grosby, "The First National Folk Festival," special issue, *Missouri Folklore Society Journal* 8–9, 1986–1987: 115–122.

20. May Kennedy McCord, unpublished notes for speech to Ozark Writer's Guild, circa 1956, McCord Personal Papers.

21. Marguerite Lyon, "Fresh from the Hills," Marge of Sunrise Mountain Farm, *Chicago Tribune,* March 14, 1948, 101.

22. Wayne Glenn, "It was the Summer of 1936," *Springfield Leader and Press,* June 29, 1975, 79; and Samantha C. Horn, "Wayfaring Stranger: Sidney Robertson, American Folk Music, and the Resettlement Administration, 1936–37" (master's thesis, University of North Carolina at Chapel Hill, 2016), https://doi.org/10.17615/vsj1-0j81.

23. Library of Congress search results, accessed July 5, 2020, https://www.loc.gov/search/?all=true&fa=contributor:mccord,+may+kennedy; and "Hobart Smith and May Kennedy McCord oral history interviews, 1963," Catalog, Library of Congress, accessed July 5, 2020, https://lccn.loc.gov/2017655232.

24. "Love Voiced for Ozarks," *Los Angeles Times,* June 20, 1935.

25. Hillbilly Queen of Ozarks Recalls Customs of Hills," *Los Angeles Times,* June 19, 1941, 25.

26. "Personalities: Five Out of the Six 'Best Known' St. Louis Radio Personalities Are on KWK," *St. Louis Globe-Democrat,* October 24, 1943, 43.

27. "World Series Jubilee," *St. Louis Globe-Democrat,* October 4, 1942, 6.

28. Unpublished, handwritten radio script dated Monday, November 27, 1944, McCord Personal Papers.

29. David E. Whisnant, *All That Is Native and Fine: The Politics of Culture in an American Region* (Chapel Hill: University of North Carolina Press, 1983).

30. For a description of the settlement movements in Appalachia and reformers'

disregard for native culture as they sought to change lives to match their own cultural values, see Whisnant, *All That is Native*, 92.

31. Jane Becker, *Selling Tradition: Appalachia and the Construction of an American Folk, 1930–1940* (Chapel Hill: University of North Carolina Press, 1998), 5.

32. Catherine S. Barker, *Yesterday Today: Life in the Ozarks* (Caldwell, ID: Caxton Printers, 1941).

33. For examples, see Hillbilly Heartbeats, *Springfield News and Leader*, November 28, 1937; *Springfield Daily News*, December 3, 1938; and December 18, 1941.

34. Hillbilly Heartbeats, *Springfield News and Leader*, October 25, 1936.

35. Dewey Jackson Short, *Congressional Record* (Washington, DC: US Government Printing Office, April 30, 1936, Seventy-Fourth Congress, Section 2), 6455.

36. The University of North Carolina, Indiana University, and the University of Oklahoma were among the first academic institutions to offer programs in folklore. For additional information see Simon J. Bronner, *Following Tradition: Folklore in the Discourse of American Culture* (Logan: University of Utah Press, 1998).

37. Susan L. Pentlin and Rebecca B. Schroeder, "H. M. Belden, The English Club and the Missouri Folk-Lore Society," *Missouri Folklore Society Journal*, 8–9 (1986–1987): 1–45. For history of development of folklore societies see Wayland D. Hand, "North American Folklore Societies," *The Journal of American Folklore* 56, no. 221 (1943): 161–91.

38. Nolan Porterfield, *Last Cavalier: The Life and Times of John A. Lomax* (Urbana and Chicago: University of Illinois Press, 1996), 141.

39. See Hillbilly Heartbeats, *Springfield Daily News*, December 20, 1938, re information provided to Dr. Sam Lloyd, Professor of Sociology, Missouri School of Mines, Rolla, Missouri.

40. Hillbilly Heartbeats, *Springfield Daily News*, March 25, 1941; and April 28, 1938.

41. *Missouri Folklore Society Journal*, 8–9 (1986–1987).

42. F. A. Behymer, "He Sings of the Gasconade," *St. Louis Post-Dispatch*, February 5, 1946.

43. Otto Ernest Rayburn, *Rayburn's Ozark Guide* 6, no. 1, Summer 1948.

44. Hillbilly Heartbeats, *Springfield News and Leader*, October 23, 1932.

45. Letter from Rayburn to McCord, August 8, 1957, McCord Personal Papers.

46. Letter from Randolph to McCord, February 6, 1958, McCord Personal Papers.

47. Letter from Sandburg to McCord, July 12, 1951, McCord Personal Papers.

48. Letter from Driftwood to McCord, February 22, 1959, McCord Personal Papers. Alan Lomax and his father, John Lomax, were ethnomusicologists whose work was important to the preservation and promotion of folklore and

folk music. As curator of the Archive of American Folk Song at the Library of Congress, John Lomax, with Alan's support, oversaw the collection of thousands of records of vocal and instrumental music from a wide diversity of national and international folk traditions. Later, Alan Lomax was a performing musician and produced concerts, radio shows, and recordings. The Lomax family is credited with identifying and promoting many others who achieved recognition in the folk field.

49. For discussion of music in settlement schools, see Whisnant; for review of folk music intended for use in the Resettlement Administration collectives, see Horn.

50. Sarah Gertrude Knott, "The National Folk Festival After Twelve Years," *California Folklore Quarterly* 5, no. 1 (January 1946): 83–93. See also Grosby, "The First National Folk Festival."

51. Robert Cochran, *Vance Randolph: An Ozark Life* (Urbana and Chicago: University of Illinois Press, 1985).

52. *Mason City Globe-Gazette*, April 3, 1934, 1; also see "Mr. Randolph Taken Back," *Springfield Leader and Press*, April 17, 1934.

53. Hillbilly Heartbeats, *Springfield Leader and Press*, April 1, 1934.

54. "Nimble Feet and Bow-Arms Swing as Hill-Folk Play," *St. Louis Star and Times*, May 1, 1934, 11.

55. "Folk Festival Pleases Mayor," *Springfield Leader and Press*, April 18, 1934.

56. Letter from Randolph to McCord, February 16, 1956, McCord Personal Papers.

57. Letter from Seeger to McCord, December 17, 1966, McCord Personal Papers.

58. "Court Learns of 75 Ways to Cure a Wart," *Chicago Tribune*, June 21, 1951, 1.

59. May Kennedy McCord, *Dial*, November 1946.

60. Knott, "The National Folk Festival After Twelve Years."

61. Hillbilly Heartbeats, *Springfield News and Leader*, February 18, 1934.

62. Hillbilly Heartbeats, *Springfield Daily News*, March 25, 1943.

63. Hillbilly Heartbeats, *Springfield News and Leader*, November 13, 1932. Patti McCord, May's granddaughter, remembers her family did not allow her to listen to country music, including Patsy Cline.

64. "Who's Who to List May Kennedy McCord for Folklore Work," *Springfield Leader and Press*, March 1942. May later quipped that all this was "a bit too many words!"

65. "The Queen is Dead," *Springfield Leader and Press*, February 25, 1979, 43; and " 'Queen' May Kennedy McCord," *St. Louis Post-Dispatch*, March 3, 1979, 4.

CHAPTER 1

1. Modern scholars use the Missouri River as the northern boundary and the Grand (or Neosho) River as the western boundary. The map illustrates the physical boundary of the Ozark uplift that is widely accepted today.
2. Though a popular trope for chroniclers of Appalachia and the Ozarks in the first half of the twentieth century, the notion that "Elizabethan English" and Anglo-Saxon culture survived in the highlands gets little traction among modern scholars.
3. Worn out.
4. Arkansas native Coral Almy Wilson was a teacher who wrote poetry and stories in hill-country dialect. She is listed as a source for poems and stories in books by Otto Ernest Rayburn and Vance Randolph, and she wrote for Rayburn's *Arcadian Magazine*. Several of her poems were published in *New Letters* magazine in the 1930s and in other publications, such as the *Kansas University Journal* and *State Journal* of Lansing, Michigan.

CHAPTER 2

1. May Kennedy McCord in talk to Pilot Club in Joplin, Missouri, "Ozarkian Folklore Described to Club," *Joplin Globe*, Tuesday, February 22, 1949, 7.
2. A similar story was printed in *The Sample Case*, September 1925; edited and retold in Hillbilly Heartbeats, *SNL*, October 8, 1933.
3. The blue hen is a breed of chicken originally bred for fighting gamecocks. During the Revolutionary War the phrase *blue hen's chickens* was used to describe a fierce and successful company commanded by a captain from Delaware who bred blue hens. The phrase has since been used to describe a formidable fighter or spirited or quick-tempered person.
4. Mae Traller (1891–1959) began teaching at age seventeen and continued for thirty years, in Everton, Missouri. In the 1940s she wrote a regular column as a special correspondent of the *St. Louis Globe-Democrat* and later had articles in the *Springfield Leader and Press*. She frequently contributed to Hillbilly Heartbeats.
5. Mary Elizabeth Prather Mahnkey (1877–1948) was an Ozarks native who spent most of her life in rural Taney County, Missouri. Daughter of one of the original Bald Knobber vigilantes and wife of a country storekeeper, she began writing community news segments for local weekly newspapers as a teenager and continued to do so throughout her life. In 1934, a collection of her poems was published as *Ozark Lyrics*, with proceeds from book sales used to found a library in Branson. The following year she received national recognition when a New York publishing company named her the country's top rural newspaper correspondent and brought her to the city for a highly publicized promotional appearance.

CHAPTER 3

1. Some of the Bald Knobbers.
2. Matthews was another convicted Bald Knobber. For a history of the founding of the Bald Knobbers and this trial, see Lucile Morris Upton, *Bald Knobbers* (Caldwell, ID: Caxton Printers, 1939) and Matthew J. Hernando, *Faces Like Devils: The Bald Knobbers Vigilantes in the* Ozarks (Columbia: University of Missouri Press, 2015).
3. See Upton, 26–29.
4. Bolin was head of a mob that was credited with many cruel murders during the Civil War, including raids on helpless freighters and small groups of Union soldiers. Several versions of Bolin's capture and death were rumored, such as that he had been killed by Union soldiers who sent his head to the state capital in order to collect a reward. This story is different from the version that has become tradition in the hills.
5. Join.
6. Who was an officer.

CHAPTER 4

1. The spook light is a paranormal enigma seen on the road west of the small town of Hornet, near Joplin, Missouri. It is the stuff of legends and lore, but also has been scientifically studied, with various theories explored, such as natural gas emitted from abandoned zinc mines, or related to an electrical charge created from an earthquake fault, or even headlights from cars as they turn a particular curve in the road. Whatever the cause, it's a tourist attraction with its own webpage: https://www.joplinmo.org/575/The-Spook-Light, accessed July 14, 2020.
2. Otto Ernest Rayburn summarizes parts of this story in *Rayburn's Ozark Guide*, Summer 1948. He noted that the story was used by Vance Randolph in *Ozark Ghost Stories*. Both credit May McCord, who "lived not far from Dead Man's Pond as a child," as the source of the story.
3. Boldly confront.

CHAPTER 5

1. Dewey and May were close friends from Galena, Missouri.
2. The mourner's bench as used in this story was popular during nineteenth-century Christian evangelical revival meetings, especially in rural areas. A bench was placed where penitents would go to pray, sing, cry, confess their wrongs, commit to a life free from sin, and seek salvation.
3. May's personal memories of Pentecostal meetings, followed by a story.

4. This is incorrect. Oneness Pentecostals baptize only in the name of Jesus, as the term *oneness* suggests.

CHAPTER 6

1. For additional information, see Abby Burnett, *Gone to the Grave: Burial Customs of the Arkansas Ozarks, 1850–1950* (Jackson: University of Mississippi Press, 2014).
2. On April 20, 1942, *Newsweek* published a short article on angel crowns that included the photo from the *St. Louis Post-Dispatch*.
3. A native of Shannon County, Missouri, May E. Doms (1884–1962) was a teacher and a member of the Hillcrofters and the Gasconade Writers' Guild. She wrote a column entitled Along the Road for the *Salem News* in Salem, Missouri, and had poems published in several anthologies. Her son, Francis J. Doms, served in the army during World War II. Two of her subsequent poems were widely published: "I Gave My Son to Uncle Sam Today" and "To Cletus Parks." These sentimental poems found an audience during the war. The fallen pilot to whom Doms refers in this poem is thirty-two-year-old Cletus Park, not Cletus Parks.
4. A newspaper based in Van Buren, Missouri.
5. This story is from the McCord Personal Papers. An earlier version—May's first published work—was printed in the *Sample Case*, December 1925.

CHAPTER 7

1. For more information, see Gilmore, *Ozark Baptizings, Hangings, and Other Diversions*.
2. Ruth Tyler (1894–1976) of Neosho, Missouri, was in May's circle of friends. She was active in the Hillcrofters and the Ozark Writers and Artists Guild, and she played the dulcimer at the National Folk Festival. Her articles and poetry were published by many major newspapers and her regular column, Pinch and Taste, syndicated in Hearst's *American Weekly*. She wrote scripts for the skit "Uncle Luke and Aunt Mirandy of Persimmon Holler" on *The National Farm and Home Hour*, a radio show broadcast nationally from Chicago in the late 1920s and early 1930s.
3. Strict religious beliefs held that dancing was immoral. Play-parties became a common alternative. No fiddle or other musical instruments were played—just singing and movement that looked like dance. For more information, see Otto Ernest Rayburn, *Ozark Country* (New York: Duell, Sloan & Pierce, 1941), 101–110; and Alan L. Spurgeon, *Waltz the Hall: The American Play Party* (Jackson: University Press of Mississippi, 2005).
4. Mrs. Hair's.

5. In Kingston, Arkansas, in 1927, thirteen writers and artists established the Ozarkians. The group adopted Otto Ernest Rayburns's magazine, *Ozark Life*, as its official publication and at its meeting in June 1931 gave May Kennedy McCord the moniker *Queen of the Hillbillies*. Rayburn and nineteen others founded the Society of Hillcrofters in Eminence, Missouri, in 1931, for the purpose of preserving the heritage of the Ozarks. These two groups merged in 1932 as the Society of Hillcrofters and elected McCord president. Over time the organization was simply called the Hillcrofters. The group had about two hundred members by 1945, many from outside the Ozarks. Meetings were not exclusive to members, and everyone was welcome. The gatherings were both festive and serious, with lectures and ceremonies that honored Ozarks heritage and the region's Native Americans, whose lives close to nature reflected the ideal embodied in the old Scottish term *crofter*. For additional information, see Mabel E. Mueller, "History of the Hillcrofters," folder 16808, US Works Projects Administration, Historical Records Survey of Missouri, 1935–1942 (C3551), State Historical Society of Missouri–Columbia.

6. McCord, "Speakin' of Fishin'," 16–17.

CHAPTER 8

1. At that time, May's father was dying far away in Arizona.
2. Seeger, Charles. "Contrapuntal Style in the Three-Voice Shape-Note Hymns." *The Musical Quarterly* 26, no. 4 (1940): 483–93, accessed July 15, 2020, www.jstor.org/stable/738918.
3. See Stephen A. Marini, *Sacred Song in America: Religion, Music, and Public Culture* (Urbana: University of Illinois Press, 2003); and John Bealle, *Public Worship, Private Faith: Sacred Harp and American Folksong* (Athens: University of Georgia Press, 1997).
4. The Meeks Murder happened in Northeast Missouri, not in the Ozarks.
5. Vance Randolph, *Ozark Folksongs* (Urbana: University of Illinois Press, 1982). Lyle Lofgren, a contemporary collector of old songs, noted on his website that he heard this song and discovered that it was well known, even recorded by Joan Baez in the 1960s. "It was variously called 'The Palace Grand,' 'Lady Mary,' and 'The Sad Song.' All versions were credited from May Kennedy McCord who must have memorized every song she ever heard. She said she heard this song about 1900 but didn't know the title, which explains why it had so many of them." "Remembering the Old Songs: The Palace Grand," Lyle Lofgren & Elizabeth Lofgren, accessed September 12, 2019, http://www.lizlyle.lofgrens.org.

CHAPTER 9

1. This article and the following one appeared in the *Springfield Daily News* prior to the opening of the Ozark Empire District Free Fair in September 1939.
2. May's friend and a fellow columnist for the *Springfield Daily News.*
3. This is the second article May wrote about the Ozark Empire District Free Fair. It was printed the day after "Old Time Ozark Hogs Knew No Law but Own."
4. An old Scotch-Irish term for a cow with no horns.

CHAPTER 10

1. For more on this topic, see Vance Randolph, *Ozark Magic and Folklore* (New York: Dover Publications, Inc., 1947).
2. This comment was written the year Hitler became chancellor of Germany and established the Third Reich.
3. Asafetida.
4. A rural mail carrier known as the Hillbilly Poet, Carl B. Ike (1900–1982) helped found several organizations dedicated to writing about and studying the Ozarks, including the Gasconade Writers' Guild, the Ozarkians, and the Hillcrofters. He was local chairman for the district folk festival in West Plains, Missouri, prior to the National Folk Festival in 1934. His work was widely published in poetry anthologies, and he was often referred to as the Poet Laureate of the Ozarks.
5. From video recording of *Pig in a Poke*, n.d.
6. Skin infection.
7. Mad stones are objects found in the intestines of deer or other animals, and they are believed to draw poison out of insect and animal bites.
8. Rabies.
9. A native and lifelong resident of Carroll County, Arkansas, Cora Pinkley Call (1892–1966) was a prolific writer of both fiction and nonfiction in the form of newspaper and magazine articles and books, most of which she self-published. Her topics ranged from gardening to local history and from cooking to wildlife. In 1935 she founded the Ozark Writers and Artists Guild, which was centered in Eureka Springs.
10. Jack in the pulpit.
11. Letter from Jones to McCord, June 13, 1939.
12. A "posthumous person" is someone born after the death of a parent.
13. Cyst.

CHAPTER 11

1. In the sign of Pisces.
2. In the sign of Gemini.
3. The local weather announcer.

CHAPTER 12

1. Born in 1844.
2. Born in 1871.

CHAPTER 13

1. Rendered pork or chicken fat.

CHAPTER 14

1. Article written by May Kennedy McCord prior to the Ozark Free Fair in Springfield, Missouri.
2. The last two lines of this ballad aren't present in the original publication. The editors chose to restore them here because May always included them when she sang the song and when she taught it to others.
3. Dora Greenwell, "Home," *Poems by Dora Greenwell (Selected)* (London: Walter Scott, 1889).

INDEX